D1148097

DEATH IN VENICE

AND OTHER STORIES

THOMAS MANN

DEATH IN VENICE
AND OTHER STORIES

A LANDMARK EDITION

A LANDMARK EDITION

A series published jointly by William Heinemann Ltd
and Martin Secker and Warburg Ltd

54 Poland Street, London W1V 3D

LONDON MELBOURNE TORONTO
JOHANNESBURG AUCKLAND

This edition 1983

436 24131 5

Printed in Finland by Werner Söderström Oy,
a member of Finnprint

CONTENTS

DEATH IN VENICE

GUSTAVE ASCHENBACH—or von Aschenbach, as he had been known officially since his fiftieth birthday—had set out alone from his house in Prince Regent Street, Munich, for an extended walk. It was a spring afternoon in that year of grace 19—, when Europe sat upon the anxious seat beneath a menace that hung over its head for months. Aschenbach had sought the open soon after tea. He was overwrought by a morning of hard, nerve-taxing work, work which had not ceased to exact his uttermost in the way of sustained concentration, conscientiousness, and tact; and after the noon meal found himself powerless to check the onward sweep of the productive mechanism within him, that *motus animi continuus* in which, according to Cicero, eloquence resides. He had sought but not found relaxation in sleep—though the wear and tear upon his system had come to make a daily nap more and more imperative—and now undertook a walk, in the hope that air and exercise might send him back refreshed to a good evening's work.

May had begun, and after weeks of cold and wet a mock summer had set in. The English Gardens, though in tenderest leaf, felt as sultry as in August and were full of vehicles and pedestrians near the city. But towards Aumeister the paths were solitary and still, and Aschenbach strolled thither, stopping awhile to watch the lively crowds in the restaurant garden with its fringe of carriages and cabs. Thence he took his homeward way outside the park and across the sunset fields. By the time he reached the North Cemetery, however, he felt tired, and a storm was brewing above Föhring; so he waited at the stopping-place for a tram to carry him back to the city.

He found the neighbourhood quite empty. Not a wagon in sight, either on the paved Ungererstrasse, with its gleaming tramlines stretching off towards Schwabing, nor on the Föhring highway. Nothing stirred behind the hedge in the stone-mason's yard, where crosses, monuments, and commemorative tablets made a supernumerary and untenanted graveyard opposite the real one. The mortuary chapel, a structure in Byzantine style, stood facing it, silent in the gleam of the ebbing day. Its façade was adorned with Greek crosses and tinted hieratic designs, and displayed a symmetrically arranged selection of scriptural texts in gilded letters, all of them with a bearing upon the future life, such as: "They are entering into the House of the Lord" and "May the Light Everlasting shine upon them." Aschenbach beguiled some minutes of his waiting with reading these formulas and letting his mind's eye lose itself in their mystical meaning. He was brought back to reality by the sight of a man standing in the portico, above the two apocalyptic beasts that guarded the staircase, and something not quite usual in this man's appearance gave his thoughts a fresh turn.

Whether he had come out of the hall through the bronze doors or mounted unnoticed from outside, it was impossible to tell. Aschenbach casually inclined to the first idea. He was of medium height, thin, beardless, and strikingly snub-nosed; he belonged to the red-haired type and possessed its milky, freckled skin. He was obviously not Bavarian; and the broad, straight-brimmed straw hat he had on even made him look distinctly exotic. True, he had the indigenous rucksack buckled on his back, wore a belted suit of yellowish woollen stuff, apparently frieze, and carried a grey mackintosh cape across his left forearm, which was propped against his waist. In his right hand, slantwise to the ground, he held an iron-shod stick, and braced himself against its crook, with his legs crossed. His chin was up, so that the Adam's apple looked very bald in the lean neck rising from the loose shirt; and he stood there sharply peering up into space out of colourless, red-lashed eyes, while two pronounced perpendicular furrows showed on his forehead in curious contrast to his little turned-up nose. Perhaps his heightened and heightening position helped out the impression Aschenbach received. At any rate, standing there as though at survey, the man had a bold and domineering, even a ruthless, air, and his lips completed the picture by seeming to curl back, either by reason of some deformity or else because he grimaced, being blinded by the sun in his face; they laid bare the long, white, glistening teeth to the gums.

Aschenbach's gaze, though unawares, had very likely been inquisitive and tactless; for he became suddenly conscious that the stranger was returning it, and indeed so directly, with such hostility, such plain intent to force the withdrawal of the other's eyes, that Aschenbach felt an unpleasant twinge and, turning his back, began to walk along the hedge, hastily resolving to give the man no further heed. He had forgotten him the next minute. Yet whether the pilgrim air the stranger wore kindled his fantasy or whether some other physical or psychical influence came in play, he could not tell; but he felt the most surprising consciousness of a widening of inward barriers, a kind of vaulting unrest, a youthfully ardent thirst for distant scenes—a feeling so lively and so new, or at least so long ago outgrown and forgot, that he stood there rooted to the spot, his eyes on the ground and his hands clasped behind him, exploring these sentiments of his, their bearing and scope.

True, what he felt was no more than a longing to travel; yet coming upon him with such suddenness and passion as to resemble a seizure, almost an hallucination. Desire projected itself visually: his fancy, not quite yet lulled since morning, imaged the marvels and terrors of the manifold earth. He saw. He beheld a landscape, a tropical marshland, beneath a reeking sky, steaming, monstrous, rank—a kind of primeval wilderness-world of islands, morasses, and alluvial channels. Hairy palm-trunks rose near and far out of lush brakes of fern, out of bottoms of crass vegetation, fat, swollen, thick with incredible bloom. There were trees, mis-shapen as a dream, that dropped their naked roots straight through the air into the ground or into water that was stagnant and shadowy and glassy-green, where mammoth milk-white blossoms floated, and strange high-shouldered birds with curious bills stood gazing sidewise without sound or stir. Among the knotted joints of a bamboo thicket the eyes of a crouching tiger gleamed—and he felt his heart throb with terror, yet with a longing inexplicable. Then the vision vanished. Aschenbach, shaking his head, took up his march once more along the hedge of the stone-mason's yard.

He had, at least ever since he commanded means to get about the world at will, regarded travel as a necessary evil, to be endured now and again willy-nilly for the sake of one's health. Too busy with the tasks imposed upon him by his own ego and the European soul, too laden with the care and duty to create, too preoccupied to be an amateur of the gay outer world, he had been content to know as much of the earth's surface as he could without stirring far outside his own sphere—had, indeed, never even been tempted to leave Europe. Now more than ever, since his life was on the wane, since he could no longer brush aside as fanciful his artist fear of not having done, of not being finished before the works ran down, he had confined himself to close range, had hardly stepped outside the charming city which he had made his home and the rude country house he had built in the mountains, whither he went to spend the rainy summers.

And so the new impulse which thus late and suddenly swept over him was speedily made to conform to the pattern of self-discipline he had followed from his youth up. He had meant to bring his work, for which he lived, to a certain point before leaving for the country, and the thought of a leisurely ramble across the globe, which should take him away from his desk for months, was too fantastic and upsetting to be seriously entertained. Yet the source of the unexpected contagion was known to him only too well. This yearning for new and distant scenes, this craving for freedom, release, forgetfulness—they were, he admitted to himself, an impulse towards flight, flight from the spot which was the daily theatre of a rigid, cold, and passionate service. That service he loved, had even almost come to love the enervating daily struggle between a proud, tenacious, well-tried will and this growing fatigue, which no one must suspect, nor the finished product betray by any faintest sign that his inspiration could ever flag or miss fire. On the other hand, it seemed the part of common sense not to span the bow too far, not to suppress summarily a need that so unequivocally asserted itself. He thought of his work, and the place where yesterday and again today he had been forced to lay it down, since it would not yield either to patient effort or a swift *coup de main*. Again and again he had tried to break or untie the knot—only to retire at last from the attack with a shiver of repugnance. Yet the difficulty was actually not a great one; what sapped his strength was distaste for the task, betrayed by a fastidiousness he could no longer satisfy. In his youth, indeed, the nature and inmost essence of the literary gift had been, to him, this very scrupulosity; for it he had bridled and tempered his sensibilities, knowing full well that feeling is prone to be content with easy gains and blithe half-perfection. So now, perhaps, feeling, thus tyrannized, avenged itself by leaving him, refusing from now on to carry and wing his art and taking away with it all the ecstasy he had known in form and expression. Not that he was doing bad work. So much, at least, the years had brought him, that at any moment he might feel tranquilly assured of mastery. But he got no joy of it—not though a nation paid it homage. To him it seemed his work had ceased to be marked by that fiery play of fancy which is the product of joy, and more, and more potently, than any intrinsic content, forms in turn the joy of the receiving world. He dreaded the summer in the country, alone with the maid who prepared his food and the man who served him; dreaded to see the familiar mountain peaks and walls that would shut him up again with his heavy discontent. What he needed was a break, an interim existence, a means of passing time, other air and a new stock of blood, to make the summer tolerable and productive. Good, then, he would go a journey. Not far—not all the way to the tigers. A night in a *wagon-lit*, three or four weeks of lotus-eating at some one of the gay world's playgrounds in the lovely south. . . .

So ran his thoughts, while the clang of the electric tram drew nearer down the Ungererstrasse; and as he mounted the platform he decided to devote the evening to a study of maps and railway guides. Once in, he bethought him to look back after the man in the straw hat, the companion of this brief interval which had after all been so fruitful. But he was not in his former place, nor in the tram itself, nor yet at the next stop; in short, his whereabouts remained a mystery.

Gustave Aschenbach was born at L—, a country town in the province of Silesia. He was the son of an upper official in the judicature, and his forebears had all been officers, judges, departmental functionaries—men who lived their strict, decent, sparing lives in the service of king and state. Only once before had a livelier mentality—in the quality of a clergyman—turned up among them;

but swifter, more perceptive blood had in the generation before the poet's flowed into the stock from the mother's side, she being the daughter of a Bohemian musical conductor. It was from her he had the foreign traits that betrayed themselves in his appearance. The union of dry, conscientious officialdom and ardent, obscure impulse, produced an artist—and this particular artist: author of the lucid and vigorous prose epic on the life of Frederick the Great; careful, tireless weaver of the richly patterned tapestry entitled *Maia*, a novel that gathers up the threads of many human destinies in the warp of a single idea; creator of that powerful narrative *The Abject*, which taught a whole grateful generation that a man can still be capable of moral resolution even after he has plumbed the depths of knowledge; and lastly—to complete the tale of works of his mature period—the writer of that impassioned discourse on the theme of Mind and Art whose ordered force and antithetic eloquence led serious critics to rank it with Schiller's *Simple and Sentimental Poetry*.

Aschenbach's whole soul, from the very beginning, was bent on fame—and thus, while not precisely precocious, yet thanks to the unmistakable trenchancy of his personal accent he was early ripe and ready for a career. Almost before he was out of high school he had a name. Ten years later he had learned to sit at his desk and sustain and live up to his growing reputation, to write gracious and pregnant phrases in letters that must needs be brief, for many claims press upon the solid and successful man. At forty, worn down by the strains and stresses of his actual task, he had to deal with a daily post heavy with tributes from his own and foreign countries.

Remote on one hand from the banal, on the other from the eccentric, his genius was calculated to win at once the adhesion of the general public and the admiration, both sympathetic and stimulating, of the connoisseur. From childhood up he was pushed on every side to achievement, and achievement of no ordinary kind; and so his young days never knew the sweet idleness and blithe *laissez aller* that belong to youth. A nice observer once said of him in company—it was at the time when he fell ill in Vienna in his thirty-fifth year: "You see, Aschenbach has always lived like this"—here the speaker closed the fingers of his left hand to a fist—"never like this"—and he let his open hand hang relaxed from the back of his chair. It was apt. And this attitude was the more morally valiant in that Aschenbach was not by nature robust—he was only called to the constant tension of his career, not actually born to it.

By medical advice he had been kept from school and educated at home. He had grown up solitary, without comradeship; yet had early been driven to see that he belonged to those whose talent is not so much out of the common as is the physical basis on which talent relies for its fulfilment. It is a seed that gives early of its fruit, whose powers seldom reach a ripe old age. But his favourite motto was "Hold fast"; indeed, in his novel on the life of Frederick the Great he envisaged nothing else than the apotheosis of the old hero's word of command, "*Durchhalten,*" which seemed to him the epitome of fortitude under suffering. Besides, he deeply desired to live to a good old age, for it was his conviction that only the artist to whom it has been granted to be fruitful on all stages of our human scene can be truly great, or universal, or worthy of honour.

Bearing the burden of his genius, then, upon such slender shoulders and resolved to go so far, he had the more need of discipline—and discipline, fortunately, was his native inheritance from the father's side. At forty, at fifty, he was still living as he had commenced to live in the years when others are prone to waste and revel, dream high thoughts and postpone fulfilment. He began his day with a cold shower over chest and back; then, setting a pair of tall wax candles in silver holders at the head of his manuscript, he sacrificed to art, in two or three hours of almost religious fervour, the powers he had assembled in sleep. Outsiders might be pardoned for believing that his *Maia* world and the epic amplitude revealed by the life of Frederick were a manifestation of great power working under high pressure, that they came forth, as it were, all in one breath. It was the more triumph for his morale; for the truth was that they were heaped up to greatness in layer after layer, in long days of work, out of hundreds and hundreds of single inspirations; they owed their excellence, both of mass and detail, to one thing and one alone: that their creator could hold out for years under the strain of the same piece of work, with an endurance and a tenacity of purpose like that which had conquered his native province of Silesia, devoting to actual composition none but his best and freshest hours.

For an intellectual product of any value to exert an immediate influence which shall also be deep and lasting, it must rest on an inner harmony, yes, an affinity, between the personal destiny of its author and that of his contemporaries in general. Men do not know why they award fame to one work of art rather than another. Without being in the faintest connoisseurs, they think to justify the warmth of their commendations by discovering in it a hundred virtues, whereas the real ground of their applause is inexplicable—it is sympathy. Aschenbach had once given direct expression—though in an unobtrusive place—to the idea that almost everything conspicuously great is great in despite: has come into being in defiance of affliction and pain, poverty, destitution, bodily weakness, vice, passion, and a thousand other obstructions. And that was more than observation—it was the fruit of experience, it was precisely the formula of his life and fame, it was the key to his work. What wonder, then, if it was also the fixed character, the outward gesture, of his most individual figures?

The new type of hero favoured by Aschenbach, and recurring many times in his works, had early been analysed by a shrewd critic: "The conception of an intellectual and virginal manliness, which clenches its teeth and stands in modest defiance of the swords and spears that pierce its side." That was beautiful, it was *spirituel*, it was exact, despite the suggestion of too great passivity it held. Forbearance in the face of fate, beauty constant under torture, are not merely passive. They are a positive achievement, an explicit triumph; and the figure of Sebastian is the most beautiful symbol, if not of art as a whole, yet certainly of the art we speak of here. Within that world of Aschenbach's creation were exhibited many phases of this theme: there was the aristocratic self-command that is eaten out within and for as long as it can conceals its biologic decline from the eyes of the world; the sere and ugly outside, hiding the embers of smouldering fire—and having power to fan them to so pure a flame as to challenge supremacy in the domain of beauty itself; the pallid languors of the flesh, contrasted with the fiery ardours of the spirit within, which can fling a whole proud people down at the foot of the Cross, at the feet of its own sheer self-abnegation; the gracious bearing preserved in the stern, stark service of form; the unreal, precarious existence of the born intriguant with its swiftly enervating alternation of schemes and desires

—all these human fates and many more of their like one read in Aschenbach's pages, and reading them might doubt the existence of any other kind of heroism than the heroism born of weakness. And, after all, what kind could be truer to the spirit of the times? Gustave Aschenbach was the poet-spokesman of all those who labour at the edge of exhaustion; of the overburdened, of those who are already worn out but still hold themselves upright; of all our modern moralizers of accomplishment, with stunted growth and scanty resources, who yet contrive by skilful husbanding and prodigious spasms of will to produce, at least for a while, the effect of greatness. There are many such, they are the heroes of the age. And in Aschenbach's pages they saw themselves; he justified, he exalted them, he sang their praise—and they, they were grateful, they heralded his fame.

He had been young and crude with the times and by them badly counselled. He had taken false steps, blundered, exposed himself, offended in speech and writing against tact and good sense. But he had attained to honour, and honour, he used to say, is the natural goal towards which every considerable talent presses with whip and spur. Yes, one might put it that his whole career had been one conscious and overweening ascent to honour, which left in the rear all the misgivings or self-derogation which might have hampered him.

What pleases the public is lively and vivid delineation which makes no demands on the intellect; but passionate and absolutist youth can only be enthralled by a problem. And Aschenbach was as absolute, as problematist, as any youth of them all. He had done homage to intellect, had overworked the soil of knowledge and ground up her seed-corn; had turned his back on the "mysteries," called genius itself in question, held up art to scorn—yes, even while his faithful following revelled in the characters he created, he, the young artist, was taking away the breath of the twenty-year-olds with his cynic utterances on the nature of art and the artist life.

But it seems that a noble and active mind blunts itself against nothing so quickly as the sharp and bitter irritant of knowledge. And certain it is that the youth's constancy of purpose, no matter how painfully conscientious, was shallow beside the mature resolution of the master of his craft, who made a right-about-face, turned his back on the realm of knowledge, and passed it by with averted face, lest it lame his will or power of action, paralyse his feelings or his passions, deprive any of these of their conviction or utility. How else interpret the oft-cited story of *The Abject* than as a rebuke to the excesses of a psychology-ridden age, embodied in the delineation of the weak and silly fool who manages to lead fate by the nose; driving his wife, out of sheer innate pusillanimity, into the arms of a beardless youth, and making this disaster an excuse for trifling away the rest of his life?

With rage the author here rejects the rejected, casts out the outcast—and the measure of his fury is the measure of his condemnation of all moral shilly-shallying. Explicitly he renounces sympathy with the abyss, explicitly he refutes the flabby humanitarianism of the phrase: "*Tout comprendre c'est tout pardonner.*" What was here unfolding, or rather was already in full bloom, was the "miracle of regained detachment," which a little later became the theme of one of the author's dialogues, dwelt upon not without a certain oracular emphasis. Strange sequence of thought! Was it perhaps an intellectual consequence of this rebirth, this new austerity, that from now on his style showed an almost exaggerated sense of beauty, a lofty purity, symmetry, and simplicity, which gave his productions a stamp of the classic, of conscious and deliberate mastery? And yet: this moral fibre, surviving the hampering and disintegrating effect of knowledge, does it not result in its turn in a dangerous simplification, in a tendency to equate the world and the human soul, and thus to strengthen the hold of the evil, the forbidden, and the ethically impossible? And has not form two aspects? Is it not moral and immoral at once: moral in so far as it is the expression and result of discipline; immoral—yes, actually hostile to morality—in that of its very essence it is indifferent to good and evil, and deliberately concerned to make the moral world stoop beneath its proud and undivided sceptre?

Be that as it may. Development is destiny; and why should a career attended by the applause and adulation of the masses necessarily take the same course as one which does not share the glamour and the obligations of fame? Only the incorrigible bohemian smiles or scoffs when a man of transcendent gifts outgrows his carefree prentice stage, recognizes his own worth and forces the world to recognize it too and pay it homage, though he puts on a courtly bearing to hide his bitter struggles and his loneliness. Again, the play of a developing talent must give its possessor joy, if of a wilful, defiant kind. With time, an official note, something almost expository, crept into Gustave Aschenbach's method. His later style gave up the old sheer audacities, the fresh and subtle nuances—it became fixed and exemplary, conservative, formal, even formulated. Like Louis XIV—or as tradition has it of him—Aschenbach, as he went on in years, banished from his style every common word. It was at this time that the school authorities adopted selections from his works into their text-books. And he found it only fitting—and had no thought but to accept—when a German prince signalized his accession to the throne by conferring upon the poet-author of the life of Frederick the Great on his fiftieth birthday the letters-patent of nobility.

He had roved about for a few years, trying this place and that as a place of residence, before choosing, as he soon did, the city of Munich for his permanent home. And there he lived, enjoying among his fellow-citizens the honour which is in rare cases the reward of intellectual eminence. He married young, the daughter of a university family; but after a brief term of wedded happiness his wife had died. A daughter, already married, remained to him. A son he never had.

Gustave von Aschenbach was somewhat below middle height, dark and smooth-shaven, with a head that looked rather too large for his almost delicate figure. He wore his hair brushed back; it was thin at the parting, bushy and grey on the temples, framing a lofty, rugged, knotty brow—if one may so characterize it. The nose-piece of his rimless gold spectacles cut into the base of his thick, aristocratically hooked nose. The mouth was large, often lax, often suddenly narrow and tense; the cheeks lean and furrowed, the pronounced chin slightly cleft. The vicissitudes of fate, it seemed, must have passed over this head, for he held it, plaintively, rather on one side; yet it was art, not the stern discipline of an active career, that had taken over the office of modelling these features. Behind this brow were born the flashing thrust and parry of the dialogue between Frederick and Voltaire on the theme of war; these eyes, weary and sunken, gazing through their glasses, had beheld the blood-stained inferno of the hospitals in the Seven Years' War. Yes, personally speaking too, art heightens life. She gives deeper joy, she consumes more swiftly. She engraves adventures of the spirit and the mind in the faces of her votaries; let them lead outwardly a life of the most cloistered calm, she will in the end produce in them a fastidiousness, an over-refinement, a nervous fever and exhaustion, such as a career of extravagant passions and pleasures can hardly show.

Eager though he was to be off, Aschenbach was kept in Munich by affairs both literary and practical for some two weeks after that walk of his. But at length he ordered his country home put ready against his return within the next few weeks, and on a day between the middle and the end of May took the evening train for Trieste, where he stopped only twenty-four hours, embarking for Pola the next morning but one.

What he sought was a fresh scene, without associations, which should yet be not too out-of-the-way; and accordingly he chose an island in the Adriatic, not far off the Istrian coast. It had been well known some years, for its splendidly rugged cliff formations on the side next the open sea, and its population, clad in a bright flutter of rags and speaking an outlandish tongue. But there was rain and heavy air; the society at the hotel was provincial Austrian, and limited; besides, it annoyed him not to be able to get at the sea—he missed the close and soothing contact which only a gentle sandy slope affords. He could not feel this was the place he sought; an inner impulse made him wretched, urging him on he knew not whither; he racked his brains, he looked up boats, then all at once his goal stood plain before his eyes. But of course! When one wanted to arrive overnight at the incomparable, the fabulous, the like-nothing-else-in-the-world, where was it one went? Why, obviously; he had intended to go there, whatever was he doing here? A blunder. He made all haste to correct it, announcing his departure at once. Ten days after his arrival on the island a swift motorboat bore him and his luggage in the misty dawning back across the water to the naval station, where he landed only to pass over the landing-stage and on to the wet decks of a ship lying there with steam up for the passage to Venice.

It was an ancient hulk belonging to an Italian line, obsolete, dingy, grimed with soot. A dirty hunchbacked sailor, smirkingly polite, conducted him at once belowships to a cavernous, lamplit cabin. There behind a table sat a man with a beard like a goat's; he had his hat on the back of his head, a cigar-stump in the corner of his mouth; he reminded Aschenbach of an old-fashioned circus-director. This person put the usual questions and wrote out a ticket to Venice, which he issued to the traveller with many commercial flourishes.

"A ticket for Venice," repeated he, stretching out his arm to dip the pen into the thick ink in a tilted ink-stand. "One first-class to Venice! Here you are, *signore mio*." He made some scrawls on the paper, strewed bluish sand on it out of a box, thereafter letting the sand run off into an earthen vessel, folded the paper with bony yellow fingers, and wrote on the outside. "An excellent choice," he rattled on. "Ah, Venice! What a glorious city! Irresistibly attractive to the cultured man for her past history as well as her present charm." His copious gesturings and empty phrases gave the odd impression that he feared the traveller might alter his mind. He changed Aschenbach's note, laying the money on the spotted table-cover with the glibness of a croupier. "A pleasant visit to you, signore," he said, with a melodramatic bow. "Delighted to serve you." Then he beckoned and called out: "Next" as though a stream of passengers stood waiting to be served, though in point of fact there was not one. Aschenbach returned to the upper deck.

He leaned an arm on the railing and looked at the idlers lounging along the quay to watch the boat go out. Then he turned his attention to his fellow-passengers. Those of the second class, both men and women, were squatted on their bundles of luggage on the forward deck. The first cabin consisted of a group of lively youths, clerks from Pola, evidently, who had made up a pleasure excursion to Italy and were not a little thrilled at the prospect, bustling about and laughing with satisfaction at the stir they made. They leaned over the railings and shouted, with a glib command of epithet, derisory remarks at such of their fellow-clerks as they saw going to business along the quay; and these in turn shook their sticks and shouted as good back again. One of the party, in a dandified buff suit, a rakish panama with a coloured scarf, and a red cravat, was loudest of the loud: he outcrowed all the rest. Aschenbach's eye dwelt on him, and he was shocked to see that the apparent youth was no youth at all. He was an old man, beyond a doubt, with wrinkles and crow's-feet round eyes and mouth; the dull carmine of the cheeks was rouge, the brown hair a wig. His neck was shrunken and sinewy, his turned-up moustaches and small imperial were dyed, and the unbroken double row of yellow teeth he showed when he laughed were but too obviously a cheapish false set. He wore a seal ring on each forefinger, but the hands were those of an old man. Aschenbach was moved to shudder as he watched the creature and his association with the rest of the group. Could they not see he was old, that he had no right to wear the clothes they wore or pretend to be one of them? But they were used to him, it seemed; they suffered him among them, they paid back his jokes in kind and the playful pokes in the ribs he gave them. How could they? Aschenbach put his hand to his brow, he covered his eyes, for he had slept little, and they smarted. He felt not quite canny, as though the world were suffering a dreamlike distortion of perspective which he might arrest by shutting it all out for a few minutes and then looking at it afresh. But instead he felt a floating sensation, and opened his eyes with unreasoning alarm to find that the ship's dark sluggish bulk was slowly leaving the jetty. Inch by inch, with the to-and-fro motion of her machinery, the strip of iridescent dirty water widened, the boat manoeuvred clumsily and turned her bow to the open sea. Aschenbach moved over to the starboard side, where the hunchbacked sailor had set up a deck-chair for him, and a steward in a greasy dress-coat asked for orders.

The sky was grey, the wind humid. Harbour and island dropped behind, all sight of land soon vanished in mist. Flakes of sodden, clammy soot fell upon the still undried deck. Before the boat was an hour out a canvas had to be spread as a shelter from the rain.

Wrapped in his cloak, a book in his lap, our traveller rested; the hours slipped by unawares. It stopped raining, the canvas was taken down. The horizon was visible right round: beneath the sombre dome of the sky stretched the vast plain of empty sea. But immeasurable unarticulated space weakens our power to measure time as well: the time-sense falters and grows dim. Strange, shadowy figures passed and repassed—the elderly coxcomb, the goat-bearded man from the bowels of the ship—with vague gesturings and mutterings through the traveller's mind as he lay. He fell asleep.

At midday he was summoned to luncheon in a corridor-like saloon with the sleeping-cabins giving off it. He ate at the head of the long table; the party of clerks, including the old man, sat with the jolly captain at the other end, where they had been carousing since ten o'clock. The meal was wretched, and soon done. Aschenbach was driven to seek the open and look at the sky—perhaps it would lighten presently above Venice.

He had not dreamed it could be otherwise, for the city had ever given him a brilliant welcome. But sky and sea remained leaden, with spurts of fine, mistlike rain; he reconciled himself to the idea of seeing a different Venice from that he had always approached on the landward side. He stood by the foremast, his gaze on the distance, alert for the first glimpse of the coast. And he thought of the melancholy and susceptible poet who had once seen the towers and turrets of his dreams rise out of these waves; repeated the rhythms born of his awe, his mingled emotions of joy and suffering—and easily susceptible to a prescience already shaped within him, he asked his own sober, weary heart if a new enthusiasm, a new preoccupation, some late adventue of the feelings could still be in store for the idle traveller.

The flat coast showed on the right, the sea was soon populous with fishing-boats. The Lido appeared and was left behind as the ship glided at half speed through the narrow harbour of the same name, coming to a full stop on the lagoon in sight of garish, badly built houses. Here it waited for the boat bringing the sanitary inspector.

An hour passed. One had arrived—and yet not. There was no conceivable haste—yet one felt harried. The youths from Pola were on deck, drawn hither by the martial sound of horns coming across the water from the direction of the Public Gardens. They had drunk a good deal of Asti and were moved to shout and hurrah at the drilling *bersaglieri*. But the young-old man was a truly repulsive sight in the condition to which his company with youth had brought him. He could not carry his wine like them: he was pitiably drunk. He swayed as he stood—watery-eyed, a cigarette between his shaking fingers, keeping upright with difficulty. He could not have taken a step without falling and knew better than to stir, but his spirits were deplorably high. He buttonholed anyone who came within reach, he stuttered, he giggled, he leered, he fatuously shook his beringed old forefinger; his tongue kept seeking the corner of his mouth in a suggestive motion ugly to behold.

Aschenbach's brow darkened as he looked, and there came over him once more a dazed sense, as though things about him were just slightly losing their ordinary perspective, beginning to show a distortion that might merge into the grotesque. He was prevented from dwelling on the feeling, for now the machinery began to thud again, and the ship took up its passage through the Canale di San Marco which had been interrupted so near the goal.

He saw it once more, that landing-place that takes the breath away, that amazing group of incredible structures the Republic set up to meet the awe-struck eye of the approaching seafarer: the airy splendour of the palace and Bridge of Sighs, the columns of lion and saint on the shore, the glory of the projecting flank of the fairy temple, the vista of gateway and clock. Looking, he thought that to come to Venice by the station is like entering a palace by the back door. No one should approach, save by the high seas as he was doing now, this most improbable of cities.

The engines stopped. Gondolas pressed alongside, the landing-stairs were let down, customs officials came on board and did their office, people began to go ashore. Aschenbach ordered a gondola. He meant to take up his abode by the sea and needed to be conveyed with his luggage to the landing-stage of the little steamers that ply between the city and the Lido. They called down his order to the surface of the water where the gondoliers were quarrelling in dialect. Then came another delay while his trunk was worried down the ladder-like stairs. Thus he was forced to endure the importunities of the ghastly young-old man, whose drunken state obscurely urged him to pay the stranger the honour of a formal farewell. "We wish you a very pleasant sojourn," he babbled, bowing and scraping. "Pray keep us in mind. *Au revoir, excusez et bon jour, votre Excellence.*" He drooled, he blinked, he licked the corner of his mouth, the little imperial bristled on his elderly chin. He put the tips of two fingers to his mouth and said thickly: "Give her our love, will you, the p-pretty little dear"—here his upper plate came away and fell down on the lower one. . . . Aschenbach escaped. "Little sweety-sweety-sweetheart" he heard behind him, gurgled and stuttered, as he climbed down the rope stair into the boat.

Is there anyone but must repress a secret thrill, on arriving in Venice for the first time—or returning thither after long absence

—and stepping into a Venetian gondola? That singular conveyance, come down unchanged from ballad times, black as nothing else on earth except a coffin—what pictures it calls up of lawless, silent adventures in the plashing night; or even more, what visions of death itself, the bier and solemn rites and last soundless voyage! And has anyone remarked that the seat in such a bark, the armchair lacquered in coffin-black and dully black-upholstered, is the softest, most luxurious, most relaxing seat in the world? Aschenbach realized it when he had let himself down at the gondolier's feet, opposite his luggage, which lay neatly composed on the vessel's beak. The rowers still gestured fiercely; he heard their harsh, incoherent tones. But the strange stillness of the water-city seemed to take up their voices gently, to disembody and scatter them over the sea. It was warm here in the harbour. The lukewarm air of the sirocco breathed upon him, he leaned back among his cushions and gave himself to the yielding element, closing his eyes for very pleasure in an indolence as unaccustomed as sweet. "The trip will be short," he thought, and wished it might last for ever. They gently swayed away from the boat with its bustle and clamour of voices.

It grew still and stiller all about. No sound but the splash of the oars, the hollow slap of the wave against the steep, black, halbert-shaped beak of the vessel, and one sound more—a muttering by fits and starts, expressed as it were by the motion of his arms, from the lips of the gondolier. He was talking to himself, between his teeth. Aschenbach glanced up and saw with surprise that the lagoon was widening, his vessel was headed for the open sea. Evidently it would not do to give himself up to sweet *far niente*; he must see his wishes carried out.

"You are to take me to the steamboat landing, you know," he said, half turning round towards it. The muttering stopped. There was no reply.

"Take me to the steamboat landing," he repeated, and this time turned quite round and looked up into the face of the gondolier as he stood there on his little elevated deck, high against the pale grey sky. The man had an unpleasing, even brutish face, and wore blue clothes like a sailor's, with a yellow sash; a shapeless straw hat with the braid torn at the brim perched rakishly on his head. His facial structure, as well as the curling blond moustache under the short snub nose, showed him to be of non-Italian stock. Physically rather undersized, so that one would not have expected him to be very muscular, he pulled vigorously at the oar, putting all his body-weight behind each stroke. Now and then the effort he made curled back his lips and bared his white teeth to the gums. He spoke in a decided, almost curt voice, looking out to sea over his fare's head: "The signore is going to the Lido."

Aschenbach answered: "Yes, I am. But I only took the gondola to cross over to San Marco. I am using the *vaporetto* from there."

"But the signore cannot use the *vaporetto*."

"And why not?"

"Because the *vaporetto* does not take luggage."

It was true. Aschenbach remembered it. He made no answer. But the man's gruff, overbearing manner, so unlike the usual courtesy of his countrymen towards the stranger, was intolerable. Aschenbach spoke again: "That is my own affair. I may want to give my luggage in deposit. You will turn round."

No answer. The oar splashed, the wave struck dull against the prow. And the muttering began anew, the gondolier talked to himself, between his teeth.

What should the traveller do? Alone on the water with this tongue-tied, obstinate, uncanny man, he saw no way of enforcing his will. And if only he did not excite himself, how pleasantly he might rest! Had he not wished the voyage might last for ever? The wisest thing—and how much the pleasantest!—was to let matters take their own course. A spell of indolence was upon him; it came from the chair he sat in—this low, black-upholstered armchair, so gently rocked at the hands of the despotic boatman in his rear. The thought passed dreamily through Aschenbach's brain that perhaps he had fallen into the clutches of a criminal; it had not power to rouse him to action. More annoying was the simpler explanation: that the man was only trying to extort money. A sense of duty, a recollection, as it were, that this ought to be prevented, made him collect himself to say:

"How much do you ask for the trip?"

And the gondolier, gazing out over his head, replied: "The signore will pay."

There was an established reply to this; Aschenbach made it, mechanically:

"I will pay nothing whatever if you do not take me where

I want to go."

"The signore wants to go to the Lido."

"But not with you."

"I am a good rower, signore. I will row you well."

"So much is true," thought Aschenbach, and again he relaxed. "That is true, you row me well. Even if you mean to rob me, even if you hit me in the back with your oar and send me down to the kingdom of Hades, even then you will have rowed me well."

But nothing of the sort happened. Instead, they fell in with company: a boat came alongside and waylaid them, full of men and women singing to guitar and mandolin. They rowed persistently bow for bow with the gondola and filled the silence that had rested on the waters with their lyric love of gain. Aschenbach tossed money into the hat they held out. The music stopped at once, they rowed away. And once more the gondolier's mutter became audible as he talked to himself in fits and snatches.

Thus they rowed on, rocked by the wash of a steamer returning citywards. At the landing two municipal officials were walking up and down with their hands behind their backs and their faces turned towards the lagoon. Aschenbach was helped on shore by the old man with a boat-hook who is the permanent feature of every landing-stage in Venice; and having no small change to pay the boatman, crossed over into the hotel opposite. His wants were supplied in the lobby; but when he came back his possessions were already on a hand-car on the quay, and gondola and gondolier were gone.

"He ran away, signore," said the old boatman. "A bad lot, a man without a licence. He is the only gondolier without one. The others telephoned over, and he knew we were on the look-out, so he made off."

Aschenbach shrugged.

"The signore has had a ride for nothing," said the old man, and held out his hat. Aschenbach dropped some coins. He directed that his luggage be taken to the Hôtel des Bains and followed the hand-car through the avenue, that white-blossoming avenue with taverns, booths, and pensions on either side it, which runs across the island diagonally to the beach.

He entered the hotel from the garden terrace at the back and passed through the vestibule and hall into the office. His arrival was expected, and he was served with courtesy and dispatch. The manager, a small, soft, dapper man with a black moustache and a caressing way with him, wearing a French frock-coat, himself took him up in the lift and showed him his room. It was a pleasant chamber, furnished in cherry-wood, with lofty windows looming out to sea. It was decorated with strong-scented flowers. Aschenbach, as soon as he was alone, and while they brought in his trunk and bags and disposed them in the room, went up to one of the windows and stood looking out upon the beach in its afternoon emptiness, and at the sunless sea, now full and sending long, low waves with rhythmic beat upon the sand.

A solitary, unused to speaking of what he sees and feels, has mental experiences which are at once more intense and less articulate than those of a gregarious man. They are sluggish, yet more wayward, and never without a melancholy tinge. Sights and impressions which others brush aside with a glance, a light comment, a smile, occupy him more than their due; they sink silently in, they take on meaning, they become experience, emotion, adventure. Solitude gives birth to the original in us, to beauty unfamiliar and perilous—to poetry. But also, it gives birth to the opposite: to the perverse, the illicit, the absurd. Thus the traveller's mind still dwelt with disquiet on the episodes of his journey hither: on the horrible old fop with his drivel about a mistress, on the outlaw boatman and his lost tip. They did not offend his reason, they hardly afforded food for thought; yet they seemed by their very nature fundamentally strange, and thereby vaguely disquieting. Yet here was the sea; even in the midst of such thoughts he saluted it with his eyes, exulting that Venice was near and accessible. At length he turned round, disposed his personal belongings and made certain arrangements with the chambermaid for his comfort, washed up, and was conveyed to the ground floor by the green-uniformed Swiss who ran the lift.

He took tea on the terrace facing the sea and afterwards went down and walked some distance along the shore promenade in the direction of Hôtel Excelsior. When he came back it seemed to be time to change for dinner. He did so, slowly and methodically as his way was, for he was accustomed to work while he dressed; but even so found himself a little early when he entered the hall, where a large number of guests had collected—strangers to each other and affecting mutual indifference, yet united in expectancy of the meal. He picked up a paper, sat down in a leather arm-chair, and took stock of the company, which compared most favourably with that he had just left.

This was a broad and tolerant atmosphere, of wide horizons. Subdued voices were speaking most of the principal European tongues. That uniform of civilization, the conventional evening dress, gave outward conformity to the varied types. There were long, dry Americans, large-familied Russians, English ladies, German children with French *bonnes*. The Slavic element predominated it seemed. In Aschenbach's neighbourhood Polish was being spoken.

Round a wicker table next him was gathered a group of young folk in charge of a governess or companion—three young girls, perhaps fifteen to seventeen years old, and a long-haired boy of about fourteen. Aschenbach noticed with astonishment the lad's perfect beauty. His face recalled the noblest moment of Greek sculpture—pale, with a sweet reserve, with clustering honey-coloured ringlets, the brow and nose descending in one line, the winning mouth, the expression of pure and godlike serenity. Yet with all this chaste perfection of form it was of such unique personal charm that the observer thought he had never seen, either in nature or art, anything so utterly happy and consummate. What struck him further was the strange contrast the group afforded, a difference in educational method, so to speak, shown in the way the brother and sisters were clothed and treated. The girls, the eldest of whom was practically grown up, were dressed with an almost disfiguring austerity. All three wore half-length slate-coloured frocks of cloister-like plainness, arbitrarily unbecoming in cut, with white turn-over collars as their only adornment. Every grace of outline was wilfully suppressed; their hair lay smoothly plastered to their heads, giving them a vacant expression, like a nun's. All this could only be by the mother's orders; but there was no trace of the same pedagogic severity in the case of the boy. Tenderness and softness, it was plain, conditioned his existence. No scissors had been put to the lovely hair that (like the Spinnario's) curled about his brows, above his ears, longer still in the neck. He wore an English sailor suit, with quilted sleeves that narrowed round the delicate wrists of his long and slender though still childish hands. And this suit, with its breast-knot, lacings, and embroideries, lent the slight figure something "rich and strange," a spoilt, exquisite air. The observer saw him in half profile, with one foot in its black patent leather advanced, one elbow resting on the arm of his basket-chair, the cheek nestled into the closed hand in a pose of easy grace, quite unlike the stiff subservient mien which was evidently habitual to his sisters. Was he delicate? His facial tint was ivory-white against the golden darkness of his clustering locks. Or was he simply a pampered darling, the object of a self-willed and partial love? Aschenbach inclined to think the latter. For in almost every artist's nature is inborn a wanton and treacherous proneness to side with the beauty that breaks hearts, to single out aristocratic pretensions and pay them homage.

A waiter announced, in English, that dinner was served. Gradually the company dispersed through the glass doors into the dining-room. Late-comers entered from the vestibule or the lifts. Inside, dinner was being served; but the young Poles still sat and waited about their wicker table. Aschenbach felt comfortable in his deep arm-chair, he enjoyed the beauty before his eyes, he waited with them.

The governess, a short, stout, red-faced person, at length gave the signal. With lifted brows she pushed back her chair and made a bow to the tall woman, dressed in palest grey, who now entered the hall. This lady's abundant jewels were pearls, her manner was cool and measured; the fashion of her gown and the arrangement of her lightly powdered hair had the simplicity prescribed in certain circles whose piety and aristocracy are equally marked. She might have been, in Germany, the wife of some high official. But there was something faintly fabulous, after all, in her appearance, though lent it solely by the pearls she wore: they were well-nigh priceless, and consisted of ear-rings and a three-stranded necklace, very long, with gems the size of cherries.

The brother and sisters had risen briskly. They bowed over their mother's hand to kiss it, she turning away from them, with a slight smile on her face, which was carefully preserved but rather sharp-nosed and worn. She addressed a few words in French to the governess, then moved towards the glass door. The children followed, the girls in order of age, then the governess, and last the boy. He chanced to turn before he crossed the threshold, and as there was no one else in the room, his strange, twilit grey eyes met

Aschenbach's, as our traveller sat there with the paper on his knee, absorbed in looking after the group.

There was nothing singular, of course, in what he had seen. They had not gone in to dinner before their mother, they had waited, given her a respectful salute, and but observed the right and proper forms on entering the room. Yet they had done all this so expressly, with such self-respecting dignity, discipline, and sense of duty that Aschenbach was impressed. He lingered still a few minutes, then he, too, went into the dining-room, where he was shown a table far off the Polish family, as he noted at once, with a stirring of regret.

Tired, yet mentally alert, he beguiled the long, tedious meal with abstract, even with transcendent matters: pondered the mysterious harmony that must come to subsist between the individual human being and the universal law, in order that human beauty may result; passed on to general problems of form and art, and came at length to the conclusion that what seemed to him fresh and happy thoughts were like the flattering inventions of a dream, which the waking sense proves worthless and insubstantial. He spent the evening in the park, that was sweet with the odours of evening—sitting, smoking, wandering about; went to bed betimes, and passed the night in deep, unbroken sleep, visited, however, by varied and lively dreams.

The weather next day was no more promising. A land breeze blew. Beneath a colourless, overcast sky the sea lay sluggish, and as it were shrunken, so far withdrawn as to leave bare several rows of long sand-banks. The horizon looked close and prosaic. When Aschenbach opened his window he thought he smelt the stagnant odour of the lagoons.

He felt suddenly out of sorts and already began to think of leaving. Once, years before, after weeks of bright spring weather, this wind had found him out; it had been so bad as to force him to flee from the city like a fugitive. And now it seemed beginning again—the same feverish distaste, the pressure on his temples, the heavy eyelids. It would be a nuisance to change again; but if the wind did not turn, this was no place for him. To be on the safe side, he did not entirely unpack. At nine o'clock he went down to the buffet, which lay between the hall and the dining-room and served as a breakfast-room.

A solemn stillness reigned here, such as it is the ambition of all large hotels to achieve. The waiters moved on noiseless feet. A rattling of tea-things, a whispered word—and no other sounds. In a corner diagonally to the door, two tables off his own, Aschenbach saw the Polish girls with their governess. They sat there very straight, in their stiff blue linen frocks with little turn-over collars and cuffs, their ash-blond hair newly brushed flat, their eyelids red from sleep; and handed each other the marmalade. They had nearly finished their meal. The boy was not there.

Aschenbach smiled. "Aha, little Phæax," he thought. "It seems you are privileged to sleep yourself out." With sudden gaiety he quoted:

"Oft veränderten Schmuck und warme Bäder und Ruhe."

He took a leisurely breakfast. The porter came up with his braided cap in his hand, to deliver some letters that had been sent on. Aschenbach lighted a cigarette and opened a few letters and thus was still seated to witness the arrival of the sluggard.

He entered through the glass doors and passed diagonally across the room to his sisters at their table. He walked with extraordinary grace—the carriage of the body, the action of the knee, the way he set down his foot in its white shoe—it was all so light, it was at once dainty and proud, it wore an added charm in the childish shyness which made him twice turn his head as he crossed the room, made him give a quick glance and then drop his eyes. He took his seat, with a smile and a murmured word in his soft and blurry tongue; and Aschenbach, sitting so that he could see him in profile, was astonished anew, yes, startled, at the godlike beauty of the human being. The lad had on a light sailor suit of blue and white striped cotton, with a red silk breast-knot and a simple white standing collar round the neck—a not very elegant effect—yet above this collar the head was poised like a flower, in incomparable loveliness. It was the head of Eros, with the yellowish bloom of Parian marble, with fine serious brows, and dusky clustering ringlets standing out in soft plenteousness over temples and ears.

"Good, oh, very good indeed!" thought Aschenbach, assuming the patronizing air of the connoisseur to hide, as artists will, their ravishment over a masterpiece. "Yes," he went on to himself, "if it were not that sea and beach were waiting for me, I should sit here as long as you do." But he went out on that, passing through the hall, beneath the watchful eye of the functionaries, down the steps and directly across the board walk to the section of the beach reserved for the guests of the hotel. The bathing-master, a barefoot old man in linen trousers and sailor blouse, with a straw hat, showed him the cabin that had been rented for him, and Aschenbach had him set up table and chair on the sandy platform before it. Then he dragged the reclining-chair through the pale yellow sand, closer to the sea, sat down, and composed himself.

He delighted, as always, in the scene on the beach, the sight of sophisticated society giving itself over to a simple life at the edge of the element. The shallow grey sea was already gay with children wading, with swimmers, with figures in bright colours lying on the sand-banks with arms behind their heads. Some were rowing in little keelless boats painted red and blue, and laughing when they capsized. A long row of *capanne* ran down the beach, with platforms, where people sat as on verandas, and there was social life, with bustle and with indolent repose; visits were paid, amid much chatter, punctilious morning *toilettes* hob-nobbed with comfortable and privileged dishabille. On the hard wet sand close to the sea figures in white bath-robes or loose wrappings in garish colours strolled up and down. A mammoth sand-hill had been built up on Aschenbach's right, the work of children, who had stuck it full of tiny flags. Vendors of sea-shells, fruit, and cakes knelt beside their wares spread out on the sand. A row of cabins on the left stood obliquely to the others and to the sea, thus forming the boundary of the enclosure on this side; and on the little veranda in front of one of these a Russian family was encamped; bearded men with strong white teeth, ripe, indolent women, a Fräulein from the Baltic provinces, who sat at an easel painting the sea and tearing her hair in despair; two ugly but good-natured children and an old maidservant in a head-cloth, with the caressing, servile manner of the born dependant. There they sat together in grateful enjoyment of their blessings: constantly shouting at their romping children, who paid not the slightest heed; making jokes in broken Italian to the funny old man who sold them sweetmeats, kissing each other on the cheeks—no jot concerned that their domesticity was overlooked.

"I'll stop," thought Aschenbach. "Where could it be better than here?" With his hands clasped in his lap he let his eyes swim in the wideness of the sea, his gaze lose focus, blur, and grow vague in the misty immensity of space. His love of the ocean had profound sources: the hard-worked artist's longing for rest, his yearning to seek refuge from the thronging manifold shapes of his fancy in the bosom of the simple and vast; and another yearning, opposed to his art and perhaps for that very reason a lure, for the unorganized, the immeasurable, the eternal—in short, for nothingness. He whose preoccupation is with excellence longs fervently to find rest in perfection; and is not nothingness a form of perfection? As he sat there dreaming thus, deep, deep into the void, suddenly the margin line of the shore was cut by a human form. He gathered up his gaze and withdrew it from the illimitable, and lo, it was the lovely boy who crossed his vision coming from the left along the sand. He was barefoot, ready for wading, the slender legs uncovered above the knee, and moved slowly, yet with such a proud, light tread as to make it seem he had never worn shoes. He looked towards the diagonal row of cabins; and the sight of the Russian family, leading their lives there in joyous simplicity, distorted his features in a spasm of angry disgust. His brow darkened, his lips curled, one corner of the mouth was drawn down in a harsh line that marred the curve of the cheek, his frown was so heavy that the eyes seemed to sink in as they uttered beneath the black and vicious language of hate. He looked down, looked threateningly back once more; then giving it up with a violent and contemptuous shoulder-shrug, he left his enemies in the rear.

A feeling of delicacy, a qualm, almost like a sense of shame, made Aschenbach turn away as though he had not seen; he felt unwilling to take advantage of having been, by chance, privy to this passionate reaction. But he was in truth both moved and exhilarated—that is to say, he was delighted. This childish exhibition of fanaticism, directed against the good-naturedest simplicity in the world—it gave to the godlike and inexpressive the final human touch. The figure of the half-grown lad, a masterpiece from nature's own hand, had been significant enough when it gratified the eye alone; and now it evoked sympathy as well—the little episode had set it off, lent it a dignity in the onlooker's eyes that was beyond its years.

Aschenbach listened with still averted head to the boy's voice announcing his coming to his companions at the sand-heap. The voice was clear, though a little weak, but they answered, shouting his name—or his nickname—again and again. Aschenbach was not without curiosity to learn it, but could make out nothing more exact than two musical syllables, something like Adgio—or, oftener still, Adjiu, with a long-drawn-out *u* at the end. He liked the melodious sound, and found it fitting; said it over to himself a few times and turned back with satisfaction to his papers.

Holding his travelling-pad on his knees, he took his fountain-pen and began to answer various items of his correspondence. But presently he felt it too great a pity to turn his back, and the eyes of his mind, for the sake of mere commonplace correspondence, to this scene which was, after all, the most rewarding one he knew. He put aside his papers and swung round to the sea; in no long time, beguiled by the voices of the children at play, he had turned his head and sat resting it against the chair-back, while he gave himself up to contemplating the activities of the exquisite Adgio.

His eye found him out at once, the red breast-knot was unmistakable. With some nine or ten companions, boys and girls of his own age and younger, he was busy putting in place an old plank to serve as a bridge across the ditches between the sand-piles. He directed the work by shouting and motioning with his head, and they were all chattering in many tongues—French, Polish, and even some of the Balkan languages. But his was the name oftenest on their lips, he was plainly sought after, wooed, admired. One lad in particular, a Pole like himself, with a name that sounded something like Jaschiu, a sturdy lad with brilliantined black hair, in a belted linen suit, was his particular liegeman and friend. Operations at the sand-pile being ended for the time, the two walked away along the beach, with their arms round each other's waists, and once the lad Jaschiu gave Adgio a kiss.

Aschenbach felt like shaking a finger at him. "But you, Critobulus," he thought with a smile, "you I advise to take a year's leave. That long, at least, you will need for complete recovery." A vendor came by with strawberries, and Aschenbach made his second breakfast of the great luscious, dead-ripe fruit. It had grown very warm, although the sun had not availed to pierce the heavy layer of mist. His mind felt relaxed, his senses revelled in this vast and soothing communion with the silence of the sea. The grave and serious man found sufficient occupation in speculating what name it could be that sounded like Adgio. And with the help of a few Polish memories he at length fixed on Tadzio, a shortened form of Thaddeus, which sounded, when called, like Tadziu or Adziu.

Tadzio was bathing. Aschenbach had lost sight of him for a moment, then descried him far out in the water, which was shallow a very long way—saw his head, and his arm striking out like an oar. But his watchful family were already on the alert; the mother and governess called from the veranda in front of their bathing-cabin, until the lad's name, with its softened consonants and long-drawn *u*-sound, seemed to possess the beach like a rallying-cry; the cadence had something sweet and wild: "Tadziu! Tadziu!" He turned and ran back against the water, churning the waves to a foam, his head flung high. The sight of this living figure, virginally pure and austere, with dripping locks, beautiful as a tender young god, emerging from the depths of sea and sky, outrunning the element—it conjured up mythologies, it was like a primeval legend, handed down from the beginning of time, of the birth of form, of the origin of the gods. With closed lids Aschenbach listened to this poesy hymning itself silently within him, and anon he thought it was good to be here and that he would stop awhile.

Afterwards Tadzio lay on the sand and rested from his bathe, wrapped in his white sheet, which he wore drawn underneath the right shoulder, so that his head was cradled on his bare right arm. And even when Aschenbach read, without looking up, he was conscious that the lad was there; that it would cost him but the slightest turn of the head to have the rewarding vision once more in his purview. Indeed, it was almost as though he sat there to guard the youth's repose; occupied, of course, with his own affairs, yet alive to the presence of that noble human creature close at hand. And his heart was stirred, it felt a father's kindness: such an emotion as the possessor of beauty can inspire in one who has offered himself up in spirit to create beauty.

At midday he left the beach, returned to the hotel, and was carried up in the lift to his room. There he lingered a little time before the glass and looked at his own grey hair, his keen and weary face. And he thought of his fame, and how people gazed respectfully at him in the streets, on account of his unerring gift of words and their power to charm. He called up all the worldly successes his genius had reaped, all he could remember, even his patent of nobility. Then went to luncheon down in the dining-room, sat at his little table and ate. Afterwards he mounted again in the lift, and a group of young folk, Tadzio among them, pressed with him into the little compartment. It was the first time Aschenbach had seen him close at hand, not merely in perspective, and could see and take account of the details of his humanity. Someone spoke to the lad, and he, answering, with indescribably lovely smile, stepped out again, as they had come to the first floor, backwards, with his eyes cast down. "Beauty makes people self-conscious," Aschenbach thought, and considered within himself imperatively why this should be. He had noted, further, that Tadzio's teeth were imperfect, rather jagged and bluish, without a healthy glaze, and of that peculiar brittle transparency which the teeth of chlorotic people often show. "He is delicate, he is sickly," Aschenbach thought. "He will most likely not live to grow old." He did not try to account for the pleasure the idea gave him.

In the afternoon he spent two hours in his room, then took the *vaporetto* to Venice, across the foul-smelling lagoon. He got out at San Marco, had his tea in the Piazza, and then, as his custom was, took a walk through the streets. But this walk of his brought about nothing less than a revolution in his mood and an entire change in all his plans.

There was a hateful sultriness in the narrow streets. The air was so heavy that all the manifold smells wafted out of houses, shops, and cook-shops—smells of oil, perfumery, and so forth—hung low, like exhalations, not dissipating. Cigarette smoke seemed to stand in the air, it drifted so slowly away. Today the crowd in these narrow lanes oppressed the stroller instead of diverting him. The longer he walked, the more was he in tortures under that state, which is the product of the sea air and the sirocco and which excites and enervates at once. He perspired painfully. His eyes rebelled, his chest was heavy, he felt feverish, the blood throbbed in his temples. He fled from the huddled, narrow streets of the commercial city, crossed many bridges, and came into the poor quarter of Venice. Beggars waylaid him, the canals sickened him with their evil exhalations. He reached a quiet square, one of those that exist at the city's heart, forsaken of God and man; there he rested awhile on the margin of a fountain, wiped his brow, and admitted to himself that he must be gone.

For the second time, and now quite definitely, the city proved that in certain weathers it could be directly inimical to his health. Nothing but sheer unreasoning obstinacy would linger on, hoping for an unprophesiable change in the wind. A quick decision was in place. He could not go home at this stage, neither summer nor winter quarters would be ready. But Venice had not a monopoly of sea and shore: there were other spots where these were to be had without the evil concomitants of lagoon and fever-breeding vapours. He remembered a little bathing-place not far from Trieste of which he had had a good report. Why not go thither? At once, of course, in order that this second change might be worth the making. He resolved, he rose to his feet and sought the nearest gondola-landing, where he took a boat and was conveyed to San Marco through the gloomy windings of many canals, beneath balconies of delicate marble traceries flanked by carven lions; round slippery corners of wall, past melancholy façades with ancient business shields reflected in the rocking water. It was not too easy to arrive at his destination, for his gondolier, being in league with various lace-makers and glass-blowers, did his best to persuade his fare to pause, look, and be tempted to buy. Thus the charm of this bizarre passage through the heart of Venice, even while it played upon his spirit, yet was sensibly cooled by the predatory commercial spirit of the fallen queen of the seas.

Once back in his hotel, he announced at the office, even before dinner, that circumstances unforeseen obliged him to leave early next morning. The management expressed its regret, it changed his money and receipted his bill. He dined, and spent the lukewarm evening in a rocking-chair on the rear terrace, reading the newspapers. Before he went to bed, he made his luggage ready against the morning.

His sleep was not of the best, for the prospect of another journey made him restless. When he opened his window next morning, the sky was still overcast, but the air seemed fresher—and there and then his rue began. Had he not given notice too soon? Had he not let himself be swayed by a slight and momentary indisposition? If he had only been patient, not lost heart so quickly, tried to adapt himself to the climate, or even waited for a change in the weather before deciding! Then, instead of the hurry and flurry of departure, he would have before him now a morning like yesterday's on the beach. Too late! He must go on wanting what he had wanted yesterday. He dressed and at eight o'clock went down to breakfast.

When he entered the breakfast-room it was empty. Guests came in while he sat waiting for his order to be filled. As he sipped his tea he saw the Polish girls enter with their governess, chaste and morning-fresh, with sleep-reddened eyelids. They crossed the room and sat down at their table in the window. Behind them came the porter, cap in hand, to announce that it was time for him to go. The car was waiting to convey him and other travellers to the Hôtel Excelsior, whence they would go by motor-boat through the company's private canal to the station. Time passed. But Aschenbach found it did nothing of the sort. There still lacked more than an hour of train-time. He felt irritated at the hotel habit of getting the guests out of the house earlier than necessary; and requested the porter to let him breakfast in peace. The man hesitated and withdrew, only to come back again five minutes later. The car could wait no longer. Good, then it might go, and take his trunk with it, Aschenbach answered with some heat. He would use the public conveyance, in his own time; he begged them to leave the choice of it to him. The functionary bowed. Aschenbach, pleased to be rid of him, made a leisurely meal, and even had a newspaper off the waiter. When at length he rose, the time was grown very short. And it so happened that at that moment Tadzio came through the glass doors into the room.

To reach his own table he crossed the traveller's path, and modestly cast down his eyes before the grey-haired man of the lofty brows—only to lift them again in that sweet way he had and direct his full soft gaze upon Aschenbach's face. Then he was past. "For the last time, Tadzio," thought the elder man. "It was all too brief!" Quite unusually for him, he shaped a farewell with his lips, he actually uttered it, and added: "May God bless you!" Then he went out, distributed tips, exchanged farewells with the mild little manager in the frock-coat, and, followed by the porter with his land-luggage, left the hotel. On foot as he had come, he passed through the white-blossoming avenue, diagonally across the island to the boat-landing. He went on board at once—but the tale of his journey across the lagoon was a tale of woe, a passage through the very valley of regrets.

It was the well-known route: through the lagoon, past San Marco, up the Grand Canal. Aschenbach sat on the circular bench in the bows, with his elbow on the railing, one hand shading his eyes. They passed the Public Gardens, once more the princely charm of the Piazzetta rose up before him and then dropped behind, next came the great row of palaces, the canal curved, and the splendid marble arches of the Rialto came in sight. The traveller gazed—and his bosom was torn. The atmosphere of the city, the faintly rotten scent of swamp and sea, which had driven him to leave—in what deep, tender, almost painful draughts he breathed it in! How was it he had not known, had not thought, how much his heart was set upon it all? What this morning had been slight regret, some little doubt of his own wisdom, turned now to grief, to actual wretchedness, a mental agony so sharp that it repeatedly brought tears to his eyes, while he questioned himself how he could have foreseen it. The hardest part, the part that more than once it seemed he could not bear, was the thought that he should never more see Venice again. Since now for the second time the place had made him ill, since for the second time he had had to flee for his life, he must henceforth regard it as a forbidden spot, to be for ever shunned; senseless to try it again, after he had proved himself unfit. Yes, if he fled it now, he felt that wounded pride must prevent his return to this spot where twice he had made actual bodily surrender. And this conflict between inclination and capacity all at once assumed, in this middle-aged man's mind, immense weight and importance; the physical defeat seemed a shameful thing, to be avoided at whatever cost; and he stood amazed at the ease with which on the day before he had yielded to it.

Meanwhile the steamer neared the station landing; his anguish of irresolution amounted almost to panic. To leave seemed to the sufferer impossible, to remain not less so. Torn thus between two alternatives, he entered the station. It was very late, he had not a moment to lose. Time pressed, it scourged him onward. He hastened to buy his ticket and looked round in the crowd to find the hotel porter. The man appeared and said that the trunk had already gone off. "Gone already?" "Yes, it has gone to Como." "To Como?" A hasty exchange of words—angry questions from Aschenbach, and puzzled replies from the porter—at length made it clear that the trunk had been put with the wrong luggage even before leaving the hotel, and in company with other trunks was now well on its way in precisely the wrong direction.

Aschenbach found it hard to wear the right expression as he heard this news. A reckless joy, a deep incredible mirthfulness shook him almost as with a spasm. The porter dashed off after the lost trunk, returning very soon, of course, to announce that his efforts were unavailing. Aschenbach said he would not travel without his luggage; that he would go back and wait at the Hôtel des Bains until it turned up. Was the company's motor-boat still outside? The man said yes, it was at the door. With his native eloquence he prevailed upon the ticket-agent to take back the ticket already purchased; he swore that he would wire, that no pains should be spared, that the trunk would be restored in the twinkling of an eye. And the unbelievable thing came to pass: the traveller, twenty minutes after he had reached the station, found himself once more on the Grand Canal on his way back to the Lido.

What a strange adventure indeed, this right-about face of destiny—incredible, humiliating, whimsical as any dream! To be passing again, within the hour, these scenes from which in profoundest grief he had but now taken leave for ever! The little swift-moving vessel, a furrow of foam at its prow, tacking with droll agility between steamboats and gondolas, went like a shot to its goal; and he, its sole passenger, sat hiding the panic and thrills of a truant schoolboy beneath a mask of forced resignation. His breast still heaved from time to time with a burst of laughter over the contretemps. Things could not, he told himself, have fallen out more luckily. There would be the necessary explanations, a few astonished faces—then all would be well once more, a mischance prevented, a grievous error set right; and all he had thought to have left for ever was his own once more, his for as long as he liked. . . . And did the boat's swift motion deceive him, or was the wind now coming from the sea?

The waves struck against the tiled sides of the narrow canal. At Hôtel Excelsior the automobile omnibus awaited the returned traveller and bore him along by the crisping waves back to the Hôtel des Bains. The little mustachioed manager in the frock-coat came down the steps to greet him.

In dulcet tones he deplored the mistake, said how painful it was to the management and himself; applauded Aschenbach's resolve to stop on until the errant trunk came back; his former room, alas, was already taken, but another as good awaited his approval. "*Pas de chance, monsieur,*" said the Swiss lift-porter, with a smile, as he conveyed him upstairs. And the fugitive was soon quartered in another room which in situation and furnishings almost precisely resembled the first.

He laid out the contents of his hand-bag in their wonted places; then, tired out, dazed by the whirl of the extraordinary forenoon, subsided into the arm-chair by the open window. The sea wore a pale-green cast, the air felt thinner and purer, the beach with its cabins and boats had more colour, notwithstanding the sky was still grey. Aschenbach, his hands folded in his lap, looked out. He felt rejoiced to be back, yet displeased with his vacillating moods, his ignorance of his own real desires. Thus for nearly an hour he sat, dreaming, resting, barely thinking. At midday he saw Tadzio, in his striped sailor suit with red breast-knot, coming up from the sea, across the barrier and along the board walk to the hotel. Aschenbach recognized him, even at this height, knew it was he before he actually saw him, had it in mind to say to himself: "Well, Tadzio, so here you are again too!" But the casual greeting died away before it reached his lips, slain by the truth in his heart. He felt the rapture of his blood, the poignant pleasure, and realized that it was for Tadzio's sake the leavetaking had been so hard.

He sat quite still, unseen at his high post, and looked within himself. His features were lively, he lifted his brows; a smile, alert, inquiring, vivid, widened the mouth. Then he raised his head, and with both hands, hanging limp over the chair-arms, he described a slow motion, palms outward, a lifting and turning movement, as though to indicate a wide embrace. It was a gesture of welcome, a calm and deliberate acceptance of what might come.

Now daily the naked god with cheeks aflame drove his four fire-breathing steeds through heaven's spaces; and with him streamed the strong east wind that fluttered his yellow locks. A sheen, like white satin, lay over all the idly rolling sea's expanse. The sand was burning hot. Awnings of rust-coloured canvas were spanned before the bathing-huts, under the ether's quivering silver-blue; one spent the morning hours within the small, sharp square of shadow they purveyed. But evening too was rarely lovely: balsamic with the breath of flowers and shrubs from the near-by park, while overhead the constellations circled in their spheres, and the murmuring of the night-girted sea swelled softly up and whispered to the soul. Such nights as these contained the joyful promise of a sunlit morrow, brim-full of sweetly ordered idleness, studded thick with countless precious possibilities.

The guest detained here by so happy a mischance was far from finding the return of his luggage a ground for setting out anew. For two days he had suffered slight inconvenience and had to dine in the large salon in his travelling-clothes. Then the lost trunk was set down in his room, and he hastened to unpack, filling presses and drawers with his possessions. He meant to stay on—and on; he rejoiced in the prospect of wearing a silk suit for the hot morning hours on the beach and appearing in acceptable evening dress at dinner.

He was quick to fall in with the pleasing monotony of this manner of life, readily enchanted by its mild soft brilliance and ease. And what a spot it is, indeed!—uniting the charms of a luxurious bathing-resort by a southern sea with the immediate nearness of a unique and marvellous city. Aschenbach was not pleasure-loving. Always, wherever and whenever it was the order of the day to be merry, to refrain from labour and make glad the heart, he would soon be conscious of the imperative summons—and especially was this so in his youth—back to the high fatigues, the sacred and fasting service that consumed his days. This spot and this alone had power to beguile him, to relax his resolution, to make him glad. At times—of a forenoon perhaps, as he lay in the shadow of his awning, gazing out dreamily over the blue of the southern sea, or in the mildness of the night, beneath the wide starry sky, ensconced among the cushions of the gondola that bore him Lidowards after an evening on the Piazza, while the gay lights faded and the melting music of the serenades died away on his ear—he would think of his mountain home, the theatre of his summer labours. There clouds hung low and trailed through the garden, violent storms extinguished the lights of the house at night, and the ravens he fed swung in the tops of the fir trees. And he would feel transported to Elysium, to the ends of the earth, to a spot most carefree for the sons of men, where no snow is, and no winter, no storms or downpours of rain; where Oceanus sends a mild and cooling breath, and days flow on in blissful idleness, without effort or struggle, entirely dedicated to the sun and the feasts of the sun.

Aschenbach saw the boy Tadzio almost constantly. The narrow confines of their world of hotel and beach, the daily round followed by all alike, brought him in close, almost uninterrupted touch with the beautiful lad. He encountered him everywhere—in the salons of the hotel, on the cooling rides to the city and back, among the splendours of the Piazza, and besides all this in many another going and coming as chance vouchsafed. But it was the regular morning hours on the beach which gave him his happiest opportunity to study and admire the lovely apparition. Yes, this immediate happiness, this daily recurring boon at the hand of circumstance, this it was that filled him with content, with joy in life, enriched his stay, and lingered out the row of sunny days that fell into place so pleasantly one behind the other.

He rose early—as early as though he had a panting press of work—and was among the first on the beach, when the sun was still benign and the sea lay dazzling white in its morning slumber. He gave the watchman a friendly good-morning and chatted with the barefoot, white-haired old man who prepared his place, spread the awning, trundled out the chair and table on to the little platform. Then he settled down; he had three or four hours before the sun reached its height and the fearful climax of its power; three or four hours while the sea went deeper and deeper blue; three or four hours in which to watch Tadzio.

He would see him come up, on the left, along the margin of the sea; or from behind, between the cabins; or, with a start of joyful surprise, would discover that he himself was late, and Tadzio already down, in the blue and white bathing-suit that was now his only wear on the beach; there and engrossed in his usual activities in the sand, beneath the sun. It was a sweetly idle, trifling, fitful life, of play and rest, of strolling, wading, digging, fishing, swimming, lying on the sand. Often the women sitting on the platform would call out to him in their high voices: "Tadziu! Tadziu!" and he would come running and waving his arms, eager to tell them what he had done, show them what he had found, what caught—shells, seahorses, jelly-fish, and sidewards-running crabs. Aschenbach understood not a word he said; it might be the sheerest commonplace, in his ear it became mingled harmonies. Thus the lad's foreign birth raised his speech to music; a wanton sun showered splendour on him, and the noble distances of the sea formed the background which set off his figure.

Soon the observer knew every line and pose of this form that limned itself so freely against sea and sky; its every loveliness, though conned by heart, yet thrilled him each day afresh; his admiration knew no bounds, the delight of his eye was unending. Once the lad was summoned to speak to a guest who was waiting for his mother at their cabin. He ran up, ran dripping wet out of the sea, tossing his curls, and put out his hand, standing with his weight on one leg, resting the other foot on the toes; as he stood there in a posture of suspense the turn of his body was enchanting, while his features wore a look half shamefaced, half conscious of the duty breeding laid upon him to please. Or he would lie at full length, with his bath-robe around him, one slender young arm resting on the sand, his chin in the hollow of his hand; the lad they called Jaschiu squatting beside him, paying him court. There could be nothing lovelier on earth than the smile and look with which the playmate thus singled out rewarded his humble friend and vassal. Again, he might be at the water's edge, alone, removed from his family, quite close to Aschenbach; standing erect, his hands clasped at the back of his neck, rocking slowly on the balls of his feet, day-dreaming away into blue space, while little waves ran up and bathed his toes. The ringlets of honey-coloured hair clung to his temples and neck, the fine down along the upper vertebræ was yellow in the sunlight; the thin envelope of flesh covering the torso betrayed the delicate outlines of the ribs and the symmetry of the breast-structure. His armpits were still as smooth as a statue's, smooth the glistening hollows behind the knees, where the blue network of veins suggested that the body was formed of some stuff more transparent than mere flesh. What discipline, what precision of thought were expressed by the tense youthful perfection of this form! And yet the pure, strong will which had laboured in darkness and succeeded in bringing this godlike work of art to the light of day—was it not known and familiar to him, the artist? Was not the same force at work in himself when he strove in cold fury to liberate from the marble mass of language the slender forms of his art which he saw with the eye of his mind and would body forth to men as the mirror and image of spiritual beauty?

Mirror and image! His eyes took in the proud bearing of that figure there at the blue water's edge; with an outburst of rapture he told himself that what he saw was beauty's very essence; form as divine thought, the single and pure perfection which resides in the mind, of which an image and likeness, rare and holy, was here raised up for adoration. This was very frenzy—and without a scruple, nay, eagerly, the ageing artist bade it come. His mind was in travail, his whole mental background in a state of flux. Memory flung up in him the primitive thoughts which are youth's inheritance, but which with him had remained latent, never leaping up into a blaze. Has it not been written that the sun beguiles our attention from things of the intellect to fix it on things of the sense? The sun, they say, dazzles; so bewitching reason and memory that the soul for very pleasure forgets its actual state, to cling with doting on the loveliest of all the objects she shines on. Yes, and then it is only through the medium of some corporeal being that it can raise itself again to contemplation of higher things. Amor, in sooth, is like the mathematician who in order to give children a knowledge of pure form must do so in the language of pictures; so, too, the god, in order to make visible the spirit, avails himself of the forms and colours of human youth, gilding it with all imaginable beauty that it may serve memory as a tool, the very sight of which then sets us afire with pain and longing.

Such were the devotee's thoughts, such the power of his emotions. And the sea, so bright with glancing sunbeams, wove in his mind a spell and summoned up a lovely picture: there was the ancient plane-tree outside the walls of Athens, a hallowed, shady spot, fragrant with willow-blossom and adorned with images and votive offerings in honour of the nymphs and Achelous. Clear ran the smooth-pebbled stream at the foot of the spreading tree. Crickets were fiddling. But on the gentle grassy slope, where one could lie yet hold the head erect, and shelter from the scorching heat, two men reclined, an elder with a younger, ugliness paired with beauty and wisdom with grace. Here Socrates held forth to youthful Phædrus upon the nature of virtue and desire, wooing him with insinuating wit and charming turns of phrase. He told him of the shuddering and unwonted heat that come upon him whose heart is open, when his eye beholds an image of eternal beauty; spoke of the impious and corrupt, who cannot conceive beauty though they see its image, and are incapable of awe; and of the fear and reverence felt by the noble soul when he beholds a godlike face or a form which is a good image of beauty: how as he gazes he worships the beautiful one and scarcely dares to look upon him, but would offer sacrifice as to an idol or a god, did he not fear to be thought stark mad. "For beauty, my Phædrus, beauty alone, is lovely and visible at once. For, mark you, it is the sole aspect of the spiritual which we can perceive through our senses, or bear so to perceive. Else what should become of us, if the divine, if reason and virtue and truth, were to speak to us through the senses? Should we not perish and be consumed by love, as Semele aforetime was by Zeus? So beauty, then, is the beauty-lover's way to the spirit—but only the way, only the means, my little Phædrus." . . . And then, sly arch-lover that he was, he said the subtlest thing of all: that the lover was nearer the divine than the beloved; for the god was in the one but not in the other—perhaps the tenderest, most mocking thought that ever was thought, and source of all the guile and secret bliss the lover knows.

Thought that can merge wholly into feeling, feeling that can merge wholly into thought—these are the artist's highest joy. And our solitary felt in himself at this moment power to command and wield a thought that thrilled with emotion, an emotion as precise and concentrated as thought: namely, that nature herself shivers with ecstasy when the mind bows down in homage before beauty. He felt a sudden desire to write. Eros, indeed, we are told, loves idleness, and for idle hours alone was he created. But in this crisis the violence of our sufferer's seizure was directed almost wholly towards production, its occasion almost a matter of indifference. News had reached him on his travels that a certain problem had been raised, the intellectual world challenged for its opinion on a great and burning question of art and taste. By nature and experience the theme was his own; and he could not resist the temptation to set it off in the glistering foil of his words. He would write, and moreover he would write in Tadzio's presence. This lad should be in a sense his model, his style should follow the lines of this figure that seemed to him divine; he would snatch up this beauty into the realms of the mind, as once the eagle bore the

Trojan shepherd aloft. Never had the pride of the word been so sweet to him, never had he known so well that Eros is in the word, as in those perilous and precious hours when he sat at his rude table, within the shade of his awning, his idol full in his view and the music of his voice in his ears, and fashioned his little essay after the model Tadzio's beauty set: that page and a half of choicest prose, so chaste, so lofty, so poignant with feeling, which would shortly be the wonder and admiration of the multitude. Verily it is well for the world that it sees only the beauty of the completed work and not its origins nor the conditions whence it sprang; since knowledge of the artist's inspiration might often but confuse and alarm and so prevent the full effect of its excellence. Strange hours, indeed, these were, and strangely unnerving the labour that filled them! Strangely fruitful intercourse this, between one body and another mind! When Aschenbach put aside his work and left the beach he felt exhausted, he felt broken—conscience reproached him, as it were after a debauch.

Next morning on leaving the hotel he stood at the top of the stairs leading down from the terrace and saw Tadzio in front of him on his way to the beach. The lad had just reached the gate in the railings, and he was alone. Aschenbach felt, quite simply, a wish to overtake him, to address him and have the pleasure of his reply and answering look; to put upon a blithe and friendly footing his relation with this being who all unconsciously had so greatly heightened and quickened his emotions. The lovely youth moved at a loitering pace—he might easily be overtaken; and Aschenbach hastened his own step. He reached him on the board walk that ran behind the bathing-cabins, and all but put out his hand to lay it on shoulder or head, while his lips parted to utter a friendly salutation in French. But—perhaps from the swift pace of his last few steps—he found his heart throbbing unpleasantly fast, while his breath came in such quick pants that he could only have gasped had he tried to speak. He hesitated, sought after self-control, was suddenly panic-stricken lest the boy notice him hanging there behind him and look round. Then he gave up, abandoned his plan, and passed him with bent head and hurried step.

"Too late! Too late!" he thought as he went by. But was it too late? This step he had delayed to take might so easily have put everything in a lighter key, have led to a sane recovery from his folly. But the truth may have been that the ageing man did not want to be cured, that his illusion was far too dear to him. Who shall unriddle the puzzle of the artist nature? Who understands that mingling of discipline and licence in which it stands so deeply rooted? For not to be able to want sobriety is licentious folly. Aschenbach was no longer disposed to self-analysis. He had no taste for it; his self-esteem, the attitude of mind proper to his years, his maturity and single-mindedness, disinclined him to look within himself and decide whether it was constraint or puerile sensuality that had prevented him from carrying out his project. He felt confused, he was afraid someone, if only the watchman, might have been observing his behaviour and final surrender—very much he feared being ridiculous. And all the time he was laughing at himself for his serio-comic seizure. "Quite crestfallen," he thought. "I was like the gamecock that lets his wings droop in the battle. That must be the Love-God himself, that makes us hang our heads at sight of beauty and weighs our proud spirits low as the ground." Thus he played with the idea—he embroidered upon it, and was too arrogant to admit fear of an emotion.

The term he had set for his holiday passed by unheeded; he had no thought of going home. Ample funds had been sent him. His sole concern was that the Polish family might leave, and a chance question put to the hotel barber elicited the information that they had come only very shortly before himself. The sun browned his face and hands, the invigorating salty air heightened his emotional energies. Heretofore he had been wont to give out at once, in some new effort, the powers accumulated by sleep or food or outdoor air; but now the strength that flowed in upon him with each day of sun and sea and idleness he let go up in one extravagant gush of emotional intoxication.

His sleep was fitful; the priceless, equable days were divided one from the next by brief nights filled with happy unrest. He went, indeed, early to bed, for at nine o'clock, with the departure of Tadzio from the scene, the day was over for him. But in the faint greyness of the morning a tender pang would go through him as his heart was minded of its adventure; he could no longer bear his pillow and, rising, would wrap himself against the early chill and sit down by the window to await the sunrise. Awe of the miracle filled his soul new-risen from its sleep. Heaven, earth, and its waters yet lay enfolded in the ghostly, glassy pallor of dawn; one paling star still swam in the shadowy vast. But there came a breath, a winged word from far and inaccessible abodes, that Eos was rising from the side of her spouse; and there was that first sweet reddening of the farthest strip of sea and sky that manifests creation to man's sense. She neared, the goddess, ravisher of youth, who stole away Cleitos and Cephalus and, defying all the envious Olympians, tasted beautiful Orion's love. At the world's edge began a strewing of roses, a shining and a blooming ineffably pure; baby cloudlets hung illumined, like attendant amoretti, in the blue and blushful haze; purple effulgence fell upon the sea, that seemed to heave it forward on its welling waves; from horizon to zenith went great quivering thrusts like golden lances, the gleam became a glare; without a sound, with godlike violence, glow and glare and rolling flames streamed upwards, and with flying hoof-beats the steeds of the sun-god mounted the sky. The lonely watcher sat, the splendour of the god shone on him, he closed his eyes and let the glory kiss his lids. Forgotten feelings, precious pangs of his youth, quenched long since by the stern service that had been his life and now returned so strangely metamorphosed—he recognized them with a puzzled, wondering smile. He mused, he dreamed, his lips slowly shaped a name; still smiling, his face turned seawards and his hands lying folded in his lap, he fell asleep once more as he sat.

But that day, which began so fierily and festally, was not like other days; it was transmuted and gilded with mythical significance. For whence could come the breath, so mild and meaningful, like a whisper from higher spheres, that played about temple and ear? Troops of small feathery white clouds ranged over the sky, like grazing herds of the gods. A stronger wind arose, and Poseidon's horses ran up, arching their manes, among them too the steers of him with the purpled locks, who lowered their horns and bellowed as they came on; while like prancing goats the waves on the farther strand leaped among the craggy rocks. It was a world possessed, peopled by Pan, that closed round the spell-bound man, and his doting heart conceived the most delicate fancies. When the sun was going down behind Venice, he would sometimes sit on a bench in the park and watch Tadzio, white-clad, with gay-coloured sash, at play there on the rolled gravel with his ball; and at such times it was not Tadzio whom he saw, but Hyacinthus, doomed to die because two gods were rivals for his love. Ah, yes, he tasted the envious pangs that Zephyr knew when his rival, bow and cithara, oracle and all forgot, played with the beauteous youth; he watched the discus, guided by torturing jealousy, strike the beloved head; paled as he received the broken body in his arms, and saw the flower spring up, watered by that sweet blood and signed for evermore with his lament.

There can be no relation more strange, more critical, than that between two beings who know each other only with their eyes, who meet daily, yes, even hourly, eye each other with a fixed regard, and yet by some whim or freak of convention feel constrained to act like strangers. Uneasiness rules between them, unslaked curiosity, a hysterical desire to give rein to their suppressed impulse to recognize and address each other; even, actually, a sort of strained but mutual regard. For one human being instinctively feels respect and love for another human being so long as he does not know him well enough to judge him; and that he does not, the craving he feels is evidence.

Some sort of relation and acquaintanceship was perforce set up between Aschenbach and the youthful Tadzio; it was with a thrill of joy the older man perceived that the lad was not entirely unresponsive to all the tender notice lavished on him. For instance, what should move the lovely youth, nowadays when he descended to the beach, always to avoid the board walk behind the bathing-huts and saunter along the sand, passing Aschenbach's tent in front, sometimes so unnecessarily close as almost to graze his table or chair? Could the power of an emotion so beyond his own so draw, so fascinate its innocent object? Daily Aschenbach would wait for Tadzio. Then sometimes, on his approach, he would pretend to be preoccupied and let the charmer pass unregarded by. But sometimes he looked up, and their glances met; when that happened both were profoundly serious. The elder's dignified and cultured mien let nothing appear of his inward state; but in Tadzio's eyes a question lay—he faltered in his step, gazed on the ground, then up again with that ineffably sweet look he had; and when he was past, something in his bearing seemed to say that only good breeding hindered him from turning round.

But once, one evening, it fell out differently. The Polish brother and sisters, with their governess, had missed the evening meal, and Aschenbach had noted the fact with concern. He was restive over their absence, and after dinner walked up and down in front of the hotel, in evening dress and a straw hat; when suddenly he saw the nunlike sisters with their companion appear in the light of the arc-lamps, and four paces behind them Tadzio. Evidently they came from the steamer-landing, having dined for some reason in Venice. It had been chilly on the lagoon, for Tadzio wore a dark-blue reefer-jacket with gilt buttons, and a cap to match. Sun and sea air could not burn his skin, it was the same creamy marble hue as at first—though he did look a little pale, either from the cold or in the bluish moonlight of the arc-lamps. The shapely brows were so delicately drawn, the eyes so deeply dark—lovelier he was than words could say, and as often the thought visited Aschenbach, and brought its own pang, that language could but extol, not reproduce, the beauties of the sense.

The sight of that dear form was unexpected, it had appeared unhoped-for, without giving him time to compose his features. Joy, surprise, and admiration might have painted themselves quite openly upon his face—and just at this second it happened that Tadzio smiled. Smiled at Aschenbach, unabashed and friendly, a speaking, winning, captivating smile, with slowly parting lips. With such a smile it might be that Narcissus bent over the mirroring pool, a smile profound, infatuated, lingering, as he put out his arms to the reflection of his own beauty; the lips just slightly pursed, perhaps half-realizing his own folly in trying to kiss the cold lips of his shadow—with a mingling of coquetry and curiosity and a faint unease, enthralling and enthralled.

Aschenbach received that smile and turned away with it as though entrusted with a fatal gift. So shaken was he that he had to flee from the lighted terrace and front gardens and seek out with hurried steps the darkness of the park at the rear. Reproaches strangely mixed of tenderness and remonstrance burst from him: "How dare you smile like that! No one is allowed to smile like that!" He flung himself on a bench, his composure gone to the winds, and breathed in the nocturnal fragrance of the garden. He leaned back, with hanging arms, quivering from head to foot, and quite unmanned he whispered the hackneyed phrase of love and longing—impossible in these circumstances, absurd, abject, ridiculous enough, yet sacred too, and not unworthy of honour even here: "I love you!"

In the fourth week of his stay on the Lido, Gustave von Aschenbach made certain singular observations touching the world about him. He noticed, in the first place, that though the season was approaching its height, yet the number of guests declined and, in particular, that the German tongue had suffered a rout, being scarcely or never heard in the land. At table and on the beach he caught nothing but foreign words. One day at the barber's—where he was now a frequent visitor—he heard something rather startling. The barber mentioned a German family who had just left the Lido after a brief stay, and rattled on in his obsequious way: "The signore is not leaving—he has no fear of the sickness, has he?" Aschenbach looked at him. "The sickness?" he repeated. Whereat the prattler fell silent, became very busy all at once, affected not to hear. When Aschenbach persisted he said he really knew nothing at all about it, and tried in a fresh burst of eloquence to drown the embarrassing subject.

That was one forenoon. After luncheon Aschenbach had himself ferried across to Venice, in a dead calm, under a burning sun; driven by his mania, he was following the Polish young folk, whom he had seen with their companion, taking the way to the landing-stage. He did not find his idol on the Piazza. But as he sat there at tea, at a little round table on the shady side, suddenly he noticed a peculiar odour, which, it seemed to him now, had been in the air for days without his being aware: a sweetish, medicinal smell, associated with wounds and disease and suspect cleanliness. He sniffed and pondered and at length recognized it; finished his tea and left the square at the end facing the cathedral. In the narrow space the stench grew stronger. At the street corners placards were stuck up, in which the city authorities warned the population against the danger of certain infections of the gastric system, prevalent during the heated season; advising them not to eat oysters or other shell-fish and not to use the canal waters. The ordinance showed every sign of minimizing an existing situation. Little groups of people stood about silently in the squares and on the bridges; the traveller moved among them, watched and listened and thought.

He spoke to a shopkeeper lounging at his door among dangling coral necklaces and trinkets of artificial amethyst, and asked him about the disagreeable odour. The man looked at him, heavy-eyed, and hastily pulled himself together. "Just a formal precaution, signore," he said, with a gesture. "A police regulation we have to put up with. The air is sultry—the sirocco is not wholesome, as the signore knows. Just a precautionary measure, you understand —probably unnecessary...." Aschenbach thanked him and passed on. And on the boat that bore him back to the Lido he smelt the germicide again.

On reaching his hotel he sought the table in the lobby and buried himself in the newspapers. The foreign-language sheets had nothing. But in the German papers certain rumours were mentioned, statistics given, then officially denied, then the good faith of the denials called in question. The departure of the German and Austrian contingent was thus made plain. As for other nationals, they knew or suspected nothing—they were still undisturbed. Aschenbach tossed the newspapers back on the table. "It ought to be kept quiet," he thought, aroused. "It should not be talked about." And he felt in his heart a curious elation at these events impending in the world about him. Passion is like crime: it does not thrive on the established order and the common round; it welcomes every blow dealt the bourgeois structure, every weakening of the social fabric, because therein it feels a sure hope of its own advantage. These things that were going on in the unclean alleys of Venice, under cover of an official hushing-up policy—they gave Aschenbach a dark satisfaction. The city's evil secret mingled with the one in the depths of his heart—and he would have staked all he possessed to keep it, since in his infatuation he cared for nothing but to keep Tadzio here, and owned to himself, not without horror, that he could not exist were the lad to pass from his sight.

He was no longer satisfied to owe his communion with his charmer to chance and the routine of hotel life; he had begun to follow and waylay him. On Sundays, for example, the Polish family never appeared on the beach. Aschenbach guessed they went to mass at San Marco and pursued them thither. He passed from the glare of the Piazza into the golden twilight of the holy place and found him he sought bowed in worship over a prie-dieu. He kept in the background, standing on the fissured mosaic pavement among the devout populace, that knelt and muttered and made the sign of the cross; and the crowded splendour of the oriental temple weighed voluptuously on his sense. A heavily ornate priest intoned and gesticulated before the altar, where little candle-flames flickered helplessly in the reek of incense-breathing smoke; and with that cloying sacrificial smell another seemed to mingle—the odour of the sickened city. But through all the glamour and glitter Aschenbach saw the exquisite creature there in front turn his head, seek out and meet his lover's eye.

The crowd streamed out through the portals into the brilliant square thick with fluttering doves, and the fond fool stood aside in the vestibule on the watch. He saw the Polish family leave the church. The children took ceremonial leave of their mother, and she turned towards the Piazzetta on her way home, while his charmer and the cloistered sisters, with their governess, passed beneath the clock tower into the Merceria. When they were a few paces on, he followed—he stole behind them on their walk through the city. When they paused, he did so too; when they turned round, he fled into inns and courtyards to let them pass. Once he lost them from view, hunted feverishly over bridges and in filthy *culs-de-sac*, only to confront them suddenly in a narrow passage whence there was no escape, and experienced a moment of panic fear. Yet it would be untrue to say he suffered. Mind and heart were drunk with passion, his footsteps guided by the dæmonic power whose pastime it is to trample on human reason and dignity.

Tadzio and his sisters at length took a gondola. Aschenbach hid behind a portico or fountain while they embarked, and directly they pushed off did the same. In a furtive whisper he told the boatman he would tip him well to follow at a little distance the other gondola, just rounding a corner, and fairly sickened at the man's quick, sly grasp and ready acceptance of the go-between's role.

Leaning back among soft, black cushions he swayed gently in the wake of the other black-snouted bark, to which the strength of his passion chained him. Sometimes it passed from his view, and then he was assailed by an anguish of unrest. But his guide appeared to have long practice in affairs like these; always, by dint of short cuts or deft manœuvres, he contrived to overtake the coveted sight. The air was heavy and foul, the sun burnt down through a slate-coloured haze. Water slapped gurgling against wood and stone. The gondolier's cry, half warning, half salute, was answered with singular accord from far within the silence of the labyrinth. They passed little gardens, high up the crumbling wall, hung with clustering white and purple flowers that sent down an odour of almonds. Moorish lattices showed shadowy in the gloom. The marble steps of a church descended into the canal, and on them a beggar squatted, displaying his misery to view, showing the whites of his eyes, holding out his hat for alms. Farther on a dealer in antiquities cringed before his lair, inviting the passer-by to enter and be duped. Yes, this was Venice, this the fair frailty that fawned and that betrayed, half fairy-tale, half snare; the city in whose stagnating air the art of painting once put forth so lusty a growth, and where musicians were moved to accords so weirdly lulling and lascivious. Our adventurer felt his senses wooed by this voluptuousness of sight and sound, tasted his secret knowledge that the city sickened and hid its sickness for love of gain, and bent an ever more unbridled leer on the gondola that glided on before him.

It came at last to this—that his frenzy left him capacity for nothing else but to pursue his flame; to dream of him absent, to lavish, loverlike, endearing terms on his mere shadow. He was alone, he was a foreigner, he was sunk deep in this belated bliss of his—all which enabled him to pass unblushing through experiences well-nigh unbelievable. One night, returning late from Venice, he paused by his beloved's chamber door in the second storey, leaned his head against the panel, and remained there long, in utter drunkenness, powerless to tear himself away, blind to the danger of being caught in so mad an attitude.

And yet there were not wholly lacking moments when he paused and reflected, when in consternation he asked himself what path was this on which he had set his foot. Like most other men of parts and attainments, he had an aristocratic interest in his forebears, and when he achieved a success he liked to think he had gratified them, compelled their admiration and regard. He thought of them now, involved as he was in this illicit adventure, seized of these exotic excesses of feeling; thought of their stern self-command and decent manliness, and gave a melancholy smile. What would they have said? What, indeed, would they have said to his entire life, that varied to the point of degeneracy from theirs? This life in the bonds of art, had not he himself, in the days of his youth and in the very spirit of those bourgeois forefathers, pronounced mocking judgment upon it? And yet, at bottom, it had been so like their own! It had been a service, and he a soldier, like some of them; and art was war—a grilling, exhausting struggle that nowadays wore one out before one could grow old. It had been a life of self-conquest, a life against odds, dour, steadfast, abstinent; he had made it symbolical of the kind of overstrained heroism the time admired, and he was entitled to call it manly, even courageous. He wondered if such a life might not be somehow specially pleasing in the eyes of the god who had him in his power. For Eros had received most countenance among the most valiant nations—yes, were we not told that in their cities prowess made him flourish exceedingly? And many heroes of olden time had willingly borne his yoke, not counting any humiliation such if it happened by the god's decree; vows, prostrations, self-abasements, these were no source of shame to the lover; rather they reaped him praise and honour.

Thus did the fond man's folly condition his thoughts; thus did he seek to hold his dignity upright in his own eyes. And all the while he kept doggedly on the traces of the disreputable secret the city kept hidden at its heart, just as he kept his own—and all that he learned fed his passion with vague, lawless hopes. He turned over newspapers at cafés, bent on finding a report on the progress of the disease; and in the German sheets, which had ceased to appear on the hotel table, he found a series of contradictory statements. The deaths, it was variously asserted, ran to twenty, to forty, to a hundred or more; yet in the next day's issue the existence of the pestilence was, if not roundly denied, reported as a matter of a few sporadic cases such as might be brought into a seaport town. After that the warnings would break out again, and the protests against the unscrupulous game the authorities were playing. No definite information was to be had.

And yet our solitary felt he had a sort of first claim on a share in the unwholesome secret; he took a fantastic satisfaction in putting leading questions to such persons as were interested to conceal it, and forcing them to explicit untruths by way of denial. One day he attacked the manager, that small, soft-stepping man in the French frock-coat, who was moving about among the guests at luncheon, supervising the service and making himself socially agreeable. He paused at Aschenbach's table to exchange a greeting, and the guest put a question, with a negligent, casual air: "Why in the world are they forever disinfecting the city of Venice?" "A police regulation," the adroit one replied; "a precautionary measure, intended to protect the health of the public during this unseasonably warm and sultry weather." "Very praiseworthy of the police," Aschenbach gravely responded. After a further exchange of meteorological commonplaces the manager passed on.

It happened that a band of street musicians came to perform in the hotel gardens that evening after dinner. They grouped themselves beneath an iron stanchion supporting an arc-light, two women and two men, and turned their faces, that shone white in the glare, up towards the guests who sat on the hotel terrace enjoying this popular entertainment along with their coffee and iced drinks. The hotel lift-boys, waiters, and office staff stood in the doorway and listened; the Russian family displayed the usual Russian absorption in their enjoyment—they had their chairs put down into the garden to be nearer the singers and sat there in a half-circle with gratitude painted on their features, the old serf in her turban erect behind their chairs.

These strolling players were adepts at mandolin, guitar, harmonica, even compassing a reedy violin. Vocal numbers alternated with instrumental, the younger woman, who had a high shrill voice, joining in a love-duet with the sweetly falsettoing tenor. The actual head of the company, however, and incontestably its most gifted member, was the other man, who played the guitar. He was a sort of baritone buffo; with no voice to speak of, but possessed of a pantomimic gift and remarkable burlesque *élan*. Often he stepped out of the group and advanced towards the terrace, guitar in hand, and his audience rewarded his sallies with bursts of laughter. The Russians in their parterre seats were beside themselves with delight over this display of southern vivacity; their shouts and screams of applause encouraged him to bolder and bolder flights.

Aschenbach sat near the balustrade, a glass of pomegranate-juice and soda-water sparkling ruby-red before him, with which he now and then moistened his lips. His nerves drank in thirstily the unlovely sounds, the vulgar and sentimental tunes, for passion paralyses good taste and makes its victim accept with rapture what a man in his senses would either laugh at or turn from with disgust. Idly he sat and watched the antics of the buffoon with his face set in a fixed and painful smile, while inwardly his whole being was rigid with the intensity of the regard he bent on Tadzio, leaning over the railing six paces off.

He lounged there, in the white belted suit he sometimes wore at dinner, in all his innate, inevitable grace, with his left arm on the balustrade, his legs crossed, the right hand on the supporting hip; and looked down on the strolling singers with an expression that was hardly a smile, but rather a distant curiosity and polite toleration. Now and then he straightened himself and with a charming movement of both arms drew down his white blouse through his leather belt, throwing out his chest. And sometimes —Aschenbach saw it with triumph, with horror, and a sense that his reason was tottering—the lad would cast a glance, that might be slow and cautious, or might be sudden and swift, as though to take him by surprise, to the place where his lover sat. Aschenbach did not meet the glance. An ignoble caution made him keep his eyes in leash. For in the rear of the terrace sat Tadzio's mother and governess; and matters had gone so far that he feared to make himself conspicuous. Several times, on the beach, in the hotel lobby, on the Piazza, he had seen, with a stealing numbness, that they called Tadzio away from his neighbourhood. And his pride revolted at the affront, even while conscience told him it was deserved.

The performer below presently began a solo, with guitar accompaniment, a street song in several stanzas, just then the rage all over Italy. He delivered it in a striking and dramatic recitative, and his company joined in the refrain. He was a man of slight build, with a thin, undernourished face; his shabby felt hat rested on the back of his neck, a great mop of red hair sticking out in front; and he stood there on the gravel in advance of his troupe, in an impudent, swaggering posture, twanging the strings of his instrument and flinging a witty and rollicking recitative up to the terrace, while the veins on his forehead swelled with the violence of his effort. He was scarcely a Venetian type, belonging rather to the race of Neapolitan jesters, half bully, half comedian, brutal, blustering, an unpleasant customer, and entertaining to the last degree. The words of his song were trivial and silly, but on his lips, accompanied with gestures of head, hands, arms, and body, with leers and winks and the loose play of the tongue in the corner of his mouth, they took on meaning; an equivocal meaning, yet vaguely offensive. He wore a white sports shirt with a suit of ordinary clothes, and a strikingly large and naked-looking Adam's apple rose out of the open collar. From that pale, snub-nosed face it was hard to judge of his age; vice sat on it, it was furrowed with grimacing, and two deep wrinkles of defiance and self-will, almost of desperation, stood oddly between the red brows, above the grinning, mobile mouth. But what more than all drew upon him the profound scrutiny of our solitary watcher was that this suspicious figure seemed to carry with it its own suspicious odour. For whenever the refrain occurred and the singer, with waving arms and antic gestures, passed in his grotesque march immediately beneath Aschenbach's seat, a strong smell of carbolic was wafted up to the terrace.

After the song he began to take up money, beginning with the Russian family, who gave liberally, and then mounting the steps to the terrace. But here he became as cringing as he had before been forward. He glided between the tables, bowing and scraping, showing his strong white teeth in a servile smile, though the two deep furrows on the brow were still very marked. His audience looked at the strange creature as he went about collecting his livelihood, and their curiosity was not unmixed with disfavour. They tossed coins with their finger-tips into his hat and took care not to touch it. Let the enjoyment be never so great, a sort of embarrassment always comes when the comedian oversteps the physical distance between himself and respectable people. This man felt it and sought to make his peace by fawning. He came along the railing to Aschenbach, and with him came that smell no one else seemed to notice.

"Listen!" said the solitary, in a low voice, almost mechanically; "they are disinfecting Venice—why?" The mountebank answered hoarsely: "Because of the police. Orders, signore. On account of the heat and the sirocco. The sirocco is oppressive. Not good for the health." He spoke as though surprised that anyone could ask, and with the flat of his hand he demonstrated how oppressive the sirocco was. "So there is no plague in Venice?" Aschenbach asked the question between his teeth, very low. The man's expressive face fell, he put on a look of comical innocence. "A plague? What sort of plague? Is the sirocco a plague? Or perhaps our police are a plague! You are making fun of us, signore! A plague! Why should there be? The police make regulations on account of the heat and the weather. . . ." He gestured. "Quite," said Aschenbach, once more, soft and low; and dropping an unduly large coin into the man's hat dismissed him with a sign. He bowed very low and left. But he had not reached the steps when two of the hotel servants flung themselves on him and began to whisper, their faces close to his. He shrugged, seemed to be giving assurances, to be swearing he had said nothing. It was not hard to guess the import of his words. They let him go at last and he went back into the garden, where he conferred briefly with his troupe and then stepped forward for a farewell song.

It was one Aschenbach had never to his knowledge heard before, a rowdy air, with words in impossible dialect. It had a laughing-refrain in which the other three artists joined at the top of their lungs. The refrain had neither words nor accompaniment, it was nothing but rhythmical, modulated, natural laughter, which the soloist in particular knew how to render with most deceptive realism. Now that he was farther off his audience, his self-assurance had come back, and this laughter of his rang with a mocking note. He would be overtaken, before he reached the end of the last line of each stanza; he would catch his breath, lay his hand over his mouth, his voice would quaver and his shoulders shake, he would lose power to contain himself longer. Just at the right moment each time, it came whooping, bawling, crashing out of him, with a verisimilitude that never failed to set his audience off in profuse and unpremeditated mirth that seemed to add gusto to his own. He bent his knees, he clapped his thigh, he held his sides, he looked ripe for bursting. He no longer laughed, but yelled, pointing his finger at the company there above as though there could be in all the world nothing so comic as they; until at last they laughed in hotel, terrace, and garden, down to the waiters, lift-boys, and servants—laughed as though possessed.

Aschenbach could no longer rest in his chair, he sat poised for flight. But the combined effect of the laughing, the hospital odour in his nostrils, and the nearness of the beloved was to hold him in a spell; he felt unable to stir. Under cover of the general commotion he looked across at Tadzio and saw that the lovely boy returned his gaze with a seriousness that seemed the copy of his own; the general hilarity, it seemed to say, had no power over him, he kept aloof. The grey-haired man was overpowered, disarmed by this docile, childlike deference; with difficulty he refrained from hiding his face in his hands. Tadzio's habit, too, of drawing himself up and taking a deep sighing breath struck him as being due to an oppression of the chest. "He is sickly, he will never live to grow up," he thought once again, with that dispassionate vision to which his madness of desire sometimes so strangely gave way. And compassion struggled with the reckless exultation of his heart.

The players, meanwhile, had finished and gone; their leader bowing and scraping, kissing his hands and adorning his leave-taking with antics that grew madder with the applause they evoked. After all the others were outside, he pretended to run backwards full tilt against a lamp-post and slunk to the gate apparently doubled over with pain. But there he threw off his buffoon's mask, stood erect, with an elastic straightening of his whole figure, ran out his tongue impudently at the guests on the terrace, and vanished in the night. The company dispersed. Tadzio had long since left the balustrade. But he, the lonely man, sat for long, to the waiters' great annoyance, before the dregs of pomegranate-juice in his glass. Time passed, the night went on. Long ago, in his parental home, he had watched the sand filter through an hour-glass—he could still see, as though it stood before him, the fragile, pregnant little toy. Soundless and fine the rust-red streamlet ran through the narrow neck, and made, as it declined in the upper cavity, an exquisite little vortex.

The very next afternoon the solitary took another step in pursuit of his fixed policy of baiting the outer world. This time he had all possible success. He went, that is, into the English travel bureau in the Piazza, changed some money at the desk, and posing as the suspicious foreigner, put his fateful question. The clerk was a tweed-clad young Britisher, with his eyes set close together, his hair parted in the middle, and radiating that steady reliability which makes his like so strange a phenomenon in the *gamin*, agile-witted south. He began: "No ground for alarm, sir. A mere formality. Quite regular in view of the unhealthy climatic conditions." But then, looking up, he chanced to meet with his own blue eyes the stranger's weary, melancholy gaze, fixed on his face. The Englishman coloured. He continued in a lower voice, rather confused: "At least, that is the official explanation, which they see fit to stick to. I may tell you there's a bit more to it than that." And then, in his good, straightforward way, he told the truth.

For the past several years Asiatic cholera had shown a strong tendency to spread. Its source was the hot, moist swamps of the delta of the Ganges, where it bred in the mephitic air of that primeval island-jungle, among whose bamboo thickets the tiger crouches, where life of every sort flourishes in rankest abundance, and only man avoids the spot. Thence the pestilence had spread throughout Hindustan, raging with great violence; moved eastwards to China, westward to Afghanistan and Persia; following the great caravan routes, it brought terror to Astrakhan, terror to Moscow. Even while Europe trembled lest the spectre be seen striding westward across country, it was carried by sea from Syrian ports and appeared simultaneously at several points on the Mediterranean littoral; raised its head in Toulon and Malaga, Palermo and Naples, and soon got a firm hold in Calabria and Apulia. Northern Italy had been spared—so far. But in May the horrible vibrions were found on the same day in two bodies: the emaciated, blackened corpses of a bargee and a woman who kept a greengrocer's shop. Both cases were hushed up. But in a week there were ten more—twenty, thirty in different quarters of the town. An Austrian provincial, having come to Venice on a few days' pleasure trip, went home and died with all the symptoms of the plague. Thus was explained the fact that the German-language papers were the first to print the news of the Venetian outbreak. The Venetian authorities published in reply a statement to the effect that the state of the city's health had never been better; at the same time instituting the most necessary precautions. But by that time the food supplies—milk, meat or vegetables—had probably been contaminated, for death unseen and unacknowledged was devouring and laying waste in the narrow streets, while a brooding, unseasonable heat warmed the waters of the canals and encouraged the spread of the pestilence. Yes, the disease seemed to flourish and wax strong, to redouble its generative powers. Recoveries were rare. Eighty out of every hundred died, and horribly, for the onslaught was of the extremest violence, and not infrequently of the "dry" type, the most malignant form of the contagion. In this form the victim's body loses power to expel the water secreted by the blood-vessels, it shrivels up, he passes with hoarse cries from convulsion to convulsion, his blood grows thick like pitch, and he suffocates in a few hours. He is fortunate indeed, if, as sometimes happens, the disease, after a slight *malaise*, takes the form of a profound unconsciousness, from which the sufferer seldom or never rouses. By the beginning of June the quarantine buildings of the *ospedale civico* had quietly filled up, the two orphan asylums were entirely occupied, and there was a hideously brisk traffic between the *Nuovo Fundamento* and the island of San Michele, where the cemetery was. But the city was not swayed by high-minded motives or regard for international agreements. The authorities were more actuated by fear of being out of pocket, by regard for the new exhibition of paintings just opened in the Public Gardens, or by apprehension of the large losses the hotels and the shops that catered to foreigners would suffer in case of panic and blockade. And the fears of the people supported the persistent official policy of silence and denial. The city's first medical officer, an honest and competent man, had indignantly resigned his office and been privily replaced by a more compliant person. The fact was known; and this corruption in high places played its part, together with the suspense as to where the walking terror might strike next, to demoralize the baser elements in the city and encourage those antisocial forces which shun the light of day. There was intemperance, indecency, increase of crime. Evenings one saw many drunken people, which was unusual. Gangs of men in surly mood made the streets unsafe, theft and assault were said to be frequent, even murder; for in two cases persons supposedly victims of the plague were proved to have been poisoned by their own families. And professional vice was rampant, displaying excesses heretofore unknown and only at home much farther south and in the east.

Such was the substance of the Englishman's tale. "You would do well," he concluded, "to leave today instead of tomorrow. The blockade cannot be more than a few days off."

"Thank you," said Aschenbach, and left the office.

The Piazza lay in sweltering sunshine. Innocent foreigners sat before the cafés or stood in front of the cathedral, the centre of clouds of doves that, with fluttering wings, tried to shoulder each other away and pick the kernels of maize from the extended hand.

Aschenbach strode up and down the spacious flags, feverishly excited, triumphant in possession of the truth at last, but with a sickening taste in his mouth and a fantastic horror at his heart. One decent, expiatory course lay open to him; he considered it. Tonight, after dinner, he might approach the lady of the pearls and address her in words which he precisely formulated in his mind: "Madame, will you permit an entire stranger to serve you with a word of advice and warning which self-interest prevents others from uttering? Go away. Leave here at once, without delay, with Tadzio and your daughters. Venice is in the grip of pestilence." Then might he lay his hand in farewell upon the head of that instrument of a mocking deity; and thereafter himself flee the accursed morass. But he knew that he was far indeed from any serious desire to take such a step. It would restore him, would give him back himself once more; but he who is beside himself revolts at the idea of self-possession. There crossed his mind the vision of a white building with inscriptions on it, glittering in the sinking sun—he recalled how his mind had dreamed away into their transparent mysticism; recalled the strange pilgrim apparition that had wakened in the ageing man a lust for strange countries and fresh sights. And these memories, again, brought in their train the thought of returning home, returning to reason, self-mastery, an ordered existence, to the old life of effort. Alas! the bare thought made him wince with a revulsion that was like physical nausea. "It must be kept quiet," he whispered fiercely. "I will not speak!" The knowledge that he shared the city's secret, the city's guilt—it put him beside himself, intoxicated him as a small quantity of wine will a man suffering from brain-fag. His thoughts dwelt upon the image of the desolate and calamitous city, and he was giddy with fugitive, mad, unreasoning hopes and visions of a monstrous sweetness. That tender sentiment he had a moment ago evoked, what was it compared with such images as these? His art, his moral sense, what were they in the balance beside the boons that chaos might confer? He kept silence, he stopped on.

That night he had a fearful dream—if dream be the right word for a mental and physical experience which did indeed befall him in deep sleep, as a thing quite apart and real to his senses, yet without his seeing himself as present in it. Rather its theatre seemed to be his own soul, and the events burst in from outside, violently overcoming the profound resistance of his spirit; passed him through and left him, left the whole cultural structure of a lifetime trampled on, ravaged, and destroyed.

The beginning was fear; fear and desire, with a shuddering curiosity. Night reigned, and his senses were on the alert; he heard loud, confused noises from far away, clamour and hubbub. There was a rattling, a crashing, a low dull thunder; shrill halloos and a kind of howl with a long-drawn *u*-sound at the end. And with all these, dominating them all, flute-notes of the cruellest sweetness, deep and cooing, keeping shamelessly on until the listener felt his very entrails bewitched. He heard a voice, naming, though darkly, that which was to come: "The stranger god!" A glow lighted up the surrounding mist and by it he recognized a mountain scene like that about his country home. From the wooded heights, from among the tree-trunks and crumbling moss-covered rocks, a troop came tumbling and raging down, a whirling rout of men and animals, and overflowed the hillside with flames and human forms, with clamour and the reeling dance. The females stumbled over the long, hairy pelts that dangled from their girdles; with heads flung back they uttered loud hoarse cries and shook their tambourines high in air; brandished naked daggers or torches vomiting trails of sparks. They shrieked, holding their breasts in both hands; coiling snakes with quivering tongues they clutched about their waists. Horned and hairy males, girt about the loins with hides, drooped heads and lifted arms and thighs in unison, as they beat on brazen vessels that gave out droning thunder, or thumped madly on drums. There were troops of beardless youths armed with garlanded staves; these ran after goats and thrust their staves against the creatures' flanks, then clung on the plunging horns and let themselves be borne off with triumphant shouts. And one and all the mad rout yelled that cry, composed of soft consonants with a long-drawn *u*-sound at the end, so sweet and wild it was together, and like nothing ever heard before! It would ring through the air like the bellow of a challenging stag, and be given back many-tongued; or they would use it to goad each other on to dance with wild excess of tossing limbs—they never let it die. But the deep, beguiling notes of the flute wove in and out and over all. Beguiling too it was to him who struggled in the grip of these sights and sounds, shamelessly awaiting the coming feast and the uttermost surrender. He trembled, he shrank, his will was steadfast to preserve and uphold his own god against this stranger who was sworn enemy to dignity and self-control. But the mountain wall took up the noise and howling and gave it back manifold; it rose high, swelled to a madness that carried him away. His senses reeled in the steam of panting bodies, the acrid stench from the goats, the odour as of stagnant waters—and another, too familiar smell—of wounds, uncleanness, and disease. His heart throbbed to the drums, his brain reeled, a blind rage seized him, a whirling lust, he craved with all his soul to join the ring that formed about the obscene symbol of the godhead, which they were unveiling and elevating, monstrous and wooden, while from full throats they yelled their rallying-cry. Foam dripped from their lips, they drove each other on with lewd gesturings and beckoning hands. They laughed, they howled, they thrust their pointed staves into each other's flesh and licked the blood as it ran down. But now the dreamer was in them and of them, the stranger god was his own. Yes, it was he who was flinging himself upon the animals, who bit and tore and swallowed smoking gobbets of flesh—while on the trampled moss there now began the rites in honour of the god, an orgy of promiscuous embraces—and in his very soul he tasted the bestial degradation of his fall.

The unhappy man woke from this dream shattered, unhinged, powerless in the demon's grip. He no longer avoided men's eyes nor cared whether he exposed himself to suspicion. And anyhow, people were leaving; many of the bathing-cabins stood empty, there were many vacant places in the dining-room, scarcely any foreigners were seen in the streets. The truth seemed to have leaked out; despite all efforts to the contrary, panic was in the air. But the lady of the pearls stopped on with her family; whether because the rumours had not reached her or because she was too proud and fearless to heed them. Tadzio remained; and it seemed at times to Aschenbach, in his obsessed state, that death and fear together might clear the island of all other souls and leave him there alone with him he coveted. In the long mornings on the beach his heavy gaze would rest, a fixed and reckless stare, upon the lad; towards nightfall, lost to shame, he would follow him through the city's narrow streets where horrid death stalked too, and at such time it seemed to him as though the moral law were fallen in ruins and only the monstrous and perverse held out a hope.

Like any lover, he desired to please; suffered agonies at the thought of failure, and brightened his dress with smart ties and handkerchiefs and other youthful touches. He added jewellery and perfumes and spent hours each day over his *toilette*, appearing at dinner elaborately arrayed and tensely excited. The presence of the youthful beauty that had bewitched him filled him with disgust of his own ageing body; the sight of his own sharp features and grey hair plunged him in hopeless mortification; he made desperate efforts to recover the appearance and freshness of his youth and began paying frequent visits to the hotel barber. Enveloped in the white sheet, beneath the hands of that garrulous personage, he would lean back in the chair and look at himself in the glass with misgiving.

"Grey," he said, with a grimace.

"Slightly," answered the man. "Entirely due to neglect, to a lack of regard for appearances. Very natural, of course, in men of affairs, but, after all, not very sensible, for it is just such people who ought to be above vulgar prejudice in matters like these. Some folk have very strict ideas about the use of cosmetics; but they never extend them to the teeth, as they logically should. And very disgusted other people would be if they did. No, we are all as old as we feel, but no older, and grey hair can misrepresent a man worse than dyed. You, for instance, signore, have a right to your natural colour. Surely you will permit me to restore what belongs to you?"

"How?" asked Aschenbach.

For answer the oily one washed his client's hair in two waters, one clear and one dark, and lo, it was as black as in the days of his youth. He waved it with the tongs in wide, flat undulations, and stepped back to admire the effect.

"Now if we were just to freshen up the skin a little," he said.

And with that he went on from one thing to another, his enthusiasm waxing with each new idea. Aschenbach sat there comfortably; he was incapable of objecting to the process—rather as it went forward it roused his hopes. He watched it in the mirror and saw his eyebrows grow more even and arching, the eyes gain in size and brilliance, by dint of a little application below the lids. A delicate carmine glowed on his cheeks where the skin had been so brown and leathery. The dry, anæmic lips grew full, they turned the colour of ripe strawberries, the lines round eyes and mouth were treated with a facial cream and gave place to youthful bloom. It was a young man who looked back at him from the glass—Aschenbach's heart leaped at the sight. The artist in cosmetic at last professed himself satisfied; after the manner of such people, he thanked his client profusely for what he had done himself. "The merest trifle, the merest, signore," he said as he added the final touches. "Now the signore can fall in love as soon as he likes." Aschenbach went off as in a dream, dazed between joy and fear, in his red neck-tie and broad straw hat with its gay striped band.

A lukewarm storm-wind had come up. It rained a little now and then, the air was heavy and turbid and smelt of decay. Aschenbach, with fevered cheeks beneath the rouge, seemed to hear rushing and flapping sounds in his ears, as though storm-spirits were abroad—unhallowed ocean harpies who follow those devoted to destruction, snatch away and defile their viands. For the heat took away his appetite and thus he was haunted with the idea that his food was infected.

One afternoon he pursued his charmer deep into the stricken city's huddled heart. The labyrinthine little streets, squares, canals, and bridges, each one so like the next, at length quite made him lose his bearings. He did not even know the points of the compass; all his care was not to lose sight of the figure after which his eyes thirsted. He slunk under walls, he lurked behind buildings or people's backs; and the sustained tension of his senses and emotions exhausted him more and more, though for a long time he was unconscious of fatigue. Tadzio walked behind the others, he let them pass ahead in the narrow alleys, and as he sauntered slowly after, he would turn his head and assure himself with a glance of his strange, twilit grey eyes that his lover was still following. He saw him—and he did not betray him. The knowledge enraptured Aschenbach. Lured by those eyes, led on the leading-string of his own passion and folly, utterly lovesick, he stole upon the footsteps of his unseemly hope—and at the end found himself cheated. The Polish family crossed a small vaulted bridge, the height of whose archway hid them from his sight, and when he climbed it himself they were nowhere to be seen. He hunted in three directions—straight ahead and on both sides of the narrow, dirty quay—in vain. Worn quite out and unnerved, he had to give over the search.

His head burned, his body was wet with clammy sweat, he was plagued by intolerable thirst. He looked about for refreshment, of whatever sort, and found a little fruit-shop where he bought some strawberries. They were overripe and soft; he ate them as he went. The street he was on opened out into a little square, one of those charmed, forsaken spots he liked; he recognized it as the very one where he had sat weeks ago and conceived his abortive plan of flight. He sank down on the steps of the well and leaned his head against its stone rim. It was quiet here. Grass grew between the stones, and rubbish lay about. Tall, weather-beaten houses bordered the square, one of them rather palatial, with vaulted windows, gaping now, and little lion balconies. In the ground floor of another was an apothecary's shop. A waft of carbolic acid was borne on a warm gust of wind.

There he sat, the master: this was he who had found a way to reconcile art and honours; who had written *The Abject*, and in a style of classic purity renounced bohemianism and all its works, all sympathy with the abyss and the troubled depths of the outcast human soul. This was he who had put knowledge underfoot to climb so high; who had outgrown the ironic pose and adjusted himself to the burdens and obligations of fame; whose renown had been officially recognized and his name ennobled, whose style was set for a model in the schools. There he sat. His eyelids were closed, there was only a swift, sidelong glint of the eyeballs now and again, something between a question and a leer; while the rouged and flabby mouth uttered single words of the sentences shaped in his disordered brain by the fantastic logic that governs our dreams.

"For mark you, Phædrus, beauty alone is both divine and visible; and so it is the sense way, the artist's way, little Phædrus, to the spirit. But, now tell me, my dear boy, do you believe that such a man can ever attain wisdom and true manly worth, for whom the path to the spirit must lead through the senses? Or do you rather think—for I leave the point to you—that it is a path of perilous sweetness, a way of transgression, and must surely lead him who walks in it astray? For you know that we poets cannot walk the way of beauty without Eros as our companion and guide. We may be heroic after our fashion, disciplined warriors of our craft, yet are we all like women, for we exult in passion, and love is still our desire—our craving and our shame. And from this you will perceive that we poets can be neither wise nor worthy citizens. We must needs be wanton, must needs rove at large in the realm of feeling. Our magisterial style is all folly and pretence, our honourable repute a farce, the crowd's belief in us is merely laughable. And to teach youth, or the populace, by means of art is a dangerous practice and ought to be forbidden. For what good can an artist be as a teacher, when from his birth up he is headed direct for the pit? We may want to shun it and attain to honour in the world; but however we turn, it draws us still. So, then, since knowledge might destroy us, we will have none of it. For knowledge, Phædrus, does not make him who possesses it dignified or austere. Knowledge is all-knowing, understanding, forgiving; it takes up no position, sets no store by form. It has compassion with the abyss—it *is* the abyss. So we reject it, firmly, and henceforward our concern shall be with beauty only. And by beauty we mean simplicity, largeness, and renewed severity of discipline; we mean a return to detachment and to form. But detachment, Phædrus, and preoccupation with form lead to intoxication and desire, they may lead the noblest among us to frightful emotional excesses, which his own stern cult of the beautiful would make him the first to condemn. So they too, they too, lead to the bottomless pit. Yes, they lead us thither, I say, us who are poets—who by our natures are prone not to excellence but to excess. And now, Phædrus, I will go. Remain here; and only when you can no longer see me, then do you depart also."

A few days later Gustave Aschenbach left his hotel rather later than usual in the morning. He was not feeling well and had to struggle against spells of giddiness only half physical in their nature, accompanied by a swiftly mounting dread, a sense of futility and hopelessness—but whether this referred to himself or to the outer world he could not tell. In the lobby he saw a quantity of luggage lying strapped and ready; asked the porter whose it was, and received in answer the name he already knew he should hear—that of the Polish family. The expression of his ravaged features did not change; he only gave that quick lift of the head with which we sometimes receive the uninteresting answer to a casual query. But he put another: "When?" "After luncheon," the man replied. He nodded, and went down to the beach.

It was an unfriendly scene. Little crisping shivers ran all across the wide stretch of shallow water between the shore and the first sand-bank. The whole beach, once so full of colour and life, looked now autumnal, out of season; it was nearly deserted and not even very clean. A camera on a tripod stood at the edge of the water, apparently abandoned; its black cloth snapped in the freshening wind.

Tadzio was there, in front of his cabin, with the three or four playfellows still left him. Aschenbach set up his chair some half-way between the cabins and the water, spread a rug over his knees, and sat looking on. The game this time was unsupervised, the elders being probably busy with their packing, and it looked rather lawless and out-of-hand. Jaschiu, the sturdy lad in the belted suit, with the black, brilliantined hair, became angry at a handful of sand thrown in his eyes; he challenged Tadzio to a fight, which quickly ended in the downfall of the weaker. And perhaps the coarser nature saw here a chance to avenge himself at last, by one cruel act, for his long weeks of subserviency: the victor would not let the vanquished get up, but remained kneeling on Tadzio's back, pressing Tadzio's face into the sand—for so long a time that it seemed the exhausted lad might even suffocate. He made spasmodic efforts to shake the other off, lay still, and then began a feeble twitching. Just as Aschenbach was about to spring indignantly to the rescue, Jaschiu let his victim go. Tadzio, very pale, half sat up, and remained so, leaning on one arm, for several minutes, with darkening eyes and rumpled hair. Then he rose and walked slowly away. The others called him, at first gaily, then imploringly; he would not hear. Jaschiu was evidently overtaken by swift remorse; he followed his friend and tried to make his peace, but Tadzio motioned him back with a jerk of one shoulder and went down to the water's edge. He was barefoot and wore his striped linen suit with the red breast-knot.

There he stayed a little, with bent head, tracing figures in the wet sand with one toe; then stepped into the shallow water, which at its deepest did not wet his knees; waded idly through it and reached the sand-bar. Now he paused again, with his face turned seaward; and next began to move slowly leftwards along the narrow strip of sand the sea left bare. He paced there, divided by an expanse of water from the shore, from his mates by his moody pride; a remote and isolated figure, with floating locks, out there in sea and wind, against the misty inane. Once more he paused to look: with a sudden recollection, or by an impulse, he turned from the waist up, in an exquisite movement, one hand resting on his hip, and looked over his shoulder at the shore. The watcher sat just as he had sat that time in the lobby of the hotel when first the twilit grey eyes had met his own. He rested his head against the chair-back and followed the movements of the figure out there, then lifted it, as it were to Tadzio's gaze. It sank on his breast, the eyes looked out beneath their lids, while his whole face took on the relaxed and brooding expression of deep slumber. It seemed to him the pale and lovely Summoner out there smiled at him and beckoned; as though, with the hand he lifted from his hip, he pointed outward as he hovered on before into an immensity of richest expectation.

Some minutes passed before anyone hastened to the aid of the elderly man sitting there collapsed in his chair. They bore him to his room. And before nightfall a shocked and respectful world received the news of his decease.

LITTLE HERR FRIEDEMANN

IT WAS the nurse's fault. When they first suspected, Frau Consul Friedemann had spoken to her very gravely about the need of controlling her weakness. But what good did that do? Or the glass of red wine which she got daily besides the beer which was needed for the milk? For they suddenly discovered that she even sank so low as to drink the methylated spirit which was kept for the spirit lamp. Before they could send her away and get someone to take her place, the mischief was done. One day the mother and sisters came home to find that little Johannes, then about a month old, had fallen from the couch and lay on the floor, uttering an appallingly faint little cry, while the nurse stood beside him quite stupefied.

The doctor came and with firm, gentle hands tested the little creature's contracted and twitching limbs. He made a very serious face. The three girls stood sobbing in a corner and the Frau Consul in the anguish of her heart prayed aloud.

The poor mother, just before the child's birth, had already suffered a crushing blow: her husband, the Dutch Consul, had been snatched away from her by sudden and violent illness, and now she was too broken to cherish any hope that little Johannes would be spared to her. But by the second day the doctor had given her hand an encouraging squeeze and told her that all immediate danger was over. There was no longer any sign that the brain was affected. The facial expression was altered, it had lost the fixed and staring look.... Of course, they must see how things went on—and hope for the best, hope for the best.

The grey gabled house in which Johannes Friedemann grew up stood by the north gate of the little old commercial city. The front door led into a large flag-paved entry, out of which a stair with a white wooden balustrade led up into the second storey. The faded wall-paper in the living-room had a landscape pattern, and straight-backed chairs and sofas in dark-red plush stood round the heavy mahogany table.

Often in his childhood Johannes sat here at the window, which always had a fine showing of flowers, on a small footstool at his mother's feet, listening to some fairy-tale she told him, gazing at her smooth grey head, her mild and gentle face, and breathing in the faint scent she exhaled. She showed him the picture of his father, a kindly man with grey side-whiskers—he was now in heaven, she said, and awaiting them there.

Behind the house was a small garden where in summer they spent much of their time, despite the smell of burnt sugar which came over from the refinery close by. There was a gnarled old walnut tree in whose shade little Johannes would sit, on a low wooden stool, cracking walnuts, while Frau Friedemann and her three daughters, now grown women, took refuge from the sun under a grey canvas tent. The mother's gaze often strayed from her embroidery to look with sad and loving eyes at her child.

He was not beautiful, little Johannes, as he crouched on his stool industriously cracking his nuts. In fact, he was a strange sight, with his pigeon breast, humped back, and disproportionately long arms. But his hands and feet were delicately formed, he had soft red-brown eyes like a doe's, a sensitive mouth, and fine, light-brown hair. His head, had it not sat so deep between his shoulders, might almost have been called pretty.

When he was seven he went to school, where time passed swiftly and uniformly. He walked every day, with the strut deformed people often have, past the quaint gabled houses and shops to the old schoolhouse with the vaulted arcades. When he had done his preparation he would read in his books with the lovely title-page illustrations in colour, or else work in the garden, while his sisters kept house for their invalid mother. They went out too, for they belonged to the best society of the town; but unfortunately they had not married, for they had not much money nor any looks to recommend them.

Johannes too was now and then invited out by his schoolmates, but it is not likely that he enjoyed it. He could not take part in their games, and they were always embarrassed in his company, so there was no feeling of good fellowship.

There came a time when he began to hear certain matters talked about, in the courtyard at school. He listened wide-eyed and large-eared, quite silent, to his companions' raving over this or that little girl. Such things, though they entirely engrossed the attention of these others, were not, he felt, for him; they belonged in the same category as the ball games and gymnastics. At times he felt a little sad. But at length he had become quite used to standing on one side and not taking part.

But after all it came about—when he was sixteen—that he felt suddenly drawn to a girl of his own age. She was the sister of a classmate of his, a blond, hilarious hoyden, and he met her when calling at her brother's house. He felt strangely embarrassed in her neighbourhood; she too was embarrassed and treated him with such artificial cordiality that it made him sad.

One summer afternoon as he was walking by himself on the wall outside the town, he heard a whispering behind a jasmine bush and peeped cautiously through the branches. There she sat on a bench beside a long-legged, red-haired youth of his acquaintance. They had their arms about each other and he was imprinting on her lips a kiss, which she returned amid giggles. Johannes looked, turned round, and went softly away.

His head was sunk deeper than ever between his shoulders, his hands trembled, and a sharp pain shot upwards from his chest to his throat. But he choked it down, straightening himself as well as he could. "Good," said he to himself. "That is over. Never again will I let myself in for any of it. To the others it brings joy and happiness, for me it can only mean sadness and pain. I am done with it. For me that is all over. Never again."

The resolution did him good. He had renounced, renounced for ever. He went home, took up a book, or else played on his violin, which despite his deformed chest he had learned to do.

At seventeen Johannes left school to go into business, like everybody else he knew. He was apprenticed to the big lumber firm of Herr Schlievogt down on the river-bank. They were kind and considerate, he on his side was responsive and friendly, time passed with peaceful regularity. But in his twenty-first year his mother died, after a lingering illness.

This was a sore blow for Johannes Friedemann, and the pain of it endured. He cherished this grief, he gave himself up to it as one gives oneself to a great joy, he fed it with a thousand childhood memories; it was the first important event in his life and he made the most of it.

Is not life in and for itself a good, regardless of whether we may call its content "happiness"? Johannes Friedemann felt that it was so, and he loved life. He, who had renounced the greatest joy it can bring us, taught himself with infinite, incredible care to take pleasure in what it had still to offer. A walk in the springtime in the parks surrounding the town; the fragrance of a flower; the song of a bird—might not one feel grateful for such things as these?

And that we need to be taught how to enjoy, yes, that our education is always and only equal to our capacity for enjoyment—he knew that too, and he trained himself. Music he loved, and attended all the concerts that were given in the town. He came to play the violin not so badly himself, no matter what a figure of fun he made when he did it; and took delight in every beautiful soft tone he succeeded in producing. Also, by much reading he came in time to possess a literary taste the like of which did not exist in the place. He kept up with the new books, even the foreign ones; he knew how to savour the seductive rhythm of a lyric or the ultimate flavour of a subtly told tale—yes, one might almost call him a connoisseur.

He learned to understand that to everything belongs its own enjoyment and that it is absurd to distinguish between an experience which is "happy" and one which is not. With a right good will he accepted each emotion as it came, each mood, whether sad or gay. Even he cherished the unfulfilled desires, the longings. He loved them for their own sakes and told himself that with fulfilment the best of them would be past. The vague, sweet, painful yearning and hope of quiet spring evenings—are they not richer in joy than all the fruition the summer can bring? Yes, he was a connoisseur, our little Herr Friedemann.

But of course they did not know that, the people whom he met on the street, who bowed to him with the kindly, compassionate air he knew so well. They could not know that this unhappy cripple, strutting comically along in his light overcoat and shiny top hat—strange to say, he was a little vain—they could not know how tenderly he loved the mild flow of his life, charged with no great emotions, it is true, but full of a quiet and tranquil happiness which was his own creation.

But Herr Friedemann's great preference, his real passion, was for the theatre. He possessed a dramatic sense which was unusually strong; at a telling theatrical effect or the catastrophe of a tragedy his whole small frame would shake with emotion. He had his regular seat in the first row of boxes at the opera-house; was an assiduous frequenter and often took his sisters with him. Since their mother's death they kept house for their brother in the old home which they all owned together.

It was a pity they were unmarried still; but with the decline of hope had come resignation—Friederike, the eldest, was seventeen years further on than Herr Friedemann. She and her sister Henriette were over-tall and thin, whereas Pfiffi, the youngest, was too short and stout. She had a funny way, too, of shaking herself as she talked, and water came in the corners of her mouth.

Little Herr Friedemann did not trouble himself overmuch about his three sisters. But they stuck together loyally and were always of one mind. Whenever an engagement was announced in their circle they with one voice said how very gratifying that was.

Their brother continued to live with them even after he became independent, as he did by leaving Herr Schlievogt's firm and going into business for himself, in an agency of sorts, which was no great tax on his time. His offices were in a couple of rooms on the ground floor of the house so that at mealtimes he had but the pair of stairs to mount—for he suffered now and then from asthma.

His thirtieth birthday fell on a fine warm June day, and after dinner he sat out in the grey canvas tent, with a new head-rest embroidered by Henriette. He had a good cigar in his mouth and a good book in his hand. But sometimes he would put the latter down to listen to the sparrows chirping blithely in the old nut tree and look at the clean gravel path leading up to the house between lawns bright with summer flowers.

Little Herr Friedemann wore no beard, and his face had scarcely changed at all, save that the features were slightly sharper. He wore his fine light-brown hair parted on one side.

Once, as he let the book fall on his knee and looked up into the sunny blue sky, he said to himself: "Well, so that is thirty years. Perhaps there may be ten or even twenty more, God knows. They will mount up without a sound or a stir and pass by like those that are gone; and I look forward to them with peace in my heart."

Now, it happened in July of the same year that a new appointment to the office of District Commandant had set the whole town talking. The stout and jolly gentleman who had for many years occupied the post had been very popular in social circles and they saw him go with great regret. It was in compliance with goodness knows what regulations that Herr von Rinnlingen and no other was sent hither from the capital.

In any case the exchange was not such a bad one. The new Commandant was married but childless. He rented a spacious villa in the southern suburbs of the city and seemed to intend to set up an establishment. There was a report that he was very rich—which received confirmation in the fact that he brought with him four servants, five riding and carriage horses, a landau and a light hunting-cart.

Soon after their arrival the husband and wife left cards on all the best society, and their names were on every tongue. But it was not Herr von Rinnlingen, it was his wife who was the centre of interest. All the men were dazed, for the moment too dazed to pass judgment; but their wives were quite prompt and definite in the view that Gerda von Rinnlingen was not their sort.

"Of course, she comes from the metropolis, her ways would naturally be different," Frau Hagenström, the lawyer's wife, said, in conversation with Henriette Friedemann. "She smokes, and she rides. That is of course. But it is her manners—they are not only free, they are positively brusque, or even worse. You see, no one could call her ugly, one might even say she is pretty; but she has not a trace of feminine charm in her looks or gestures or her laugh—they completely lack everything that makes a man fall in love with a woman. She is not a flirt—and goodness knows I would be the last to disparage her for that. But it is strange to see so young a woman—she is only twenty-four—so entirely wanting in natural charm. I am not expressing myself very well, my dear, but I know what I mean. All the men are simply bewildered. In a few weeks, you will see, they will be disgusted."

"Well," Fräulein Friedemann said, "she certainly has everything she wants."

"Yes," cried Frau Hagenström, "look at her husband! And how does she treat him? You ought to see it—you will see it! I would be the first to approve of a married woman behaving with a certain reserve towards the other sex. But how does she behave to her own husband? She has a way of fixing him with an ice-cold stare and saying 'My dear friend!' with a pitying expression that drives me mad. For when you look at him—upright, correct, gallant, a brilliant officer and a splendidly preserved man of forty! They have been married four years, my dear."

Herr Friedemann was first vouchsafed a glimpse of Frau von Rinnlingen in the main street of the town, among all the rows of shops, at midday, when he was coming from the Bourse, where he had done a little bidding.

He was strolling along beside Herr Stephens, looking tiny and important, as usual. Herr Stephens was in the wholesale trade, a huge stocky man with round side-whiskers and bushy eyebrows. Both of them wore top hats; their overcoats were unbuttoned on account of the heat. They tapped their canes along the pavement and talked of the political situation; but half-way down the street Stephens suddenly said:

"Deuce take it if there isn't the Rinnlingen driving along."

"Good," answered Herr Friedemann in his high, rather sharp voice, looking expectantly ahead. "Because I have never yet set eyes on her. And here we have the yellow cart we hear so much about."

It was in fact the hunting-cart which Frau von Rinnlingen was herself driving today with a pair of thoroughbreds; a groom sat behind her, with folded arms. She wore a loose beige coat and skirt and a small round straw hat with a brown leather band, beneath which her well-waved red-blond hair, a good, thick crop, was drawn into a knot at the nape of her neck. Her face was oval, with a dead-white skin and faint bluish shadows lurking under the close-set eyes. Her nose was short but well-shaped, with a becoming little saddle of freckles; whether her mouth was as good or not could not be told, for she kept it in continual motion, sucking the lower and biting the upper lip.

Herr Stephens, as the cart came abreast of them, greeted her with a great show of deference; little Herr Friedemann lifted his hat too and looked at her with wide-eyed attention. She lowered her whip, nodded slightly, and drove slowly past, looking at the houses and shop-windows.

After a few paces Herr Stephens said:

"She has been taking a drive and was on her way home."

Little Herr Friedmann made no answer, but stared before him at the pavement. Presently he started, looked at his companion, and asked: "What did you say?"

And Herr Stephens repeated his acute remark.

Three days after that Johannes Friedemann came home at midday from his usual walk. Dinner was at half past twelve, and he would spend the interval in his office at the right of the entrance door. But the maid came across the entry and told him that there were visitors.

"In my office?" he asked.

"No, upstairs with the mistresses."

"Who are they?"

"Herr and Frau Colonel von Rinnlingen."

"Ah," said Johannes Friedemann. "Then I will—"

And he mounted the stairs. He crossed the lobby and laid his hand on the knob of the high white door leading into the "landscape room". And then he drew back, turned round, and slowly returned as he had come. And spoke to himself, for there was no one else there, and said: "No, better not."

He went into his office, sat down at his desk, and took up the paper. But after a little he dropped it again and sat looking to one side out of the window. Thus he sat until the maid came to say that luncheon was ready; then he went up into the dining-room where his sisters were already waiting, and sat down in his chair, in which there were three music-books.

As she ladled the soup Henriette said:

"Johannes, do you know who were here?"

"Well?" he asked.

"The new Commandant and his wife."

"Indeed? That was friendly of them."

"Yes," said Pfiffi, a little water coming in the corners of her mouth. "I found them both very agreeable."

"And we must lose no time in returning the call," said Friederike. "I suggest that we go next Sunday, the day after tomorrow."

"Sunday," Henriette and Pfiffi said.

"You will go with us, Johannes?" asked Friederike.

"Of course he will," said Pfiffi, and gave herself a little shake. Herr Friedemann had not heard her at all; he was eating his soup, with a hushed and troubled air. It was as though he were listening to some strange noise he heard.

Next evening *Lohengrin* was being given at the opera, and everybody in society was present. The small auditorium was crowded, humming with voices and smelling of gas and perfumery. And every eye-glass in the stalls was directed towards box thirteen, next to the stage; for this was the first appearance of Herr and Frau von Rinnlingen and one could give them a good looking-over.

When little Herr Friedemann, in flawless dress clothes and glistening white pigeon-breasted shirt-front, entered his box, which was number thirteen, he started back at the door, making a gesture with his hand towards his brow. His nostrils dilated feverishly. Then he took his seat, which was next to Frau von Rinnlingen's.

She contemplated him for a little while, with her under lip stuck out; then she turned to exchange a few words with her husband, a tall, broad-shouldered gentleman with a brown, good-natured face and turned-up moustaches.

When the overture began and Frau von Rinnlingen leaned over the balustrade Herr Friedemann gave her a quick, searching side glance. She wore a light-coloured evening frock, the only one in the theatre which was slightly low in the neck. Her sleeves were full and her white gloves came up to her elbows. Her figure was statelier than it had looked under the loose coat; her full bosom slowly rose and fell and the knot of red-blond hair hung low and heavy at the nape of her neck.

Herr Friedemann was pale, much paler than usual, and little

beads of perspiration stood on his brow beneath the smoothly parted brown hair. He could see Frau von Rinnlingen's left arm, which lay upon the balustrade. She had taken off her glove and the rounded, dead-white arm and ringless hand, both of them shot with pale blue veins, were directly under his eye—he could not help seeing them.

The fiddles sang, the trombones crashed, Telramund was slain, general jubilation reigned in the orchestra, and little Herr Friedemann sat there motionless and pallid, his head drawn in between his shoulders, his forefinger to his lips and one hand thrust into the opening of his waistcoat.

As the curtain fell, Frau von Rinnlingen got up to leave the box with her husband. Johannes Friedemann saw her without looking, wiped his handkerchief across his brow, then rose suddenly and went as far as the door into the foyer, where he turned, came back to his chair, and sat down in the same posture as before.

When the bell rang and his neighbours re-entered the box he felt Frau von Rinnlingen's eyes upon him, so that finally against his will he raised his head. As their eyes met, hers did not swerve aside; she continued to gaze without embarrassment until he himself, deeply humiliated, was forced to look away. He turned a shade paler and felt a strange, sweet pang of anger and scorn. The music began again.

Towards the end of the act Frau von Rinnlingen chanced to drop her fan; it fell at Herr Friedemann's feet. They both stooped at the same time, but she reached it first and gave a little mocking smile as she said: "Thank you."

Their heads were quite close together and just for a second he got the warm scent of her breast. His face was drawn, his whole body twitched, and his heart thumped so horribly that he lost his breath. He sat without moving for half a minute, then he pushed back his chair, got up quietly, and went out.

He crossed the lobby, pursued by the music; got his top hat from the cloak-room, his light overcoat and his stick, went down the stairs and out of doors.

It was a warm, still evening. In the gas-lit street the gabled houses towered towards a sky where stars were softly beaming. The pavement echoed the steps of a few passers-by. Someone spoke to him, but he heard and saw nothing; his head was bowed and his deformed chest shook with the violence of his breathing. Now and then he murmured to himself:

"My God, my God!"

He was gazing horror-struck within himself, beholding the havoc which had been wrought with his tenderly cherished, scrupulously managed feelings. Suddenly he was quite overpowered by the strength of his tortured longing. Giddy and drunken he leaned against a lamp-post and his quivering lips uttered the one word: "Gerda!"

The stillness was complete. Far and wide not a soul was to be seen. Little Herr Friedemann pulled himself together and went on, up the street in which the opera-house stood and which ran steeply down to the river, then along the main street northwards to his home.

How she had looked at him! She had forced him, actually, to cast down his eyes! She had humiliated him with her glance. But was she not a woman and he a man? And those strange brown eyes of hers—had they not positively glittered with unholy joy?

Again he felt the same surge of sensual, impotent hatred mount up in him; then he relived the moment when her head had touched his, when he had breathed in the fragrance of her body—and for the second time he halted, bent his deformed torso backwards, drew in the air through clenched teeth, and murmured helplessly, desperately, uncontrollably:

"My God, my God!"

Then went on again, slowly, mechanically, through the heavy evening air, through the empty echoing streets until he stood before his own house. He paused a minute in the entry, breathing the cool, dank inside air; then he went into his office.

He sat down at his desk by the open window and stared straight ahead of him at a large yellow rose which somebody had set there in a glass of water. He took it up and smelt it with his eyes closed, then put it down with a gesture of weary sadness. No, no. That was all over. What was even that fragrance to him now? What any of all those things that up to now had been the well-springs of his joy?

He turned away and gazed into the quiet street. At intervals steps passed and the sound died away. The stars stood still and glittered. He felt so weak, so utterly tired to death. His head was quite vacant, and suddenly his despair began to melt into a gentle, pervading melancholy. A few lines of a poem flickered through his head, he heard the *Lohengrin* music in his ears, he saw Frau von Rinnlingen's face and her round white arm on the red velvet —then he fell into a heavy fever-burdened sleep.

Often he was near waking, but feared to do so and managed to sink back into forgetfulness again. But when it had grown quite light, he opened his eyes and looked round him with a wide and painful gaze. He remembered everything, it was as though the anguish had never been intermitted by sleep.

His head was heavy and his eyes burned. But when he had washed up and bathed his head with cologne he felt better and sat down in his place by the still open window. It was early, perhaps only five o'clock. Now and then a baker's boy passed; otherwise there was no one to be seen. In the opposite house the blinds were down. But birds were twittering and the sky was luminously blue. A wonderfully beautiful Sunday morning.

A feeling of comfort and confidence came over little Herr Friedemann. Why had he been distressing himself? Was not everything just as it had been? The attack of yesterday had been a bad one. Granted. But it should be the last. It was not too late, he could still escape destruction. He must avoid every occasion of a fresh seizure, he felt sure he could do this. He felt the strength to conquer and suppress his weakness.

It struck half past seven and Friederike came in with the coffee, setting it on the round table in front of the leather sofa against the rear wall.

"Good morning, Johannes," said she; "here is your breakfast."

"Thanks," said little Herr Friedemann. And then: "Dear Friederike, I am sorry, but you will have to pay your call without me, I do not feel well enough to go. I have slept badly and have a headache—in short, I must ask you—"

"What a pity!" answered Friederike. "You must go another time. But you do look ill. Shall I lend you my menthol pencil?"

"Thanks," said Herr Friedemann. "It will pass." And Friederike went out.

Standing at the table he slowly drank his coffee and ate a croissant. He felt satisfied with himself and proud of his firmness. When he had finished he sat down again by the open window, with a cigar. The food had done him good and he felt happy and hopeful. He took a book and sat reading and smoking and blinking into the sunlight.

Morning had fully come, wagons rattled past, there were many voices and the sound of the bells on passing trams. With and among it all was woven the twittering and chirping; there was a radiant blue sky, a soft mild air.

At ten o'clock he heard his sisters cross the entry; the front door creaked, and he idly noticed that they passed his window. An hour went by. He felt more and more happy.

A sort of hubris mounted in him. What a heavenly air—and how the birds were singing! He felt like taking a little walk. Then suddenly, without any transition, yet accompanied by a terror namelessly sweet came the thought: "Suppose I were to go to her!" And suppressing, as though by actual muscular effort, every warning voice within him, he added with blissful resolution: "I will go to her!"

He changed into his Sunday clothes, took his top hat and his stick, and hurried with quickened breath through the town and into the southern suburbs. Without looking at a soul he kept raising and dropping his head with each eager step, completely rapt in his exalted state until he arrived at the avenue of chestnut trees and the red brick villa with the name of Commandant von Rinnlingen on the gate-post.

But here he was seized by a tremor, his heart throbbed and pounded in his breast. He went across the vestibule and rang at the inside door. The die was cast, there was no retreating now. "Come what come may," thought he, and felt the stillness of death within him.

The door suddenly opened and the maid came towards him across the vestibule; she took his card and hurried away up the red-carpeted stair. Herr Friedemann gazed fixedly at the bright colour until she came back and said that her mistress would like him to come up.

He put down his stick beside the door leading into the salon and stole a look at himself in the glass. His face was pale, the eyes red, his hair was sticking to his brow, the hand that held his top hat kept on shaking.

The maid opened the door and he went in. He found himself in a rather large, half-darkened room, with drawn curtains. At his right was a piano, and about the round table in the centre stood several arm-chairs covered in brown silk. The sofa stood along the left-hand wall, with a landscape painting in a heavy gilt frame hanging above it. The wall-paper too was dark in tone. There was an alcove filled with potted palms.

A minute passed, then Frau von Rinnlingen opened the portières on the right and approached him noiselessly over the thick brown carpet. She wore a simply cut frock of red and black plaid. A ray of light, with motes dancing in it, streamed from the alcove and fell upon her heavy red hair so that it shone like gold. She kept her strange eyes fixed upon him with a searching gaze and as usual stuck out her under lip.

"Good morning, Frau Commandant," began little Herr Friedemann, and looked up at her, for he came only as high as her chest. "I wished to pay you my respects too. When my sisters did so I was unfortunately out . . . I regretted sincerely . . ."

He had no idea at all what else he should say; and there she stood and gazed ruthlessly at him as though she would force him to go on. The blood rushed to his head. "She sees through me," he thought, "she will torture and despise me. Her eyes keep flickering. . . ."

But at last she said, in a very high, clear voice:

"It is kind of you to have come. I have also been sorry not to see you before. Will you please sit down?"

She took her seat close beside him, leaned back, and put her arm along the arm of the chair. He sat bent over, holding his hat between his knees. She went on:

"Did you know that your sisters were here a quarter of an hour ago? They told me you were ill."

"Yes," he answered, "I did not feel well enough to go out, I thought I should not be able to. That is why I am late."

"You do not look very well even now," said she tranquilly, not shifting her gaze. "You are pale and your eyes are inflamed. You are not very strong, perhaps?"

"Oh," said Herr Friedemann, stammering, "I've not much to complain of, as a rule."

"I am ailing a good deal too," she went on, still not turning her eyes from him, "but nobody notices it. I am nervous, and sometimes I have the strangest feelings."

She paused, lowered her chin to her breast, and looked up expectantly at him. He made no reply, simply sat with his dreamy gaze directed upon her. How strangely she spoke, and how her clear and thrilling voice affected him! His heart beat more quietly and he felt as though he were in a dream. She began again:

"I am not wrong in thinking that you left the opera last night before it was over?"

"Yes, madam."

"I was sorry to see that. You listened like a music-lover—though the performance was only tolerable. You are fond of music, I am sure. Do you play the piano?"

"I play the violin, a little," said Herr Friedemann. "That is, really not very much—"

"You play the violin?" she asked, and looked past him consideringly. "But we might play together," she suddenly said. "I can accompany a little. It would be a pleasure to find somebody here—would you come?"

"I am quite at your service—with pleasure," said he, stiffly. He was still as though in a dream. A pause ensued. Then suddenly her expression changed. He saw it alter for one of cruel, though hardly perceptible mockery, and again she fixed him with that same searching, uncannily flickering gaze. His face burned, he knew not where to turn; drawing his head down between his shoulders he stared confusedly at the carpet, while there shot through him once more that strangely sweet and torturing sense of impotent rage.

He made a desperate effort and raised his eyes. She was looking over his head at the door. With the utmost difficulty he fetched out a few words:

"And you are so far not too dissatisfied with your stay in our city?"

"Oh, no," said Frau Rinnlingen indifferently. "No, certainly not; why should I not be satisfied? To be sure, I feel a little hampered, as though everybody's eyes were upon me, but—oh, before I forget it," she went on quickly, "we are entertaining a few people next week, a small, informal company. A little music, perhaps, and conversation.... There is a charming garden at the back, it runs down to the river. You and your sisters will be receiving an invitation in due course, but perhaps I may ask you now to give us the pleasure of your company?"

Her Friedemann was just expressing his gratitude for the invitation when the door-knob was seized energetically from without and the Commandant entered. They both rose and Frau von Rinnlingen introduced the two men to each other. Her husband bowed to them both with equal courtesy. His bronze face glistened with the heat.

He drew off his gloves, addressing Herr Friedemann in a powerful, rather sharp-edged voice. The latter looked up at him with large vacant eyes and had the feeling that he would presently be clapped benevolently on the shoulder. Heels together, inclining from the waist, the Commandant turned to his wife and asked, in a much gentler tone:

"Have you asked Herr Friedemann if he will give us the pleasure of his company at our little party, my love? If you are willing I should like to fix the date for next week and I hope that the weather will remain fine so that we can enjoy ourselves in the garden."

"Just as you say," answered Frau von Rinnlingen, and gazed past him.

Two minutes later Herr Friedemann got up to go. At the door he turned and bowed to her once more, meeting her expressionless gaze still fixed upon him.

He went away, but he did not go back to the town; unconsciously he struck into a path that led away from the avenue towards the old ruined fort by the river, among well-kept lawns and shady avenues with benches.

He walked quickly and absently, with bent head. He felt intolerably hot, as though aware of flames leaping and sinking within him, and his head throbbed with fatigue.

It was as though her gaze still rested on him—not vacantly as it had at the end, but with that flickering cruelty which went with the strange still way she spoke. Did it give her pleasure to put him beside himself, to see him helpless? Looking through and through him like that, could she not feel a little pity?

He had gone along the river-bank under the moss-grown wall; he sat down on a bench within a half-circle of blossoming jasmine.

The sweet, heavy scent was all about him, the sun brooded upon the dimpling water.

He was weary, he was worn out; and yet within him all was tumult and anguish. Were it not better to take one last look and then to go down into that quiet water; after a brief struggle to be free and safe at peace? Ah, peace, peace—that was what he wanted! Not peace in an empty and soundless void, but a gentle, sunlit peace, full of good, of tranquil thoughts.

All his tender love of life thrilled through him in that moment, all his profound yearning for his vanished "happiness". But then he looked about him into the silent, endlessly indifferent peace of nature, saw how the river went its own way in the sun, how the grasses quivered and the flowers stood up where they blossomed, only to fade and be blown away; saw how all that was bent submissively to the will of life; and there came over him all at once that sense of acquaintance and understanding with the inevitable which can make those who know it superior to the blows of fate.

He remembered the afternoon of his thirtieth birthday and the peaceful happiness with which he, untroubled by fears or hopes, had looked forward to what was left of his life. He had seen no light and no shadow there, only a mild twilight radiance gently declining into the dark. With what a calm and superior smile had he contemplated the years still to come—how long ago was that?

Then this woman had come, she had to come, it was his fate that she should, for she herself was his fate and she alone. He had known it from the first moment. She had come—and though he had tried his best to defend his peace, her coming had roused in him all those forces which from his youth up he had sought to suppress, feeling, as he did, that they spelled torture and destruction. They had seized upon him with frightful, irresistible power and flung him to the earth.

They were his destruction, well he knew it. But why struggle, then, and why torture himself? Let everything take its course. He would go his appointed way, closing his eyes before the yawning void, bowing to his fate, bowing to the overwhelming, anguishingly sweet, irresistible power.

The water glittered, the jasmine gave out its strong, pungent scent, the birds chattered in the tree-tops that gave glimpses among them of a heavy, velvety-blue sky. Little hump-backed

Herr Friedemann sat long upon his bench; he sat bent over, holding his head in his hands.

Everybody agreed that the Rinnlingens entertained very well. Some thirty guests sat in the spacious dining-room, at the long, prettily decorated table, and the butler and two hired waiters were already handing round the ices. Dishes clattered, glasses rang, there was a warm aroma of food and perfumes. Here were comfortable merchants with their wives and daughters; most of the officers of the garrison; a few professional men, lawyers and the popular old family doctor—in short, all the best society.

A nephew of the Commandant, on a visit, a student of mathematics, sat deeply in conversation with Fräulein Hagenström, whose place was directly opposite Herr Friedemann's, at the lower end of the table. Johannes Friedemann sat there on a rich velvet cushion, beside the unbeautiful wife of the Colonial Director and not far off Frau von Rinnlingen, who had been escorted to table by Consul Stephens. It was astonishing, the change which had taken place in little Herr Friedemann in these few days. Perhaps the incandescent lighting in the room was partly to blame; but his cheeks looked sunken, he made a more crippled impression even than usual, and his inflamed eyes, with their dark rings, glowed with an inexpressibly tragic light. He drank a great deal of wine and now and then addressed a remark to his neighbour.

Frau von Rinnlingen had not so far spoken to him at all; but now she leaned over and called out:

"I have been expecting you in vain these days, you and your fiddle."

He looked vacantly at her for a while before he replied. She wore a light-coloured frock with a low neck that left the white throat bare; a Maréchal Niel rose in full bloom was fastened in her shining hair. Her cheeks were a little flushed, but the same bluish shadows lurked in the corners of her eyes.

Herr Friedemann looked at his plate and forced himself to make some sort of reply; after which the school superintendent's wife asked him if he did not love Beethoven and he had to answer that too. But at this point the Commandant, sitting at the head of the table, caught his wife's eye, tapped on his glass and said:

"Ladies and gentlemen, I suggest that we drink our coffee in the next room. It must be fairly decent out in the garden too, and whoever wants a little fresh air, I am for him."

Lieutenant von Deidesheim made a tactful little joke to cover the ensuing pause, and the table rose in the midst of laughter. Herr Friedemann and his partner were among the last to quit the room; he escorted her through the "old German" smoking-room to the dim and pleasant living-room, where he took his leave.

He was dressed with great care: his evening clothes were irreproachable, his shirt was dazzlingly white, his slender, well-shaped feet were encased in patent-leather pumps, which now and then betrayed the fact that he wore red silk stockings.

He looked out into the corridor and saw a good many people descending the steps into the garden. But he took up a position at the door of the smoking-room, with his cigar and coffee, where he could see into the living-room.

Some of the men stood talking in this room, and at the right of the door a little knot had formed round a small table, the centre of which was the mathematics student, who was eagerly talking. He had made the assertion that one could draw through a given point more than one parallel to a straight line; Frau Hagenström had cried that this was impossible, and he had gone on to prove it so conclusively that his hearers were constrained to behave as though they understood.

At the rear of the room, on the sofa beside the red-shaded lamp, Gerda von Rinnlingen sat in conversation with young Fräulein Stephens. She leaned back among the yellow silk cushions with one knee slung over the other, slowly smoking a cigarette, breathing out the smoke through her nose and sticking out her lower lip. Fräulein Stephens sat stiff as a graven image beside her, answering her questions with an assiduous smile.

Nobody was looking at little Herr Friedemann, so nobody saw that his large eyes were constantly directed upon Frau von Rinnlingen. He sat rather droopingly and looked at her. There was no passion in his gaze nor scarcely any pain. But there was something dull and heavy there, a dead weight of impotent, involuntary adoration.

Some ten minutes went by. Then as though she had been secretly watching him the whole time, Frau von Rinnlingen approached and paused in front of him. He got up as he heard her say:

"Would you care to go into the garden with me, Herr Friedemann?"

He answered:

"With pleasure, madam."

"You have never seen our garden?" she asked him as they went down the steps. "It is fairly large. I hope that there are not too many people in it; I should like to get a breath of fresh air. I got a headache during supper; perhaps the red wine was too strong for me. Let us go this way." They passed through a glass door, the vestibule, and a cool little courtyard, whence they gained the open air by descending a couple more steps.

The scent of all the flower-beds rose into the wonderful, warm, starry night. The garden lay in full moonlight and the guests were strolling up and down the white gravel paths, smoking and talking as they went. A group had gathered round the old fountain, where the much-loved old doctor was making them laugh by sailing paper boats.

With a little nod Frau von Rinnlingen passed them by, and pointed ahead of her, where the fragrant and well-cared-for garden blended into the darker park.

"Shall we go down this middle path?" asked she. At the beginning of it stood two low, squat obelisks.

In the vista at the end of the chestnut alley they could see the river shining green and bright in the moonlight. All about them was darkness and coolness. Here and there side paths branched off, all of them probably curving down to the river. For a long time there was not a sound.

"Down by the water," she said, "there is a pretty spot where I often sit. We could stop and talk a little. See the stars glittering here and there through the trees."

He did not answer, gazing, as they approached it, at the river's shimmering green surface. You could see the other bank and the park along the city wall. They left the alley and came out on the grassy slope down to the river, and she said:

"Here is our place, a little to the right, and there is no one there."

The bench stood facing the water, some six paces away, with its back to the trees. It was warmer here in the open. Crickets chirped among the grass, which at the river's edge gave way to sparse reeds.

The moonlit water gave off a soft light.

For a while they both looked in silence. Then he heard her voice; it thrilled him to recognize the same low, gentle, pensive tone of a week ago, which now as then moved him so strangely:

"How long have you had your infirmity, Herr Friedemann? Were you born so?"

He swallowed before he replied, for his throat felt as though he were choking. Then he said, politely and gently:

"No, *gnädige Frau*. It comes from their having let me fall, when I was an infant."

"And how old are you now?" she asked again.

"Thirty years old."

"Thirty years old," she repeated. "And these thirty years were not happy ones?"

Little Herr Friedemann shook his head, his lips quivered.

"No," he said, "that was all lies and my imagination."

"Then you have thought that you were happy?" she asked.

"I have tried to be," he replied, and she responded:

"That was brave of you."

A minute passed. The crickets chirped and behind them the boughs rustled lightly.

"I understand a good deal about unhappiness," she told him. "These summer nights by the water are the best thing for it."

He made no direct answer, but gestured feebly across the water, at the opposite bank, lying peaceful in the darkness.

"I was sitting over there not long ago," he said.

"When you came from me?" she asked. He only nodded.

Then suddenly he started up from his seat, trembling all over; he sobbed and gave vent to a sound, a wail which yet seemed like a release from strain, and sank slowly to the ground before her. He had touched her hand with his as it lay beside him on the bench, and clung to it now, seizing the other as he knelt before her, this little cripple, trembling and shuddering; he buried his face in her lap and stammered between his gasps in a voice which was scarcely human:

"You know, you understand . . . let me . . . I can no longer . . . my God, oh, my God!"

She did not repulse him, neither did she bend her face towards him. She sat erect, leaning a little away, and her close-set eyes, wherein the liquid shimmer of the water seemed to be mirrored, stared beyond him into space.

Then she gave him an abrupt push and uttered a short, scornful laugh. She tore her hands from his burning fingers, clutched his arm, and flung him sidewise upon the ground. Then she sprang up and vanished down the wooded avenue.

He lay there with his face in the grass, stunned, unmanned, shudders coursing swiftly through his frame. He pulled himself together, got up somehow, took two steps, and fell again, close to the water. What were his sensations at this moment? Perhaps he was feeling that same luxury of hate which he had felt before when she had humiliated him with her glance, degenerated now, when he lay before her on the ground and she had treated him like a dog, into an insane rage which must at all costs find expression even against himself—a disgust, perhaps of himself, which filled him with a thirst to destroy himself, to tear himself to pieces, to blot himself utterly out.

On his belly he dragged his body a little further, lifted its upper part, and let it fall into the water. He did not raise his head nor move his legs, which still lay on the bank.

The crickets stopped chirping a moment at the noise of the little splash. Then they went on as before, the boughs lightly rustled, and down the long alley came the faint sound of laughter.

TONIO KRÖGER

THE WINTER sun, poor ghost of itself, hung milky and wan behind layers of cloud above the huddled roofs of the town. In the gabled streets it was wet and windy and there came in gusts a sort of soft hail, not ice, not snow.

School was out. The hosts of the released streamed over the paved court and out at the wrought-iron gate, where they broke up and hastened off right and left. Elder pupils held their books in a strap high on the left shoulder and rowed, right arm against the wind, towards dinner. Small people trotted gaily off, splashing the slush with their feet, the tools of learning rattling amain in their walrus-skin satchels. But one and all pulled off their caps and cast down their eyes in awe before the Olympian hat and ambrosial beard of a master moving homewards with measured stride....

"Ah, there you are at last, Hans," said Tonio Kröger. He had been waiting a long time in the street and went up with a smile to the friend he saw coming out of the gate in talk with other boys and about to go off with them.... "What?" said Hans, and looked at Tonio. "Right-oh! We'll take a little walk, then."

Tonio said nothing and his eyes were clouded. Did Hans forget, had he only just remembered that they were to take a walk together today? And he himself had looked forward to it with almost incessant joy.

"Well, good-bye, fellows," said Hans Hansen to his comrades. "I'm taking a walk with Kröger." And the two turned to their left, while the others sauntered off in the opposite direction.

Hans and Tonio had time to take a walk after school because in neither of their families was dinner served before four o'clock.

Their fathers were prominent business men, who held public office and were of consequence in the town. Hans's people had owned for some generations the big wood-yards down by the river, where powerful machine-saws hissed and spat and cut up timber; while Tonio was the son of Consul Kröger, whose grain-sacks with the firm name in great black letters you might see any day driven through the streets; his large, old ancestral home was the finest house in all the town. The two friends had to keep taking off their hats to their many acquaintances; some folk did not even wait for the fourteen-year-old lads to speak first, as by rights they should.

Both of them carried their satchels across their shoulders and both were well and warmly dressed: Hans in a short sailor jacket, with the wide blue collar of his sailor suit turned out over shoulders and back, and Tonio in a belted grey overcoat. Hans wore a Danish sailor cap with black ribbons, beneath which streamed a shock of straw-coloured hair. He was uncommonly handsome and well built, broad in the shoulders and narrow in the hips, with keen, far-apart, steel-blue eyes; while beneath Tonio's round fur cap was a brunette face with the finely chiselled features of the south; the dark eyes, with delicate shadows and too heavy lids, looked dreamily and a little timorously on the world. Tonio's walk was idle and uneven, whereas the other's slim legs in their black stockings moved with an elastic, rhythmic tread.

Tonio did not speak. He suffered. His rather oblique brows were drawn together in a frown, his lips were rounded to whistle, he gazed into space with his head on one side. Posture and manner were habitual.

Suddenly Hans shoved his arm into Tonio's, with a sideways look—he knew very well what the trouble was. And Tonio, though he was silent for the next few steps, felt his heart soften.

"I hadn't forgotten, you see, Tonio," Hans said, gazing at the pavement, "I only thought it wouldn't come off today because it was so wet and windy. But I don't mind that at all, and it's jolly of you to have waited. I thought you had gone home, and I was cross...."

Everything in Tonio leaped and jumped for joy at the words.

"All right; let's go over the wall," he said with a quaver in his voice. "Over the Millwall and the Holstenwall, and I'll go as far as your house with you, Hans. Then I'll have to walk back alone, but that doesn't matter; next time you can go round my way."

At bottom he was not really convinced by what Hans said; he quite knew the other attached less importance to this walk than he did himself. Yet he saw Hans was sorry for his remissness and willing to be put in a position to ask pardon, a pardon that Tonio was far indeed from withholding.

The truth was, Tonio loved Hans Hansen, and had already suffered much on his account. He who loves the more is the inferior and must suffer; in this hard and simple fact his fourteen-year-old soul had already been instructed by life; and he was so organized that he received such experiences consciously, wrote them down as it were inwardly, and even, in a certain way, took pleasure in them, though without ever letting them mould his conduct, indeed, or drawing any practical advantage from them. Being what he was, he found this knowledge far more important and far more interesting than the sort they made him learn in school; yes, during his lesson hours in the vaulted Gothic classrooms he was mainly occupied in feeling his way about among these intuitions of his and penetrating them. The process gave him the same kind of satisfaction as that he felt when he moved about in his room with his violin—for he played the violin—and made the tones, brought out as softly as ever he knew how, mingle with the splashing of the fountain that leaped and danced down there in the garden beneath the branches of the old walnut tree.

The fountain, the old walnut tree, his fiddle, and away in the distance the North Sea, within sound of whose summer murmurings he spent his holidays—these were the things he loved, within these he enfolded his spirit, among these things his inner life took its course. And they were all things whose names were effective in verse and occurred pretty frequently in the lines Tonio Kröger sometimes wrote.

The fact that he had a note-book full of such things, written by himself, leaked out through his own carelessness and injured him no little with the masters as well as among his fellows. On the one hand, Consul Kröger's son found their attitude both cheap and silly, and despised his schoolmates and his masters as well, and in his turn (with extraordinary penetration) saw through and disliked their personal weaknesses and bad breeding. But then, on the other hand, he himself felt his verse-making extravagant and out of place and to a certain extent agreed with those who considered it an unpleasing occupation. But that did not enable him to leave off.

As he wasted his time at home, was slow and absent-minded at school, and always had bad marks from the masters, he was in the habit of bringing home pitifully poor reports, which troubled and angered his father, a tall, fastidiously dressed man, with thoughtful blue eyes, and always a wild flower in his buttonhole. But for his mother, she cared nothing about the reports—Tonio's beautiful black-haired mother, whose name was Consuelo, and who was so absolutely different from the other ladies in the town, because father had brought her long ago from some place far down on the map.

Tonio loved his dark, fiery mother, who played the piano and mandolin so wonderfully, and he was glad his doubtful standing among men did not distress her. Though at the same time he found his father's annoyance a more dignified and respectable attitude and despite his scoldings understood him very well, whereas his mother's blithe indifference always seemed just a little wanton. His thoughts at times would run something like this: "It is true enough that I am what I am and will not and cannot alter: heedless, self-willed, with my mind on things nobody else thinks of. And so it is right they should scold and punish me and not smother things all up with kisses and music. After all, we are not gypsies living in a green wagon; we're respectable people, the family of Consul Kröger." And not seldom he would think: "Why is it I am different, why do I fight everything, why am I at odds with the masters and like a stranger among the other boys? The good scholars, and the solid majority—they don't find the masters funny, they don't write verses, their thoughts are all about things that people do think about and can talk about out loud. How regular and comfortable they must feel, knowing that everybody knows just where they stand! It must be nice! But what is the matter with me, and what will be the end of it all?"

These thoughts about himself and his relation to life played an important part in Tonio's love for Hans Hansen. He loved him in the first place because he was handsome; but in the next because he was in every respect his own opposite and foil. Hans Hansen was a capital scholar, and a jolly chap to boot, who was head at drill, rode and swam to perfection, and lived in the sunshine of popularity. The masters were almost tender with him, they called him Hans and were partial to him in every way; the other pupils curried favour with him; even grown people stopped him on the street, twitched the shock of hair beneath his Danish sailor cap, and said: "Ah, here you are, Hans Hansen, with your pretty blond hair! Still head of the school? Remember me to your father and mother, that's a fine lad!"

Such was Hans Hansen; and ever since Tonio Kröger had known him, from the very minute he set eyes on him, he had burned inwardly with a heavy, envious longing. "Who else has blue eyes like yours, or lives in such friendliness and harmony with all the world? You are always spending your time with some right and proper occupation. When you have done your prep you take your riding-lesson, or make things with a fret-saw; even in the holidays, at the seashore, you row and sail and swim all the time, while I wander off somewhere and lie down in the sand and stare at the strange and mysterious changes that whisk over the face of the sea. And all that is why your eyes are so clear. To be like you..."

He made no attempt to be like Hans Hansen, and perhaps hardly even seriously wanted to. What he did ardently, painfully want was that, just as he was, Hans Hansen should love him; and he wooed Hans Hansen in his own way, deeply, lingeringly, devotedly, with a melancholy that gnawed and burned more terribly than all the sudden passion one might have expected from his exotic looks.

And he wooed not in vain. Hans respected Tonio's superior power of putting certain difficult matters into words; moreover, he felt the lively presence of an uncommonly strong and tender feeling for himself; he was grateful for it, and his response gave Tonio much happiness—though also many pangs of jealousy and disillusion over his futile efforts to establish a communion of spirit between them. For the queer thing was that Tonio, who after all envied Hans Hansen for being what he was, still kept on trying to draw him over to his own side; though of course he could succeed in this at most only at moments and superficially....

"I have just been reading something so wonderful and splendid..." he said. They were walking and eating together out of a bag of fruit toffees they had bought at Iverson's sweet-shop in Mill Street for ten pfennigs. "You must read it, Hans, it is Schiller's *Don Carlos* . . . I'll lend it you if you like. . . ."

"Oh, no," said Hans Hansen, "you needn't, Tonio, that's not anything for me. I'll stick to my horse books. There are wonderful cuts in them, let me tell you. I'll show them to you when you come to see me. They are instantaneous photography—the horse in motion; you can see him trot and canter and jump, in all positions, that you never can get to see in life, because they happen so fast. . . ."

"In all positions?" asked Tonio politely. "Yes, that must be great. But about *Don Carlos*—it is beyond anything you could possibly dream of. There are places in it that are so lovely they make you jump . . . as though it were an explosion—"

"An explosion?" asked Hans Hansen. "What sort of an explosion?"

"For instance, the place where the king has been crying because the marquis betrayed him . . . but the marquis did it only out of love for the prince, you see, he sacrifices himself for his sake. And the word comes out of the cabinet into the antechamber that the king has been weeping. 'Weeping? The king been weeping?' All the courtiers are fearfully upset, it goes through and through you, for the king has always been so frightfully stiff and stern. But it is so easy to understand why he cried, and I feel sorrier for him than for the prince and the marquis put together. He is always so alone, nobody loves him, and then he thinks he has found one man, and then *he* betrays him. . . ."

Hans Hansen looked sideways into Tonio's face, and something in it must have won him to the subject, for suddenly he shoved his arm once more into Tonio's and said:

"How had he betrayed him, Tonio?"

Tonio went on.

"Well," he said, "you see all the letters for Brabant and Flanders—"

"There comes Irwin Immerthal," said Hans.

Tonio stopped talking. If only the earth would open and swallow Immerthal up! "Why does he have to come disturbing us? If he only doesn't go with us all the way and talk about the riding-lessons!" For Irwin Immerthal had riding-lessons too. He was the son of the bank president and lived close by, outside the city wall. He had already been home and left his bag, and now he walked towards them through the avenue. His legs were crooked and his eyes like slits.

"'lo, Immerthal," said Hans. "I'm taking a little walk with Kröger...."

"I have to go into town on an errand," said Immerthal. "But I'll walk a little way with you. Are those fruit toffees you've got? Thanks, I'll have a couple. Tomorrow we have our next lesson, Hans." He meant the riding-lesson.

"What larks!" said Hans. "I'm going to get the leather gaiters for a present, because I was top lately in our papers."

"You don't take riding-lessons, I suppose, Kröger?" asked Immerthal, and his eyes were only two gleaming cracks.

"No..." answered Tonio, uncertainly.

"You ought to ask your father," Hans Hansen remarked, "so you could have lessons too, Kröger."

"Yes ..." said Tonio. He spoke hastily and without interest; his throat had suddenly contracted, because Hans had called him by his last name. Hans seemed conscious of it too, for he said by way of explanation: "I call you Kröger because your first name is so crazy. Don't mind my saying so, I can't do with it all. Tonio—why, what sort of name is that? Though of course I know it's not your fault in the least."

"No, they probably called you that because it sounds so foreign and sort of something special," said Immerthal, obviously with intent to say just the right thing.

Tonio's mouth twitched. He pulled himself together and said: "Yes, it's a silly name—Lord knows I'd rather be called Heinrich or Wilhelm. It's all because I'm named after my mother's brother Antonio. She comes from down there, you know...."

There he stopped and let the others have their say about horses and saddles. Hans had taken Immerthal's arm; he talked with a fluency that *Don Carlos* could never have roused in him.... Tonio felt a mounting desire to weep pricking his nose from time to time; he had hard work to control the trembling of his lips.

Hans could not stand his name—what was to be done? He himself was called Hans, and Immerthal was called Irwin; two good, sound, familiar names, offensive to nobody. And Tonio was foreign and queer. Yes, there was always something queer about him, whether he would or no, and he was alone, the regular and usual would none of him; although after all he was no gypsy in a green wagon, but the son of Consul Kröger, a member of the Kröger family. But why did Hans call him Tonio as long as they were alone and then feel ashamed as soon as anybody else was by? Just now he had won him over, they had been close together, he was sure. "How had he betrayed him, Tonio?" Hans asked, and took his arm. But he had breathed easier directly Immerthal came up, he had dropped him like a shot, even gratuitously taunted him with his outlandish name. How it hurt to have to see through all this! . . . Hans Hansen did like him a little, when they were alone, that he knew. But let a third person come, he was ashamed, and offered up his friend. And again he was alone. He thought of King Philip. The king had wept. . . .

"Goodness, I have to go," said Irwin Immerthal. "Good-bye, and thanks for the toffee." He jumped upon a bench that stood by the way, ran along it with his crooked legs, jumped down, and trotted off.

"I like Immerthal," said Hans, with emphasis. He had a spoilt and arbitrary way of announcing his likes and dislikes, as though graciously pleased to confer them like an order on this person and that. . . . He went on talking about the riding-lessons where he had left off. Anyhow, it was not very much farther to his house; the walk over the walls was not a long one. They held their caps and bent their heads before the strong, damp wind that rattled and groaned in the leafless trees. And Hans Hansen went on talking, Tonio throwing in a forced yes or no from time to time. Hans talked eagerly, had taken his arm again; but the contact gave Tonio no pleasure. The nearness was only apparent, not real; it meant nothing. . . .

They struck away from the walls close to the station, where they saw a train puff busily past, idly counted the coaches, and waved to the man who was perched on top of the last one bundled in a leather coat. They stopped in front of the Hansen villa on the Lindenplatz, and Hans went into detail about what fun it was to stand on the bottom rail of the garden gate and let it swing on its creaking hinges. After that they said good-bye.

"I must go in now," said Hans. "Good-bye, Tonio. Next time I'll take you home, see if I don't."

"Good-bye, Hans," said Tonio. "It was a nice walk."

They put out their hands, all wet and rusty from the garden gate. But as Hans looked into Tonio's eyes, he bethought himself, a look of remorse came over his charming face.

"And I'll read *Don Carlos* pretty soon, too," he said quickly. "That bit about the king in his cabinet must be nuts." Then he took his bag under his arm and ran off through the front garden. Before he disappeared he turned and nodded once more.

And Tonio went off as though on wings. The wind was at his back; but it was not the wind alone that bore him along so lightly.

Hans would read *Don Carlos*, and then they would have something to talk about, and neither Irwin Immerthal nor another could join in. How well they understood each other! Perhaps—who knew?—some day he might even get Hans to write poetry! ... No, no, that he did not ask. Hans must not become like Tonio, he must stop just as he was, so strong and bright, everybody loved him as he was, and Tonio most of all. But it would do him no harm to read *Don Carlos*.... Tonio passed under the squat old city gate, along by the harbour, and up the steep, wet, windy, gabled street to his parents' house. His heart beat richly: longing was awake in it, and a gentle envy; a faint contempt, and no little innocent bliss.

Ingeborg Holm, blonde little Inge, the daughter of Dr. Holm, who lived on Market Square opposite the tall old Gothic fountain with its manifold spires—she it was Tonio Kröger loved when he was sixteen years old.

Strange how things come about! He had seen her a thousand times; then one evening he saw her again; saw her in a certain light, talking with a friend in a certain saucy way, laughing and tossing her head; saw her lift her arm and smooth her back hair with her schoolgirl hand, that was by no means particularly fine or slender, in such a way that the thin sleeve slipped down from her elbow; heard her speak a word or two, a quite indifferent phrase, but with a certain intonation, with a warm ring in her voice; and his heart throbbed with ecstasy, far stronger than that he had once felt when he looked at Hans Hansen long ago, when he was still a little, stupid boy.

That evening he carried away her picture in his eye: the thick blond plait, the longish, laughing blue eyes, the saddle of pale freckles across the nose. He could not go to sleep for hearing that ring in her voice; he tried in a whisper to imitate the tone in which she had uttered the commonplace phrase, and felt a shiver run through and through him. He knew by experience that this was love. And he was accurately aware that love would surely bring him much pain, affliction, and sadness, that it would certainly destroy his peace, filling his heart to overflowing with melodies which would be no good to him because he would never have the time or tranquillity to give them permanent form. Yet he received this love with joy, surrendered himself to it, and cherished it with all the strength of his being; for he knew that love made one vital and rich, and he longed to be vital and rich, far more than he did to work tranquilly on anything to give it permanent form.

Tonio Kröger fell in love with merry Ingeborg Holm in Frau Consul Hustede's drawing-room on the evening when it was emptied of furniture for the weekly dancing-class. It was a private class, attended only by members of the first families; it met by turns in the various parental houses to receive instruction from Knaak, the dancing-master, who came from Hamburg expressly for the purpose.

François Knaak was his name, and what a man he was! "*J'ai l'honneur de me vous représenter,*" he would say, "*mon nom est Knaak*. . . . This is not said during the bowing, but after you have finished and are standing up straight again. In a low voice, but distinctly. Of course one does not need to introduce oneself in French every day in the week, but if you can do it correctly and faultlessly in French you are not likely to make a mistake when you do it in German." How marvellously the silky black frock-coat fitted his chubby hips! His trouser-legs fell down in soft folds upon his patent-leather pumps with their wide satin bows, and his brown eyes glanced about him with languid pleasure in their own beauty.

All this excess of self-confidence and good form was positively overpowering. He went trippingly—and nobody tripped like him, so elastically, so weavingly, rockingly, royally—up to the mistress of the house, made a bow, waited for a hand to be put forth. This vouchsafed, he gave murmurous voice to his gratitude, stepped buoyantly back, turned on his left foot, swiftly drawing the right one backwards on its toe-tip, and moved away, with his hips shaking.

When you took leave of a company you must go backwards out at the door; when you fetched a chair, you were not to shove it along the floor or clutch it by one leg; but gently, by the back, and set it down without a sound. When you stood, you were not to fold your hands on your tummy or seek with your tongue the corners of your mouth. If you did, Herr Knaak had a way of showing you how it looked that filled you with disgust for that particular gesture all the rest of your life.

This was deportment. As for dancing, Herr Knaak was, if possible, even more of a master at that. The salon was emptied of furniture and lighted by a gas-chandelier in the middle of the ceiling and candles on the mantel-shelf. The floor was strewn with talc, and the pupils stood about in a dumb semicircle. But in the next room, behind the portières, mothers and aunts sat on plush-upholstered chairs and watched Herr Knaak through their lorgnettes, as in little springs and hops, curtsying slightly, the hem of his frock-coat held up on each side by two fingers, he demonstrated the single steps of the mazurka. When he wanted to dazzle his audience completely he would suddenly and unexpectedly spring from the ground, whirling his two legs about each other with bewildering swiftness in the air, as it were trilling with them, and then, with a subdued bump, which nevertheless shook everything within him to its depths, returned to earth.

"What an unmentionable monkey!" thought Tonio Kröger to himself. But he saw the absorbed smile on jolly little Inge's face as she followed Herr Knaak's movements; and that, though not that alone, roused in him something like admiration of all this wonderfully controlled corporeality. How tranquil, how imperturbable was Herr Knaak's gaze! His eyes did not plumb the depth of things to the place where life becomes complex and melancholy; they knew nothing save that they were beautiful brown eyes. But that was just why his bearing was so proud. To be able to walk like that, one must be stupid; then one was loved, then one was lovable. He could so well understand how it was that Inge, blonde, sweet little Inge, looked at Herr Knaak as she did. But would never a girl look at him like that?

Oh, yes, there would, and did. For instance, Magdalena Vermehren, Attorney Vermehren's daughter, with the gentle mouth and the great, dark, brilliant eyes, so serious and adoring. She often fell down in the dance; but when it was "ladies' choice" she came up to him; she knew he wrote verses and twice she had asked him to show them to her. She often sat at a distance, with drooping head, and gazed at him. He did not care. It was Inge he loved, blonde, jolly Inge, who most assuredly despised him for his poetic effusions . . . he looked at her, looked at her narrow blue eyes full of fun and mockery, and felt an envious longing; to be shut away from her like this, to be for ever strange—he felt it in his breast, like a heavy, burning weight.

"First couple *en avant*," said Herr Knaak; and no words can tell how marvellously he pronounced the nasal. They were to practise the quadrille, and to Tonio Kröger's profound alarm he found himself in the same set with Inge Holm. He avoided her where he could, yet somehow was for ever near her; kept his eyes away from her person and yet found his gaze ever on her. There she came, tripping up hand-in-hand with red-headed Ferdinand Matthiessen; she flung back her braid, drew a deep breath, and took her place opposite Tonio. Herr Heinzelmann, at the piano, laid bony hands upon the keys, Herr Knaak waved his arm, the quadrille began.

She moved to and fro before his eyes, forwards and back, pacing and swinging; he seemed to catch a fragrance from her hair or the folds of her thin white frock, and his eyes grew sadder and sadder. "I love you, dear, sweet Inge," he said to himself, and put into his words all the pain he felt to see her so intent upon the dance with not a thought of him. Some lines of an exquisite poem by Storm came into his mind: "I would sleep, but thou must dance." It seemed against all sense, and most depressing, that he must be dancing when he was in love. . . .

"First couple *en avant*," said Herr Knaak; it was the next figure. "*Compliment! Moulinet des dames! Tour de main!*" and he swallowed the silent *e* in the "*DE*", with quite indescribable ease and grace.

"Second couple *en avant*!" This was Tonio Kröger and his partner. "*Compliment!*" And Tonio Kröger bowed. "*Moulinet des dames!*" And Tonio Kröger, with bent head and gloomy brows, laid his hand on those of the four ladies, on Ingeborg Holm's hand, and danced the *moulinet*.

Roundabout rose a tittering and laughing. Herr Knaak took a ballet pose conventionally expressive of horror. "Oh, dear! Oh, dear!" he cried. "Stop! Stop! Kröger among the ladies! *En arrière*, Fräulein Kröger, step back, *fi donc!* Everybody else understood it but you. Shoo! Get out! Get away!" He drew out his yellow silk handkerchief and flapped Tonio Kröger back to his place.

Everyone laughed, the girls and the boys and the ladies beyond the portières; Herr Knaak had made something too utterly funny out of the little episode, it was as amusing as a play. But Herr Heinzelmann at the piano sat and waited, with a dry, business-like air, for a sign to go on; he was hardened against Herr Knaak's effects.

Then the quadrille went on. And the intermission followed. The parlourmaid came clinking in with a tray of wine-jelly glasses, the cook followed in her wake with a load of plum-cake. But Tonio Kröger stole away. He stole out into the corridor and stood there, his hands behind his back, in front of a window with the blind down. He never thought that one could not see through the blind and that it was absurd to stand there as though one were looking out.

For he was looking within, into himself, the theatre of so much pain and longing. Why, why was he here? Why was he not sitting by the window in his own room, reading Storm's *Immensee* and lifting his eyes to the twilight garden outside, where the old walnut tree moaned? That was the place for him! Others might dance, others bend their fresh and lively minds upon the pleasure in hand! ... But no, no, after all, his place was here, where he could feel near Inge, even although he stood lonely and aloof, seeking to distinguish the warm notes of her voice amid the buzzing, clattering, and laughter within. Oh, lovely Inge, blonde Inge of the narrow, laughing blue eyes! So lovely and laughing as you are one can only be if one does not read *Immensee* and never tries to write things like it. And that was just the tragedy!

Ah, she *must* come! She *must* notice where he had gone, must feel how he suffered! She must slip out to him, even pity must bring her, to lay her hand on his shoulder and say: "Do come back to us, ah, don't be sad—I love you, Tonio." He listened behind him and waited in frantic suspense. But not in the least. Such things did not happen on this earth.

Had she laughed at him too like all the others? Yes, she had, however gladly he would have denied it for both their sakes. And yet it was only because he had been so taken up with her that he had danced the *moulinet des dames*. Suppose he had—what did that matter? Had not a magazine accepted a poem of his a little while ago—even though the magazine had failed before his poem could be printed? The day was coming when he would be famous, when they would print everything he wrote; and *then* he would see if that made any impression on Inge Holm! No, it would make no impression at all; that was just it. Magdalena Vermehren, who was always falling down in the dances, yes, she would be impressed. But never Ingeborg Holm, never blue-eyed, laughing Inge. So what was the good of it?

Tonio Kröger's heart contracted painfully at the thought. To feel stirring within you the wonderful and melancholy play of strange forces and to be aware that those others you yearn for are blithely inaccessible to all that moves you—what a pain is this! And yet! He stood there aloof and alone, staring hopelessly at a drawn blind and making, in his distraction, as though he could look out. But yet he was happy. For he lived. His heart was full; hotly and sadly it beat for thee, Ingeborg Holm, and his soul embraced thy blonde, simple, pert, commonplace little personality in blissful self-abnegation.

Often after that he stood thus, with burning cheeks, in lonely corners, whither the sound of the music, the tinkling of glasses and fragrance of flowers came but faintly, and tried to distinguish the ringing tones of thy voice amid the distant happy din; stood suffering for thee—and still was happy! Often it angered him to think that he might talk with Magdalena Vermehren, who always fell down in the dance. She understood him, she laughed or was serious in the right places; while Inge the fair, let him sit never so near her, seemed remote and estranged, his speech not being her speech. And still—he was happy. For happiness, he told himself, is not in being loved—which is a satisfaction of the vanity and mingled with disgust. Happiness is in loving, and perhaps in snatching fugitive little approaches to the beloved object. And he took inward note of this thought, wrote it down in his mind; followed out all its implications and felt it to the depths of his soul.

"Faithfulness," thought Tonio Kröger. "Yes, I will be faithful, I will love thee, Ingeborg, as long as I live!" He said this in the honesty of his intentions. And yet a still small voice whispered misgivings in his ear: after all, he had forgotten Hans Hansen utterly, even though he saw him every day! And the hateful, the pitiable fact was that this still, small, rather spiteful voice was right: time passed and the day came when Tonio Kröger was no longer so unconditionally ready as once he had been to die for the lively Inge, because he felt in himself desires and powers to accomplish in his own way a host of wonderful things in this world.

And he circled with watchful eye the sacrificial altar, where flickered the pure, chaste flame of his love; knelt before it and tended and cherished it in every way, because he so wanted to be faithful. And in a little while, unobservably, without sensation or stir, it went out after all.

But Tonio Kröger still stood before the cold altar, full of regret and dismay at the fact that faithfulness was impossible upon this earth. Then he shrugged his shoulders and went his way.

He went the way that go he must, a little idly, a little irregularly, whistling to himself, gazing into space with his head on one side; and if he went wrong it was because for some people there is no such thing as a right way. Asked what in the world he meant to become, he gave various answers, for he was used to say (and had even already written it) that he bore within himself the possibility of a thousand ways of life, together with the private conviction that they were all sheer impossibilities.

Even before he left the narrow streets of his native city, the threads that bound him to it had gently loosened. The old Kröger family gradually declined, and some people quite rightly considered Tonio Kröger's own existence and way of life as one of the signs of decay. His father's mother, the head of the family, had died, and not long after his own father followed, the tall, thoughtful, carefully dressed gentleman with the field-flower in his buttonhole. The great Kröger house, with all its stately tradition, came up for sale, and the firm was dissolved. Tonio's mother, his beautiful, fiery mother, who played the piano and mandolin so wonderfully and to whom nothing mattered at all, she married again after a year's time; married a musician, moreover, a virtuoso with an Italian name, and went away with him into remote blue distances. Tonio Kröger found this a little irregular, but who was he to call her to order, who wrote poetry himself and could not even give an answer when asked what he meant to do in life?

And so he left his native town and its tortuous, gabled streets with the damp wind whistling through them; left the fountain in the garden and the ancient walnut tree, familiar friends of his youth; left the sea too, that he loved so much, and felt no pain to go. For he was grown up and sensible and had come to realize how things stood with him; he looked down on the lowly and vulgar life he had led so long in these surroundings.

He surrendered utterly to the power that to him seemed the highest on earth, to whose service he felt called, which promised him elevation and honours: the power of intellect, the power of the Word, that lords it with a smile over the unconscious and inarticulate. To this power he surrendered with all the passion of youth, and it rewarded him with all it had to give, taking from him inexorably, in return, all that it is wont to take.

It sharpened his eyes and made him see through the large words which puff out the bosoms of mankind; it opened for him men's souls and his own, made him clairvoyant, showed him the inwardness of the world and the ultimate behind men's words and deeds. And all that he saw could be put in two words: the comedy and the tragedy of life.

And then, with knowledge, its torment and its arrogance, came solitude; because he could not endure the blithe and innocent with their darkened understanding, while they in turn were troubled by the sign on his brow. But his love of the word kept growing sweeter and sweeter, and his love of form; for he used to say (and had already said it in writing) that knowledge of the soul would unfailingly make us melancholy if the pleasure of expression did not keep us alert and of good cheer.

He lived in large cities and in the south, promising himself a luxuriant ripening of his art by southern suns; perhaps it was the blood of his mother's race that drew him thither. But, his heart being dead and loveless, he fell into adventures of the flesh, descended into the depths of lust and searing sin, and suffered unspeakably thereby. It might have been his father in him, that tall, thoughtful, fastidiously dressed man with the wild flower in his buttonhole, that made him suffer so down there in the south; now and again he would feel a faint, yearning memory of a certain joy that was of the soul; once it had been his own, but now, in all his joys, he could not find it again.

Then he would be seized with disgust and hatred of the senses; pant after purity and seemly peace, while still he breathed the air of art, the tepid, sweet air of permanent spring, heavy with fragrance where it breeds and brews and burgeons in the mysterious bliss of creation. So for all result he was flung to and fro for ever between two crass extremes: between icy intellect and scorching sense, and what with his pangs of conscience led an exhausting life, rare, extraordinary, excessive, which at bottom he, Tonio Kröger, despised. "What a labyrinth!" he sometimes thought. "How could I possibly have got into all these fantastic adventures? As though I had a wagonful of travelling gypsies for my ancestors!"

But as his health suffered from these excesses, so his artistry was sharpened; it grew fastidious, precious, *raffiné*, morbidly sensitive in questions of tact and taste, rasped by the banal. His first appearance in print elicited much pleasure; there was joy among the elect, for it was a good and workmanlike performance, full of humour and acquaintance with pain. In no long time his name—the same by which his masters had reproached him, the same he had signed to his earliest verses on the walnut tree and the fountain and the sea, those syllables compact of the north and the south, that good middle-class name with the exotic twist to it—became a synonym for excellence; for the painful thoroughness of the experiences he had gone through, combined with a tenacious ambition and a persistent industry, joined battle with the irritable fastidiousness of his taste and under grinding torments issued in work of a quality quite uncommon.

He worked, not like a man who works that he may live; but as one who is bent on doing nothing but work; having no regard for himself as a human being but only as a creator; moving about grey and unobtrusive among his fellows like an actor without his make-up, who counts for nothing as soon as he stops representing something else. He worked withdrawn out of sight and sound of the small fry, for whom he felt nothing but contempt, because to them a talent was a social asset like another; who, whether they were poor or not, went about ostentatiously shabby or else flaunted startling cravats, all the time taking jolly good care to amuse themselves, to be artistic and charming without the smallest notion of the fact that good work only comes out under pressure of a bad life; that he who lives does not work; that one must die to life in order to be utterly a creator.

"Shall I disturb you?" asked Tonio Kröger on the threshold of the atelier. He held his hat in his hand and bowed with some ceremony, although Lisabeta Ivanovna was a good friend of his, to whom he told all his troubles.

"Mercy on you, Tonio Kröger! Don't be so formal," answered she, with her lilting intonation. "Everybody knows you were taught good manners in your nursery." She transferred her brush to her left hand, that held the palette, reached him her right, and looked him in the face, smiling and shaking her head.

"Yes, but you are working," he said. "Let's see. Oh, you've been getting on," and he looked at the colour-sketches leaning against chairs at both sides of the easel and from them to the large canvas covered with a square linen mesh, where the first patches of colour were beginning to appear among the confused and schematic lines of the charcoal sketch.

This was in Munich, in a back building in Schellingstrasse, several storeys up. Beyond the wide window facing the north were blue sky, sunshine, birds twittering; the young sweet breath of spring streaming through an open pane mingled with the smells of paint and fixative. The afternoon light, bright golden, flooded the spacious emptiness of the atelier; it made no secret of the bad flooring or the rough table under the window, covered with little bottles, tubes, and brushes; it illumined the unframed studies on the unpapered walls, the torn silk screen that shut off a charmingly furnished little living-corner near the door; it shone upon the inchoate work on the easel, upon the artist and the poet there before it.

She was about the same age as himself—slightly past thirty. She sat there on a low stool, in her dark-blue apron, and leant her chin in her hand. Her brown hair, compactly dressed, already a little grey at the sides, was parted in the middle and waved over the temples, framing a sensitive, sympathetic, dark-skinned face, which was Slavic in its facial structure, with flat nose, strongly accentuated cheek-bones, and little bright black eyes. She sat there measuring her work with her head on one side and her eyes screwed up; her features were drawn with a look of misgiving, almost of vexation.

He stood beside her, his right hand on his hip, with the other furiously twirling his brown moustache. His dress, reserved in cut and a soothing shade of grey, was punctilious and dignified to the last degree. He was whistling softly to himself, in the way he had, and his slanting brows were gathered in a frown. The dark-brown hair was parted with severe correctness, but the laboured forehead beneath showed a nervous twitching, and the chiselled southern features were sharpened as though they had been gone over again with a graver's tool. And yet the mouth—how gently curved it was, the chin how softly formed! ... After a little he drew his hand across his brow and eyes and turned away.

"I ought not to have come," he said.

"And why not, Tonio Kröger?"

"I've just got up from my desk, Lisabeta, and inside my head it looks just the way it does on this canvas. A scaffolding, a faint first draft smeared with corrections and a few splotches of colour; yes, and I come up here and see the same thing. And the same conflict and contradiction in the air," he went on, sniffing, "that has been torturing me at home. It's extraordinary. If you are possessed by an idea, you find it expressed everywhere, you even *smell* it. Fixative and the breath of spring; art and—what? Don't say nature, Lisabeta, 'nature' isn't exhausting. Ah, no, I ought to have gone for a walk, though it's doubtful if it would have made me feel better. Five minutes ago, not far from here, I met a man I know, Adalbert, the novelist. 'God damn the spring!' says he in the aggressive way he has. 'It is and always has been the most ghastly time of the year. Can you get hold of a single sensible idea, Kröger? Can you sit still and work out even the smallest effect, when your blood tickles till it's positively indecent and you are teased by a whole host of irrelevant sensations that when you look at them turn out to be unworkable trash? For my part, I am going to a café. A café is neutral territory, the change of the seasons doesn't affect it; it represents, so to speak, the detached and elevated sphere of the literary man, in which one is only capable of refined ideas.' And he went into the café . . . and perhaps I ought to have gone with him."

Lisabeta was highly entertained.

"I like that, Tonio Kröger. That part about the indecent tickling is good. And he is right too, in a way, for spring is really not very conducive to work. But now listen. Spring or no spring, I will just finish this little place—work out this little effect, as your friend Adalbert would say. Then we'll go into the 'salon' and have tea, and you can talk yourself out, for I can perfectly well see you are too full for utterance. Will you just compose yourself somewhere—on that chest, for instance, if you are not afraid for your aristocratic garments—"

"Oh, leave my clothes alone, Lisabeta Ivanovna! Do you want me to go about in a ragged velveteen jacket or a red waistcoat? Every artist is as bohemian as the deuce, inside! Let him at least wear proper clothes and behave outwardly like a respectable being. No, I am not too full for utterance," he said as he watched her mixing her paints. "I've told you, it is only that I have a problem and a conflict, that sticks in my mind and disturbs me at my work. . . . Yes, what was it we were just saying? We were talking about Adalbert, the novelist, that stout and forthright man. 'Spring is the most ghastly time of the year,' says he, and goes into a café. A man has to know what he needs, eh? Well, you see he's not the only one; the spring makes me nervous, too; I get dazed with the triflingness and sacredness of the memories and feelings it evokes; only that I don't succeed in looking down on it; for the truth is it makes me ashamed; I quail before its sheer naturalness and triumphant youth. And I don't know whether I should envy Adalbert or despise him for his ignorance. . . .

"Yes, it is true; spring is a bad time for work; and why? Because we are feeling too much. Nobody but a beginner imagines that he who creates must feel. Every real and genuine artist smiles at such naïve blunders as that. A melancholy enough smile, perhaps, but still a smile. For what an artist talks about is never the main point; it is the raw material, in and for itself indifferent, out of which, with bland and serene mastery, he creates the work of art. If you care too much about what you have to say, if your heart is too much in it, you can be pretty sure of making a mess. You get pathetic, you wax sentimental; something dull and doddering, without roots or outlines, with no sense of humour—something tiresome and banal grows under your hand, and you get nothing out of it but apathy in your audience and disappointment and misery in yourself. For so it is, Lisabeta; feeling, warm, heartfelt feeling, is always banal and futile; only the irritations and icy ecstasies of the artist's corrupted nervous system are artistic. The artist must be unhuman, extra-human; he must stand in a queer aloof relationship to our humanity; only so is he in a position, I ought to say only so would he be tempted, to represent it, to present it, to portray it to good effect. The very gift of style, of form and expression, is nothing else than this cool and fastidious attitude towards humanity; you might say there has to be this impoverishment and devastation as a preliminary condition. For sound natural feeling, say what you like, has no taste. It is all up with the artist as soon as he becomes a man and begins to feel. Adalbert knows that; that's why he betook himself to the café, the neutral territory—God help him!"

"Yes, God help him, Batuschka," said Lisabeta, as she washed her hands in a tin basin. "You don't need to follow his example."

"No, Lisabeta, I am not going to; and the only reason is that I am now and again in a position to feel a little ashamed of the springtime of my art. You see sometimes I get letters from strangers, full of praise and thanks and admiration from people whose feelings I have touched. I read them and feel touched myself at these warm if ungainly emotions I have called up; a sort of pity steals over me at this naïve enthusiasm; and I positively blush at the thought of how these good people would freeze up if they were to get a look behind the scenes. What they, in their innocence, cannot comprehend is that a properly constituted, healthy, decent man never writes, acts, or composes—all of which does not hinder me from using his admiration for my genius to goad myself on; nor from taking it in deadly earnest and aping the airs of a great man. Oh, don't talk to me, Lisabeta. I tell you I am sick to death of depicting humanity without having any part or lot in it.... Is an artist a male, anyhow? Ask the females! It seems to me we artists are all of us something like those unsexed papal singers ... we sing like angels; but—"

"Shame on you, Tonio Kröger. But come to tea. The water is just on the boil, and here are some *papyros*. You were talking about singing soprano, do go on. But really you ought to be ashamed of yourself. If I did not know your passionate devotion to your calling and how proud you are of it—"

"Don't talk about 'calling', Lisabeta Ivanovna. Literature is not a calling, it is a curse, believe me! When does one begin to feel the curse? Early, horribly early. At a time when one ought by rights still to be living in peace and harmony with God and the world. It begins by your feeling yourself set apart, in a curious sort of opposition to the nice, regular people; there is a gulf of ironic sensibility, of knowledge, scepticism, disagreement, between you and the others; it grows deeper and deeper, you realize that you are alone; and from then on any *rapprochement* is simply hopeless! What a fate! That is, if you still have enough heart, enough warmth of affections, to feel how frightful it is! . . . Your self-consciousness is kindled, because you among thousands feel the sign on your brow and know that everyone else sees it. I once knew an actor, a man of genius, who had to struggle with a morbid self-consciousness and instability. When he had no rôle to play, nothing to represent, this man, consummate artist but impoverished human being, was overcome by an exaggerated consciousness of his ego. A genuine artist—not one who has taken up art as a profession like another, but artist foreordained and damned—you can pick out, without boasting very sharp perceptions, out of a group of men. The sense of being set apart and not belonging, of being known and observed, something both regal and incongruous shows in his face. You might see something of the same sort on the features of a prince walking through a crowd in ordinary clothes. But no civilian clothes are any good here, Lisabeta. You can disguise yourself, you can dress up like an attaché or a lieutenant of the guard on leave; you hardly need to give a glance or speak a word before everyone knows you are not a human being, but something else: something queer, different, inimical.

"But what is it, to be an artist? Nothing shows up the general human dislike of thinking, and man's innate craving to be comfortable, better than his attitude to this question. When these worthy people are affected by a work of art, they say humbly that that sort of thing is a 'gift'. And because in their innocence they assume that beautiful and uplifting results must have beautiful and uplifting causes, they never dream that the 'gift' in question is a very dubious affair and rests upon extremely sinister foundations. Everybody knows that artists are 'sensitive' and easily wounded; just as everybody knows that ordinary people, with a normal bump of self-confidence, are not. Now you see, Lisabeta, I cherish at the bottom of my soul all the scorn and suspicion of the artist gentry—translated into terms of the intellectual—that my upright old forebears there on the Baltic would have felt for any juggler or mountebank that entered their houses. Listen to this. I know a banker, grey-haired business man, who has a gift for writing stories. He employs this gift in his idle hours, and some of his stories are of the first rank. But despite—I say despite—this excellent gift his withers are by no means unwrung: on the contrary, he has had to serve a prison sentence, on anything but trifling grounds. Yes, it was actually first *in prison* that he became conscious of his gift, and his experiences as a convict are the main theme in all his works. One might be rash enough to conclude that a man has to be at home in some kind of jail in order to become a poet. But can you escape the suspicion that the source and essence of his being an artist had less to do with his life in prison than they had with the reasons that *brought him there*? A banker who writes—that is a rarity, isn't it? But a banker who isn't a criminal, who is irreproachably respectable, and yet writes—he doesn't exist. Yes, you are laughing, and yet I am more than half serious. No problem, none in the world, is more tormenting than this of the artist and his human aspect. Take the most miraculous case of all, take the most typical and therefore the most powerful of artists, take such a morbid and profoundly equivocal work as *Tristan and Isolde*, and look at the effect it has on a healthy young man of thoroughly normal feelings. Exaltation, encouragement, warm, downright enthusiasm, perhaps incitement to 'artistic' creation of his own. Poor young dilettante! In us artists it looks fundamentally different from what he wots of, with his 'warm heart' and 'honest enthusiasm'. I've seen women and youths go mad over artists ... and I *knew* about them ... ! The origin, the accompanying phenomena, and the conditions of the artist life—good Lord, what I haven't observed about them, over and over!"

"Observed, Tonio Kröger? If I may ask, only 'observed'?"

He was silent, knitting his oblique brown brows and whistling softly to himself.

"Let me have your cup, Tonio. The tea is weak. And take another cigarette. Now, you perfectly know that you are looking at things as they do not necessarily have to be looked at...."

"That is Horatio's answer, dear Lisabeta. ' 'Twere to consider too curiously, to consider so.' "

"I mean, Tonio Kröger, that one can consider them just exactly as well from another side. I am only a silly painting female, and if I can contradict you at all, if I can defend your own profession a little against you, it is not by saying anything new, but simply by reminding you of some things you very well know yourself: of the purifying and healing influence of letters, the subduing of the passions by knowledge and eloquence; literature as the guide to understanding, forgiveness, and love, the redeeming power of the word, literary art as the noblest manifestation of the human mind, the poet as the most highly developed of human beings, the poet as saint. Is it to consider things not curiously enough, to consider them so?"

"You may talk like that, Lisabeta Ivanovna, you have a perfect right. And with reference to Russian literature, and the works of your poets, one can really worship them; they really come close to being that elevated literature you are talking about. But I am not ignoring your objections, they are part of the things I have in my mind today.... Look at me, Lisabeta. I don't look any too cheerful, do I? A little old and tired and pinched, eh? Well, now to come back to the 'knowledge'. Can't you imagine a man, born orthodox, mild-mannered, well-meaning, a bit sentimental, just simply over stimulated by his psychological clairvoyance, and going to the dogs? Not to let the sadness of the world unman you; to read, mark, learn, and put to account even the most torturing things and to be of perpetual good cheer, in the sublime consciousness of moral superiority over the horrible invention of existence —yes, thank you! But despite all the joys of expression once in a while the thing gets on your nerves. '*Tout comprendre c'est tout pardonner.*' I don't know about that. There is something I call being sick of knowledge, Lisabeta: when it is enough for you to see through a thing in order to be sick to death of it, and not in the least in a forgiving mood. Such was the case of Hamlet the

Dane, that typical literary man. He knew what it meant to be called to knowledge without being born to it. To see things clear, if even through your tears, to recognize, notice, observe—and have to put it all down with a smile, at the very moment when hands are clinging, and lips meeting, and the human gaze is blinded with feeling—it is infamous, Lisabeta, it is indecent, outrageous—but what good does it do to be outraged?

"Then another and no less charming side of the thing, of course, is your ennui, your indifferent and ironic attitude towards truth. It is a fact that there is no society in the world so dumb and hopeless as a circle of literary people who are hounded to death as it is. All knowledge is old and tedious to them. Utter some truth that it gave you considerable youthful joy to conquer and possess—and they will all chortle at you for your naïveté. Oh, yes, Lisabeta, literature is a wearing job. In human society, I do assure you, a reserved and sceptical man can be taken for stupid, whereas he is really only arrogant and perhaps lacks courage. So much for 'knowledge'. Now for the 'Word'. It isn't so much a matter of the 'redeeming power' as it is of putting your emotions on ice and serving them up chilled! Honestly, don't you think there's a good deal of cool cheek in the prompt and superficial way a writer can get rid of his feelings by turning them into literature? If your heart is too full, if you are overpowered with the emotions of some sweet or exalted moment—nothing simpler! Go to the literary man, he will put it all straight for you *instanter*. He will analyse and formulate your affair, label it and express it and discuss it and polish it off and make you indifferent to it for time and eternity—and not charge you a farthing. You will go home quite relieved, cooled off, enlightened; and wonder what it was all about and why you were so mightily moved. And will you seriously enter the lists in behalf of this vain and frigid charlatan? What is uttered, so runs this *credo*, is finished and done with. If the whole world could be expressed, it would be saved, finished and done. . . . Well and good. But I am not a nihilist—"

"You are not a—" said Lisabeta. . . . She was lifting a teaspoonful of tea to her mouth and paused in the act to stare at him.

"Come, come, Lisabeta, what's the matter? I say I am not a nihilist, with respect, that is, to lively feeling. You see, the literary man does not understand that life may go on living, unashamed, even after it has been expressed and therewith finished. No matter how much it has been redeemed by becoming literature, it keeps right on sinning—for all action is sin in the mind's eye—

"I'm nearly done, Lisabeta. Please listen. I love life—this is an admission. I present it to you, you may have it. I have never made it to anyone else. People say—people have even written and printed—that I hate life, or fear or despise or abominate it. I liked to hear this, it has always flattered me; but that does not make it true. I love life. You smile; and I know why, Lisabeta. But I implore you not to take what I am saying for literature. Don't think of Caesar Borgia or any drunken philosophy that has him for a standard-bearer. He is nothing to me, your Caesar Borgia. I have no opinion of him, and I shall never comprehend how one can honour the extraordinary and daemonic as an ideal. No, life as the eternal antinomy of mind and art does not represent itself to us as a vision of savage greatness and ruthless beauty; we who are set apart and different do not conceive it as, like us, unusual; it is the normal, respectable, and admirable that is the kingdom of our longing: life, in all its seductive banality! That man is very far from being an artist, my dear, whose last and deepest enthusiasm is the *raffiné*, the eccentric and satanic; who does not know a longing for the innocent, the simple, and the living, for a little friendship, devotion, familiar human happiness—the gnawing, surreptitious hankering, Lisabeta, for the bliss of the commonplace....

"A genuine human friend. Believe me, I should be proud and happy to possess a friend among men. But up to now all the friends I have had have been daemons, kobolds, impious monsters, and spectres dumb with excess of knowledge—that is to say, literary men.

"I may be standing upon some platform, in some hall in front of people who have come to listen to me. And I find myself looking round among my hearers, I catch myself secretly peering about the auditorium, and all the while I am thinking who it is that has come here to listen to me, whose grateful applause is in my ears, with whom my art is making me one.... I do not find what I seek, Lisabeta, I find the herd. The same old community, the same old gathering of early Christians, so to speak: people with fine souls in uncouth bodies, people who are always falling down in the dance, if you know what I mean; the kind to whom poetry serves as a sort of mild revenge on life. Always and only the poor and suffering, never any of the others, the blue-eyed ones, Lisabeta —they do not need mind. . . .

"And, after all, would it not be a lamentable lack of logic to want it otherwise? It is against all sense to love life and yet bend all the powers you have to draw it over to your own side, to the side of finesse and melancholy and the whole sickly aristocracy of letters. The kingdom of art increases and that of health and innocence declines on this earth. What there is left of it ought to be carefully preserved; one ought not to tempt people to read poetry who would much rather read books about the instantaneous photography of horses.

"For, after all, what more pitiable sight is there than life led astray by art? We artists have a consummate contempt for the dilettante, the man who is leading a living life and yet thinks he can be an artist too if he gets the chance. I am speaking from personal experience, I do assure you. Suppose I am in a company in a good house, with eating and drinking going on, and plenty of conversation and good feeling; I am glad and grateful to be able to lose myself among good regular people for a while. Then all of a sudden—I am thinking of something that actually happened —an officer gets up, a lieutenant, a stout, good-looking chap, whom I could never have believed guilty of any conduct unbecoming his uniform, and actually in good set terms asks the company's permission to read some verses of his own composition. Everybody looks disconcerned, they laugh and tell him to go on, and he takes them at their word and reads from a sheet of paper he has up to now been hiding in his coat-tail pocket—something about love and music, as deeply felt as it is inept. But I ask you: a lieutenant! A man of the world! He surely did not need to. . . . Well, the inevitable result is long faces, silence, a little artificial applause, everybody thoroughly uncomfortable. The first sensation I am conscious of is guilt—I feel partly responsible for the disturbance this rash youth has brought upon the company; and no wonder, for I, as a member of the same guild, am a target for some of the unfriendly glances. But next minute I realize something else: this man for whom just now I felt the greatest respect has suddenly sunk in my eyes. I feel a benevolent pity. Along with some other brave and good-natured gentlemen I go up and speak to him. 'Congratulations, Herr Lieutenant,' I say, 'that is a very pretty talent you have. It was charming.' And I am within an ace of clapping him on the shoulder. But is that the way one is supposed to feel towards a lieutenant—benevolent? . . . It was his own fault. There he stood, suffering embarrassment for the mistake of thinking that one may pluck a single leaf from the laurel tree of art without paying for it with his life. No, there I go with my colleague, the convict banker—but don't you find, Lisabeta, that I have quite a Hamlet-like flow of oratory today?"

"Are you done, Tonio Kröger?"

"No. But there won't be any more."

"And quite enough too. Are you expecting a reply?"

"Have you one ready?"

"I should say. I have listened to you faithfully, Tonio, from beginning to end, and I will give you the answer to everything you have said this afternoon and the solution of the problem that has been upsetting you. Now: the solution is that you, as you sit there, are, quite simply, a bourgeois."

"Am I?" he asked a little crestfallen.

"Yes; that hits you hard, it must. So I will soften the judgment just a little. You are a bourgeois on the wrong path, a bourgeois *manqué*."

Silence. Then he got up resolutely and took his hat and stick.

"Thank you, Lisabeta Ivanovna; now I can go home in peace. I am expressed."

Towards autumn Tonio Kröger said to Lisabeta Ivanovna:

"Well, Lisabeta, I think I'll be off. I need a change of air. I must get away, out into the open."

"Well, well, well, little Father! Does it please your Highness to go down to Italy again?"

"Oh, get along with your Italy, Lisabeta. I'm fed up with Italy, I spew it out of my mouth. It's a long time since I imagined I could belong down there. Art, eh? Blue-velvet sky, ardent wine, the sweets of sensuality. In short, I don't want it—I decline with thanks. The whole *bellezza* business makes me nervous. All those frightfully animated people down there with their black animal-like eyes; I don't like them either. These Romance peoples have no soul in their eyes. No, I'm going to take a trip to Denmark."

"To Denmark?"

"Yes. I'm quite sanguine of the results. I happen never to have been there, though I lived all my youth so close to it. Still I have always known and loved the country. I suppose I must have this northern tendency from my father, for my mother was really more for the *bellezza*, in so far, that is, as she cared very much one way or the other. But just take the books that are written up there, that clean, meaty, whimsical Scandinavian literature, Lisabeta, there's nothing like it, I love it. Or take the Scandinavian meals, those incomparable meals, which can only be digested in strong sea air (I don't know whether I can digest them in any sort of air); I know them from my home too, because we ate that way up there. Take even the names, the given names that people rejoice in up north; we have a good many of them in my part of the country too: Ingeborg, for instance, isn't it the purest poetry—like a harp-tone? And then the sea—up there it's the Baltic! ... In a word, I am going, Lisabeta. I want to see the Baltic again and read the books and hear the names on their native heath; I want to stand on the terrace at Kronberg, where the ghost appeared to Hamlet, bringing despair and death to that poor, noble-souled youth...."

"How are you going, Tonio, if I may ask? What route are you taking?"

"The usual one," he said, shrugging his shoulders, and blushed perceptibly. "Yes, I shall touch my—my point of departure, Lisabeta, after thirteen years, and that may turn out rather funny."

She smiled.

"That is what I wanted to hear, Tonio Kröger. Well, be off, then, in God's name. Be sure to write to me, do you hear? I shall expect a letter full of your experiences in—Denmark."

And Tonio Kröger travelled north. He travelled in comfort (for he was wont to say that anyone who suffered inwardly more than other people had a right to a little outward ease); and he did not stay until the towers of the little town he had left rose up in the grey air. Among them he made a short and singular stay.

The dreary afternoon was merging into evening when the train pulled into the narrow, reeking shed, so marvellously familiar. The volumes of thick smoke rolled up to the dirty glass roof and wreathed to and fro there in long tatters, just as they had, long ago, on the day when Tonio Kröger, with nothing but derision in his heart, had left his native town.—He arranged to have his luggage sent to his hotel and walked out of the station.

There were the cabs, those enormously high, enormously wide black cabs drawn by two horses, standing in a rank. He did not take one, he only looked at them, as he looked at everything: the narrow gables, and the pointed towers peering above the roofs close at hand; the plump, fair, easy-going populace, with their broad yet rapid speech. And a nervous laugh mounted in him, mysteriously akin to a sob. He walked on, slowly, with the damp wind constantly in his face, across the bridge, with the mythological statues on the railings, and some distance along the harbour.

Good Lord, how tiny and close it all seemed! The comical little gabled streets were climbing up just as of yore from the port to the town! And on the ruffled waters the smoke-stacks and masts of the ships dipped gently in the wind and twilight. Should he go up that next street, leading, he knew, to a certain house? No, tomorrow. He was too sleepy. His head was heavy from the journey, and slow, vague trains of thought passed through his mind.

Sometimes in the past thirteen years, when he was suffering from indigestion, he had dreamed of being back home in the echoing old house in the steep, narrow street. His father had been there too, and reproached him bitterly for his dissolute manner of life, and this, each time, he had found quite as it should be. And now the present refused to distinguish itself in any way from one of those tantalizing dream-fabrications in which the dreamer asks himself if this be delusion or reality and is driven to decide for the latter, only to wake up after all in the end.... He paced through the half-empty streets with his head inclined against the wind, moving as though in his sleep in the direction of the hotel, the first hotel in the town, where he meant to sleep. A bow-legged man, with a pole at the end of which burned a tiny fire, walked before him with a rolling, seafaring gait and lighted the gas-lamps.

What was at the bottom of this? What was it burning darkly beneath the ashes of his fatigue, refusing to burst out into a clear blaze? Hush, hush, only no talk. Only don't make words! He would have liked to go on so, for a long time, in the wind, through the dusky, dreamily familiar streets—but everything was so little and close together here. You reached your goal at once.

In the upper town there were arc-lamps, just lighted. There was the hotel with the two black lions in front of it; he had been afraid of them as a child. And there they were, still looking at each other as though they were about to sneeze; only they seemed to have grown much smaller. Tonio Kröger passed between them into the hotel.

As he came on foot, he was received with no great ceremony. There was a porter, and a lordly gentleman dressed in black, to do the honours; the latter, shoving back his cuffs with his little fingers, measured him from the crown of his head to the soles of his boots, obviously with intent to place him, to assign him to his proper category socially and hierarchically speaking and then mete out the suitable degree of courtesy. He seemed not to come to any clear decision and compromised on a moderate display of politeness. A mild-mannered waiter with yellow-white side-whiskers, in a dress suit shiny with age, and rosettes on his soundless shoes, led him up two flights into a clean old room furnished in patriarchal style. Its windows gave on a twilit view of courts and gables, very mediaeval and picturesque, with the fantastic bulk of the old church close by. Tonio Kröger stood awhile before this window; then he sat down on the wide sofa, crossed his arms, drew down his brows, and whistled to himself.

Lights were brought and his luggage came up. The mild-mannered waiter laid the hotel register on the table, and Tonio Kröger, his head on one side, scrawled something on it that might be taken for a name, a station, and a place of origin. Then he ordered supper and went on gazing into space from his sofa-corner. When it stood before him he let it wait long untouched, then took a few bites and walked up and down an hour in his room, stopping from time to time and closing his eyes. Then he very slowly undressed and went to bed. He slept long and had curiously confused and ardent dreams.

It was broad day when he woke. Hastily he recalled where he was and got up to draw the curtains; the pale-blue sky, already with a hint of autumn, was streaked with frayed and tattered cloud; still, above his native city the sun was shining.

He spent more care than usual upon his toilette, washed and shaved and made himself fresh and immaculate as though about to call upon some smart family where a well-dressed and flawless appearance was *de rigueur*; and while occupied in this wise he listened to the anxious beating of his heart.

How bright it was outside! He would have liked better a twilight air like yesterday's, instead of passing through the streets in the broad sunlight, under everybody's eye. Would he meet people he knew, be stopped and questioned and have to submit to be asked how he had spent the last thirteen years? No, thank goodness, he was known to nobody here; even if anybody remembered him, it was unlikely he would be recognized—for certainly he had changed in the meantime! He surveyed himself in the glass and felt a sudden sense of security behind his mask, behind his work-worn face, that was older than his years.... He sent for breakfast, and after that he went out; he passed under the disdainful eyes of the porter and the gentleman in black, through the vestibule and between the two lions, and so into the street.

Where was he going? He scarcely knew. It was the same as yesterday. Hardly was he in the midst of this long-familiar scene, this stately conglomeration of gables, turrets, arcades, and fountains, hardly did he feel once more the wind in his face, that strong current wafting a faint and pungent aroma from far-off dreams, than the same mistiness laid itself like a veil about his senses.... The muscles of his face relaxed, and he looked at men and things with a look grown suddenly calm. Perhaps right there, on that street corner, he might wake up after all....

Where was he going? It seemed to him the direction he took had a connection with his sad and strangely rueful dreams of the night. ... He went to Market Square, under the vaulted arches of the Rathaus, where the butchers were weighing out their wares red-handed, where the tall old Gothic fountain stood with its manifold spires. He paused in front of a house, a plain narrow building, like many another, with a fretted baroque gable; stood there lost in contemplation. He read the plate on the door, his eyes rested a little while on each of the windows. Then slowly he turned away.

Where did he go? Towards home. But he took a roundabout way outside the walls—for he had plenty of time. He went over the Millwall and over the Holstenwall, clutching his hat, for the wind was rushing and moaning through the trees. He left the wall near the station, where he saw a train puffing busily past, idly counted the coaches, and looked after the man who sat perched upon the last. In the Lindenplatz he stopped at one of the pretty villas, peered long into the garden and up at the windows, lastly conceived the idea of swinging the gate to and fro upon its hinges till it creaked. Then he looked awhile at his moist, rust-stained hand and went on, went through the squat old gate, along the harbour, and up the steep, windy street to his parents' house.

It stood aloof from its neighbours, its gable towering above them; grey and sombre, as it had stood these three hundred years; and Tonio Kröger read the pious, half-illegible motto above the entrance. Then he drew a long breath and went in.

His heart gave a throb of fear, lest his father might come out of one of the doors on the ground floor, in his office coat, with the pen behind his ear, and take him to task for his excesses. He would have found the reproach quite in order; but he got past unchidden. The inner door was ajar, which appeared to him reprehensible though at the same time he felt as one does in certain broken dreams, where obstacles melt away of themselves, and one presses onward in marvellous favour with fortune. The wide entry, paved with great square flags, echoed to his tread. Opposite the silent kitchen was the curious projecting structure, of rough boards, but cleanly varnished, that had been the servants' quarters. It was quite high up and could only be reached by a sort of ladder from the entry. But the great cupboards and carven presses were gone. The son of the house climbed the majestic staircase, with his hand on the white-enamelled, fret-work balustrade. At each step he lifted his hand, and put it down again with the next as though testing whether he could call back his ancient familiarity with the stout old railing.... But at the landing of the entresol he stopped. For on the entrance door was a white plate; and on it in black letters he read: "Public Library."

"Public Library?" thought Tonio Kröger. What were either literature or the public doing here? He knocked... heard a "Come in," and obeying it with gloomy suspense gazed upon a scene of most unhappy alteration.

The storey was three rooms deep, and all the doors stood open. The walls were covered nearly all the way up with long rows of books in uniform bindings, standing in dark-coloured bookcases. In each room a poor creature of a man sat writing behind a sort of counter. The farthest two just turned their heads, but the nearest got up in haste and, leaning with both hands on the table, stuck out his head, pursed his lips, lifted his brows, and looked at the visitor with eagerly blinking eyes.

"I beg pardon," said Tonio Kröger without turning his eyes from the book-shelves. "I am a stranger here, seeing the sights. So this is your Public Library? May I examine your collection a little?"

"Certainly, with pleasure," said the official, blinking still more violently. "It is open to everybody. . . . Pray look about you. Should you care for a catalogue?"

"No, thanks," answered Tonio Kröger, "I shall soon find my way about." And he began to move slowly along the walls, with the appearance of studying the rows of books. After a while he took down a volume, opened it, and posted himself at the window.

This was the breakfast-room. They had eaten here in the morning instead of in the big dining-room upstairs, with its white statues of gods and goddesses standing out against the blue walls. . . . Beyond there had been a bedroom, where his father's mother had died—only after a long struggle, old as she was, for she had been of a pleasure-loving nature and clung to life. And his father too had drawn his last breath in the same room: that tall, correct, slightly melancholy and pensive gentleman with the wild flower in his buttonhole. . . . Tonio had sat at the foot of his death-bed, quite given over to unutterable feelings of love and grief. His mother had knelt at the bedside, his lovely, fiery mother, dissolved in hot tears; and after that she had withdrawn with her artist into the far blue south. . . . And beyond still, the small third room, likewise full of books and presided over by a shabby man—that had been for years on end his own. Thither he had come after school and a walk—like today's; against that wall his table had stood with the drawer where he had kept his first clumsy, heartfelt attempts at verse. . . . The walnut tree . . . a pang went through him. He gave a sidewise glance out at the window. The garden lay desolate, but there stood the old walnut tree where it used to stand, groaning and creaking heavily in the wind. And Tonio Kröger let his gaze fall upon the book he had in his hands, an excellent piece of work, and very familiar. He followed the black lines of print, the paragraphs, the flow of words that flowed with so much art, mounting in the ardour of creation to a certain climax and effect and then as artfully breaking off....

"Yes, that was well done," he said; put back the book and turned away. Then he saw that the functionary still stood bolt-upright, blinking with a mingled expression of zeal and misgiving.

"A capital collection, I see," said Tonio Kröger. "I have already quite a good idea of it. Much obliged to you. Good-bye." He went out; but it was a poor exit, and he felt sure the official would stand there perturbed and blinking for several minutes.

He felt no desire for further researches. He had been home. Strangers were living upstairs in the large rooms behind the pillared hall; the top of the stairs was shut off by a glass door which used not to be there, and on the door was a plate. He went away, down the steps, across the echoing corridor, and left his parental home. He sought a restaurant, sat down in a corner, and brooded over a heavy, greasy meal. Then he returned to his hotel.

"I am leaving," he said to the fine gentleman in black. "This afternoon." And he asked for his bill, and for a carriage to take him down to the harbour where he should take the boat for Copenhagen. Then he went up to his room and sat there stiff and still, with his cheek on his hand, looking down on the table before him with absent eyes. Later he paid his bill and packed his things. At the appointed hour the carriage was announced and Tonio Kröger went down in travel array.

At the foot of the stairs the gentleman in black was waiting.

"Beg pardon," he said, shoving back his cuffs with his little fingers.... "Beg pardon, but we must detain you just a moment. Herr Seehaase, the proprietor, would like to exchange two words with you. A matter of form.... He is back there.... If you will have the goodness to step this way.... It is *only* Herr Seehaase, the proprietor."

And he ushered Tonio Kröger into the background of the vestibule.... There, in fact, stood Herr Seehaase. Tonio Kröger recognized him from old time. He was small, fat, and bow-legged. His shaven side-whisker was white, but he wore the same old low-cut dress coat and little velvet cap embroidered in green. He was not alone. Beside him, at a little high desk fastened into the wall, stood a policeman in a helmet, his gloved right hand resting on a document in coloured inks; he turned towards Tonio Kröger with his honest, soldierly face as though he expected Tonio to sink into the earth at his glance.

Tonio Kröger looked at the two and confined himself to waiting.

"You came from Munich?" the policeman asked at length in a heavy, good-natured voice.

Tonio Kröger said he had.

"You are going to Copenhagen?"

"Yes, I am on the way to a Danish seashore resort."

"Seashore resort? Well, you must produce your papers," said the policeman. He uttered the last word with great satisfaction.

"Papers . . . ?" He had no papers. He drew out his pocket-book and looked into it; but aside from notes there was nothing there but some proof-sheets of a story which he had taken along to finish reading. He hated relations with officials and had never got himself a passport. . . .

"I am sorry," he said, "but I don't travel with papers."

"Ah!" said the policeman. "And what might be your name?"

Tonio replied.

"Is that a fact?" asked the policeman, suddenly erect, and expanding his nostrils as wide as he could. . . .

"Yes, that is a fact," answered Tonio Kröger.

"And what are you, anyhow?"

Tonio Kröger gulped and gave the name of his trade in a firm voice. Herr Seehaase lifted his head and looked him curiously in the face.

"H'm," said the policeman. "And you give out that you are not identical with an individdle named"—he said "individdle" and then, referring to his document in coloured inks, spelled out an involved, fantastic name which mingled all the sounds of all the races—Tonio Kröger forgot it next minute—"of unknown parentage and unspecified means," he went on, "wanted by the Munich police for various shady transactions, and probably in flight towards Denmark?"

"Yes, I give out all that, and more," said Tonio Kröger, wriggling his shoulders. The gesture made a certain impression.

"What? Oh, yes, of course," said the policeman. "You say you can't show any papers—"

Herr Seehaase threw himself into the breach.

"It is only a formality," he said pacifically, "nothing else. You must bear in mind the official is only doing his duty. If you could only identify yourself somehow—some document ..."

They were all silent. Should he make an end of the business, by revealing to Herr Seehaase that he was no swindler without specified means, no gypsy in a green wagon, but the son of the late Consul Kröger, a member of the Kröger family? No, he felt no desire to do that. After all, were not these guardians of civic order within their right? He even agreed with them—up to a point. He shrugged his shoulders and kept quiet.

"What have you got, then?" asked the policeman. "In your portfoly, I mean?"

"Here? Nothing. Just a proof-sheet," answered Tonio Kröger.

"Proof-sheet? What's that? Let's see it."

And Tonio Kröger handed over his work. The policeman spread it out on the shelf and began reading. Herr Seehaase drew up and shared it with him. Tonio Kröger looked over their shoulders to see what they read. It was a good moment, a little effect he had worked out to a perfection. He had a sense of self-satisfaction.

"You see," he said, "there is my name. I wrote it, and it is going to be published, you understand."

"All right, that will answer," said Herr Seehaase with decision, gathered up the sheets and gave them back. "That will have to answer, Peterson," he repeated crisply, shutting his eyes and shaking his head as though to see and hear no more. "We must not keep the gentleman any longer. The carriage is waiting. I implore you to pardon the little inconvenience, sir. The officer has only done his duty, but I told him at once he was on the wrong track...."

"Indeed!" thought Tonio Kröger.

The officer seemed still to have his doubts; he muttered something else about individdle and document. But Herr Seehaase, overflowing with regrets, led his guest through the vestibule, accompanied him past the two lions to the carriage, and himself, with many respectful bows, closed the door upon him. And then the funny, high, wide old cab rolled and rattled and bumped down the steep, narrow street to the quay.

And such was the manner of Tonio Kröger's visit to his ancestral home.

Night fell and the moon swam up with silver gleam as Tonio Kröger's boat reached the open sea. He stood at the prow wrapped in his cloak against a mounting wind, and looked beneath into the dark going and coming of the waves as they hovered and swayed and came on, to meet with a clap and shoot erratically away in a bright gush of foam.

He was lulled in a mood of still enchantment. The episode at the hotel, their wanting to arrest him for a swindler in his own home, had cast him down a little, even although he found it quite in order—in a certain way. But after he came on board he had watched, as he used to do as a boy with his father, the lading of goods into the deep bowels of the boat, amid shouts of mingled Danish and Plattdeutsch; not only boxes and bales, but also a Bengal tiger and a polar bear were lowered in cages with stout iron bars. They had probably come from Hamburg and were destined for a Danish menagerie. He had enjoyed these distractions. And as the boat glided along between flat river-banks he quite forgot Officer Petersen's inquisition; while all the rest—his sweet, sad, rueful dreams of the night before, the walk he had taken, the walnut tree—had welled up again in his soul. The sea opened out and he saw in the distance the beach where he as a lad had been let to listen to the ocean's summer dreams; saw the flashing of the lighthouse tower and the lights of the Kurhaus where he and his parents had lived.... The Baltic! He bent his head to the strong salt wind; it came sweeping on, it enfolded him, made him faintly giddy and a little deaf; and in that mild confusion of the senses all memory of evil, of anguish and error, effort and exertion of the will, sank away into joyous oblivion and were gone. The roaring, foaming, flapping, and slapping all about him came to his ears like the groan and rustle of an old walnut tree, the creaking of a garden gate.... More and more the darkness came on.

"The stars! Oh, by Lord, look at the stars!" a voice suddenly said, with a heavy singsong accent that seemed to come out of the inside of a tun. He recognized it. It belonged to a young man with red-blond hair who had been Tonio Kröger's neighbour at dinner in the salon. His dress was very simple, his eyes were red, and he had the moist and chilly look of a person who has just bathed. With nervous and self-conscious movements he had taken unto himself an astonishing quantity of lobster omelet. Now he leaned on the rail beside Tonio Kröger and looked up at the skies, holding his chin between thumb and forefinger. Beyond a doubt he was in one of those rare and festal and edifying moods that cause the barriers between man and man to fall; when the heart opens even to the stranger, and the mouth utters that which otherwise it would blush to speak. . . .

"Look, by dear sir, just look at the stars. There they stahd and glitter; by goodness, the whole sky is full of theb! And I ask you, when you stahd ahd look up at theb, ahd realize that bany of theb are a huddred tibes larger thad the earth, how does it bake you feel? Yes, we have idvehted the telegraph and the telephode and all the triuphs of our bodern tibes. But whed we look up there, after all we have to recogdize and uhderstad that we are worbs, biserable worbs, ahd dothing else. Ab I right, sir, or ab I wrog? Yes, we are worbs," he answered himself, and nodded meekly and abjectly in the direction of the firmament.

"Ah, no, he has no literature in his belly," thought Tonio Kröger. And he recalled something he had lately read, an essay by a famous French writer on cosmological and psychological philosophies, a very delightful *causerie*.

He made some sort of reply to the young man's feeling remarks, and they went on talking, leaning over the rail, and looking into the night with its movement and fitful lights. The young man, it seemed, was a Hamburg merchant on his holiday.

"Y'ought to travel to Copedhagen on the boat, thigks I, and so here I ab, and so far it's been fide. But they shouldn't have given us the lobster obelet, sir, for it's going to be storby—the captain said so hibself—and that's do joke with indigestible food like that in your stobach. . . ."

Tonio Kröger listed to all this engaging artlessness and was privately drawn to it.

"Yes," he said, "all the food up here is too heavy. It makes one lazy and melancholy."

"Belancholy?" repeated the young man, and looked at him, taken aback. Then he asked, suddenly: "You are a stradger up here, sir?"

"Yes, I come from a long way off," answered Tonio Kröger vaguely, waving his arm.

"But you're right," said the youth; "Lord kdows you are right about the belancholy. I am dearly always belancholy, but specially on evedings like this when there are stars in the sky." And he supported his chin again with thumb and forefinger.

"Surely this man writes verses," thought Tonio Kröger; "business man's verses, full of deep feeling and single-mindedness."

Evening drew on. The wind had grown so violent as to prevent them from talking. So they thought they would sleep a bit, and wished each other good-night.

Tonio Kröger stretched himself out on the narrow cabin bed, but he found no repose. The strong wind with its sharp tang had power to rouse him; he was strangely restless with sweet anticipations. Also he was violently sick with the motion of the ship as she glided down a steep mountain of wave and her screw vibrated as in agony, free of the water. He put on all his clothes again and went up to the deck.

Clouds raced across the moon. The sea danced. It did not come on in full-bodied, regular waves; but far out in the pale and flickering light the water was lashed, torn, and tumbled; leaped upward like great licking flames; hung in jagged and fantastic shapes above dizzy abysses, where the foam seemed to be tossed by the playful strength of colossal arms and flung upward in all directions. The ship had a heavy passage; she lurched and stamped and groaned through the welter; and far down in her bowels the tiger and the polar bear voiced their acute discomfort. A man in an oilskin, with the hood drawn over his head and a lantern strapped to his chest, went straddling painfully up and down the deck. And at the stern, leaning far out, stood the young man from Hamburg suffering the worst. "Lord!" he said in a hollow, quavering voice, when he saw Tonio Kröger. "Look at the uproar of the elebents, sir!" But he could say no more—he was obliged to turn hastily away.

Tonio Kröger clutched at a taut rope and looked abroad into the arrogance of the elements. His exultation outvied storm and wave; within himself he chanted a song to the sea, instinct with love of her: "O thou wild friend of my youth, Once more I behold thee—" But it got no further, he did not finish it. It was not fated to receive a final form nor in tranquillity to be welded to a perfect whole. For his heart was too full. . . .

Long he stood; then stretched himself out on a bench by the pilot-house and looked up at the sky, where stars where flickering.

He even slept a little. And when the cold foam splashed his face it seemed in his half-dreams like a caress.

Perpendicular chalk-cliffs, ghostly in the moonlight, came in sight. They were nearing the island of Möen. Then sleep came again, broken by salty showers of spray that bit into his face and made it stiff. . . . When he really roused, it was broad day, fresh and palest grey, and the sea had gone down. At breakfast he saw the young man from Hamburg again, who blushed rosy-red for shame of the poetic indiscretions he had been betrayed into by the dark, ruffled up his little red-blond moustache with all five fingers, and called out a brisk and soldierly good-morning—after that he studiously avoided him.

And Tonio Kröger landed in Denmark. He arrived in Copenhagen, gave tips to everybody who laid claim to them, took a room at a hotel, and roamed the city for three days with an open guide-book and the air of an intelligent foreigner bent on improving his mind. He looked at the king's New Market and the "Horse" in the middle of it, gazed respectfully up the columns of the Frauenkirch, stood long before Thorwaldsen's noble and beautiful statuary, climbed the round tower, visited castles, and spent two lively evenings in the Tivoli. But all this was not exactly what he saw.

The doors of the houses—so like those in his native town, with open-work gables of baroque shape—bore names known to him of old; names that had a tender and precious quality, and withal in their syllables an accent of plaintive reproach, of repining after the lost and gone. He walked, he gazed, drawing deep, lingering draughts of moist sea air, and everywhere he saw eyes as blue, hair as blond, faces as familiar, as those that had visited his rueful dreams the night he had spent in his native town. There in the open street it befell him that a glance, a ringing word, a sudden laugh would pierce him to his marrow.

He could not stand the bustling city for long. A restlessness, half memory and half hope, half foolish and half sweet, possessed him; he was moved to drop this rôle of ardently inquiring tourist and lie somewhere, quite quietly, on a beach. So he took ship once more and travelled under a cloudy sky, over a black water, northwards along the coast of Seeland towards Helsingör. Thence he drove, at once, by carriage, for three-quarters of an hour, along and above the sea, reaching at length his ultimate goal, the little white "bath-hotel" with green blinds. It stood surrounded by a settlement of cottages, and its shingled turret tower looked out on the beach and the Swedish coast. Here he left the carriage, took possession of the light room they had ready for him, filled shelves and presses with his kit, and prepared to stop awhile.

It was well on in September; not many guests were left in Aalsgaard. Meals were served on the ground floor, in the great beamed dining-room, whose lofty windows led out upon the veranda and the sea. The landlady presided, an elderly spinster with white hair and faded eyes, a faint colour in her cheek and a feeble twittering voice. She was for ever arranging her red hands to look well upon the table-cloth. There was a short-necked old gentleman, quite blue in the face, with a grey sailor beard; a fish-dealer he was, from the capital, and strong at the German. He seemed entirely congested and inclined to apoplexy; breathed in short gasps, kept putting his beringed first finger to one nostril, and snorting violently to get a passage of air through the other. Notwithstanding, he addressed himself constantly to the whisky-bottle, which stood at his place at luncheon and dinner, and breakfast as well. Besides him the company consisted only of three tall American youths with their governor or tutor, who kept adjusting his glasses in unbroken silence. All day long he played football with his charges, who had narrow, taciturn faces and reddish-yellow hair parted in the middle. "Please pass the *wurst,*" said one. "That's not *wurst,* it's *schinken,*" said the other, and this was the extent of their conversation, as the rest of the time they sat there dumb, drinking hot water.

Tonio Kröger could have wished himself no better table-companions. He revelled in the peace and quiet, listened to the Danish palatals, the clear and the clouded vowels in which the fish-dealer and the landlady desultorily conversed; modestly exchanged views with the fish-dealer on the state of the barometer, and then left the table to go through the veranda and on to the beach once more, where he had already spent long, long morning hours.

Sometimes it was still and summery there. The sea lay idle and smooth, in stripes of blue and russet and bottle-green, played all across with glittering silvery lights. The seaweed shrivelled in the sun and the jelly-fish lay steaming. There was a faintly stagnant smell and a whiff of tar from the fishing-boat against which Tonio Kröger leaned, so standing that he had before his eyes not the Swedish coast but the open horizon, and in his face the pure, fresh breath of the softly breathing sea.

Then grey, stormy days would come. The waves lowered their heads like bulls and charged against the beach; they ran and ramped high up the sands and left them strewn with shining wet sea-grass, driftwood, and mussels. All abroad beneath an overcast sky extended ranges of billows, and between them foaming valleys palely green; but above the spot where the sun hung behind the cloud a patch like white velvet lay on the sea.

Tonio Kröger stood wrapped in wind and tumult, sunk in the continual dull, drowsy uproar that he loved. When he turned away it seemed suddenly warm and silent all about him. But he was never unconscious of the sea at his back; it called, it lured, it beckoned him. And he smiled.

He went landward, by lonely meadow-paths, and was swallowed up in the beech-groves that clothed the rolling landscape near and far. Here he sat down on the moss, against a tree, and gazed at the strip of water he could see between the trunks. Sometimes the sound of surf came on the wind—a noise like boards collapsing at a distance. And from the tree-tops over his head a cawing—hoarse, desolate, forlorn. He held a book on his knee, but did not read a line. He enjoyed profound forgetfulness, hovered disembodied above space and time; only now and again his heart would contract with a fugitive pain, a stab of longing and regret, into whose origin he was too lazy to inquire.

Thus passed some days. He could not have said how many and had no desire to know. But then came one on which something happened; happened while the sun stood in the sky and people were about; and Tonio Kröger, even, felt no vast surprise.

The very opening of the day had been rare and festal. Tonio Kröger woke early and suddenly from his sleep, with a vague and exquisite alarm; he seemed to be looking at a miracle, a magic illumination. His room had a glass door and balcony facing the sound; a thin white gauze curtain divided it into living- and sleeping-quarters, both hung with delicately tinted paper and furnished with an airy good taste that gave them a sunny and friendly look. But now to his sleep-drunken eyes it lay bathed in a serene and roseate light, an unearthly brightness that gilded walls and furniture and turned the gauze curtain to radiant pink cloud. Tonio Kröger did not at once understand. Not until he stood at the glass door and looked out did he realize that this was the sunrise.

For several days there had been clouds and rain; but now the sky was like a piece of pale-blue silk, spanned shimmering above sea and land, and shot with light from red and golden clouds. The sun's disk rose in splendour from a crisply glittering sea that seemed to quiver and burn beneath it. So began the day. In a joyous daze Tonio Kröger flung on his clothes and, breakfasting in the veranda before everybody else, swam from the little wooden bath-house some distance out into the sound, then walked for an hour along the beach. When he came back, several omnibuses were before the door, and from the dining-room he could see people in the parlour next door where the piano was, in the veranda, and on the terrace in front; quantities of people sitting at little tables enjoying beer and sandwiches amid lively discourse. There were whole families, there were old and young, there were even a few children.

At second breakfast—the table was heavily laden with cold viands, roast, pickled, and smoked—Tonio Kröger inquired what was going on.

"Guests," said the fish-dealer. "Tourists and ball-guests from Helsingör. Lord help us, we shall get no sleep this night! There will be dancing and music, and I fear me it will keep up till late. It is a family reunion, a sort of celebration and excursion combined; they all subscribe to it and take advantage of the good weather. They came by boat and bus and they are having breakfast. After that they go on with their drive, but at night they will all come back for a dance here in the hall. Yes, damn it, you'll see we shan't get a wink of sleep."

"Oh, it will be a pleasant change," said Tonio Kröger.

After that there was nothing more said for some time. The landlady arranged her red fingers on the cloth, the fish-dealer blew through his nostril, the Americans drank hot water and made long faces.

Then all at once a thing came to pass: *Hans Hansen and Inge-*

borg Holm walked through the room.

Tonio Kröger, pleasantly fatigued after his swim and rapid walk, was leaning back in his chair and eating smoked salmon on toast; he sat facing the veranda and the ocean. All at once the door opened and the two entered hand-in-hand—calmly and unhurried. Ingeborg, blonde Inge, was dressed just as she used to be at Herr Knaak's dancing-class. The light flowered frock reached down to her ankles and it had a tulle fichu draped with a pointed opening that left her soft throat free. Her hat hung by its ribbons over her arm. She, perhaps, was a little more grown up than she used to be, and her wonderful plait of hair was wound round her head; but Hans Hansen was the same as ever. He wore his sailor overcoat with gilt buttons, and his wide blue sailor collar lay across his shoulders and back; the sailor cap with its short ribbons he was dangling carelessly in his hand. Ingeborg's narrow eyes were turned away; perhaps she felt shy before the company at table. But Hans Hansen turned his head straight towards them, and measured one after another defiantly with his steel-blue eyes; challengingly, with a sort of contempt. He even dropped Ingeborg's hand and swung his cap harder than ever, to show what manner of man he was. Thus the two, against the silent, blue-dyed sea, measured the length of the room and passed through the opposite door into the parlour.

This was at half past eleven in the morning. While the guests of the house were still at table the company in the veranda broke up and went away by the side door. No one else came into the dining-room. The guests could hear them laughing and joking as they got into the omnibuses, which rumbled away one by one.... "So they are coming back?" asked Tonio Kröger.

"That they are," said the fish-dealer. "More's the pity. They have ordered music, let me tell you—and my room is right above the dining-room."

"Oh, well, it's a pleasant change," repeated Tonio Kröger. Then he got up and went away.

That day he spent as he had the others, on the beach and in the wood, holding a book on his knee and blinking in the sun. He had but one thought; they were coming back to have a dance in the hall, the fish-dealer had promised they would; and he did nothing but be glad of this, with a sweet and timorous gladness such as he had not felt through all these long dead years. Once he happened, by some chance association, to think of his friend Adalbert, the novelist, the man who had known what he wanted and betaken himself to the café to get away from the spring. Tonio Kröger shrugged his shoulders at the thought of him.

Luncheon was served earlier than usual, also supper, which they ate in the parlour because the dining-room was being got ready for the ball, and the whole house flung in disorder for the occasion. It grew dark; Tonio Kröger sitting in his room heard on the road and in the house the sounds of approaching festivity. The picnickers were coming back; from Helsingör, by bicycle and carriage, new guests were arriving; a fiddle and a nasal clarinet might be heard practising down in the dining-room. Everything promised a brilliant ball....

Now the little orchestra struck up a march; he could hear the notes, faint but lively. The dancing opened with a polonaise. Tonio Kröger sat for a while and listened. But when he heard the march-time go over into a waltz he got up and slipped noiselessly out of his room.

From his corridor it was possible to go by the side stairs to the side entrance of the hotel and thence to the veranda without passing through a room. He took this route, softly and stealthily as though on forbidden paths, feeling along through the dark, relentlessly drawn by this stupid jigging music, that now came up to him loud and clear.

The veranda was empty and dim, but the glass door stood open into the hall, where shone two large oil lamps, furnished with bright reflectors. Thither he stole on soft feet; and his skin prickled with the thievish pleasure of standing unseen in the dark and spying on the dancers there in the brightly lighted room. Quickly and eagerly he glanced about for the two whom he sought....

Even though the ball was only half an hour old, the merriment seemed in full swing; however, the guests had come hither already warm and merry, after a whole day of carefree, happy companionship. By bending forward a little, Tonio Kröger could see into the parlour from where he was. Several old gentlemen sat there smoking, drinking, and playing cards; others were with their wives on the plush-upholstered chairs in the foreground watching the dance. They sat with their knees apart and their hands resting on them, puffing out their cheeks with a prosperous air; the mothers, with bonnets perched on their parted hair, with their hands folded over their stomachs and their heads on one side, gazed into the whirl of dancers. A platform had been erected on the long side of the hall, and on it the musicians were doing their utmost. There was even a trumpet, that blew with a certain caution, as though afraid of its own voice, and yet after all kept breaking and cracking. Couples were dipping and circling about, others walked arm-in-arm up and down the room. No one wore ballroom clothes; they were dressed as for an outing in the summertime: the men in countrified suits which were obviously their Sunday wear; the girls in light-coloured frocks with bunches of field-flowers in their bodices. Even a few children were there, dancing with each other in their own way, even after the music stopped. There was a long-legged man in a coat with a little swallow-tail, a provincial lion with an eye-glass and frizzed hair, a post-office clerk or some such thing; he was like a comic figure stepped bodily out of a Danish novel; and he seemed to be the leader and manager of the ball. He was everywhere at once, bustling, perspiring, officious, utterly absorbed; setting down his feet, in shiny, pointed, military half-boots, in a very artificial and involved manner, toes first; waving his arms to issue an order, clapping his hands for the music to begin; here, there, and everywhere, and glancing over his shoulder in pride at his great bow of office, the streamers of which fluttered grandly in his rear.

Yes, there they were, those two, who had gone by Tonio Kröger in the broad light of day; he saw them again—with a joyful start he recognized them almost at the same moment. Here was Hans Hansen by the door, quite close; his legs apart, a little bent over, he was eating with circumspection a large piece of sponge-cake, holding his hand cupwise under his chin to catch the crumbs. And there by the wall sat Ingeborg Holm, Inge the fair; the post-office clerk was just mincing up to her with an exaggerated bow and asking her to dance. He laid one hand on his back and gracefully shoved the other into his bosom. But she was shaking her head in token that she was a little out of breath and must rest awhile, whereat the post-office clerk sat down by her side.

Tonio Kröger looked at them both, these two for whom he had in time past suffered love—at Hans and Ingeborg. They were Hans and Ingeborg not so much by virtue of individual traits and similarity of costume as by similarity of race and type. This was the blond, fair-haired breed of the steel-blue eyes, which stood to him for the pure, the blithe, the untroubled in life; for a virginal aloofness that was at once both simple and full of pride.... He looked at them. Hans Hansen was standing there in his sailor suit, lively and well built as ever, broad in the shoulders and narrow in the hips; Ingeborg was laughing and tossing her head in a certain high-spirited way she had; she carried her hand, a schoolgirl hand, not at all slender, not at all particularly aristocratic, to the back of her head in a certain manner so that the thin sleeve fell away from her elbow—and suddenly such a pang of home-sickness shook his breast that involuntarily he drew farther back into the darkness lest someone might see his features twitch.

"Had I forgotten you?" he asked. "No, never. Not thee, Hans, not thee, Inge the fair! It was always you I worked for; when I heard applause I always stole a look to see if you were there.... Did you read *Don Carlos*, Hans Hansen, as you promised me at the garden gate? No, don't read it! I do not ask it any more. What have you to do with a king who weeps for loneliness? You must not cloud your clear eyes or make them dreamy and dim by peering into melancholy poetry.... To be like you! To begin again, to grow up like you, regular like you, simple and normal and cheerful, in conformity and understanding with God and man, beloved of the innocent and happy. To take you, Ingeborg Holm, to wife, and have a son like you, Hans Hansen—to live free from the curse of knowledge and the torment of creation, live and praise God in blessed mediocrity! Begin again? But it would do no good. It would turn out the same—everything would turn out the same as it did before. For some go of necessity astray, because for them there is no such thing as a right path."

The music ceased; there was a pause in which refreshments were handed round. The post-office assistant tripped about in person with a trayful of herring salad and served the ladies; but before Ingeborg Holm he even went down on one knee as he passed her the dish, and she blushed for pleasure.

But now those within began to be aware of a spectator behind the glass door; some of the flushed and pretty faces turned to measure him with hostile glances; but he stood his ground. Ingeborg and Hans looked at him too, at almost the same time, both with that utter indifference in their eyes that looks so like contempt. And he was conscious too of a gaze resting on him from a different quarter; turned his head and met with his own the eyes that had sought him out. A girl stood not far off, with a fine, pale little face—he had already noticed her. She had not danced much, she had few partners, and he had seen her sitting there against the wall, her lips closed in a bitter line. She was standing alone now too; her dress was a thin light stuff, like the others, but beneath the transparent frock her shoulders showed angular and poor, and the thin neck was thrust down so deep between those meagre shoulders that as she stood there motionless she might almost be thought a little deformed. She was holding her hands in their thin mitts across her flat breast, with the finger-tips touching; her head was drooped, yet she was looking up at Tonio Kröger with black swimming eyes. He turned away....

Here, quite close to him, were Ingeborg and Hans. He had sat down beside her—she was perhaps his sister—and they ate and drank together surrounded by other rosy-cheeked folk; they chattered and made merry, called to each other in ringing voices, and laughed aloud. Why could he not go up and speak to them? Make some trivial remark to him or her, to which they might at least answer with a smile? It would make him happy—he longed to do it; he would go back more satisfied to his room if he might feel he had established a little contact with them. He thought out what he might say; but he had not the courage to say it. Yes, this too was just as it had been: they would not understand him, they would listen like strangers to anything he was able to say. For their speech was not his speech.

It seemed the dance was about to begin again. The leader developed a comprehensive activity. He dashed hither and thither, adjuring everybody to get partners; helped the waiters to push chairs and glasses out of the way, gave orders to the musicians, even took some awkward people by the shoulders and shoved them aside.... What was coming? They formed squares of four couples each.... A frightful memory brought the colour to Tonio Kröger's cheeks. They were forming for a quadrille.

The music struck up, the couples bowed and crossed over. The leader called off; he called off—Heaven save us—in French! And pronounced the nasals with great distinction. Ingeborg Holm danced close by, in the set nearest the glass door. She moved to and fro before him, forwards and back, pacing and turning; he caught a waft from her hair or the thin stuff of her frock, and it made him close his eyes with the old, familiar feeling, the fragrance and bitter-sweet enchantment he had faintly felt in all these days, that now filled him utterly with irresistible sweetness. And what was the feeling? Longing, tenderness? Envy? Self-contempt? ... *Moulinet des dames!* "Did you laugh, Ingeborg the blonde, did you laugh at me when I disgraced myself by dancing the *moulinet*? And would you still laugh today even after I have become something like a famous man? Yes, that you would, and you would be right to laugh. Even if I in my own person had written the nine symphonies and *The World as Will and Idea* and painted the Last Judgment, you would still be eternally right to laugh...." As he looked at her he thought of a line of verse once so familiar to him, now long forgotten: "I would sleep, but thou must dance." How well he knew it, that melancholy northern mood it evoked—its heavy inarticulateness. To sleep.... To long to be allowed to live the life of simple feeling, to rest sweetly and passively in feeling alone, without compulsion to act and achieve —and yet to be forced to dance, dance the cruel and perilous sword-dance of art; without even being allowed to forget the melancholy conflict within oneself; to be forced to dance, the while one loved. . . .

A sudden wild extravagance had come over the scene. The sets had broken up, the quadrille was being succeeded by a gallop, and all the couples were leaping and gliding about. They flew past Tonio Kröger to a maddeningly quick tempo, crossing, advancing, retreating, with quick, breathless laughter. A couple came rushing and circling towards Tonio Kröger; the girl had a pale, refined face and lean, high shoulders. Suddenly, directly in front of him, they tripped and slipped and stumbled.... The pale girl fell, so hard and violently it almost looked dangerous; and her partner with her. He must have hurt himself badly, for he quite forgot her, and, half rising, began to rub his knee and grimace; while she, quite dazed, it seemed, still lay on the floor. Then Tonio Kröger came forward, took her gently by the arms, and lifted her up. She looked dazed, bewildered, wretched; then suddenly her delicate face flushed pink.

"*Tak, O, mange tak!*" she said, and gazed up at him with dark, swimming eyes.

"You should not dance any more, Fräulein," he said gently. Once more he looked round at *them*, at Ingeborg and Hans, and then he went out, left the ball and the veranda and returned to his own room.

He was exhausted with jealousy, worn out with the gaiety in which he had had no part. Just the same, just the same as it had always been. Always with burning cheeks he had stood in his dark corner and suffered for you, you blond, you living, you happy ones! And then quite simply gone away. Somebody *must* come now! Ingeborg *must* notice he had gone, must slip after him, lay a hand on his shoulder and say: "Come back and be happy. I love you!" But she came not at all. No, such things did not happen. Yes, all was as it had been, and he too was happy, just as he had been. For his heart was alive. But between that past and this present what had happened to make him become that which he now was? Icy desolation, solitude: mind, and art, forsooth!

He undressed, lay down, put out the light. Two names he whispered into his pillow, the few chaste northern syllables that meant for him his true and native way of love, of longing and happiness; that meant to him life and home, meant simple and heartfelt feeling. He looked back on the years that had passed. He thought of the dreamy adventures of the senses, nerves, and mind in which he had been involved; saw himself eaten up with intellect and introspection, ravaged and paralysed by insight, half worn out by the fevers and frosts of creation, helpless and in anguish of conscience between two extremes, flung to and fro between austerity and lust; *raffiné*, impoverished, exhausted by frigid and artificially heightened ecstasies; erring, forsaken, martyred, and ill—and sobbed with nostalgia and remorse.

Here in his room it was still and dark. But from below life's lulling, trivial waltz-rhythm came faintly to his ears.

Tonio Kröger sat up in the north, composing his promised letter to his friend Lisabeta Ivanovna.

"Dear Lisabeta down there in Arcady, whither I shall shortly return," he wrote: "Here is something like a letter, but it will probably disappoint you, for I mean to keep it rather general. Not that I have nothing to tell; for indeed, in my way, I have had experiences; for instance, in my native town they were even going to arrest me . . . but of that by word of mouth. Sometimes now I have days when I would rather state things in general terms than go on telling stories.

"You probably still remember, Lisabeta, that you called me a *bourgeois*, a *bourgeois manqué?* You called me that in an hour when, led on by other confessions I had previously let slip, I confessed to you my love of life, or what I call life. I ask myself if you were aware how very close you came to the truth, how much my love of 'life' is one and the same thing as my being a *bourgeois*. This journey of mine has given me much occasion to ponder the subject.

"My father, you know, had the temperament of the north: solid, reflective, puritanically correct, with a tendency to melancholia. My mother, of indeterminate foreign blood, was beautiful, sensuous, naïve, passionate, and careless at once, and, I think, irregular by instinct. The mixture was no doubt extraordinary and bore with it extraordinary dangers. The issue of it, a *bourgeois* who strayed off into art, a bohemian who feels nostalgic yearnings for respectability, an artist with a bad conscience. For surely it is my *bourgeois* conscience makes me see in the artist life, in all irregularity and all genius, something profoundly suspect, profoundly disreputable; that fills me with this lovelorn *faiblesse* for the simple and good, the comfortably normal, the average unendowed respectable human being.

"I stand between two worlds. I am at home in neither, and I suffer in consequence. You artists call me a *bourgeois*, and the *bourgeois* try to arrest me. . . . I don't know which makes me feel worse. The *bourgeois* are stupid; but you adorers of the beautiful, who call me phlegmatic and without aspirations, you ought to realize that there is a way of being an artist that goes so deep and is so much a matter of origins and destinies that no longing seems to it sweeter and more worth knowing than longing after the bliss of the commonplace.

"I admire those proud, cold beings who adventure upon the paths of great and daemonic beauty and despise 'mankind'; but I do not envy them. For if anything is capable of making a poet of a literary man, it is my *bourgeois* love of the human, the living and usual. It is the source of all warmth, goodness, and humour; I even almost think it is itself that love of which it stands written that one may speak with the tongues of men and of angels and yet having it not is as sounding brass and tinkling cymbals.

"The work I have so far done is nothing or not much—as good as nothing. I will do better, Lisabeta—this is a promise. As I write, the sea whispers to me and I close my eyes. I am looking into a world unborn and formless, that needs to be ordered and shaped; I see into a whirl of shadows of human figures who beckon to me to weave spells to redeem them: tragic and laughable figures and some that are both together—and to these I am drawn. But my deepest and secretest love belongs to the blond and blue-eyed, the fair and living, the happy, lovely, and commonplace.

"Do not chide this love, Lisabeta; it is good and fruitful. There is longing in it, and a gentle envy; a touch of contempt and no little innocent bliss."

FIORENZA

TIME: the afternoon of the 8th of April 1492
PLACE: the Villa Medicea, Careggi, near Florence

ACT ONE

The study of Cardinal Giovanni de' Medici, a private apartment on the top floor of the villa. Tapestries on the walls; between them book-shelves are built in, sparsely filled with books and scrolls. Windows high up in the walls, with deep sills. Entrance centre back, covered by a tapestry. On the left a table with a heavy brocade cover; on it an ink-pot, pens, and paper. Before it an armchair with a high back. Down stage right a sofa decorated with the Medici arms; leaning against it a lute. On the right wall a large painting with a mythological subject. In front of it an étagère with ornaments.

1

On the sofa sits the young Cardinal Giovanni—seventeen years old, in red skull-cap and mantle with broad white turn-over collar. He has a charming, whimsical, effeminate face. On a chair beside him Angelo Poliziano, *in a long, dark, flowing robe with full sleeves, finished at the neck with a narrow white collar. His shrewd, sensual face, framed in grey curls, with a powerful aquiline nose and a mouth with deep folds at the corners, is turned towards the Cardinal. The latter, being short-sighted, is using a lorgnon shaped like a pair of scissors. Books lie heaped on the carpet, some of them open.* Poliziano *holds a book in his hands.*

POLIZIANO: ... and at this point, Giovanni, my friend and son of my great and beloved friend Lorenzo, I come back to the hope, the justifiable and well-founded wish which the whole wisdom-loving world, like myself, is looking to you to gratify. Do not think I forget the respect I owe to your lofty position in the hierarchy ...

GIOVANNI: Pardon me, Messer Angelo! Have you not heard that Fra Girolamo said of late in the cathedral that in the spiritual hierarchy the Christian priesthood follows after the lowest of the angels? (*He giggles.*)

POLIZIANO: What? ... Perhaps ... yes, I may have heard it. But no matter. What I wish to make clear to you is this: that Christ's vicar on earth, whose tiara in the course of events you will very likely be called upon to wear, does nothing incompatible with his holy office in carrying out the plan I have in mind, which is that of all lovers of wisdom. You are aware, Giovanni, that I refer to the canonization of Plato. He is divine, thus it is but obeying the dictates of reason to make him a god. Star-gazers have read in the heavens that the performance of this reasonable and meritorious act has been reserved to the enlightened dynasty of the Medicis; not only so, but it is altogether a fitting and logical thing to do. And for Christ. He Himself doubtless could but sanction the canonization of the ancient philosopher. More than once did the Sibyls explicitly prophesy the coming of Christ; I do not need to remind my pupil of Virgil's pregnant lines. Plato himself, as we have on the best authority, spoke of it in no ambiguous terms; and we read in Porphyrius that the gods recognized the rare piety and religiosity of the Nazarene; they confirmed the fact of His immortality and were on the whole favourably disposed towards Him. ... In short, my dear Giovanni, I pray that the gods will let me live to see the day which will bring to fulfilment my oft-expressed hope. That day will be the ultimate fruition of our Platonic studies together. (*He sees that the Cardinal is chuckling to himself.*) Might I ask what it is that amuses you?

GIOVANNI: Nothing, nothing, Messer Angelo—really nothing at all. I was only reminded of what Fra Girolamo said of late in the cathedral: "Plato's *Symposium* is marked by an indecent pseudo-morality." That is good, isn't it? (*Laughs.*) I find it a shrewd observation. All the same . . .

POLIZIANO (*after a pause*): I am grieved, Giovanni, and I think justifiably. You are inattentive this afternoon, you were extremely inattentive all the time we were reading. I put it down to the unfavourable circumstances, and the care which sits heavy upon us all. Your glorious father is ill, and very ill, there are fears for his life. But we place our hopes on the costly medicine which the Jewish doctor from Pavia has administered to him; and, moreover, it seems to me that philosophy, in our hour of need, should be our loftiest and most grateful consolation. I might but too well understand it if the thought of your father should distract you from your studies. But since I am driven to realize that your mind is taken up with this absurd and fantastic mendicant friar, this Fra Girolamo—

GIOVANNI: Whose mind is not taken up with him? Forgive me, Messer Angelo! Do not be angry—look kindly at me; anger does not become you. Only the beautiful, the formal, the pellucid should be the subject of your talk. Do I love you or do I not? Who knows all your verses, and almost your whole vintage of Latin hexameters off by heart? Well, then! But this man from Ferrara—I should like to talk about him a little. You must agree that after all he is an original and arresting figure. He is the prior of a mendicant order and as such despicable. These orders are the object of general mirth and as often as I have been in Rome I have been told that they are nothing but an embarrassment to the Church. But when by reason of his own rare gifts one of these despised Frati not only overcomes the existing prejudice against his class but turns it into admiration for his person—

POLIZIANO: Admiration! Who admires him? Not I. Certainly not I. The rabble honours itself in his image.

GIOVANNI: No, no, no, Messer Angelo—he does not belong to the rabble. And not only because he comes of an old and highly respected Ferrarese family. I have heard him more than once in Santa Maria del Fiore and I assure you that he impressed me as a many-sided man. I grant you that he lacks culture and elegance to an astounding degree. But a close view shows that even so he must be constitutionally sensitive in both mind and body. Often in the pulpit he has to sit down, so shaken is he by his own passion—they say that he is so exhausted after every sermon that he has to go to bed. His voice is marvellously soft, it is only his eyes and his gestures that sometimes make it seem like crashing thunder. I will even admit to you—when I am alone, sometimes, I take up my Venetian mirror and try to imitate the way he hurls his lightnings against the clergy. (*Imitating*) "But now I will stretch out My hand, saith the Lord; I will fall upon thee, thou adulterous, thou infamous, thou shameless Church! My sword shall fall upon thy favourites, upon the places of thy shame, thy palaces and thy harlots, and I will visit My justice upon thee. . . ." So it goes—but you see I cannot do it. I should be a poor hand at preaching repentance. Florence would laugh me to scorn, pert wench that she is! Even less—though I am a cardinal and shall come to be a pope—could I foretell events like him, who is but a begging friar, Messer Angelo. More than a year ago he prophesied the coming deaths of my father the Magnifico and of the Pope; may God forfend that this prophecy be fulfilled. But even now so much has come to pass that the jovial man who with such a pretty wit took the name of Innocent has been lying for weeks in a stupor so that the whole court has at times thought him dead; and my father is so ill that this morning they gave him the sacrament. Anyhow, that seems to have revived him; he was able to make a joke about it, although in a very feeble voice. But . . .

POLIZIANO: Your father overdid during carnival, that is all. There was great excess at the artist balls, and Lorenzo loves beauty and pleasure with such a burning love that he is too ready to forget considerations of health. He plies the cup of love and joy as though his body were as puissant as his wonderful soul. But it is not. . . . A child could foretell that some day he would have to learn his lesson—and you attribute a miracle to this monk of yours? Fie, Giovanni! Either you are a fool or you want to make one of me, which is more likely. You would tell me of his visions; how now and again he sees the heavens open, hears voices, and beholds the rain of fire, of swords and arrows. I am willing to believe that this good Brother believes in his own revelations, I will not laugh at their simplicity. But I hardly think that they would visit him if he were a little more educated and disciplined, if his gifts and his learning were not so hopelessly disorderly and muddled.

GIOVANNI: I am convinced of that, it is perfectly true. All of us are far too cultured and instructed to see visions; if we did have them we would not believe in them. But he succeeds where we fail, Messer Angelo!

POLIZIANO: You cannot talk of success where only the rabble is won over, and that by flattering its miserable instincts. Otherwise Florence must blush indeed in the sight of all Italy at the success of this disgusting monk. I have been once in the Duomo when he preached, this much-admired Prior of San Marco—and, by all the Graces, Muses, and Nymphs, I will not go again! I have always flattered myself that I knew something about eloquence—but it seems I was mistaken. There was a time in Florence when a preacher was admired for his choice and measured use of gesture, word and phrase, his familiarity with the classic authors as displayed in apposite quotation; for his pregnant sayings, the clarity and elegance of his language, the masterly structure of his sentences, and for a voice of pure quality uttering harmonious cadences. But these it seems are all nothing. Real superiority is the achievement of a sickly boor with eyes like coals of fire, whose gestures are out of all compass, who sheds tears over the decay of chastity, cries down culture and the arts, vilifies the poets and philosophers, quotes exclusively from the Bible, as though the Latinity of that book were not execrable—and to cap all dares to inveigh against the life and the government of our great Lorenzo. (*He has risen and strides excitedly up and down the room, the Cardinal surveying him complacently through his lorgnon.*)

GIOVANNI: By the Holy Virgin, Messer Angelo, how splendidly wroth you are! You look at things with such conviction from a single point of view—Brother Girolamo himself could not improve upon your single-mindedness. Go on! I listen with the utmost enjoyment. Speak even more bitingly, more crushingly. "Epicureans and swine"—he spoke of "epicureans and swine". The phrase is in everybody's mouth. He referred to my father's friends, to Ficino, to Messer Pulci, to the artists, presumably also to you. (*Laughs.*)

POLIZIANO: Hearken, my Lord Cardinal—

GIOVANNI: Now, now! What ails you? Do I love you or do I not? You are as right as you can be....

POLIZIANO: I do not say that I am right, but I say that I despise this worm for imagining that he thinks he holds the truth in his hands. One little smile, ye gods! One single sly ironic word! One subtle sceptical allusion to raise him above the masses and put him in touch with the cultured among his congregation! Then I could forgive him all. But nothing, nothing, nothing of the kind. One dismal indiscriminate condemnation of unbelief, immorality, blasphemy, vice, luxury, and the lusts of the flesh—

GIOVANNI (*shaking with laughter*): *Vaccæ pingues*—oh, my God, did you hear what he said about the fat cows that graze on the hills of Samaria? He spoke of them when he was expounding Amos. "These fat cows," said he, "would you hear what they mean? They mean the courtesans, all the thousands and thousands of fat courtesans in Italy!" That is good—it is capital. Do not deny it. It takes imagination to think of a thing like that, it is a witty figure that sticks in the memory. *Vaccæ pingues.* I shall never see a fat cow again without thinking of a daughter of joy; no, nor a priestess of Venus without thinking of a fat cow. I will tell you a little discovery I have made. In wit, in the humorous point of view, lies the strongest antidote to fleshly desire. I am not a hang-dog, am I? I delight in statues, pictures, architecture, verse, music, and the jest and have no other wish than to live tranquilly in the enjoyment of these beautiful things; but I assure you that I not infrequently find the temptations of love an inconvenience. They destroy my balance, they cloud my happiness, they inflame me more than is agreeable. . . . Well, yesterday on the Piazza fat Penthesilea went past my litter, the one that lives by Porta San Gallo. I looked at her, and actually I did not feel the slightest temptation. I was simply seized with such a fit of laughter that I had to draw the curtains. She walked just like a fat cow that grazes on the hills of Samaria!

POLIZIANO (*indulgently*): What a child you are, Giovanni, you with your cows! Donna Penthesilea is a very beautiful woman, versed in the arts and humanities, who does not at all deserve the comparison. But I rejoice to hear that you can see the funny side of your exhorter to penitence.

GIOVANNI: You are wrong there. I take him with all possible seriousness. One must. He is a famous man. Our beloved Florence knows well, I should say, how to annihilate with her wit people who being without talents are so foolhardy as to expose themselves. He has made her quake. At least one must grant that in religious matters he has great gifts and much experience.

POLIZIANO: Much experience! Splendid! When a man has no knowledge, then his inner experience, his inner light, make up for everything. He disowns the ancients, he will naught of Crassus or Hortensius or Cicero. He has not even the degree of Doctor of Theology and he disdains all the wisdom of the world. He knows, recognizes, and wants only himself, himself alone; he talks of himself whatever he may be speaking of—yes, sometimes he deals with episodes out of his private life and seeks to give them deep significance—as though anybody of any education or good taste could attach significance to what happened to this black bat of a begging monk. A few days ago at Antonio Miscomini the printer's I came across a copy of his pamphlet *On Love to Jesus Christ*—there have been absurdly enough, seven editions of it within a short time. Since our good Frate rejects the glorious dialogue of Plato, I was curious to see what he himself would have to say about love. What I read, my friend, was disgusting beyond all expectation. A perfervid and chaotic mixture of gloomy and fevered and drunken emotions, forebodings, and introspections which struggled in vain for clear expression. It made me reel, I felt actually nauseated. In all seriousness, I can well believe that this sort of study must be a wearing occupation. I understand his collapses and his fainting fits. Instead of running away from his honoured parents and taking refuge in a cloister, to sit between bare walls and stare into his own murky soul, this idiot ought to have submitted to teaching and sharpened his own perceptions of the colour and variety of the glorious material world. Then he would realize that work is not a castigation and martyrdom but a joyous thing, and that all that is good is blithely and easily accomplished. I wrote my drama *Orpheus* in a few days; and in face of the beauty of this world my songs flow from my lips as I drink, at the festal board—I do not need to go to bed after them.

GIOVANNI: Unless the wine were to blame! Yes, Messer Angelo, you are the light of the age. Who can equal you? Who sees the world so beauteous as you do? No one sings as sweetly as you. No one so sweetly sings the praises of a lovely boy. Perhaps Fra Girolamo has said to himself that an ambitious man must succeed by contrast if he wants to compete with you....

POLIZIANO: Are you mocking me?

GIOVANNI: That I cannot tell. You ask too much. I never know when I am mocking and when I am serious. . . . Who is there?

AN USHER (*lifting the portière at the entrance door*): The Prince of Mirandola.

GIOVANNI: Pico! Let him come in. Shall he not, Messer Angelo? He is welcome, is he not? (*The usher withdraws.*) Come hither, do not be angry—do I love you, or do I not? You are in the right, I own myself defeated. Brother Girolamo is a bat—there, are you content? One must argue a bit, eh? If you had taken his side I should have abused him with all my strength. Here is Pico. Good day, Pico!

POLIZIANO: If you were less charming, you rogue, one might be angry with you!

2

Giovanni Pico della Mirandola enters briskly, leaving his cloak in the hands of the page and coming gaily forward. He is an exuberant youth, elegantly and capriciously dressed in silken garments, with long, well-dressed blond locks, a delicate nose, a feminine mouth, and a double chin.

PICO: How is the Magnifico? Good day, Vannino! Greeting, Messer Angelo! . . . Whew! How hot I am! If you love me, signori, get me a lemonade, cold as the waters of the Cocytus. (*The Cardinal, making a sign to Politian to remain, goes obligingly to the door and gives the order in person.*) By Bacchus, my tongue is sticking to my teeth! What a warm April! The clock at San Stephano in Pane said three, and it is as hot as ever. You must know that I come from Florence, as fast as my horse would carry me. I dined at your kinsmen's the Tornabuonis, Giovanni, and I tarried there all too long. The Tornabuonis certainly set a good table. We had fat French capons, my lad, very tender-fleshed, you would have appreciated them. Yes, life has its charms. And Lorenzo—tell me the truth, how is he since this morning?

POLIZIANO: His condition seems unchanged since you saw him, my Lord. The Cardinal and I are waiting for the court physician's report on the effect of the draught of distilled precious stones which Sor Lazzaro from Pavia has administered. To beguile the heavy time we have been giving ourselves to our studies—from which, to be sure, we were distracted by an unworthy subject—

but we have had no fresh report from Messer Pierleoni. Ah, my gracious Lord, I am beginning to doubt the miraculous efficacy of this much-lauded draught. He who brewed it forsook Careggi at once—after receiving, by the by, a sinfully high fee, and left it to us to await the result of his ministrations. Would that they might be manifest! My great, my beloved Master! Did I save you, fourteen years ago in the cathedral, from the daggers of the Pazzi, that you might be torn from me by a malignant illness? Alas, wretch that I am, whither shall I turn if you join the shades? I am but a vine which twines itself about you, the laurel, and must pine away when you do. And Florence, what will become of her? She is your mistress. I see her fading in her widow's weeds—

PICO: Messer Angelo, I beseech you! This is a dirge and comes too soon. Lorenzo lives, the while you sing his death. Your genius carries you away. . . . Tell me, has Messer Pierleoni yet expressed himself decisively as to the nature of the illness?

POLIZIANO: No, my Lord. He explains, in phrases which the lay mind finds hard to grasp, that the marrow of life is attacked by decay. A horrible thought!

PICO: The marrow of life?

POLIZIANO: And most frightful of all is the inward unrest which despite his weakness possesses the beloved patient. He refuses to remain in bed. Today he has had himself carried in a litter into the garden, into the loggia of the Platonic Academy, into various rooms in the villa, and finds nowhere rest.

PICO: Strange. Were you with your father today, Giovanni?

GIOVANNI: No, Pico. And, between ourselves, being with him is become so hard for me that I avoid it all I can. Father is so changed. He has a way of looking at you—he rolls his eyes first upwards and then turns them aside, with an agonizing expression. . . . You do not know how frightful the proximity of illness and suffering is to me. I become ill myself. No, it was Father brought us up to brush calmly aside everything ugly, sad, or painful and to keep our souls receptive only to the beautiful and the joyous. It should not surprise him now—

PICO: I understand. But you should seek to overcome your reluctance. . . . Where is your brother?

GIOVANNI: Piero? How should I know? Riding, fencing (*in an effort to strike a lighter key again*), perhaps with a fat cow—

PICO: With a—Ah, ha! Well, well, hark at little Giovanni! I shall tell my prior that the Cardinal de' Medici no longer quotes Aristotle but certain sermons. . . . (*A servant brings the lemonade and goes out.*) But now tell me, tell me! How did Lorenzo take this latest news?

POLIZIANO: Which news, my Lord?

PICO: Brother Girolamo's latest joke . . . the scandal in the cathedral.

GIOVANNI AND POLIZIANO: In the cathedral?

PICO: He doesn't know? Nor you either? So much the better. Then I can tell it to you. Let me drink and I will.—That is a beautiful spoon.

GIOVANNI: Let me see. Yes, it is charming. Ercole the goldsmith made it. Clever man.

PICO: Lovely, lovely! The golden balls—what delicate foliage! A very successful piece of work. Ercole? I'll give him an order. He has taste.

GIOVANNI: The scandal, Pico!

PICO: I'll tell you. In the first place, it is about *her*.

POLIZIANO: Ah, about *her*. . . .

GIOVANNI: Go on!

PICO: You know she attends the Frate's sermons?

POLIZIANO: I know—without comprehending why.

PICO: Oh, I comprehend it perfectly. In the first place it is the women who are his most passionate worshippers, and particularly women who have loved much are the most powerfully swayed by him—as is only natural. Besides, what do you want, our Brother has become the fashion. His success goes beyond all my expectations. And it is increasing steadily among the people as well as among the aristocracy; even the fat bourgeoisie is beginning to take notice. It is quite the fashion to attend his sermons—I find it rather fanatical of you, Messer Angelo, if you will forgive me, to keep aloof as you do. But to the point. The divine Fiore is less self-willed. She has lately been going with fair regularity to sit at the Frate's feet—which in itself would be a perfectly gratifying and even an exhilarating thing. The trouble is that she does it in such an ostentatious and challenging way. What she does is to appear in the cathedral nearly a half-hour too late, when the sermon is in full swing; and even that might pass, for, after all, she could do it quietly and unobtrusively. But here comes in the fact that our divinity enjoys making itself felt and is even more given to the pomp and splendour of a regal progress than even her great lover Lorenzo himself; she shows much less restraint. A whole brilliantly dressed cortège surrounds her litter and accompanies her ladyship into the middle of the church to make a way for her through the crowd—which they do with no great tact. I was present the first time when she made her entrance, in the middle of the sermon. Her appearance would always attract attention—but in the manner of its doing it made quite a little commotion. The crowd pushed and shoved, whispered and pointed, the people who had just been bowing to the lash of the Frate's frightful prophecies twisted their necks round to enjoy the proud and revivifying spectacle of this famous, sumptuous, divinely beautiful woman as she advanced with her imperious air. As for the Frate, I was afraid, at the moment he saw her, he would lose his poise and the thread of his discourse. The word he had on his lips took so long to utter, it seemed to be frozen. He is always pale, but his face took on a waxen pallor, and never shall I forget the uncanny flicker of his eyes, in which a flame seemed to leap up, die down, and then blaze up again.

POLIZIANO: You tell the tale well, my lord—it is a veritable pleasure to listen to the harmonious flow of your periods.

PICO: By Hercules, Messer Angelo, in the present case what I have to tell is certainly rather more telling than the way it is told and I would pray you to fix your attention more upon the matter than upon the manner of the tale.

GIOVANNI: Matter, manner, tale, telling—bravo, Pico, bravo!

PICO: Hear me to the end. Since that day a silent, bitter struggle has gone on between the divine Fiore and Brother Girolamo. Her late appearance might seem the first time an aristocratic caprice, but she has persisted in it so obstinately as to make it obvious that she seeks to annoy the prior and his congregation. He on his side took various measures to counteract her late appearance. He spoke louder and more emphatically to drown out the noise her retainers made. He lowered his voice to a mysterious whisper to draw attention upon himself. He paused and let the condemnation of his silence speak for him until Donna Fiore reached her place and quiet was restored, when he resumed more violently than before.

The rest of us reap from the situation this advantage, that when *she* is there *he* outdoes himself. Terror and tears accompany his words; his audience quivers at the punishments he calls down upon Florence for her luxury and frivolity; after such a sermon people move about the streets half-dead and speechless. Often when he talks of the world's extremity and of pity and redemption the very scribe who takes down his words must break off in his task overcome by sobbing. The Frate has the art to touch the conscience with a single word uttered with such uncanny stress that the throng shudders as one man; it is very interesting to see this and at the same time feel the shuddering within one's proper breast. Naturally all this has made people attend the sermons in greater crowds than ever. . . . Our lovely mistress has not desisted from her provocative behaviour—and today things came to a climax, a catastrophe. Brother Girolamo has gone too far; I would not defend him. He was carried away by his own performance—listen to what happened. Even before dawn the cathedral was full of people who wanted to make sure of a good place. At sermon hour the crush inside and out was so great that a pin could not have fallen to the ground. At the very least, ten thousand people were present; those from outside of Florence have been reckoned at more than two thousand. From villas and from the countryside lords and peasants came by night not to miss the sermon hour—there were even people from Bologna. The crush between the Duomo and San Marco was frightful. The authorities had a hard time protecting the Prior from the demonstrations of the masses who wanted to kiss his hands and feet and cut pieces from his frock. In Via Larga, near your palace, Giovanni, a woman shrieked out that she had been healed of an issue of blood by touching the prophet's hem. There was an outcry that a miracle had happened and the crowd screamed *Misericordia*. All the Fathers of San Marco, all the brotherhoods, and all the world besides were gathered in the Duomo. There were members of the Signoria and the red-caps of the College of Eight; men and women of every rank and age, boys clambering on the pillars, workmen, poets, philosophers. At last Brother Girolamo mounted the pulpit. His gaze, that strangely fixed and burning gaze, was directed upon the throng as he began to speak amid a breathless and oppressive stillness. He spoke to Florence, addressed her with the thou and in a frightfully slow, quiet voice questioned her how she spent her days and how her nights. In chastity, in fear of sensual lusts, in the spirit, in peace? He paused, awaiting an answer. And this Florence, this thousand-headed host, bends beneath his intolerable eye that sees through all, guesses all, knows all. "Thou answerest me not?" he says. . . . He draws up his sickly frame and cries out in a terrible voice: "Let me tell thee!" Then begins a pitiless reckoning, a Last Judgment in words, under which the crowd writhes as under the rod. In his mouth every weakness of the flesh becomes an intolerable, abominable sin. He names them all by name, ruthlessly, with dreadful emphasis: vices which till then have never been mentioned in holy places. And all are guilty, he declares: Pope, clergy, princes, humanists, poets, artists, and makers of feasts. He lifts his arms, and lo, a hideous vision, a devilish, alluring picture rises from the maw of revelation: the whore sitting upon many waters, the woman on the beast! She is arrayed in purple and scarlet colour and decked with gold and precious stones and pearls, having a golden cup in her hand full of abominations and filthiness of her fornication. And upon her forehead was a name written, Mystery, Babylon the Great, the Mother of Harlots. "That woman art thou, Florence, thou shameless wanton and strumpet! Very delicate art thou, arrayed in fine linen, painted and scented. Thy speech is wit and elegant euphony. Thy hand rejects any instrument that bears not the mark of beauty, thine eye rests voluptuously upon costly paintings and the statues of nude heathen gods. But the Lord hath spewed thee out of His mouth. Hark! Hearest thou not the voices in the air? Hearest thou not the wings of destruction? Yea, then, the time hath come. It is past. Remorse cometh too late. Judgment is at hand. I have prophesied it unto thee a hundred times, Florence, but in thy pleasures thou wouldest not hearken to the voice of the poor, wise monk. Gone are the days of dancing, of pageantry, of obscene songs. . . . Unhappy one, thou art lost. The frightful darkness falls. Thunder fills the air. The sword of the Most High flashes down. . . . Save thyself! Repent! Atone! . . . Too late! For the Lord looses His waters over the kingdoms of the earth. The flood carries away the masks and costumes of thy carnivals, thy books of Latin and Italian poesy, thine adornments and thy tirings, thy perfumes and thy veils, thy unchaste paintings, thy heathen statuary. Seest thou the flames gleaming blood-red? Thou art overrun with savage armies. Famine stalks grinning through thy streets. The plague breathes over thee her stinking breath. . . . The end cometh, the end cometh! Thou shalt be rooted out, rooted out amid torments." —No, my friends, I am giving no proper picture—my words cannot make you see his face, his gestures, cannot make you hear his voice, cannot bring you under the domination of his personal dæmon. The multitudes groaned as though on the rack. I saw bearded men spring up in a panic and take to flight. A desperate, long-drawn wail for mercy was wrung from the centre of the crowd: "Have pity!" And a deathly stillness. . . . And then—his eyes grow dim. At the very moment of uttermost terror a miracle comes to pass. The annihilating wrath upon his countenance melts away. In overflowing love he stretches forth his arms. "The miracle of grace!" he cries. "It comes to pass! Florence, my city, my people, let me announce it unto thee, grace is vouchsafed thee if thou dost penance, if thou renouncest thy infamous revellings, if thou wilt dedicate thyself as a bride to the King of humility and suffering. Lo, He, He"—and he lifts the crucifix aloft—"He, Florence, would be thy King. Wilt thou accept Him? Ye who are tortured by sin and marked for affliction, ye poor in spirit, ye who know naught of Cicero and naught of the philosophers, ye who are cast down and rejected, ailing and wretched, He will lift you up, will comfort, refresh, and give you cheer. Did not our blessed Thomas Aquinas declare that the blessed in the heavenly kingdom will look down and see the sufferings of the damned that their bliss might be augmented? So shall it be. But the city which chooses Jesus as its King is blest already in this earthly life. No more shall some famish while others dwell among beautiful furnishings set upon floors of mosaic. Jesus will have it and I as His vicar announce that the price of meat be reduced to a minimum, to a few soldi the pound; He wills that those who must pay a penance of five measures of meal to a cloister shall give it to the poor instead. He wills that the splendid gold vessels and the paintings in the churches be turned into money and the proceeds distributed among the people. He wills"—and just at that point, Giovanni, Messer Angelo, in that moment of universal emotion, contrition, abasement—just at that moment happened the thing which will give the Florentines food for talk for many a month to come. There was a noise at the entrance, a clatter, a murmuring, a sound of feet, which echoed and increased. The slanting rays of light from the windows shone on steel, as the pike-bearers forced their way into the nave, crying to the startled crowd to make way. And into the path they opened stepped the divine Fiore with majestic tread, among her retinue. The great pearl which Lorenzo lately gave her gleamed like milk on her flawless brow. Her hands were folded before her, her eyes lowered, yet seeing all, her lips curved in an incomparable smile; she advanced slowly to her chosen position opposite the pulpit. But he, the Ferrarese, broke off his sentence abruptly, leaned his prophetic wrath far out over the pulpit, pointing down with arm outstretched straight into her face: "Behold!" he cried, "turn ye and behold! She comes, she is here, the harlot with whom kings have dallied on earth, the mother of abominations, the woman on the beast, the great Babylon!"

POLIZIANO: Terrible! The foul-mouthed wretch!

GIOVANNI: A little severe—but all's one.

PICO: No, no, do not judge, gentlemen! Since, unluckily for you, you were not present, do not try to form an idea of the tremendousness of that moment. Bear in mind that whatever he sees becomes truth and presentness when he utters it. His white hand stretching out of the dark sleeve of his habit trembled, as he gazed straight and fixedly into her face, and until he let it fall the exquisite Fiore was in very truth the apocalyptic woman, the great Babylon in all its shameless splendour. The crowd, torn to and fro by conflicting feelings, between damnation and grace, overwrought and on fire, made no doubt of it at all. Hatred, fear, and disgust spoke out of the thousand faces turned upon her. A hoarse groaning sound arose, it seemed to thirst for her blood. I too was looking at her and I swear to you, *in verbo Domini*, I felt my hair rise on my head and cold shivers run down my back.

POLIZIANO: You look for such shivers, admit it, my Lord!

GIOVANNI: And she? And she?

PICO: She stood for perhaps the space of an Ave Maria rooted to the spot. Then she drew herself up with a furious exclamation, motioned to her following, and left the church. Rumours flew about that she had ordered her people to murder him there in the pulpit, but no one dared to approach. It is said too that a secret messenger went from her to San Marco after the sermon. Certainly his frenzy led him seriously astray. I am in no wise defending him. Whatever provocation she gave, it was not the way to treat such a woman. To curse her before all the people! Is she a courtesan, then?

GIOVANNI (*with a giggle*): Yes!

PICO: By the great Eros, she is the Magnifico's mistress. That is, I mean, it is not as though she were one of those who must wear the yellow veil and live in certain streets. A flawless woman! We know that, though born abroad, she is the natural seed of a noble Florentine family. But even did we not know this, her brilliant mind, her diverse gifts, her lofty humanistic culture would daily and hourly bear witness to her origins. Her terza rimas and sonnets are ravishing, her lute-playing has moved me to tears. She knows by heart countless beautiful verses from Virgil, Ovid, and Horace; and the grace with which she recited that very free story from the *Decamerone* the other day after luncheon, in the garden—I could have worshipped her for it! And if all this be not enough to assure her of universal admiration, she is the woman to whom our great Lorenzo's love belongs.

POLIZIANO: You have said it, my Lord. And I, is it I who must teach you to interpret in the light of this fact the events you have just described? Your penetration finds out so many things in heaven and on earth, you are the phœnix of the intellect, the savant of princes, the prince of savants—and you will not see what all this means? The latest atrocity of this Ferrarese is nothing else than a new act of hostility, a fresh piece of malice and impertinence against the Magnifico himself and his house. Our divine mistress has served the monk with no more contempt than he deserves; but the unbridled character of his revenge did not follow the blind dictates of rage, it seized with intent and forethoughtedly the occasion for one of his insidious attacks on the man at whose feet Florence has for two decades been lying transported, the man whom even with his own cowardly tongue he names "the Strong". You are a great man, who could rule a city and conduct a war, did you not prefer to lead the life of a free lover of wisdom; I am but a poor poet, possessing naught on earth but my burning love for the house of the Medici, source of light, of beauty, and of joy. But this love of mine bids me speak, bids me snatch you back when in the rashness of youth you approach the snake lying hidden in the grass. The conspiracy of the Pazzi, when the beautiful Giuliano was slain in the cathedral and Lorenzo himself would have suffered the same fate had not some god given me strength at the last moment to close the door of the sacristy behind him—that conspiracy was child's-play beside the infernal machinations which—again in the same place, again in Santa Maria del Fiore—are on foot against the Medici and their blithe sway. The cheap successes which this viper has had from laying bare the meannesses of his character to the masses have simply turned his head. His zeal for human hearts, his craving to win souls for his own ends, is daily more and more undisguised. My Lord, do not fail to understand: his lowering face is set towards power! And what if it should fall into his hands? Open your eyes to what is happening and you will shiver with fright to see how shockingly the number swells of those who throng about this sorry despot and swallow the perverted and disingenuous mildness of his doctrine. These pitiful, self-denying, beauty-hating folk have been christened by more cheerful mortals with the nick-name "The Weepers"—as one calls the paid mourners at a funeral, you know. But in their self-abasement they have taken the name as an honour, and it now forms the style of a political party, opposed to the Medicis, whose head our monk reckons himself to be. But more: young sons from the first families of the city, a Gondi, a Salviati, brilliant and elegant youths, darlings of the gods like yourself, have crawled to this sorcerer's feet and applied for admission to San Marco as novices. The common folk are kept stirred up and baited with promises; it has gone so far that some good-for-nothings have stuck up lampoons in the form of sonnets against Piero de' Medici at the cathedral and the palace. Oh, my Lord, what did you do, what are you doing, calling this man to Florence and paving his way by your complaisance!

PICO: May we laugh at you a little, Messer Angelo, or will you take it amiss? If you could only see your own face! Go look at yourself in the glass! It looks as though you yourself belonged to the "Weepers", to that very political party of which you speak! Ha ha! Ye gods! A comic political party! So very important! I beg you to teach me the nature of our Florentines. I know them not, I have not studied them. They seem to me an uncommonly tough and solid folk, and with passions one would best not stir up. No, no, forgive me but I cannot take all this so seriously. For so long as my observation holds, Piero has been unloved in Florence. His brusque and domineering way makes him unpopular here; but certainly it is a bit too much to suppose a connection between the lame sonnets against him and Fra Girolamo's sermons. If Andrea Gondi and little Salviati find it the height of good taste to don the cowl—do you want to prevent them? I confess that I myself have already toyed with the idea. I believe we are living in an age free from prejudice. Is it true that here in Florence I can dress myself as I like, and express my personality as strikingly as I choose without anybody pointing the finger? Yes, it is true, true figuratively as well as literally. And if I tired of sky-blue and purple and preferred the colourless sobriety of the monk's habit? Why did you not object to the famous Procession of the Dead, in which after so many high-coloured carnivals we had corpses rising from their coffins? The effect was that of a savoury after too much sweet. What did I do when I persuaded Lorenzo to send for Fra Girolamo to Florence? I made the city the present of a great man, by Zeus, and I am proud of it! Lorenzo, I am sure, would be first to thank me. Did he not lately send to Spoleto to ask that the body of Fra Lippo Lippi be sent to our cathedral, that yet another might be added to our tombs of illustrious dead? When Brother Girolamo is once a dead body, the Ferrarese and perhaps even the Romans will send us ambassadors to beg for his ashes. But we will not surrender them. All Italy will visit the grave of the much-talked-of monk and I shall be able to say that it was I first discovered and fostered his genius. Yes, my good sirs, I have won my game. I was far from certain of it—for who can measure Fiorenza's whims? In that Dominican chapter-house where I first saw him no one paid him much heed. I sat in a circle of scholars and savants taking part in the chapter; he held aloof, among his brethren, so long as the discussion turned on scholastic matters. But when the question of discipline came up he suddenly projected himself into it and astounded the whole chapter by the almost superhuman originality of his words and point of view. The state of the Church and of public morals all at once appeared in a glaring and malefic light; I was extraordinarily shaken by the glowing enthusiasm and fanatic narrow-mindedness of his discourse. And I was not alone. Several men of superior intellect and rank, even princes, wrote to him afterwards. But I sought his personal acquaintance and only strengthened thereby my first impression. Everywhere I went I sang his praises. But then I moved to Florence and became absorbed in the stimulating observation of this mobile, cultured, sharp-tongued people, this restless little community for ever seeking after new things. And in a happy hour I conceived the plan of making my influence felt to the point of having Brother Girolamo summoned hither. His reputation was established, my praise had run before him, he would have the chance to produce his effect. It was a bold attempt, it involved a certain risk. I said to myself: "This man, in this city, will either be drowned in laughter and spitted on the point of a thousand jests—or he will have the greatest success of the century." Sirs, it is the latter that has happened. I spoke with my friend the Magnifico; the Magnifico spoke with the Fathers of San Marco. Brother Girolamo was sent for. He began by instructing the novices. But in order to gratify the curiosity of certain privileged persons he was asked to admit them to the lessons. The audience increased daily, he made no protest—my faith, he certainly did not, for he was overwhelmed with requests to mount the pulpit; connoisseurs, elegant dames, everybody implored him. He resisted at first, then he gave way. The little Church of San Marco was full to overflowing, he preached to an audience overwhelmed. His name was in every mouth. Platonists and Aristotelians laid by their quarrel for the time to dispute over these standards of Christian ethics. The monastery church became presently too small for the throngs, and he moved over to Santa Maria del Fiore. At first it was the cultivated amateur who came; but now it is the lowly who are on fire, upon whose spirits he practises with his melancholy gift of prophecy, his profound judgment of life. The monks elected him prior; and San Marco, which was no better and no worse then than other cloisters, became a sanctuary of holiness. His writings are read with eagerness. He is the talk of the town. Next to Lorenzo de' Medici he is the most famous, the most talked-of, the greatest man in Florence. And all this I behold with the liveliest satisfaction, in which, good Messer Angelo, I mean not to allow your misgivings to disturb me.

POLIZIANO: They shall not, my gracious Lord. Florence knows

me too, I believe, as anything but an alarmist. Let us assume that it was merely envy whispering to me when I spoke—that I grudge you a pleasure I do not understand and cannot share. For I admit that I do not in the least grasp what is going on. Often have I given thanks to the gods that I was born in this time of dawning and new birth which seems to me as enchanting as the sunrise. The world wakes and smiles, she draws a full breath and opens her chalice to the light, she is like a flower new blossoming. All the dim, hollow-eyed spectres, the cruel and hateful prejudices which have haunted men for so long a night, melt away to nothing. Everything is born afresh. A boundless, alluring kingdom of new studies, long forgotten and undreamed-of, opens out. The labouring earth presents to us fortunate ones all the treasures of antique beauty. The individual is enlightened and set free to rejoice in his own personality. Great and ruthless deeds are crowned with glory. Art, innocent, nude, unfettered, paces through the land, and all that she touches is ennobled. All human beings are filled with the intoxication emanating from the divine; they follow their smiling leader and their jubilation makes a cult of beauty and life. And then—what happens? What next? A man, too ugly and rigid to join in the dance of the elements, embittered, churlish, full of ill will, rises to lodge a protest against our godlike state, and the poison of his zeal is such that the ranks of the joyous thin, the deserters crowd about him and behave as though what he says is something vastly new, something unheard-of. And what is it he says? What is it his whole being exhales? Morality! But morality is the oldest, the boresomest, the most exposed and exploded idea in the world. It is ridiculous. Or isn't it? Do you mean it isn't? Speak, my Lord—what is your answer?

PICO: Nothing. For the moment nothing, Messer Angelo. For I must savour in silence the after-taste of your exquisite words. Glorious, glorious, what you said of the times we live in! "Like a flower new blossoming." . . . I do beseech you to put it into verse. I wonder if the ottava . . . or perhaps Latin hexameters—

GIOVANNI: You must answer, Pico, or own yourself beaten.

PICO: Answer? Willingly. But it seems to me that I have already inquired whether we live in a time that is free from prejudice or whether we do not. And if we do, then shall we set limits to our freedom? Must our free-thinking become a religion and lack of morals a species of fanaticism? I would repudiate the idea. If morality has been made impossible, if it has become ridiculous—well, then! Since in Florence the ridiculous is the greatest danger of all, then the bravest man is he who does not fear it. He would startle everybody. And in Florence to startle everybody is going far towards winning the game. Ah, my friends, sin has lost much of its charm since we got rid of our consciences! Look about you: everything is permissible; at least nothing is disgraceful. There is no atrocity that could make our hair stand on end. Today the place swarms with atheists and people who assert that Christ performed His miracles by the aid of the stars. But who has dared, this long time, to make any head against beauty or art? Am I blaspheming? Pray understand me. I am full of praise for those who devoted themselves to art when it was the possession of a few, and morality sat stolidly entrenched on her throne. But since beauty has been crying aloud in the streets, the price of virtue has gone up. Let me whisper a little piece of news in your ear, Messer Angelo: morality is possible once more!

GIOVANNI (*who had been looking out of the window through his lorgnon*): Wait, Pico! I see some guests down there in the garden—you simply must say all this to them.

PICO (*looking out*): Guests? Why, so there are. They are artists, a whole host of them. There is Aldobrandino ... and Grifone ... and the great Francesco Romano. Talk to them? Not to them, my dear Giovanni. It is not for them. But let us go down all the same. Come, Cardinal—and you too, singer of the glories of the house of the Medici. Let us enjoy ourselves with the brave lads.

POLIZIANO: You hear naught, you will hear naught. But I see sinister things coming to pass.

ACT TWO

The garden. A view of the palace, behind which the open campagna, covered with cypresses, stone pines, and olive trees, melting into the grey-green rolling horizon. A wide centre path, with smaller ones branching right and left, flanked by hermæ and potted plants, runs from the house to the front of the stage, where it opens into a rondel, with a fountain in a stone basin, where water-

lilies float. Right and left front stand marble benches shaded by flat bowers of foliage like little canopies.

1

A group of eleven persons appear on the left-hand path and move forward, in lively conversation. They are the painter and sculptor Grifone, a fair man who walks with a bent, slouching gait—he wears a beard and has large bony hands; Francesco Romano, an impressive figure with a capacious forehead like a Roman portrait bronze, full, smiling mouth, and black, animal eyes which rove calmly from side to side; Ghino, blue-eyed, boyish, and sunshiny; Leone, with a round head like a fawn's, a powerful nose, little eyes set close together, and a satyr-beard through which one can see his curling lips; Aldobrandino, a noisy swaggering fellow with a red, smirking face; the embroiderer Andreuccio, a man already grey and with a gentle, feminine air; Guidantonio, the cabinet-maker; Ercole, the goldsmith; Simonetto, the architect; Pandolfo and Dioneo, of whom the one makes arabesque sculpture and the other portrait busts in wax. With the exception of Ghino, who is rather a dandy, they are negligently and comfortably dressed, with headgear of varying sorts, square, round, and peaked. As they come forward on the middle path they are discussing with some excitement, pushing each other out of the way, approaching their faces to each other, and gesticulating.

ALDOBRANDINO: We shall see, we shall see the face Lorenzo will make! I am his friend, I am justified in hoping that he will see me avenged.

GUIDANTONIO: If I were you I would not make so much noise about the beating you got.

ALDOBRANDINO: Nobody is talking about a beating, you numbskull. It was a buffeting.

GRIFONE: On my soul, you are right, there. The crowd gave you such a plenty of buffets that you could drive a donkey to Rome with them.

ALDOBRANDINO: Shall I pass them on to you, you funny man, you Jack-of-all-trades? They were buffets—and even had they been a beating they could not have shaken the honour of a man like me! The silly mob had been stirred up by that owl of a Fra

Girolamo, an ignoramus who knows as much about artistry as an ox does about playing the lute. What does he want anyhow? Can I paint the Madonna looking a ragged old woman as this prayer-mumbler demands? No, I must have colour, I must have brightness. And since the Holy Virgin will not do me the honour of sitting for me, I must be satisfied if a mortal maiden will serve my turn.

LEONE (*delighted*): "Serve his turn"—if a maiden will serve his turn—oh, you sly fellow!

ALDOBRANDINO: You are pleased to be very merry, my dear Leone. However, everybody knows that your pretty little Lauretta, who is sitting as your model for the Magdalena, promptly bore you a child. But you probably have some charm against beatings.

GRIFONE: Buffets, buffets! We do not speak of beatings.

LEONE: That is different. I did not take her to sit for the Magdalena and then abuse her for my own pleasure; I keep her for my pleasure and happen to be using her for a model. That is very different—the Madonna could take no exception to that.

ALDOBRANDINO: But Brother Girolamo can, you numbskull, and that's enough, in these days.

ERCOLE: Yes. God keep us, he is so strict, he would give Saint Dominic himself the strappado for nothing at all. He pretends to the people that like Moses he has spoken face to face with God; since then they listen abjectly to him; he can say anything he likes.

SIMONETTO: That is true. We saw today in the Duomo how horribly he sat in judgment upon Madonna Fiore.

DIONEO: Where is she? Does anyone know where she is?

PANDOLFO: She is with the Magnifico, telling him the whole story.

GUIDANTONIO: No, she cannot be in Careggi yet. Before we came away she was seen in the city.

ALDOBRANDINO: Messer Francesco, you stand there and say nothing, as your way is, smiling as usual too. But the world knows that your house is furnished in pagan style, like an ancient Roman's, and that your paintings are a different kind from the blessed Angelico's.

GRIFONE: You are furious because it was you who received the beating.

ALDOBRANDINO: Oh, Grifone, not for nothing are you nicknamed Buffone, for you are indeed but a buffoon. You can do nothing but organize pageants and wait upon princes with your jests; and so you are annoyed with me because I am a clever painter. Sew ass's ears on your cap, fool! I go now to the Magnifico.

ANDREUCCIO: No, wait, listen! Lorenzo is very ill; we may not crowd in on him as we used to, like carnival masks. When we came, I saw the Cardinal at the window. He made a sign as though he would come down. We ought to wait.

GHINO (*in a loud, clear voice*): Listen to me! We must go at the business all together. The guild of Florentine painters must lodge a protest against Brother Girolamo with the Council of Eight. And those of us who belong to Lorenzo's musical club must combine to demand that the Ferrarese's mouth be stopped.

ALDOBRANDINO: You may do as you like. But I shall appeal to Lauro alone. He is master, the priest is not. Those scoundrels who dared to lay their filthy hands on me—he will have their ears cut off, he will order them trussed up outside the palace. I am his best friend, he loves me, I came back from Rome expressly because he was ill. I came back from Rome in eight hours!

GRIFONE: What! In eight hours from Rome?

ALDOBRANDINO: Yes, in seven and a half.

GRIFONE: What, what? And Lauro's best friend? When is he supposed to have distinguished you thus? And did not I come back from Bologna and Rimini, where I have work at the court, on purpose because of his illness?

ALDOBRANDINO: Silence, buffoon! You hate me, I know, you are my deadly enemy, because you are from Pistoia, and our subject, whereas I am a Florentine and by birthright your overlord.

GRIFONE: What, what? My overlord? You are a braggart. A beaten braggart!

ALDOBRANDINO: Draw, draw, you empty-headed fool, draw the sword at your side and defend yourself or I will murder you with no more ado. I have been mortally insulted and am ready to commit a frightful deed.

ANDREUCCIO: Stop! Keep the peace! Look over there!

LEONE: By Venus! By the Mother of God! It is she—she comes!

GHINO (*rapturously*): Let us salute her! Let us all serve her!

2

A gilded and decorated litter, hung with lanterns and silken curtains, comes to a stop at the back of the stage. Fiore descends, casts a glance over her shoulder at the group of artists, and signs to the bearers to carry it away. She stands still for a moment, then comes slowly front, in the attitude Pico has described, with arms bent at right angles, hands folded before her, slender, straight, with her head back and her eyes cast down. She has a splendid and curiously artificial beauty. The impression she gives is of height, slenderness, symmetry, poise; she is almost masklike. Her hair is confined in a thin veil, from which it flows down upon her cheeks in blond, regular curls. The brows above her rather long eyes have been artificially removed or made invisible, so that the hairless part above the drooping lids seems drawn upwards with a searching expression. The skin of her face is taut and as it were polished, her delicately chiselled lips are closed in an ambiguous smile. About her long white throat is a fine gold chain. She wears a gown of stiff brocade, with tight, dark sleeves a little slashed. It is so cut as to make the abdomen prominent and is open at the breast to display the laces of her bodice.

THE ARTISTS (*pressing towards her with loud homage, some of them even kneeling and raising their arms in greeting*): Hail, Fiore! Hail to our divine mistress! Hail!

FIORE (*still without raising her eyes, with chill authority, so quietly that all grow still as she speaks*): You will lay aside your weapons.

ALDOBRANDINO: Yes, mistress! We will put them up—see, they are gone.

FIORE: You call yourselves artists?

GRIFONE: Madama, you know well that we are artists.

FIORE: But it seems you yourselves know it not, since you are capable of taking something very different so seriously. (*Pause.*) A light art, a childish art, that leaves untasked so much blood, so much virility.

ALDOBRANDINO: Mistress, I have been mortally insulted.

FIORE (*scornfully and still very softly*): Oh, of course, then, if you were mortally insulted—

GHINO: You speak very strangely today, madama.

FIORE: Really? Do I confuse you? Do I confound your feeble brain, poor thing, poor little . . . Let me see, what is your name?

GHINO (*offended*): You usually know me.

FIORE: It is true. You are Ghino, the amiable Ghino, the perfect cavalier, Ghino the dancer, who always smells so sweet. One hears that even your horse is scented when you ride out. And over there is Guidantonio, who makes the beautiful chairs. Look, and there is Leone. Good day, sir. I hope you had a delightful night. . . .

ALDOBRANDINO (*unable to keep still*): Madonna . . . you too have been mortally insulted today.

FIORE: I insulted? By whom?

ALDOBRANDINO: Dear and most beautiful lady—this friar. . . .

FIORE: What friar? A real story-book friar? Oh, I know. Did I not see you today in the cathedral? And you? And you? I went to amuse myself. You were quite a sight. I saw you go white up to your eyes.

ALDOBRANDINO: With anger, lady, with anger.

FIORE: Of course. You could not even compress your lips—you felt quite weak with the strength of your heroism. I saw.

ALDOBRANDINO: The villain! The Jew! The knave—who dared to slander you—

FIORE: Hark, what a fine flow of words! Before long you will equal your Frate himself, my stout Aldobrandino. Come, join in, you others! Do not lag behind. It will mightily relieve you to rave, for your wrath in the cathedral left you no strength for deeds.

ALDOBRANDINO: Deeds! By all the gods, madonna, you do ill to mock us. Just now before you came we were taking counsel how to put a stop to this abuse. But what can we do? Lorenzo loves us; but a word from you carries more weight than all our protestations. If you so willed, the doom of the Ferrarese would be sealed. They would cut off his tongue that slandered you, batter in his chest as he deserves—in short, they would kill him.

FIORE (*with a sudden outburst of violence*): Kill him, then! (*With a swift movement she has drawn a stiletto from her bodice and holds it out to Aldobrandino.)* Do you see this dainty little weapon? Here at the tip the blade is a little brown. . . . Take it! The stain is from a powerful potion in which I have dipped it. One scratch is enough. Take it! Instead of standing there rolling your eyes. Take it. Ghino the *preux chevalier!* Or you, Guidantonio, maker of beautiful chairs! Or Francesco the Roman! You that look like a butcher of antiquity. He is only a feeble priest. . . .

ALDOBRANDINO: Madonna, we could not get to him. He stops in San Marco. And the people love him. . . . And he is guarded when he goes to the Duomo.

FIORE *(looking at him)*: He is coming here.

THE ARTISTS *(together)*: He is coming here? Who? Who?

FIORE: Brother Girolamo. Here. Today.

ALDOBRANDINO: Brother Girolamo . . . coming here?

FIORE *(puts away the dagger; in a changed voice)*: I was jesting. I was having my joke with you. No, it is not true—a fantastic idea! Brother Girolamo—here!—Let me now take my leave of you.

ALDOBRANDINO *(still a little out of countenance)*: You are going to Lorenzo?

FIORE: Lorenzo lies groaning in his bed. It goes very ill with the great Lorenzo. I feel like walking a little in the garden.

GHINO: And may we not enjoy the delights of your society?

FIORE: All praise to your courtesy. But even at the risk of seeming moody and unsocial in your eyes I would forgo the treasure of your company. *(She withdraws.)*

3

GHINO *(returning after having escorted her a little way)*: She is magnificent, she is divine, she is marvellous beyond all belief!

GUIDANTONIO: Well, she was not too polite about getting rid of you.

GHINO: That is nothing. Nothing at all. One is in raptures, just seeing her.

ALDOBRANDINO: One is in raptures if she takes the smallest notice of one. And if she will not, one struggles even more to win just a single second of her attention, to lure from her one single smile, one nod of approval. If we watch ourselves we shall find that we think of her when we work. It is her beauty that moves us to create. . . .

THE OTHERS: Yes, yes!

ALDOBRANDINO: Ye gods, how happy must he be to whom she belongs, before whom she kneels, by whom she was subdued!

ERCOLE: Did you hear how strangely she spoke of Lorenzo?

SIMONETTO: All that she said was strange to hear.

ANDREUCCIO: All that she said seemed to conceal something else.

LEONE: She asked me how I enjoyed last night. That was rather strong.

ALDOBRANDINO: She may say anything. She says the most impudent things in so charming a way that it is like angels' music.

PANDOLFO: I did not know that she was armed.

DIONEO: A dangerous mistress!

ALDOBRANDINO: She is a bold, mature, and independent woman. The weapon suits her gloriously.

ANDREUCCIO: Perhaps it was the very tool with which her father once threatened the Medici, when he was exiled, in Luca Pitti's time.

LEONE: I did not believe that story. I do not believe that she is the natural child of any exiled nobleman. When Zeus dethroned Chronos he robbed him of a member, an important one, and threw it in the sea. So strangely wed, the sea brought forth—our Lady.

GRIFONE: Not bad! In that case she would be a pretty age!

LEONE: Do you know how old she is? No one knows. If it is possible for her to age she conceals it well.

GHINO: That is true. They tell wonderful things about her beauty lotions and potions. They say she stays all day in the sun, to bleach her hair. They say that she even paints her teeth.

ALDOBRANDINO: Many people say that she uses magic. They tell it for a fact that she has bewitched Lorenzo, so that he is consuming himself with love of her. She boiled the navels of dead children in oil taken out of the sacramental lamps and gave them to him to eat.

GRIFONE: Rubbish—I don't believe any of that.

ALDOBRANDINO: You do not believe any further than the end of your nose, and you are proud of it! It is true, people are enlightened enough today not to take everything for gospel truth, as they used to. But there is such a thing as going too far. I don't believe in transubstantiation—no, it is a ridiculous doctrine, and my cousin Pasquino, who is a priest, told me expressly that he does not believe it either. But that there are witches in Fiesole and many courtesans resort to magic arts to ensnare men are proven facts.

LEONE: Proven facts! All women are witches—I know it, I!

ALDOBRANDINO: Believe me, there are miracles in the world, and if I cared to tell—

GHINO: There is our worshipful Lord Cardinal.

4

Cardinal Giovanni, Pico della Mirandola, and Angelo Poliziano walk down the centre path from the palace. Poliziano has a peaked cloth cap on one side of his head, Pico a round head-covering turned up a little in the back. There are lively greetings; on the part of the artists a sort of intimate or ironically exaggerated respect. They group themselves easily on the seats at both sides and on the border of the fountain.

GIOVANNI: Greetings, gentlemen. We find you in weighty converse?

ALDOBRANDINO: Philosophic matters, questions of faith, revered sir. We were discussing the supernatural.

PICO: About which, I trust, your views accord with the teachings of Holy Church.

ALDOBRANDINO: Absolutely, illustrious sir! In all essentials, perfectly. I think I may call myself a pious man. I observe the usages of religion and always when I finish a painting I burn a candle. I was at the sermon in the cathedral today. But I got a sorry reward, my dear sirs, let me tell you that!

GIOVANNI: A sorry reward? How so, Aldobrandino?

ALDOBRANDINO: I will tell you, worshipful sir; I will tell you and your glorious father, for to that end I came hither. I have been mishandled.

POLIZIANO: Mishandled?

GUIDANTONIO: The populace beat him, before the cathedral, after the sermon.

POLIZIANO: After the sermon? (*Reproachfully, to Pico*) My good Lord!

PICO: They beat you, Aldobrandino *mio?* Come hither. Where have they struck you? Who has struck you? Tell me all.

ALDOBRANDINO: That will I, sir, and my own innocence will leap to the eye. Well, I was in the cathedral, where I had managed to get a small space to set my feet. It was frightfully hot in the press, I could scarce breathe and the sweat poured off me; but what will not one endure for the glory of God?

PICO: And to satisfy one's curiosity.

ALDOBRANDINO: Of course. I wept a good deal too, though I could not even see Brother Girolamo from where I was. But everyone was weeping and it was edifying to the last degree. I was most shocked at what occurred with Madonna Fiore; and I had scarce recovered from my surprise when I heard Brother Girolamo talking about art and pricked up my ears with a vengeance. His point of view is strange, it differs from mine in essentials. He said that it is wrong and wicked to paint the blessed Virgin in sumptuous robes of velvet, silk, and gold, for so he told us angrily, she wore the garments of the poor. Very good; but what if the garments of the poor have not the faintest interest for me? What then? I have the greatest respect for the Holy Virgin—may she pray for me, poor sinner, before the throne of God! Amen, amen! But when I am at work I am less concerned with her than I am that a certain green should look well next a certain red—you can understand that, my Lord!

PICO: Certainly I can, my Aldobrandino.

ALDOBRANDINO: But he maintains that it is vicious, and a mortal sin, to paint prostitutes and dissolute women and give them out as Madonnas and Saint Sebastians as we do today. He demands that it be punished by torture and death. Well, all Florence knows that I have just finished a Madonna for which a very beautiful girl sat to me, who lives with me for my pleasure. Laugh at me if I am boasting, sirs, but it is a glorious painting. I wrote a sonnet about it when it was done, and while I worked upon it I constantly felt that a halo of light hovered about my head.

PICO (*gravely*): You are right, Aldobrandino, your Madonna is a masterpiece.

ALDOBRANDINO: Pico Mirandola, you are a great connoisseur,

I bend my knee before you. Good. Well, when the sermon was over and I was outside in the crowd that accompanied the father back to San Marco, some scoundrel looks me in the face and cries: "Here is one of those sons of Belial who paint the Madonna as a prostitute!" And at that the whole crowd turned against me in a brutish rage, struck at me with the peaks of their hoods, belaboured me with their elbows, almost trod me underfoot—I could not raise my arms, my whole body was tightly wedged in. I spat in the face of the man next me, but that was a poor defence. It is a miracle, I tell you, that I escaped with my life. God must desire me to make a few more things of beauty, since He saved me.

POLIZIANO: You see now, my Lord, to what we have come?

PICO: That I knew nothing, my Aldobrandino—that I could not come to your aid! For I cannot have been far off.

ALDOBRANDINO: Let me have my arms free, my Lord, and I need no saviour. I have a stout heart in my breast, as I have shown in more than one adventure. I have defended myself against three—it was yesterday it befell me, on my way from Rome, where I had commissions. You know that I hurried hither without stopping, on account of my patron's illness. Well, I was not far from Florence; already I could see in my mind's eye the gate of Saint Peter Gattolini. It was growing dark; I was on foot and alone. I was striding vigorously through the pass you know when two villainous-looking creatures, who had been hiding in the bushes, flung themselves upon my path, and as I turned I saw a third behind me. Do you understand what the game was? Three rogues tall as cypress trees, fearful to behold, armed to the teeth. They may have been bravoes hired by envious rivals, or common thieves with an eye on my money—in any case my situation was desperate. "Well," thought I, "if I must die, they shall not get my life for nothing!" I drew most nimbly, set my back to the wall of the defile, struck up a *Miserere* at the top of my lungs, and when the first one made a pass at me I dealt him such a blow on the head that the sparks flew out of his eyes and he sank lifeless to the ground. The others were seized with terror at my ferocity. They crossed their arms on their breasts and begged me of my mercy to let them go—which I did, in charity, as a Christian man. So they made themselves scarce, with the corpse of their accomplice, while I continued on my journey safe and sound.

GRIFONE: Now, by all the angels, what a thumping lie!

ALDOBRANDINO: God send me my death with a plague of tumours—

PICO (*coolly*): Oh, are you there, Grifone? I overlooked you until now. Seems to me, though, you ought to be on your travels?

GRIFONE: So I have been, and in your service, my Lord. What a memory you have! I *was* on my travels. I got back only yesterday. I have been given honourable and important commissions. I have arranged a pageant for the Malatesta in honour of the name-day of his illustrious wife; also Messer Giovanni Bentivoglio found employment for my diverting talents. A witty and generous prince! He gave me a present of doubloons to sit at table and imitate all the dialects of Italy or assume the facial expression of various famous men. It is undeniable, my Lord, men like me must go a journeying to learn to set off their talents. In Florence there is already too much wit. But in Lombardy or the Romagna one can come into one's own.

PICO: I congratulate you. But tell me—you are a painter, are you not?

GRIFONE: Certainly, my Lord, that is my trade.

PICO: And it happens from time to time that you paint a picture?

GRIFONE: From time to time. Yes, my Lord, it happens. But not often, since I am active in so many fields. Lately I have been making violins, that is a joy. But first and foremost I am a designer of carnivals, the organizing of festivals is my proper sphere of art. I have hurried hither to Florence because the May-day festival in Piazza Santa Trinità is close at hand. Good God, it is the eighth of April, high time to begin! Easter is not far off either; and I must think up something new for the next carnival.

PICO: But it seems to me carnival is just over.

GRIFONE: Yes, it was a little while ago. But my friends and I are racking our brains over the next one. The carnival procession, my Lord—Orpheus with his beasts, Cæsar with the seven virtues, Perseus and Andromeda, Bacchus and Ariadne, all that is stale as nuts. The crowd whistles and boos when we serve it up such stuff. And now, after our Procession of the Dead—truly I am at a loss.

PICO: Florence counts upon your creative energy. But I was talking with Aldobrandino, and you interrupted us. Retire, my friend.—Aldobrandino, let us return to your affairs. If I understand you, you are come to complain to the Magnifico....

ALDOBRANDINO: By my salvation, my Lord, that I am!

PICO: Do not, Aldobrandino, I implore you. You shall have satisfaction—or, rather, you bear your satisfaction within yourself. A man like you! So exceptional an artist knows that the esteem of all knowledgeable men is on his side. What do you care for the ephemeral hatred of the ignorant herd?

ALDOBRANDINO: Yours are glorious words, my Lord. I only—

PICO: But as for Lorenzo, he must on no account be disturbed. You know that he is ill—in what degree one dares not think, who loves him. It is essential to shield him from aught that might cloud or weaken his spirits....

ALDOBRANDINO: If that is so, I gladly spare him, though it is ill to forget an injury which one has borne in silence. But the gods know that I love him in my heart above all men.

PICO: Well said, my Aldobrandino. You are a shrewd and industrious man. Keep your word and it shall bear fruit....

POLIZIANO (*at some distance, to some other artists*): Truly, dear friends, we know nothing. We await the judgment of the doctor from Spoleto on the effect of the precious draught.

ANDREUCCIO: It is desirable that we should be able to spread good reports about the city. The people are restless.

GUIDANTONIO: Yes, they are in pessimistic mood. Evil signs have been seen.

GHINO: In the lion's cage at the palace one of the animals tore another to pieces. There are people who put a sinister interpretation on that.

ERCOLE: Some purport to have heard the saints sighing at times in the churches.

SIMONETTO: Many witness to it. And a fruit-seller in Piazza San Domenico swears that the Madonna in his shop has several times rolled her eyes.

ALDOBRANDINO: Quiet there, let me speak. All that is nothing compared to what I have seen. This morning when I was taking a walk outside the gates, it rained blood.

GRIFONE: Nonsense. It never rains blood. There is no blood in the clouds.

ALDOBRANDINO: My Lord Giovanni, will you instruct this

heretic that according to our holy religion such a thing is quite possible?

GIOVANNI: Possible or not, when my father is well again it will rain good Trebbiano, a liquid which for my part I greatly prefer.

ALDOBRANDINO: To blood. Aha, that is capital! Liquid! Trebbiano is a liquid, of course, but the joke is to call it one.

ANDREUCCIO: No, no, gentlemen, the thing is that the Padre prophesied the death of the Magnifico. That is what makes the people restless.

PANDOLFO: The scoundrel! He sings the same dirge in every sermon. And threatens war, starvation, and pestilence to boot.

ANDREUCCIO: He has a saturnine temper.

DIONEO: What rubbish! It is hatred speaks out of him, green-eyed envy.

ERCOLE: All the Ferrarese are avaricious and envious.

ANDREUCCIO: You cannot say that he is avaricious. He brought back poverty into San Marco and goes about in a worn-out habit.

LEONE: Do defend him, Brother Andreuccio the art-embroiderer. You are an old woman.

GUIDANTONIO: Easy to see he has made an impression on you. You belong to the Weepers, the bead-tellers, the head-hangers.

ANDREUCCIO: That I do not, certainly not, dear friends. But my mind is full of misgiving, and my heart is heavy. You know, gracious Prince, and you, Lord Cardinal, that I not only serve the arts with my hands, making beautiful embroideries and carpets, but also sometimes speak in public in favour of the manual arts and the beautifying of our whole life. Everything, it has seemed to me, must become art and good taste under the house of the Medici my masters. And I still think so. But there is a thorn in my flesh. You see, not long ago I was speaking to a great concourse of people about the artistic progress that has been made in the production of gingerbread; for, as you know, we now make gingerbread in all sorts of charming and amusing shapes, after the modern ideas. Well, Brother Girolamo must have got wind of my dissertation, for when I attended one of his last sermons in the Duomo he came to speak of it and looked at me as he did so. He said that whoever tried to turn higher things into common things had no conception of their significance; that it is frivolous and childish to talk about making beautiful gingerbread when thousands have not even the coarsest bread to eat to satisfy their hunger. The congregation sobbed and I hid my face. For his words are like whizzing arrows, my lords, they hit the mark! Since then I have been going about grieving and in doubt; for I know not whether my work and my activity were right all this time, or wrong.

POLIZIANO: Shame, shame, Andreuccio! You have not the heart of an artist, else you would not give ear to this creature who daily calumniates art with his vulgar hatred.

ANDREUCCIO: Does he hate art? I do not know. He speaks lovingly of the work of the blessed Angelico. Believe me, his thoughts are on fire with inward fervour. (*With an effort*) Suppose he has such reverence for art that he thinks it blasphemous to apply it to gingerbread?

ERCOLE: Whoever can understand that may! What I understand is that this loathsome mendicant friar would like to suppress all joy and light-heartedness in Florence. The feast of San Giovanni is to be abolished, the carnival—

GRIFONE: What, what? The carnival?

ERCOLE: Yes, he wants to abolish it. You would have to look to it, Grifone, how to earn your bread, after that. You will have to start painting pictures.

GIOVANNI: Come, tell me more about him. I want to hear what else he says. He is a most extraordinary man.

GUIDANTONIO: Well, I can assure your Eminence that the Frate uses some pretty strong language. He treats the Pope more scurvily than a Turk, and the Italian princes worse than heretics. He prophesies a speedy fall for you and your family; prophesies in a roundabout and uncanny way. He speaks of certain great wings which he will break. He speaks of the city of Babylon, the city of fools, which the Lord will destroy; but everybody knows that he means your father's house and his power. He describes precisely the architecture of this city: he says it is built of the twelve follies of the godless—

GRIFONE: Wait! What? Twelve follies? That would be something for my pageant. Listen! (*Pleased and excited, he draws aside another artist and begins to talk and gesticulate to him.*)

GHINO: I, your Eminence, have received the commission from the printer Antonio Miscomini to make woodcuts for the new edition of the Frate's works.

POLIZIANO: What? And you have accepted the commission?

GHINO: Certainly.

PICO: He was right, I think, Messer Angelo. The dissertations on prayer, humility, and love of Jesus Christ are capital literary performances. And they will be enhanced by Ghino's pictures.

GHINO: That last was not Brother Girolamo's view, I may say. Imagine: he protested against the adornment of his works. He wanted no pictures. Did you ever hear the like? But Signor Miscomini was shrewd enough to insist that the book have a suitably elegant appearance. I ask you: who would read a book today that has no satisfaction for the eye and only contains the bare text? I have already finished some quite good things for it, I shall cut the Frate's seal in wood—

GIOVANNI: What is his seal?

GHINO: A Madonna, your Eminence, a Virgin with the letters *F H* on either side.

LEONE: Now I know why Lorenzo cannot endure Brother Girolamo. Or at least he has always done his best not to leave any virgins in Florence. (*They all burst out laughing.*)

GIOVANNI (*slapping his knee in his relish of the joke; then, quite touched*): Come hither, Leone. That was very good. No Medici could resist it. Here, take this ducat, you long-nosed satyr. You may model me, if you wish. I like you well.

ALDOBRANDINO: That is all very fine, but after what has happened, Ghino, you must refuse the commission.

GHINO: Refuse it? A commission?

ALDOBRANDINO: Beyond any doubt. I have been insulted. In my person our whole craft is insulted, and the Frate incited to the insult. The devil can illustrate his books for him, but not one of us. You must decline.

GHINO: Not at all. Are you mad? What are you thinking of? I should refuse such a fat offer as that? Miscomini isn't stingy with his pay; he knows that he has made a tidy sum with the Frate's writings. They go everywhere. Everybody will see my woodcuts. I shall have much praise and get fresh orders. I need them, I must live. I have social obligations. And my little Ermelina wants presents, otherwise she goes with a shopkeeper behind my back. I have to bring her a silk cap, a horn of rouge and white lead if I want her to be yielding to me. I need money; I take it where I can get it.

ALDOBRANDINO: Traitor! You have no honour in your whole body. I spit on you—I despise you from the bottom of my heart.

GHINO: Ridiculous! I am an artist. A free artist. I have no opinions. I adorn with my art what is given me to adorn and would as leave illustrate Boccaccio as our holy Thomas Aquinas. There are the books, they make their impression on me, I give out again what I have received, as best I can. As for views and judgments, I leave them to Fra Girolamo.

ANDREUCCIO (*broodingly*): But hard, hard it must be, a lofty and painful task that you commit to him. To have to deal with and judge of everything, of all life and morals—seems to me it needs great courage—and freedom.

POLIZIANO: Freedom, Andreuccio? Your mind is confused. Ghino calls himself free and he is right, for the creative man is free—he over whose birth Saturn presided will always be at odds with the world in whatever state he may have found it. But truly it is better to be able to make a chair or anything of beauty than to be born to set things right.

PICO: Well, I do not know. As a collector and amateur I prize things according to their rarity. In Florence there is a legion of brave fellows who can make beautiful chairs; but only one Brother Girolamo.

POLIZIANO: You are pleased to be witty, my Lord.

PICO: No, I am serious.—Who is that coming?

5

PIERLEONI (*comes hastily through the garden from the palace, beckoning as he comes. His long robe makes him take tiny steps. He is an eccentric old man, in clothing that suggests the charlatan and magic-worker. He wears a peaked cap and has a short ivory wand in his hand.*): Lord Angelo! Messer Politian! He is asking for you.

POLIZIANO: Lorenzo! I come!

PIERLEONI: He wants you to recite to him. He has thought of a passage in your *Rusticus* and would like to hear it from your lips.

PICO: So he is awake, Messer Pierleoni? He is conscious?

PIERLEONI: He was, just a minute ago. But God knows if he will not have forgotten his wish and himself again by now.

POLIZIANO: And the draught? The healing draught of distilled precious stones? Did it help?

PIERLEONI: The draught? Very much.... I don't mean that it helped Lorenzo, exactly. Most likely the reverse. But the man who brewed it, Messer Lazzarro from Pavia, him it helped very much, it brought him in a fee of five hundred scudi.

(*Giovanni giggles.*)

PIERLEONI: You laugh, Lord Giovanni. You spirits are blithe. But I get red with anger when I think that this ignorant impostor from Pavia got away unpunished. Why was he called in? They did not ask me, they went over my head. He got a double handful of pearls and precious stones delivered to him out of the household treasury, among them diamonds of more than thirty-five carats; he certainly stuck half of them in his pocket, then he ground up the rest and dissolved them and gave our master the brew to drink, without even taking count of the position of the planets, for he has no knowledge of astral influences, whereas I never order a powder or apply a leech without carefully noting the position of the planets....

PICO: You are a great and learned physician, Messer Pierleoni. We know that our illustrious master is well looked after in your hands. But now tell us, instruct us, remove us out of our uncertainty. What is the illness that has laid Lorenzo low? Give us its name. A name can be so consoling!

PIERLEONI: Mother of God, console us all! I can name you no name, my good Lord. This sickness is nameless, like our fears. If one give a name, it sounds short and dreadful.

PICO: You wrap yourself in silence, entrench yourself behind riddling words, and have done ever since the hour when my friend took to his bed. I insist on knowing: is there a secret here?

PIERLEONI (*breaking down*): The weightiest.

PICO: I will confess the suspicion which I have had long before today and which must overwhelm everybody who sees matters from close at hand. Lorenzo, like every strong man, has enemies.

PIERLEONI: He was never strong. He lived despite himself.

PICO: He lived like a god! His life was a triumph, an Olympian feast. His life was a great flame blazing boldly and royally to the skies. And one fine day this flame dwindles, crackles, smokes, smoulders, threatens to die down. Between ourselves we have seen the like before; such surprises are not foreign to our time. We have heard of letters, of books, the confiding receiver of which read himself over into the kingdom of the shades without knowing it; of litters wherein one sat down a joyful man and descended pining and plague-stricken; of dishes in which the hand of some generous friend had mingled diamond-dust so that the eater got an indigestion for all eternity.

GIOVANNI: Very true. Very true. My father always took these things too lightly. One should taste no banquet in the house of a friend without taking at least one's own wine and cellarer along. Certainly no good host is annoyed at that. It is a well-established custom.

PICO: In short, Pierleoni, my friend, be open with us. Speak as a man among men. Are my fears justified? Plays poison a rôle in the affair?

PIERLEONI (*evasively*): Poison—that depends . . . that depends, my dear sir. Will you follow me, Messer Angelo? (*He bows and withdraws. Poliziano joins him; they move quickly down the garden.*)

6

PICO: Strange old man!

GIOVANNI: Things look bad. I am afraid, I feel sad. If my father only did not roll his eyes so strangely . . .

ALDOBRANDINO: Do not grieve, your Eminence, dear Lord Giovanni. If the illness is strange, so also shall be the cure. There are extraordinary cures. Just listen what once happened to me. It will distract you. I am often ill, as sensitive people always are; but once, some years ago, I was mortally so. The trouble was in my nose, a gnawing pain inside that noble organ. No doctor knew what to do. All internal and external means had been sought in vain. I have even used the excrement of wolves with powdered cinnamon dissolved in the slime of snails and I was completely exhausted from blood-letting. But the air passages were closing and I thought there was nothing for it but I must suffocate. Then in my hour of need my friends took me to a master of the secret sciences, Eratosthenes of Syracuse, a marvellously skilled necromancer, alchemist, and healer. He examined me, spoke not a word, put five different kinds of powder in a pan and lighted them. He said an incantation over them and left me alone in his laboratory. Then there arose so frightful and irritating a smoke that I completely lost my breath and thought I should die upon the spot. I summoned my last ounce of strength to reach the door and escape. But when I stood up I was taken with such an immoderate sneezing as I have never had in all my life before, and as I shook and quivered from head to foot, there came out of my nose an animal, a polyp or a worm, as long as my middle finger, very ugly, hairy, striped, all slippery, with suckers and pincers. But my nose was free, I breathed in air and realized that I was entirely cured.

PICO (*looking down the garden to the right*): Listen, Vannino, I must leave you. I see your brother Piero. You know I do not love his ways. Let me avoid him. I will see if they will let me in to your father. Farewell, we shall see each other soon. Good day, my lords. (*He goes.*)

GIOVANNI: Well, and the worm, the polyp, Aldobrandino? Did you catch it?

ALDOBRANDINO: No, it got away. It ran into a crack in the floor.

GIOVANNI: Too bad. You could have tamed it and taught it to do tricks, perhaps.

7

PIERO DE' MEDICI (*comes with rapid, imperious gait along the right-hand side path. He is a tall, strong, supple youth of one-and-twenty years, with a smooth, well-proportioned, arrogant face and brown curls, falling thick and soft at the nape of his neck. He is armed with dagger and sword, and wears a velvet cap with an agraffe and plume, and a tight blue silk doublet fastened in front with quantities of little buttons. His bearing is offensive, his speech loud and commanding, his whole personality uncontrolled and violent.*): Giovanni! Where are you? I am looking for you!

GIOVANNI: And lo, you have found me out, Piero. What is the good news?

PIERO: You have company . . . have you been here long?

GRIFONE: About an hour, your Excellency, or thereabouts.

PIERO: Then it seems to me that at the moment you are not needed further. If you should wish to take leave you will not be hindered. (*Stamping with his foot*) You are invited to go to the devil!

ERCOLE: Your Eminence, we crave your permission.

GIOVANNI: God be with you, dear friends; do not go far off. I am convinced my father will ask for you. Farewell, Aldobrandino ... Grifone ... Francesco. ... (*He accompanies them as they go, then returning*) You do wrong, Piero, to treat such distinguished men as you did.

PIERO: I should not know how otherwise to treat buffoons and suchlike of the artist tribe.

GIOVANNI: Yes, you see, that is wrong. In every artist, it may be, there is something of the fool and the vagabond, but that is not all of him, for each is after all something of a leader who directs the taste of the many into fresh channels and, so to speak, puts in currency new coinage of pleasure.

PIERO: Glorious leaders, forsooth! This Aldobrandino—

GIOVANNI: Yes, yes, this Aldobrandino. I admit that I like best the society of his sort. The humanists are tedious and irreligious, and the poets for the most part pathetic and conceited; the artist is my man. They are cultured without being tiresome. They dress well and they have wit, originality, and a sense of fitness. And what mobility, what lively fantasy! Messer Pulci has no more, I declare. Before you can say a rosary this Aldobrandino can kill you three giants, make it rain blood and blow monsters out of his nose, without entertaining a single doubt of the truth of his boasts.

PIERO: You are welcome to all the pleasure you get out of it. But I must speak to you alone and so I made bold to send your friends packing.

GIOVANNI: You want to speak to me? I have no money, Piero!

PIERO: Don't lie! You always have money.

GIOVANNI: By the blood of Christ, I have had large expenses—for musical instruments and for a dwarf Moor, the quaintest creature on the face of the earth. Should you like to see him? Come, I will show him to you. Why stand here and talk of money—

PIERO: I need some. You must lend me for a little while.

GIOVANNI: I can't, Piero. Certainly not. The little I have I must keep together.

PIERO: Your Highness is probably saving up for the Conclave? But it is not your turn yet, most illustrious prince of the Church. You cannot vie with Roderigo Borgia. They say he sends asses laden with gold to those cardinals whom he has not yet poisoned, to attune the Holy Ghost in his favour. Your Eminence will have to have patience.

GIOVANNI: What are you talking about, Piero? Of couse I shall have patience. I am hardly seventeen. But the growth of simony is a very interesting subject, which I should like to discuss with you.

PIERO: Well, I need a hundred ducats, to buy a horse to ride at our next tourney, the second day of Easter week—

GIOVANNI: A hundred ducats! You are stupid. A horse—when you have so many horses! And your silly tourneys! How you can be so mad about them! Running at each other and getting hurt—no sense in that. Did you ever read that Cæsar or Scipio rode tourneys? Such a dangerous passion! Petrarch—

PIERO: A fig for your Petrarch! I would not take advice about a knightly and elegant career from a sonnet-tinker like that. The times are past when the princes of Italy and Europe considered us shopkeepers and money-changers; they were past when we learned to wear armour and bear a lance. Our court shall lag behind none other in Europe—and what is a court without tourneys? Anyhow, will you advance me the hundred ducats or not?

GIOVANNI: No, Piero, certainly not. It's no good. Don't be angry, but giving you money is like pouring into the cask of the Danaids. You squander it all with your boon companions and your fat cows—

PIERO: What—fat cows?

GIOVANNI: A phrase all Florence knows. You do not seem to be informed about the latest witticisms. And besides, you are so far in the hands of usurers that you do not spend a florin without it costing you eight lire. Where will that end, I should like to know? The times are bad enough, anyhow. The sparrows on the house-tops know that our house has been going to the dogs since Grandfather died. They say that our banks in Lyons and Bruges are shaky. People are whispering that the bank of deposit for the dowries of burghers' daughters has had to limit its payments because Father spent a lot of the money for works of art and festivals. Many people have taken that amiss.

PIERO: Taken it amiss! Who dares grumble? The factions are scattered, the refractory have been consigned to exile or a dungeon. We are masters. Today it is Lorenzo, tomorrow or day after it is myself. Then, trust me, there will be an end of small shopkeeping. If the banks crash, let them. I'll give them a kick to finish them. The important thing is landownership. We must get more and more property. We are princes. Charles of France called my father his favourite cousin—he must call me his brother! Just let me be master once! Not a law shall be left that gives the people the shadow of a right or even seems to set limits to our will. We will have no nobility near the throne. There will be confiscations, condemnations. Lorenzo has never gone about this matter firmly enough. He has been too poor-spirited to give our position the title it deserves. I do not care to be the first citizen of Florence; duke and king is what they shall call me throughout Tuscany.

GIOVANNI: Ah, your Grace, your Majesty!—You are a braggart. Is that all your political theory you are showing off? Are you so sure that Madonna Fiorenza will take you for her lord and lover, when our father—which may God forbid—is dead? You have a wonderful understanding of physical exercise and affairs of gallantry; but your knowledge of public matters is to seek. Did you know that Brother Girolamo preaches against you? That the people cannot stand you? That they stick up lampoons against you on the palace?

PIERO: Listen, my lad, I advise you not to make me angry. Give me the hundred ducats I need and keep your political dissertations to yourself.

GIOVANNI: No, Piero. I gladly give you my blessing; receive it, dear brother, I pray you. But I lend you no more money. Finis, signed and sealed.

PIERO: You mule! You Sodomite! Sanctified son of a pig! What prevents me from boxing your ears, you purple ape!

GIOVANNI: Nothing prevents you, you are quite vulgar and ungentle enough. So I will go away and withdraw myself from the vicinity of your bad manners. You will find me with our father if you should be looking for me to beg my pardon. Farewell. (*He goes off up the centre path.*)

PIERO: Go, go, you weakling! Red hat on your head, wet

swaddling-clouts on your breech! I do not need you. Soon I shall be master; then the rejoicing world will see a prince to make its teeth chatter! Wagons ... wagons ... towers on wheels ... a swaying, shimmering purple progress in the dust, between carpets, under awnings, through the heart of the yelling mob! Youths poising lances, on prancing, whinnying steeds ... flying genii strewing roses ... Scipio, Hannibal, the Olympian gods descending to pay homage, rolling up to the triumph of Piero the divine! ... And on a gilded car high as a house—I, I! The orb of the earth revolving at my feet, Cæsar's laurel wreath on my brow, and in my arms she ... my creature, my handmaid, my blissfully blushing slave ... Fiorenza. ... Ah! ... You are there, madonna?

8

Fiore has appeared on the right-hand path and now stands in the centre one, her hands folded on her advanced abdomen, her head thrown back, and her eyes cast down, calmly symmetrical, in mute and mysterious loveliness.

PIERO (*going up to her*): Is it you, madonna?

FIORE: You behold me in the flesh, noble sir.

PIERO: I was unaware of your nearness. I was busy with my thoughts.

FIORE: Thoughts?

PIERO: Still I will say that I am glad, that I am inexpressibly rejoiced, to meet you.

FIORE: I beg you, spare me. I am a woman, and such words in the mouth of the glorious Piero must abash any woman. ...

PIERO: Most gracious Fiore! Ravishing Anadyomene!

FIORE: Audacious flatterer! The Grand Turk sent us some of his sweets, and when I ate of them after the meal I thought there was nothing sweeter on earth. I think so no more, now I have heard your words.

PIERO: Sweet simpleton! Come, we shall chat, you and I. ... What would I say? ... It grows cool. ... You have been walking in the garden, lovely Fiore?

FIORE: Your keen perceptions have told you as much. I walked between the hedgerows. And gazed sometimes out into the country, to see if guests were coming from the town, one guest perhaps, to bring a little diversion to the villa. . . .

PIERO: Yes, yes . . . I quite understand your longing for variety, beautiful lady! Nothing more fatiguing than a country sojourn, since Lorenzo got the bad idea of stopping in bed. Just between us, I am surprised that you have not sooner thought of having a change.

FIORE: What do you mean, my Lord?

PIERO: I mean—I mean, sweet Fiore, that you would not have far to seek to find people downright willing to take over the sweet duties of which my father has seemed now for a while no longer capable. Your beauty blooms untasted, your mouth, your bosom orphaned. . . . Be assured, not you alone are vexed. Look up and see a man who yearns immoderately to be in every way of service to you.

FIORE: Forgive me, the sight is not novel enough to lure my gaze from the ground. All long for me; do you say it of yourself in hope to win me?

PIERO: In hope? Am I a boy? Am I a tyro in the lists of love? I would and shall possess thee, divine creature. . . .

FIORE (*slowly lifting her eyes and looking with inexpressibly languid contempt into his face*): If you knew how you weary me!

PIERO: What are you saying? In my arms you would forget your weariness.

FIORE (*repulsing him scornfully*): I will not belong to you, Piero de' Medici!

PIERO: Not to me? Why not? I am strong, you would have naught to complain of. I control the wildest stallion with my thighs, needing no saddle nor bridle. I have challenged the best players in Italy to wrestling, to ball, to boxing, and you have seen that I was victor. If you will lie with me, sweet Fiore, I will tell you of my triumphs in the gymnasia of Eros.

FIORE: I will not belong to you, Piero de' Medici.

PIERO: Hell and Hades, does that mean that you scorn me?

FIORE: It means that you bore me inexpressibly.

PIERO: Hearken, madama, I speak to you as to a lady whose charm and culture one considers, but I am not minded to whimper after your love as though you were a bashful and dutiful burgher's wife. If you would play the prude, it will but sweeten my love; but I beg you not to ask me to take your cruelty to heart. Who are you, to give yourself the air of repelling my advances? You are of noble Florentine blood, but your father begot you without priestly blessing and died in exile as a reward for his bargain with Luca Pitti. You live and confer your favours in the service of Aphrodite; and Lorenzo conceived you as a partner of his pleasures when they were feasting him in Ferrara. You need not doubt that Piero will know how to reward you for your caresses as richly as Lorenzo.

FIORE: I will not belong to you, Piero de' Medici.

PIERO (*furiously*): To whom, then? To whom? You have another lover already, you shameless courtesan?

FIORE: I will not belong to you, Piero de' Medici.

PIERO: To a hero? I am a hero! Italy knows it.

FIORE: You are no hero; you are only strong. And you bore me.

PIERO: Only strong? Only strong? And is not the strong man a hero?

FIORE: No. He who is weak, but of so glowing a spirit that even so he wears the garland—he is a hero.

PIERO: You gave yourself to my father—is he a hero?

FIORE: He is one. But another has arisen, to tear the garland from him.

PIERO: You? You? I will have you. Who is he, who is he, the weakling with the glowing soul, that I may flout him, and choke him with two of my fingers?

FIORE: He is coming. I have seen to it that he should come. They shall confront each other. But as for you—withdraw, when heroes quarrel!

PIERO (*raging*): I will have you, I will have you, sweet insolence, flower of all the world—

FIORE: You will not have me. You bore me. Make way, that I may go and await your father's rival.

ACT THREE

A room adjoining the sleeping-chamber of the Magnifico. In the background, left, between heavy half-open portières, a view of the bedchamber; steps occupy the rest of the rear of the stage, leading up to a gallery. Centre left a splendid marble chimney-

piece with a relief supported by columns, and the Medici arms. In front of it chairs. Left front an étagère with antique vases. Right front a door hung with a gold-embroidered tapestry. Right back a curtained window. Between door and windows, drawn a little forward, a bust of Julius Cæsar on a pedestal. Smaller busts, without pedestals, on the chimney-piece and above the doors. Slender columns are let into the walls. The subdued light of the late afternoon sun filters through the window curtain.

1

Lorenzo de' Medici sits in a high-backed arm-chair in front of the fire, asleep, with his head on his chest, a cushion at his back, and a rug over his knees. He is ugly; with a yellowish-olive complexion and a sinister expression due to the wrinkles in his brow. He has a broad, flat face with a flattened nose and a large projecting mouth with flabby wrinkles round it. His cheeks are marked from nose to fleshless chin by two deep slack furrows; these are the more prominent because he cannot breathe through his nose but must keep his mouth open. Yet his eyes as he awakes are clear and full of fire despite his weakness and seem to seize upon men and things with vigour and avidity. His lofty and speaking brow triumphs over the rest of his facial ugliness; his motions are the perfection of aristocracy. Sometimes a charming expression of fascinatingly innocent merriment comes out upon his ravaged features, seeming to purify them entirely and give them a childlike look. He wears a voluminous fur-bordered garment like a dressing-gown, closed high round his short neck. His hair is brown, with white threads; it is parted in the middle and waves against his cheek and neck. He speaks with studied clarity, in a nasal voice.—Watching his uneasy sleep are Pico della Mirandola, Poliziano, Pierleoni, Marsilio Ficino, and Luigi Pulci. Old Ficino has the worn face of a scholar, a withered neck, and scant white locks coming out beneath his pointed cap; he wears the usual voluminous garment closed to the throat and sits in the centre of the room, surrounded by the others. Pulci, a comic type, with little red-rimmed eyes and inflamed pockets beneath them, a pointed nose, prominent ears, and a mole on his cheek, is pressing his finger to his lips as he gazes with the others into Lorenzo's face.

PIERLEONI (*going cautiously up to the invalid and feeling his pulse*): It is very irregular. I am considering whether this is not the time to bleed him once more.

PICO: You will kill him with your blood-lettings. It is not twelve hours since you took a basinful from him.

PIERLEONI: The man does not need a tenth of the blood he carries round with him.

POLIZIANO: Where is his spirit? It seems to move upon strange paths far from ours. I would gladly hear your opinion of its experiences, dear Marsilius.

FICINO: It is likely that at this hour contact with the divine unity is established in his brain.

PULCI (*lowering his strident and comically cracked voice*I: Look, look, all that is mirrored upon his countenance! I wager that he is dreaming the most extraordinary things. If he feels no pain, then I envy him. The fever causes the strangest fancies, far better than are produced by strong wine. Sometimes one may dream in verse, but is prone to forget it.

PIERLEONI: This sleep is not the sort that feeds the natural resources of the man. If his faintness continue, then I must hold the little fingers and toes of His Magnificence while I anoint his heart and his pulse with the oil which I have ready here.

PICO: Hush! He is stirring, he wakes.

PULCI: He will tell us of his adventures.

FICINO: Do you know us, Laurentius, my dear pupil?

LORENZO: Water.... (*They give him to drink.*)

LORENZO: The water-seller had a skull....

POLIZIANO: What water-seller, my Lauro?

LORENZO: Angelo ... is it you? Good, good, I will control myself. Shall not one master this madness? I met a water-seller with his laden ass and full jugs; but when he put a wooden goblet to my parched lips there was fire in it and on the villain's shoulders sat a grinning death's-head.

PULCI: Well, that is a modest invention.

LORENZO (*recognizing him*): Good day, Morgante. Are you there, old good-for-nothing? And my Pico with the ambrosial locks? And even great Marsilius, wooer and messenger between me and wisdom—you are all with me, friends. The frightful old man was only in my own blood.

PULCI: A frightful old man?

LORENZO: Rubbish! Worthless rubbish! I dreamed so hard of a bald-headed old man who wanted me to ride in his rotten bark...

POLIZIANO (*shaken*): Charon?

LORENZO: I was asleep.... What time is it?

PICO: You slept about an hour. It is three o'clock. The sun has begun to set.

LORENZO: Already? (*Seized by sudden unrest*) Listen, my friends, I should like my carrying-chair. The air here is stifling. ... Carry me ... carry me into the loggia; take me up on the battlements....

PIERLEONI: Dear and gracious Lord, that would be folly. You need rest.

LORENZO: Rest? I cannot rest. Why can I not rest, doctor? Why do I feel that I must strain myself to think and arrange manifold matters before it is too late?

PIERLEONI: You have a little fever, my Lord.

LORENZO: I do not deny it. But I would say that the fever is no ground for my being tortured by these ridiculous fears. You see, I think logically. But I do not conceal that I am heavy with cares. I have never pretended—Pico, there are no more Pazzi in Florence, are there? And the Nieroni Diotisalvi are either in exile or put safely away?

PULCI: Save those you sent to hear the grass grow!

LORENZO: Yes, come here, Margutte! Make jokes, you wild rhapsodist! Yes, in truth, much blood has flowed. It had to.—I implore you, Pico, for the time I am not able, to keep an eye on the collections in Via Larga and the villas. You will do it for me? A couple of lovely little trifles, two terracottas and a medallion, have just been acquired; they must be kept in Poggio a Cajano, you know, my dear fellow? And the Sforza has presented me with a glorious antique from Pesaro, an Ares with breastplate. It should be set up in my public garden and serve the young sculptors as a model. Will you see to it? Thanks. That is all that was troubling me.—Is Angelo here still?

POLIZIANO: Here, my Lauro.

LORENZO: Angelo, the Pliny which my grandfather got from a cloister in Lübeck is in the Signoria, is it not? I should like to see it. It is bound in red velvet with silver mountings. Let a responsible person go at once—no, wait. That seems to me less important than something else on my mind. Wait. One of my searchers has been offered a Cato manuscript for five hundred gulden. I am in doubt over the genuineness of the script. There are cases where some rascal has made up something out of his own head and put it on the market under an ancient name. I beg you to test the manuscript very carefully and if it be genuine procure it for me without bargaining. They must not say that I let a Cato escape me. May I burden you with this?—You lift a load from my heart. Come, my friends, now I feel easier. I can think of nothing to depress me. Let us talk. Let us discuss. Who was greater, Mirandola, Cæsar or Scipio? I say Cæsar, and ye shall see how I defend my thesis! But our great Marsilius Ficinus wants an abstract theme, of course!

FICINO: Let your mind have repose, Laurentius! You will wear yourself out.

LORENZO: Wisdom is worthy the sacrifice of one's last strength. There is so much to clear up! It often used to seem to me as though everything lay clear and open before me; but now I see only darkness and confusion. How is it with the immortality of the soul? Tell me!

PULCI: An old, a treacherous question—and not to be answered *ex abrupto* like that. They say that Aristotle himself, even in the kingdom of the shades, was still going about with equivocal phrases, in order not to commit himself—though he was as dead as a door-nail and yet alive. Let anyone try to make it out from his writings!

LORENZO (*laughing heartily*): Good! But now, Angelo, say something serious.

POLIZIANO: You are immortal, my Lauro! Must I tell you so? Not everybody is. Not the masses, not the small and unknown man. But you shall share the enlightened society of the laurel-crowned spirits.

LORENZO: And why I?

PICO: Now, by the blue-eyed Athene! You have written carnival songs which I have not scrupled to place above Alighieri's great poem!

FICINO: You have divine origins, forget it not. The six balls in your arms signify the apples of the Hesperides, where your stock had its rise.

POLIZIANO: They will know how to welcome you, singer of the "Rencia", *pater patriæ!* They will celebrate your coming. Cicero, the Fabians, Curius, Fabricius, and all the others will surround you and lead you into the hall of fame, which echoes with the music of the spheres.

LORENZO: That is poesy, poesy, my friend! That is beauty, beauty—but neither knowledge nor consolation!

PULCI: Yes, yes, it is a little thin, your music of the spheres, Messer Politian. It is small comfort. Do not die, Lauro, it would be stupid. You know Achilles' answer, when Odysseus visited him in Hades and asked how he fared. "I assure you," said he, "that we departed have the strongest desire to return to life." The body, lad! The body is the main thing. The body cannot be substituted for by any music of the spheres! Oh, forgive me! Are you worse?

LORENZO (*very pale*): Doctor—a coldness is coming round my heart—do you hear? A horror seizes upon me—help! It is death. ... What does it mean, that suddenly all power is gone from my brain and my entrails? I am lost ... I am forsaken. ... Dry the sweat from my brow. ... Do not despise me. My spirit is steadfast, this fear is in my body.

PIERLEONI: It is nothing. Drink this good beaker of Greek wine. I have been begging your Magnificence to go to bed.

LORENZO: If you want me to be able to breathe, let me sit in a chair. I must see about me all you who love me. I must hear your voices. Death is horrible, Pico. You cannot grasp it. No one here can grasp it, save myself, who must die. I have so dearly loved life that I held death to be the triumph of life. That was poetry and extravagance. It is gone, it fails one at the pinch. For I have seen dissolution unroll before me, the decay of the tomb.—Quick, Ficino, quick, dear, wise old Ficino! What have you taught me, that I might face death with fortitude? I have forgotten. What is your uttermost wisdom, Ficino?

FICINO: I taught you that Plato's "Idea" and the "First Form" of Aristotle are one and the same; that is, the sensitive soul, the *tertia essentia* of bodies, which in man, the microcosm of creation, is distinguished from the intellectual soul in that it—

LORENZO: Stop, wait a minute. I am confused. I understood that once; perhaps I felt it. But now I struggle in vain to do so. I am tired. I long to have something simple to hold fast to. Purgatory is simpler than Plato; you will have to admit that, Marsilius. Was it not a Franciscan father who came to me today?

POLIZIANO: Yes, beloved, a confessor came from that order.

LORENZO: A rascal. A clever head. I was ashamed to take the business seriously before him. I turned a few good Florentine phrases when he waited on me with his sacraments and he smiled like the man of the world he was. I confess that the ceremony did not soothe me much. The Father's morals were all too complaisant. He forgave me my sins as though they were boyish pranks. But I doubt if such absolution be quite valid in high places. I might have confessed that I had murdered my father and mother and he would have signed the cross over me with the greatest obligingness. No wonder. I am the master. But when the end comes, there are drawbacks about being the master whom nobody dare offend. I need a confessor who would be as priest what I have been as mocker and sinner.... What is it your eyes say, Pico? You have something in your mind. You are hiding your thoughts.

PICO: What thoughts, my Lorenzo?

LORENZO: You are thinking of a priest who would be fit to be my confessor, who would dare to damn me, who has already dared, Pico....

PICO: What priest—?

LORENZO: *The* priest. What say, Marsilius? The Platonic idea of the priest, become person and will—

POLIZIANO: I implore you, my dear Lord, turn your thoughts to gayer pictures! You cloud your spirits with thoughts unworthy for you to think. Do not forget yourself, Lorenzo de' Medici!

LORENZO: Truly, that will I not. Thanks, my Angelo. I feel better. We will be gay. We will laugh. Laughter is a sunbeam of the soul, so says a classic. We will let our souls shine in the recollection of what has been.

PICO: And what will be again.

LORENZO: Enough that it has been. This was wont to be the hour when we walked together to a spring. You remember? We lay in a ring upon the rolling sward, with the childlike prattle of the water in our midst. And we spent the time till the evening meal with each of us telling a tale.

PICO: What a charming hour! And how we admired you! Perhaps in the forenoon you may have been working out a new law for the statutes, designed to give power more fully into your hands, that you might be in a position to bless Florence still more freely with beauty and joy; perhaps uttered the death sentence upon some noble adversary; argued in the Platonic Academy upon virtue; presided over a symposium in a group of artists and lovely women; at table solved theoretic questions in art and poetry—and in all that you had brought your whole mind to bear and now were sharing the evening play of our minds, as fresh and detached as though you had not given out any part of your vital energy.

PIERLEONI: Yes, you were never niggard with your strength, my gracious Lord.

LORENZO: Was I not, my astronomical doctor? Did I not bend them to my will, despite stars and portents, which had destined me to your careful charge? Yes, I have lived. Come, let us remember. Remember with me, my friends. Remember the drunken starry nights, when we rose from our wine, you, Pico, Luigi, Angelo, you, mad Ugolino, Cardiere the ecstatic musician, and all the rest—when singing and twanging the lute we stormed the sleeping streets and inflamed maidens in their chambers by the verses we sent up to them.

POLIZIANO (*rapturously*): Alcibiades!

LORENZO: And the carnival, remember the carnival! When pleasure like a torrent overflowed the bounds of everyday, when wine ran in the streets and the populace in the squares danced and shouted the songs I composed for them; when Florence surrendered to the god of love, and men's dignity and women's modesty reeled in one intoxicated shout: Evoe! When the holy madness seized even children and kindled their senses to love before its time.

POLIZIANO: You were Dionysus.

LORENZO: And the kingdom was mine! And the sway of my soul went abroad! And the fire of my longing kindled the woman's breast, so that she fell to me, and the ugly weakling became lord of her beauty—

PICO: Lord of beauty—in that name we salute you! Speak not as though you *had been* all that!

LORENZO (*after a moment of silence, gesturing with his head behind him*): Someone wants to come in.

A PAGE (*half-way down the stairs*): Signor Niccolo Cambi has come from Florence and begs to be admitted to your Grace.

PIERLEONI: The Magnifico is receiving nobody.

LORENZO: Why not? Signor Niccolo is my friend. He comes from Florence—I feel quite well. I want to see him.

2

The page conducts the merchant Niccolo Cambi from the gallery down the steps into the room, leads him to Lorenzo, and withdraws with a low bow. Cambi is a citizen, respectable, well dressed, already a little stout, with a lively Florentine face. His shoes and stockings are dusty. He wears a light-grey cloak over darker undergarments.

LORENZO: A welcome visit, Messer Niccolo. Do not take it for discourtesy that I remain seated. I am a little unwell these days.

CAMBI: Enough to see you! To hear your voice again! My heart is lightened thereby. Good evening, gentlemen. You in particular, illustrious Prince, you, Messer Pulci, Master Poliziano! My faith, the great translator of Plato too! Messer Pierleoni! To see you again, Magnifico! To hear you speak! To feel the living pressure of your hand!

LORENZO: Then you had not expected it?

CAMBI: Why not? Certainly, of course.

LORENZO: Sit down. Push your chair close to mine. You rode up? You are overheated; did you ride so fast, then? Are you on business? Messages from Florence?

CAMBI: But why? Must one always have business with you, messages for you, in order to feel impelled to see you? My business is to look you a little while in the eye, witness my love to you, and assure myself afresh of yours. My message, to tell in all the streets of Florence that you are of good cheer, that soon we shall be able to celebrate your return to health.

LORENZO: So Florence busies itself about my illness?

CAMBI: It certainly does! One cannot say that it is exactly indifferent to it, ha ha! The Magnifico is naïve in his question. But I mean to give those rascals the lie who disquiet the people without reason and make them prey to sinister rumours.

LORENZO: There are such rascals, then?

CAMBI: There are, there are! And, Magnifico, you would do well, you would do very well, to put a stop to their activities without delay. I see you up, I see you out of bed—could you not come to Florence? Even for an hour? Just to show yourself five seconds long at a window?

LORENZO: Master Niccolo Cambi, what is going on in Florence?

CAMBI: Nothing, nothing. God keep me! Messer Pierleoni—my visit is untimely. Shall I withdraw?

LORENZO: My desire, my will, are what count here. (*With an effort at gentleness*) You will oblige me very much, honest Messer Niccolo, by speaking briefly and without reserve.

CAMBI: Then I will do so. To whom should one speak, to whom bring these fears and cares, if not to you? Things are not in Florence as they were, Magnifico! Vile machinations are afoot. The source whence these rumours are disseminated is known, which report you to be either already dead or sickened beyond cure: they come from the monkish party, from the "Weepers," from the party of the Ferrarese....

LORENZO (*who has started at mention of the Ferrarese, with forced lightness*): You hear, Pico? They come from your discovery, our monk.

CAMBI: Pardon me, illustrious Prince, it is the truth. I know that you fostered him, that you first drew attention to his strange new works, I know it. And I would not assert, either, that I do not know how to value his gifts. I am not so behind the times. His performances are titbits for a spoilt and licensed taste, that is beyond a doubt. I am not speaking of him. I am speaking of the influence he wields, which is—it is possible—independent of his intentions.

POLIZIANO: Do you think so?

CAMBI: The people, Magnifico, the people! We can afford to smile when young sprigs of the nobility forswear dancing, singing and all frivolity, and enter a cloister. But the people! All day they run irresolute through the streets, they look darkly at the beautiful houses of the rich and know nothing better to do than to throng the cathedral to hear the sermons—a dense, silent crowd, inwardly distraught, a great acreage of muddled heads, all turned in his direction, in the direction of the lean little monk up above them. When the Frate is carried back in triumph to San Marco, the masses choke the streets again and resume their obstinate, mischief-breeding activities. Before the house of Guidi, chancellor of the city archives, and in front of Miniati's the administrator of municipal debts, they have been disorderly and insulting; for Brother Girolamo designated both of these citizens as your tools, Magnifico, as people who connived with you how to squeeze new taxes from the poor for your festivities. Barbarous, insane things are happening. Before I left Florence I heard that a group of mechanics forced themselves into the house of a wealthy and art-loving citizen and broke a statue in the vestibule—*(Pained exclamations from his audience.)*

LORENZO: Hush! An antique?

CAMBI: No, it seems to have been new and not very valuable. But, O Magnifico, it is not that which you must hear! There have been noisy demonstrations before the palace all day. I was in the Piazza, I was present. There were shouts from the people, which I could have wished not to hear, not to understand. It sounded like "Down with the golden balls!"

POLIZIANO: That is treason! That is ingratitude and treachery!

PICO: It is the childish love of the populace for political cries—and nothing more! They should be dispersed with the pikes.

CAMBI: And yet another cry rose above these—a strange cry, never heard before—once, twice, and again. I did not understand, I am as you know a little deaf in one ear. But when I listened very carefully, I heard it clear and plain: *"Evviva Christo!"*

(Silence)

CAMBI: You are silent, Magnifico.

LORENZO: What was the cry?

CAMBI: The one against your arms?

LORENZO: The other.

CAMBI: *Evviva Christo!*

(Silence. Lorenzo has collapsed into the cushions; his eyes are closed.)

PIERLEONI: Go, gentlemen! In God's name, go! You see, he is exhausted.

CAMBI: Magnifico, I wish you good repose. I have done my mission. You had to know how things stand with us. You are not angry?

LORENZO: Go, friend. ... No, I am not angry with you. Go. ... Tell Florence—no, tell her nothing. She is a woman, one must take care what one says or has said to her. She runs after you with burning desire when you seem cool and strong and despises you when you betray that you are lost in love for her. Go, friend, say nothing. Say that I am well and that I laugh at what I have heard.

CAMBI: That will I. By Bacchus, that will I say. That is a good message, by my faith. And so be in good health, Laurentius Medici. And come to Florence so soon as you can. Farewell! (*He hurries off.*)

3

LORENZO (*after a pause*): Pico!

PICO: I am at your side, my Lorenzo.

LORENZO: Look at me. Seems to me you look a little embarrassed, eh, my subtle Pico? What have you to say now?

PICO: Nothing at all. What should I say? The people are drunk—with drunkenness of a sort different from that you have known so long how to cause in them. Tell the Bargello, it will know how to sober them.

LORENZO: Pico! Mæcenas! My subtle innovator! To call in the hangman's services against the spirit? That was not subtle!

PICO: One counsel or the other. Call *him* in, then. Bewitch him. Do you think this petty and solitary soul can withstand the brilliant allurement of your offers of friendliness?

LORENZO: It will, my Pico, it will! I know it better than do you, whose inquiring spirit discovered it for us. It is full of hate and mean opposition. Its gifts do not make it blithe or friendly—only more obstinate. Do you understand that? He did not come to me when he became prior—prior in that San Marco which my own grandfather built. He stuck dumbly to his priestly independence. See, thought I to myself, a stranger enters my house and has not even the decency to pay me a visit. But I was silent. I shrugged my shoulders at the little man's incivility. He reviled me from the pulpit, indirectly and by name. I went—you did not know it—to seek him out. More than once I attended mass at San Marco and afterward stopped some hour in the cloister garden, awaiting his summons. Do you think he paused in his literary labours to be hospitable to a guest who was after all more than a guest? I went further. I am not used to have men deny themselves to me. I sent presents to the cloister and gifts to charity. He took them as signs of yielding and never once thanked me. I let them find gold coins in the offertory boxes. He gave them to the poor-wardens of San Martino; the copper and silver, he said, were enough for the needs of the cloister. Do you understand? He wants war. He wants hostility. Approaches, homage, he pockets, and gives nothing in return. He cannot be shamed. Success does not soften him nor his mood. He came a nothing, a beggar, to Florence. What he is after today is a decision between me and him.

PICO: Dear friend, what fancies! He is ill and wretched. His digestion is ruined, from watching, from ecstasies. He lives on salad and water. May he enjoy them! Is he Lorenzo, who even in suffering is courteous and full of charm? Do you expect pleasant social intercourse with a father confessor? Let him have his way. And let the childish populace have theirs. Any measures you would take would give the situation a serious complexion which it has not got. Only get well, only show your face again to your city.

(There is a general backward movement. A pale and breathless youth, in a distracted condition, appears rushing down the steps. It is Ognibene, a young painter. He leans on the balustrade a moment, quite exhausted, one foot a step lower than the other.)

OGNIBENE: Lorenzo! You are here. Thank God, I have found him. Your Excellency, dear and gracious Lord, forgive me for my urgent haste; I pressed onwards, I would not let them bar the way to you. I must speak to you. I ran—Oh, my God! *(He kneels beside the Magnifico and takes his hand imploringly in both his own.)*

LORENZO: Ognibene! Indeed, you alarm me. No, let him lie

where he is. He has audience. He is a gifted youth and moreover Botticelli's pupil. What is it, Ognibene?

OGNIBENE: I ran—I came—from Florence, from my master's shop. Ah, my master! Ah, the picture! The wonderful, beautiful new picture! Forgive me! I had not time to put on my cloak. I ran as I was. The monk! My master! Lauro, win him back to you!

LORENZO (*in alarm, threateningly*): Pico! ... Hush! I will hear nothing. I will not hear it. Withdraw. ... Speak, boy, speak low. What of Botticelli?

OGNIBENE: You know that he was painting a new picture. What am I asking—he was painting it for you! I was allowed to help him ... and trembled for joy as I saw it grow. Often I slipped alone into the workshop and knelt down in the stillness where it stood and gleamed—it was more beautiful than the Primavera, more beautiful than the Pallas, lovelier than the Birth of Aphrodite. It was youth, it was bliss, it was ravishment, painted with sunshine—

LORENZO: And now? You must part?

OGNIBENE: Since he first heard Brother Girolamo in the cathedral he has worked heavily and without joy. Often he sat silent on a stool with his head in both hands and brooded. And when he raised his head he stared at the picture with eyes full of conflicting horrors. And today—

LORENZO: And today?

OGNIBENE: Today he was in San Marco after the sermon. In the Frate's cell. Two hours or three, I do not know. And when he came home he was as though dead—full of peace, but dead. "Ognibene," he said, "God has called me with a frightful voice. There is no healing in beauty and in the delight of the eyes. Tell the Magnifico that I served Satan and that from now I will serve Jesus the King, whose representative in Florence is His prophet Girolamo. When I take my brush now I will paint in deep humility the Mother of Sorrows—tell the Medici that. Now will I save my soul." And as he said that he took a knife from the colour table and cut and slashed it across and across so that the tatters hung down. ... (*He sobs with his head in his hands, as though his heart would break.*)

LORENZO (*with clenched fists, rigid with pain and rage*): Sandro....

OGNIBENE: Lauro, Lauro, what shall we do? I mean—what does your Excellency command? Will you summon him? Will you speak to him? I think if he saw you—Command me, order me what to do. I will run back. I will bring my master to you despite the darkness. You can do anything. You will lighten and set free his spirit.

LORENZO (*gloomy and exhausted*): No. Let it go. It is too late, for today. I mean, it is too late in the afternoon. Be brave and go. Go to your work. Or to your wine. Take a girl—forget. I would be alone. Go, till I call you. No, Pico, you too. And listen: send me the boys. I want to talk to Gino and Piero. They may come in now. And then go.

(They all leave, some by the stairs, some by the door front right. Lorenzo remains alone, sunk in his chair, clutching the lions' heads on the arms with his emaciated hands. His chin rests on his breast, his gaze seems to burrow deep into his own thoughts.)

4

LORENZO (*dully and brokenly, between pauses*): Jealousy—I have never known what it was.—I was alone. Where was there a purpose like to mine ... a knowledge of power? Here!—Often I marvelled.—And I made it serve.—It was beautiful, here within me.—Distraction—suffering—burning—smiling? All in vain. I hate him. I hate him too. He triumphs. For he is upright. He is effective. He wasted himself, like me, he was not wise. But he had enough left—just enough left, to do it. Perhaps because he is of commoner stuff.—The picture? Let it go. A small matter here—where we are dealing with souls. We are dealing with the kingdom. (*His eyes rest on the bust between the door and the window. He continues to muse. Piero and Giovanni come cautiously through the portières of the door right front, approach him, and kiss his hands.*)

GIOVANNI (*kneeling*): How are you, Father?

LORENZO: Oh, so it is you. You don't often come, gentlemen. Why has one sons? For show? To make an appearance? To make one look more imposing? Just as one marries a wife, of noble Roman blood, marries her in Rome by proxy and gets children with her hardly knowing her, for reasons of ṣtate? Is that the way?

GIOVANN: Father, you have been sincerely in our thoughts.

PIERO: We were impatiently awaiting your summons.

LORENZO: You are most courteous. Very well brought up. It would be exacting to ask more, I suppose. How true it is that father and son are furthest of all from each other. Relations between them are stranger and more uncomfortable than between man and wife. Well, let that be. One must not give anything away. Must not seek love too eagerly. Still, I confess, I have had you in my mind, I have thought of your welfare. That is why I had you summoned. . . . It seemed to me I had a few words to say to you, and that I should like to have you stand before me. You look at me searchingly—how do you find me?

GIOVANNI: Better, Father, much better. You have a little colour.

LORENZO: Really? My friendly little Giovanni. See, I lift my hand. I will to do it, and do it. It trembles—and falls. And falls. There it lies; quite white. I could not hold it up. Come here, Nino; bend over, Piero. I stand with one foot in Charon's bark.

GIOVANNI: No, no, Father! Do not speak like that. Pierleoni—

LORENZO: Pierleoni is a ninny. He and his rival with his draught of precious stones. I am at my last hour. I am going to hear the grass grow, as Pulci says. I am going, and you remain. Now, Piero, what have you to say to that?

PIERO: God grant you a long life, Father.

LORENZO: Very polite. But to come to the point: Are you ready to step into my shoes?

PIERO: If it must be so, yes, Father.

LORENZO: Fiorenza—you love her? Patience a little. My thoughts are confused, that I admit. I see everything in a lurid light, as in a conflagration; one thing flows into another in my mind.

GIOVANNI: Perhaps we ought to go, Father?

LORENZO: Ah, the little one is afraid. No, stay here, Nino. The fever gives me courage to speak out my feelings boldly. What I say sounds odd. But reason is at work. Piero, I speak to you. Your expectancy of power is great, and well founded—but it is not sure, not unimpeachable. You cannot rest idly upon it. We are not kings, not princes in Florence. We have no document on which our power is secured. We rule without a crown, by natural right, by our own strength. We became great of ourselves, by industry, by struggle, by self-discipline; the idle throng stood amazed and then submitted. But such power, my son, must daily be won afresh. Glory, love, the submission of others—these are all false and fickle things. If you think to rule, to shine without shining deeds, Florence will be lost to you. You will hear your name cried aloud, they will strew the laurel at your feet, they will lift you on their shields, recount your great deeds with slavish exaggeration; that is but for the moment, for what you have done up to now; it secures not a single morrow, promises no future like the past—even as they shout you may be losing ground. Be on your guard. Be cool-headed. Be aloof. They think only of themselves. They need to pay homage—homage is so easy to pay! But no one will think of sharing your struggles, your pains, your cares, your own deep fears. Guard yourself from the injurious contempt of these same idle acclamations. You stand alone, you stand entirely by yourself. Do you understand? Be stern with yourself. Do not be rendered soft and careless, for if you do, Florence will be lost to you. Do you understand?

PIERO: Yes, Father.

LORENZO: Count as nothing the outward glitter of power. Cosimo the Great shunned the eyes and the homage of the crowd, that its love might not exhaust itself in acclamations. Oh, how wise he was! How much shrewdness passion needs, to be creative! And you are foolish—I know you. You are too much like your mother. You have too much Orsini blood in your veins. You want to be painted in armour, play the prince in all the streets of Florence. Do not be a fool. Take care! Florence is sharp-eyed and loose-tongued. Be reserved—and reign! . . . Remember, too, that we are of burgher, not noble stock; that we are what we are only because of the people; that our only foe is he who would estrange the people from us—do you understand?

PIERO: Yes, Father.

LORENZO: "Yes, Father." Polite, soothing, knowing better. A perfect son. I am certain you do not believe a syllable. Hearken, Piero, things may turn out badly, I foresee it. We might fall, be driven out, when I am gone. It might be so—be quiet. Florence is false; she is a strumpet. Lovely, indeed—ah, lovely, but a strumpet. She might come to give herself to a wooer who wooed her with scorpions. So, if that should hap, Piero, if the foolish people should rise in wrath against us, then, Piero, listen, save our treasure, save the treasure of beauty which through three generations we have gathered together. I see it spread out in the palace, in the villas. I could touch the marble limbs, drink in with my eyes the glowing colour of the paintings—put my hands on the splendid vases, the gems, the inlay work, the coins, the gay majolica. You see, my children, it was not only my money and my zeal, it was my worth as a citizen I spent upon them. Who does not understand me would condemn. I made no scruple to seize the property of the state when I needed money to pay for my collections and my feasts. Unrighteous goods? Rubbish! I was the state. The state was I. Pericles himself took public money unhesitatingly when he needed it. And beauty is above law and virtue. Enough. But when they rave against it, then, Piero, save our treasures of beauty. Rescue them. Let all else go, but protect them with your life. This is my last will. You promise me?

PIERO: Be without care, Father.

LORENZO: But have a care yourself! Be shrewd. I do not believe you will be shrewd, but that is my advice.—And you, Vannino, my friendly little Giovanni! With a quiet heart I leave you. For you I have no misgivings. Your path is marked out. It will lead you to the throne of Saint Peter. You will add to our arms the triple tiara and the crossed keys. Have you any idea what that means? Why I put that in train with all my skill? A Medici in the seat of Christ? Do you understand? Do not speak. But if you understand, smile with your eyes into mine. He smiles—see, he smiles. Come, let me kiss you on your brow. Farewell. Live joyously. I summon you to no great deeds. You are not made for bearing heavy burdens of guilt and greatness. Keep yourself free of deeds of violence and crime too great for you. Be innocent, be undisturbed. Cover yourself not with blood. Be a happy father to the populace. Let the Vatican ring with merriment and the sound of lutes. Let jests and jollity be the lightnings that flash from the throne of this son of Zeus. May beauty and the arts flourish beneath your staff of power, and joy go out from your throne into all the lands. I have your promise?

GIOVANNI: I will ever be dutifully mindful of your words, dear Father.

LORENZO: Then leave me now. And thanks to you both—go now. I am very weary. My soul yearns for deep stillness. Farewell, my sons. Love one another. Think of me, and farewell.

(The brothers quietly leave the room by the same door. Giovanni with a charming gesture makes way for Piero to pass.)

5

LORENZO (*alone*): "Yes, Father." He understood not a word. I was talking to myself. It has not eased my mind. There is one to whom to speak out all one's mind would avail. Impossible. Ah, Florence, Florence! If she were to yield herself to him, this frightful Christian! She loved me, she for whom we wrestle, this sombre monk and I. O world! O deep desire! O love-dream of power, sweeter, more consuming—one must not possess. Longing is a giant's power, owning unmans. Our bliss was mutual so long as my slender strength sufficed. The wanton responds to the hero's mighty charms. Now that I am broken, she despises me.... She is vulgar, boundlessly vulgar and cruel. Why do we vie for her favour? Ah, I am weary unto death!

(Fiore appears in the background, at the top of the steps; her hands crossed over her abdomen, artificial, symmetrical, mysterious. From where she stands she flashes a quick glance across at Lorenzo from beneath her lowered lids, then descends slowly into the room, with a smile.)

FIORE: How goes it with the Lord of Florence?

LORENZO (*starts and struggles to sit upright. A painful, pathetic smile spreads over his features*): Well, very well, excellently well, my beauty! Is it you? I am well. Why should I not be so? Did I seem a little absorbed in thought as I sat here? I was composing a poem. I was conceiving a little sonnet to the exquisiteness of your nostrils when they dilate in mockery. And since I was composing poetry, it follows I am well; I am as sound as a fish swimming in its native element. For he who versifies thereby evinces a plenitude of fancy.

FIORE: Then I congratulate you.

LORENZO: And I thank you, my gracious goddess. I do not see

you; yet your sweet, cool voice laves and refreshes my heart. And now, now I will see you; ah, your loveliness! Will you sit down beside me? Here on this stool? Though it would be more fitting were I to take my place at your feet. You see, they have left me alone—and I complain not. Indeed, I may have sent them on their way, I needed them not. I could meditate more profoundly upon your charms, and love you better, being alone.

FIORE: So you still love me, Lorenzo de' Medici?

LORENZO: Love you still? I should perhaps love you no more. You do not know that all the strength of my being and my understanding are consumed in love of you?

FIORE: Then I do not understand why you do not stir out of your cushions to make fêtes for me.

LORENZO: Fêtes? Certainly. But—fêtes—you see, I am a little tired.

FIORE: Of me?

LORENZO: Sharp and sweet! I love your scorn.

FIORE: How should you be tired, if not of me?

LORENZO: Permit me to lay my hand upon your brow. It is hot, is it not? This fever—Pierleoni says it comes from the unfavourable position of Jupiter and Venus with respect to the sun and to each other, which is harmful to me. Pierleoni knows nothing. This fever inflamed my blood when I first caught sight of you, when my soul first comprehended all your charms. Since that hour it has not ceased to glow. Do you remember? Ferrara? The Duke came to meet me on the Po in a gilded gondola, surrounded by gay little barks where banners fluttered, music sounded, and I was greeted by a choir of singers. The shores were strewn with flowers, the statues of the joyous gods gleamed white; and between them stood slender boys holding garlands in their hands. But every bark bore a lovely woman, adorned each differently, for these were the cities of Italy, who came to meet me. And one, one I saw among them all, laurel in her hair and lilies in her hand; and the minstrels sang to me in saucy strophes: "Thou are Fiorenza, thou, the only one, the sweet one, the glory and the brilliance, the love and the power, the goal of yearning, thou the flower of the world, thou wilt be mine. . . ." I looked at you and pain seized my heart, an ache, a deep oppression and a stubborn grief—what shall I call it? A longing for thee! For thee! To possess thee, thou flower of the world, thou many-hued seduction, and of thee to die!

FIORE: Poor victor! What would you not give to receive this pain back again for your weariness!

LORENZO: I feel it. It never left me again. Does one possess you? Does the struggle to win you ever end? Is there ever repose in your arms? ... You came to me, you wonderful creature. Do you remember the evening after the fête? You came. ... You came in to me through the marble doorway. And when for the first time I embraced you in the golden darkness of the room and won your lips with my mouth—then I felt the dagger you carry in your bodice and thought of Judith. Your father hated us Medici. He joined the Pitti, we sent him away to misery, and his exile saw your beauty reach its flower. Perhaps you only gave yourself to be revenged? Perhaps in the moment of deepest desire the poisoned death found its mark? How often, let us be never so drunken with love, I searched your unfathomable eyes, listened to what lay behind your cool and polished words. ... Have you ever loved me? Ever loved anyone to whom you gave yourself? Or do you only out of curiosity obey the power of desire, which may never slumber satiated, which having once possessed must ever be born anew, if it will not lose you ignominiously? For him, madonna, who has once tasted of your charms, there can be no more repose, in conning either memories of the past or dreams of the future. Only a constant, piercing present, wakeful, fateful, perilous, and—consuming.

FIORE: Hearken, my Lord Lorenzo. I am not come to argue with you about the art of love. I am a woman; yet it often seemed that you laid stress upon my view and voice even in serious matters?

LORENZO: Speak, I beg you.

FIORE: Well, then, I came to express to you my astonishment at the negligence with which you look on at the evil course which public affairs are taking. ... You have never heard of a monk. Hieronymus Ferrarensis by name and Prior of San Marco?

LORENZO (*looking at her*): I have heard of him.

FIORE: And heard that he subdues the city to himself with words, brings youth to his feet, makes artists repent in sackcloth and ashes, stirs up the populace against you and your rule, and lets himself be the object of worship as envoy of the Crucified?

LORENZO: I have heard of it.

FIORE: Indeed—and you suffer all this mildly, sitting in weakness amid your cushions?

LORENZO: If Florence loves him, I cannot and I will not hinder it.

FIORE: He insults Florence.

LORENZO: And Florence loves him for it.

FIORE: Would you endure to have him insult me too?

LORENZO: Did he do so?

FIORE: I will tell you all the tale from the beginning. It lies further back than events in Santa Maria del Fiore.

LORENZO: You were in the cathedral?

FIORE: Like the rest of the world.

LORENZO: You went often to the cathedral?

FIORE: As often as it pleased me. And from a curiosity better grounded than that of others. I know this monk from early days.

LORENZO: From early days?

FIORE: From days when your glory's crown still hovered invisible high above your head. It is quickly told. At Ferrara, near the hut where my father and I found refuge from your bravoes, there lived a citizen named Niccolo, learned, wealthy, and of ancient lineage, in favour at court. He lived there with his wife, Monna Helena, and two daughters and four sons. The eldest son had gone for a soldier. I was a child still, or almost a child, twelve years, thirteen—yet I was already beautiful (if you can believe it) and youths gazed after me. I was on friendly terms with my neighbours. We visited each other, we talked at the windows, walked together in summer outside the city walls, played games in the fields, wove wreaths for each other's heads. But one of our neighbour's sons shut himself away from our merry company, the second eldest, about eighteen years old, I think: small, weak, ugly as darkness. He feared people. When all Ferrara streamed out of doors to the public festivals, he buried himself in his books, played mournful melodies upon his lute, and wrote what no one was allowed to read. They thought to make a physician of him, and he applied himself to the study of philosophy, sitting in his little chamber bowed over Thomas Aquinas and the expounders of Aristotle. Often we teased him and threw orange-peel through the window on his writing-desk; he would look up with an uneasy and contemptuous smile. Between us two, things stood very strangely. He seemed to flee the sight of me with fear and loathing, yet to be condemned to meet me for ever, indoors and out and everywhere I went. Then he seemed to play the coward and avoid me, yet he would force himself, pressing his thick lips together as he came towards me, passed and greeted me, blushing red and bending on me a sour and injured gaze. In this wise I came to understand that he was in love with me, and I rejoiced in the power I had over his gloomy arrogance. I played with him and led him on, I gave him hope and dashed it with a look. It thrilled me to know that my eyes could control the flow of his blood. He grew more lean and silent still, he began a fast that hollowed out the caverns of his eyes; one saw him sitting long hours in church, bruising his brow against the altar step. But one day, out of curiosity, I brought it about that he was alone with me in a room at twilight. I sat silent and waited. Then he groaned and was as though pulled towards me, and whispered and confessed. I made as though astonished and repulsed him; he seemed then to rave, almost like an animal, begging me with gasps and panting with parched lips to yield me to him. With horror and disgust I thrust him from me—it may even be I struck at him, since he would not leave his avid clinging. And when I did so, he tore himself away and stood up with a shriek, inarticulate and hoarse, and rushed off, his fists before his eyes.

LORENZO: I understand, I understand.

FIORE: He was named Girolamo. That night he fled to Bologna, and entered a cloister of Dominicans. He preached repentance in unheard-of accents. Folk laughed, they stared, they were subdued. His name went through all Italy. And your spoilt curiosity, gentlemen of Florence, drew him hither. And he waxes great in this Florence.

LORENZO: You have made him great.

FIORE: I—have made him? Then hear how he rewards me. He has insulted me before the populace, today, in the cathedral ... pointed at me with his finger, spat upon me with words, compared me to the great Babylon, with whom kings have commerce!

LORENZO: Kings! You made him great. Greater than I, to whom you gave yourself.

FIORE: Greater than you? That I find still undecided; it will be decided. Hearken, my friend—if you summoned him? Here before you? Be it only to see how the poor little monk stumbles over the carpet when in the presence of the Magnifico. For his Rhodus would be here. Hear him, answer him. Let him measure himself against you. And if you see his worthlessness, then send him back to his cell, back to his pulpit. Let him insult you further as he will, you—and me. And if you feel his power predominant, then it lies with you to deny it out of existence with arguments of the sternest and coldest. He is in your grasp; if you are a man he will never escape from it. . . .

LORENZO: And if I should shame to employ such arguments? You know that I should thus shame.

FIORE: I know nothing. I wait. I wait to see how each one shows himself. I await the event. From me, indeed, expect no thanks if you feel shame to show yourself the stronger!

LORENZO: He would not come. On what pretext could one call him hither?

FIORE: Indeed, you are very ailing. Have you never lied? You call the priest. You feel ill. You want to confess. You seek for spiritual counsel.

LORENZO: In very truth I seek it. I yearn for it. Emptiness and horror are all about me at this moment. I see you not, madonna. I see not that you are beautiful. No longer do I understand what desire is. I should like to despise you, but I only shudder at you. Whither shall I turn? Call Ficino! Ah, that is naught. Call Brother Girolamo. You are right. Let him come.

FIORE: He is coming.

LORENZO: How then—he is coming?

FIORE: I sent for him to you. I knew you desired him. I sent for him today after the sermon. After he had insulted me. He is on the way. He may be here at any moment.

LORENZO: At any moment. By God, you know how to act! Your zeal for this meeting is great. At any moment . . . the enemy in Careggi! Today, at once. Good, then, let him come. Am I afraid? If he comes I will not send him away. If I will still hear him; it may be the time has come. But first call someone about me. Summon my companions. Have Pico come and the others. (*Fiore touches a bell.*) Thank you, madonna. I love you. I were ill armed against this prophet did I not love you. . . . Ah, there you are, my friends! Lend me yet awhile the pleasure of your blithe company!

6

Pico, Ficino, Poliziano, Pulci, and Pierleoni come down the steps.

PICO: Ah, Lauro! We thought you resting quietly and alone, and you have just finished, so it seems, an appointment and a love-scene. Humble good day, madonna. But, Lauro, seriously: then you must not deny yourself to the jovial youth who have been hours long awaiting your pleasure: a group of artists, with Francesco Romano at their head, Aldobrandino—

LORENZO: He too? Good, good, I will see them. I need them. Let them come. (*A message is sent out by the gallery.*) I am in a good mood, gentlemen. I have had good news. I am receiving a visit. I expect today a charming and famous guest. No, you could not guess. Not even you, Pico. But I await him with impatience and am highly gratified that my artists have come to shorten the time before his entrance to my chamber. There they are. See Aldobrandino's innocent red face. And Leone's amorous nose. And Ghino, the bright darling of the gods. Welcome, children!

(*The eleven artists come in, making low bows.*)

ALDOBRANDINO: Health and blessings to your Excellency!

GRIFONE: Healing and joy to the godlike Laurentius Medici!

(*They press round him, kneel down, or bend over his hand.*)

LORENZO: I thank you. Be sure that I rejoice to see you all. Let me see, who are there here? Ercole, my brave goldsmith, and Guidantonio, who makes the beautiful chairs. . . . Yes, and I see Simonetto, the glorious architect, and Dioneo, who shapes wax in men's images. How is it with art, Pandolfo? I have not said, but I saw Messer Francesco at first glance.

ALDOBRANDINO: Truly, your Excellency, Messer Francesco is a great painter, and despite the closeness of his mouth far ahead of us all in his art; yet in love to you, gracious Lord, not one of us stands behind him, and some, perhaps, might even be before. May

I mention, since it just occurs to me, that I have not long since come back to breathe my native air?

LORENZO: Yes, yes, my good Aldobrandino, you are right. You were away. You were in Rome. I remember quite clearly. You had work there, did you not?

ALDOBRANDINO: I did indeed, sir, and for lovers of art in high places, if I may say so. But then I heard a report that Lorenzo de' Medici, my good and great patron, was not well, and I dropped everything where it was and hastened to Florence with such zeal that I covered the ground in less than eight hours.

GRIFONE: He is only boasting, my Lord; it is shameless of him, I say. Nobody could cover that distance in eight hours; it is a lie.

ALDOBRANDINO: You hear, my gracious Lord, how this man tries to harm me before you and in your eyes.

LORENZO: Peace, children, there is no cause for hard words. Even if it is impossible to come hither from Rome in eight hours. Aldobrandino in saying so merely shows that he wants to give evidence of his love to me, and that in some vivid and poetical way. I cannot chide him for it.

ALDOBRANDINO: That is a splendid setting out, my Lord. But yet you do not know the depth of my devotion, nor what I am ready to do and suffer in silence for you. . . . So much I must be allowed to say, your Excellency. Good, good, I don't want to make a fuss.

GRIFONE: You are right there. We came here on a more important errand. We must discuss the festivities to be arranged in honour of your recovery, Magnifico.

LORENZO: My recovery—

GRIFONE: That is my suggestion—with your magnanimous permission I ask leave to suggest it. We must consider what a fine opportunity Lorenzo's restoration to health gives us for organizing a beautiful pageant and a ball and public banquet afterwards. My head is full of ideas. Let me manage the whole thing and you shall see a fête the printed descriptions of which will spread throughout Italy.

LORENZO: Good, good, Grifone. Thank you, my lad. I will count on you. We will take up the matter together later. Now I must ask what Ercole has been doing since I saw him last. . . . What are you peering about the room like that for, Guidantonio?

GUIDANTONIO: Pardon, my Lord, I was looking at the furnishing. Some of it is good. The chair your Excellency is sitting on at this minute was made by me. A fine piece. But the other things are quite out of fashion and not the height of good taste. I am working on a room for you which shall most wonderfully combine the classic motifs with the most modern comfort. May I bring you the drawings?

LORENZO: Pray do so one of these days. I shall not be able to resist ordering the room, if it is a genuine Guidantonio in taste and comfort. And now, Ercole, let me hear from you.

ERCOLE: I have done only trifles, sir; still, there are pretty conceits among them. A charming set for salt and pepper, with figures and foliage, I made especially for your table. You will pay me anything I ask, so soon as you see it. Also I have made a medallion with your likeness, with Moses on the reverse striking water from the rock. The inscription runs: *Ut bibat populus.*

LORENZO: And it has drunk, the people! Cast me the medal, my Ercole. Cast it in silver and in copper. I must praise it without even having seen it. You have chosen your motto well—*Ut bibat populus.*

ERCOLE: But the finest of all is a little breviary to the honour of God's Mother, with covers in heavy gold most richly worked. There is an image of the Mother of God on the front, you see, in precious stones—they alone are worth six thousand scudi.

ALDOBRANDINO: Pack up, Ercole! Lorenzo will not buy your breviary.

LORENZO: And why will he not?

ALDOBRANDINO: Because he does not care for the sign of the Virgin. At least he has done his best to have as few as possible of them in Florence. (*Laughter and applause.*)

LEONE: What cheek, Magnifico! That is a shameless piece of plagiarism. I made that joke myself an hour ago, down in the garden. I call these gentlemen to witness.

ALDOBRANDINO: You should not make such an ugly display of your envy, Leone. You may have said something of the sort, I admit it. But it was in quite a different connection, and anyhow it shows a bad character to grudge me the applause these gentlemen would pay to my quickwittedness.

LEONE: If Lauro were not sitting here, and Madonna Fiore, you braggart, you, I would tell you to your face that you are an empty-headed rattlepate.

ALDOBRANDINO: And I would counter with the absolute truth that you are like nothing so much as a stinking billy-goat.

LORENZO: Aldobrandino! Leone! Enough! I declare the subject closed. I know that you are both of you very witty. Come here, Leone. Tell us a story. Tell us one of your adventures, you jokesmith, you! We will make up for your lost applause. Look how our mistress prays you with her eyes. She loves your historiettes. And our Messer Francesco—his wishes are written on his face. Would you like Leone to tell us a tender tale—yes or no?

FRANCESCO ROMANO (*rolls his black eyes, simpers, then opens his mouth for the first time and says in a loud, naïve voice*): Yes.

LORENZO (*much diverted*): Did you hear, Leone? The master understands painting better than making words; but what he says is weighty and solid. Impossible to refuse. Begin! Madonna is queen of the day. She summons you, and this noble circle waits to hear.

LEONE: Well, then, listen. But I must beg the learned gentlemen to bear one thing in mind. I talk as it comes to me, without art. I am no tale-writer, I make no fables, nor need to fable as a poet does. A poet, it is well known, loves and enjoys only with his inky goose-quill—but I do it with another kind of productive stub. (*Hilarity, cries of "Bravo!"*) And accordingly I will tell you truly how Dan Cupid has favoured me of late. Listen: I was of late in Lombardy, at the house of a friend, which neighbours a convent famed for its abbess, who lives in great piety and in the odour of sanctity. Now, my friend's cousin, named Fiammetta was a nun in this abbey, and I went with him to visit her one day at the grating. Hardly had I set eyes on her when I was enflamed by love for her youth and beauty and in her eyes I read that I was no less attractive to her. From then on I bent all my powers to see how I could gain her intimacy, and as I am not inexperienced in these matters I had soon conceived a plan to take advantage of the fact that a gardener was needed for the convent gardens. I took the precaution of changing my appearance a little, shaved my beard, put on ragged clothing, and applied to the holy and austere abbess for the vacant place. I made out that I was dumb, a capital idea, since it reassured the chaste madame that I was completely harmless to her flock. I was taken on and went at once to work. And it soon fell out that I met the lovely Fiammetta in the garden, made myself known and explained to her that I was not only not dumb but also not suffering from any other physical lacks—the which she begged me to demonstrate to her more convincingly. And since her desire most fully coincided with mine, she took me into her cell on the first evening that offered, and I remained there the night. And I assure you that whatever skill I lacked in my tasks by day, I was most punctual and adroit at my nightly ones. Yes, the charms of my lovely Fiammetta roused me on more than one night to heroic deeds, and would have gone on doing so, had not envy made an end to our joys. There were two ugly little nuns who had no lovers and had privately to go about as best they could to satisfy their needs. They made the discovery that here in the cloister the goat had been made the gardener; filled with ill will against their sweet sister, they scrupled not to bring their suspicions to the ear of the abbess. In order that no doubt remain, it was decided to take us in the act. They watched; and one evening late, when Fiammetta had opened her door to me, the two envious nuns hastened to the cell of the abbess, pounded on the door, and announced that the fox was in the trap. It may have disturbed the abbess's rest to be thus summoned in the night—as the sequel will show. But at all events she sprang from her bed, flung on her clothes, and rushed with the two spies to Fiammetta's cell. They burst open the door, brought lights, and exposed our embraces to the public eye. Fiammetta and I were stiff with fright. But when I had pulled myself together and looked at the abbess, who was exhausting all the curses and vile names in her vocabulary, I noticed an extraordinary circumstance. The holy female, that is, when she had thought in the darkness to set her hood on her head, had stuck on a priest's small-clothes instead, so that the kneebands hung down on her shoulders in the most singular way. "Madonna," said I, interrupting the stream of her cursings, "will perhaps first button up her headgear and then say on what pleases her to say." Then she noticed what she had done and stood crimson with blushes, for she knew where he was to whom the garment belonged. She rushed off in a fury and with her the two spies, and my Fiammetta and I were left alone to enjoy once more unvexed all the bliss of heaven.

(The general merriment has increased as he talks, certain places being warmly applauded by the artists and humanists. Even Fiore joins in. Lorenzo, completely diverted, has followed the tale with childlike enjoyment. Towards the end of it the whole room resounds with tumultuous mirth. Lorenzo laughs heartily; the artists fit to split themselves. But suddenly the narrator breaks off and there comes an abrupt silence.)

A PAGE *(entering through the curtained door front right, announces in a clear, very audible voice)*: The Prior of San Marco.

(Pause.)

POLIZIANO *(horrified, not trusting his ears)*: What did you say, boy?

PAGE *(abashed)*: The Prior of San Marco.

(Stillness. All present seek Lorenzo helplessly with their eyes. All mouths are open, all eyebrows raised.)

LORENZO *(to the page)*: Come nearer. What do they call you?

PAGE: My name is Gentile, gracious Lord.

LORENZO: Gentile. That is pretty. Go back to the door, Gentile, and come in again. I like to look at you, you walk so well. You have pretty hips. Stand so, as you are. Aldobrandino, notice the line. Take this ring, Gentile, because you have pleased my eyes. And him whom you have announced, let him now come in.

POLIZIANO: You would not!

LORENZO: I will.

(The page goes out. Deathlike stillness reigns. The portière is lifted. The sallow, woebegone, fanatical profile of the Ferrarese is projected slowly into the room. It is irredeemably ugly; its savage expression and large bony structure are in startling contrast to the smallness and sickliness of the rest of his figure. His head is framed in the cowl of the black mantle he wears over his white habit. There is an abrupt depression between the great hooked nose and the narrow peaked forehead. The thick lips are compressed with a sort of finality, emphasized still more by the hollow ashen cheeks. The eyebrows are thick and grow together over the nose, also they are perpetually raised, making horizontal wrinkles in the forehead and giving the little eyes, ringed with the black shadows of exhaus-

tion, a staring and yet vacant expression. He is out of breath from walking at a quick pace through the long passages, but tries to conceal the fact. His hands, now hanging down inside his mantle, look waxen and shake when he raises them. His voice has a nervous, frightened note, yet sometimes inexplicably takes on a hard and savage power.

As he enters, the artists retreat backwards, giving him more than enough room. They form a group; one of them takes his neighbour's arm, turns half round, and stares over his shoulder at the monk, with lifted brows, his lips distorted with amazement, disgust, and fear. They retreat gradually leftwards up the steps and through the gallery, and with them the humanists. Pico is the last to go, casting inquisitive glances back at the group of three persons who remain. At last he goes off, treading softly.

The Ferrarese looks straight ahead and his gaze meets Fiore as she sits in her composed and studied posture at Lorenzo's feet. He starts back, for a moment his face is visited by a tormented expression; then he straightens himself, fixes his eye on Lorenzo, and with his head and the upper part of his body makes a vague gesture of salutation.)

FIORE (*has risen. Her hands are folded on her prominent abdomen, her eyes are lowered as she moves towards the Ferrarese and speaks in a high, monotonous murmur*): Welcome to Careggi, Master Prior. May I congratulate you on your sermon today? I was a little late, yet not too late to hear the best of it. Be assured that I was highly edified. Your performance is very powerful indeed.—Well? Why are you so silent? It is not fitting that an artist should so stiffly and haughtily pocket the praise he gets, without even the tribute of a disclaiming smile.

THE PRIOR (*still breathless, tormented and harsh*): I spoke to you in the Duomo. I will speak to you only from my pulpit.

FIORE (*affecting a pout*): Not everybody is so stern. From the cathedrals of all the arts they speak to me—they make me smile or I give them my ear—and still have enough flesh and blood left over to treat me as a human being.

THE PRIOR: I live only in my pulpit.

FIORE (*pretending to shudder*): So down here you are dead? Ha, yes, so you are. You are pale and cold. I am here in this room with a sick man and a dead man. But once on a time, Mr. Dead Man, a long time ago, you were alive, were you not, and spoke to me here below.

THE PRIOR: I spoke. I shrieked. You smiled. You laughed. You lashed me with opprobrium. You drove me up—up to my pulpit. And now you pay me homage.

FIORE: You use large words. That is the orator's art. I pay you homage? People pay me homage, and I incline to him who knows how to pay it in the best and finest way.

THE PRIOR: I pay you no homage. I revile you. I call you abandoned and an abomination. I call you the bait of Satan, the poison of the spirit, the sword of souls, wolf's milk for him who drinks it, occasion of destruction, nymph, witch, Diana I call you.

FIORE: And you say well. It takes as much talent to revile as to praise. And what if all that seems to me but the last and extremest kind of homage? Can you imagine that? Tell me! You felt it yourself!

THE PRIOR: I understand you not. You heard me in the Duomo. I am unskilled and cannot trifle. But you heard me in the Duomo. The Word is hard and it is holy. He who closes his lips with his finger, Peter Martyr, he is my master.

FIORE: Work and be silent. . . . I find, Magnifico, much resemblance between your guest and Messer Francesco Romano. But, Mr. Dead Man, you came to talk to this sick man here. So I will go, wishing the gentlemen the pleasantest entertainment. I wish you good accord and rich experience. It would seem that it cannot lack.

(She goes up the steps and disappears through the gallery. During the following scene it grows dark.)

7

LORENZO *(seems entirely to have forgotten the Ferrarese, who keeps his burning gaze directed upon him. With bowed head the Magnifico gazes up into space. At length, coming back to himself, he makes a charming effort to assume his man-of-the-world manner and says)*: Will you not sit down, Padre?

THE PRIOR *(tempted by weariness to sink down upon a chair near the door, but recovering himself and standing stiffly erect)*:

Let me tell you this one thing, Lorenzo de' Medici! I have seen the world. I know the treachery of princes, their accustomed practice of bloody violence. If this is a snare, if I have been lured hither to be enforced and done away with—then have a care. I am beloved. My words have won souls to me. The people stand behind me. You dare not touch me.

LORENZO (*suppressing a smile*): You are afraid? But no! Have no fear. It would be far from my mind to lay traitorous hands on a man so extraordinary as yourself. Am I a Malatesta, a Baglioni? You do me less than justice to compare me with these. I am not savage, not without honour. I know how to value your life and work as well as any of your own flock. May I not ask in return that you will look upon mine as direct and fairly?

THE PRIOR: What have you to say to me?

LORENZO: Oh, I have already said some of it. But you speak grudgingly. And you look worn and weary. I do not deceive myself. My eye is sharp for such signs. (*With genuine sympathy*) You are not well?

THE PRIOR: I preached in the cathedral today. Afterwards I was ill. I lay abed. I left my bed only on your summons.

LORENZO: On my—yes, yes, quite right. I am sorry. So your work consumes you, then, so much?

THE PRIOR: My life is tortured. Fever, dysentery, and continuous mental labour for the weal of this city have so weakened all my internal organs that I can no longer bear the least hardship.

LORENZO: By God, you should spare yourself—you ought to rest.

THE PRIOR (*scornfully*): I know no rest. Rest the many know who have no mission. For them it is easy. But an inward fire burns in my limbs and urges me to the pulpit.

LORENZO: An inward fire—I know, I know! I know this fire. I have called it dæmon, will, frenzy—but it has no name. It is the madness of him who offers himself up to an unknown god. He despises the base, cautious, home-keeping folk and lets them stare amazed at one for choosing a wild, brief, burning life instead of their long, wretched, frightened one.

THE PRIOR: Choosing? I have not chosen. God summoned me to greatness and to pain and I obeyed.

LORENZO: God—or passion. Ah, Padre, we understand each

other. We shall understand each other.

THE PRIOR: You and I? You blaspheme. Why did you send for the priest? You who have worked evil all your life long!

LORENZO: What do you call evil?

THE PRIOR: All that is against spirit—within us and without.

LORENZO: Against spirit. . . . I will gladly follow you. I called you to listen to you. I beg you, Brother, have faith in my good-will. Tell me, pray: What do you mean by spirit?

THE PRIOR: The power, Lorenzo Medici, which makes for purity and freedom.

LORENZO: That sounds strong—and mild. And yet—why do I shudder? But I will hear you. In us, you say? And so in you as well? You struggle also with yourself?

THE PRIOR: I am born of woman. No flesh is pure. One must know sin, feel it, understand it, in order to hate it. The angels do not hate sin. They are ignorant of it. There have been hours when I rebelled against the order of spirits. It seemed to me that I was higher than the angels.

LORENZO (*with unaccustomed light irony*): A question so daring, so enthralling, that it is worthy being put by you. Yet, dear Brother, a question concerning you alone, and so today we can put it aside. See, I am ill, and fear is in my heart—I make no bones of telling you this. Fear for the world, for myself—who knows? —for truth. I have sought consolation with my Platonists, my artists—and I have found none. Why not? Because they are none of them my sort. They admire me, perhaps, they love me, and they know nothing of me. Courtiers, orators, children—what use is all that to me? You see, I count on you, Padre. I must hear you —about you and about me; I must compare myself, must come to terms with you; then I should have peace—I feel it. You are not like the others. You do not crawl prattling to my feet. You have risen up beside me, you breathe the same air as myself. You hate me, you repulse me, you work against me with all your art—and see, I am in my soul not far from calling you brother.

THE PRIOR (*whose lank cheeks, at the words, have taken on a glow*): I will not be your brother. I am not your brother. There you have it. I am a poor monk, a priest, scorned and despised like all my kind by the whole insolent world of the flesh, and yet I have raised myself and through me my kind to honour, so that I throw your brotherliness in your face, Magnifico though you be and a lord of this earth.

LORENZO: You see me inclined to admire you for it.

THE PRIOR: You shall not admire me, you shall hate me. And as I must be frightful to you, so must you fear me. I have heard much of your charm, Lorenzo Medici. It shall not ensnare me. Once more: why did you send for me? You shuddered before the heaped-up measure of your sins, and fear urges you to treat with God—you thirst to learn the conditions of grace. Am I not right?

LORENZO: Not quite—perhaps almost. And treat—yes, you see, that is what I want to do, that is what I am doing. But you are impatient. Let me understand you. You say I have all my life worked against the spirit?

THE PRIOR: Do you ask? Is your soul utterly insensitive, then, as they say your nose is? You have made more the temptations of this earth, the allurements of Satan which he makes run through the flesh like a luscious torment. You have set up the pride of the eye as a god, you have made pleasure spurt from the very walls of Florence—and called it beauty. You have beguiled the masses to believe the rankest lies which paralyse the desire for salvation; you have instigated feasts of gallantry in honour of the glistening surface of life—and called that art.

LORENZO: I perceive a strange contradiction here: You are zealous against art, and yet, Brother, you yourself—you too are an artist!

THE PRIOR: The people see more clearly—they call me a prophet.

LORENZO: What is a prophet, then?

THE PRIOR: An artist who is at the same time a saint.—I have nothing in common with your art of the eyes, Lorenzo de' Medici. My art is holy, for it is knowledge and a flaming denial. Long ago, when I suffered agony, I dreamed of a torch which should light up with mercy all the frightful depths, all the shameful and sorrowful abysses of being, of a divine fire which should be laid to all the world that it might blaze up and perish, together with all its shame and martyrdom in redeeming pity. It was art of which I dreamt.

LORENZO (*musing*): The earth seemed fair to me.

THE PRIOR: I saw! I saw through the fairness and the appearance! I suffered too much not to insist proudly upon my vision. Shall I tell you a parable? It was in Ferrara. Once my father took me to court with him. I saw the castle of the Estes. I saw the prince with his companions—women, dwarfs, jesters, and enlightened spirits—revelling at table. Music and the dance, sweet odours and feasting were all. Yet sometimes, very low, awesomely faint, another and strange sound rose above the tumult and the luxury: a sound of torment, a groaning and moaning—it came from below, out of frightful dungeons, where the prisoners lay and languished. I saw them too, I asked and was taken down below whence the howling and the horror came. And the sound of the feasting came down to them below; and I knew that those above felt no shame, that not one conscience was even uneasy. And suddenly it seemed as though I must choke with hatred and resistance. ... And I saw a great bird in the air, beautiful, bold, and blithe of spirit it hovered there. And my heart was gripped by a pain, an aching, a defiance and a profound urge, a fervid wish, a gigantic resolve: could I but break those great pinions!

LORENZO: So that was your one desire?

THE PRIOR: I looked into the heart of the time and saw its forehead with the mark of the whore; shameless was she, gladsome and shameless—can you understand? She would not be ashamed. She took the tapers from the altar of the Crucified and bore them to the sepulchre of one who had created beauty. Beauty—what is beauty? Is it possible not to fathom what she is? If not—who could realize a state of things on earth without being prevented by pain and disgust from still willing it to be? Who? Who? The time! All of you! But not I—I alone! I fled, fled from the abominable sight of such complacency, which laughed at feeling and suffering and redemption. I fled into the monastery, I saved myself in the austere twilight of Holy Church. Here, thought I, in the sanctified precincts of the Cross, here suffering has power to move. Here, so I thought, holiness and wisdom reign, the *sacræ litteræ*. What did I see? Here too I saw the Cross betrayed. The wearers of stole and cowl, whom I thought to be my brothers in the company of suffering—I saw them fallen away from the majesty of the spirit. They had compounded with the foe, with the great Babylon. Here also I was alone. Lo, I understood this too: I had to make myself, my very self, great in opposition against the world

—for I was chosen Christ's vicar. The spirit was born again in me!

LORENZO: Against beauty? Brother, Brother, you are leading me astray. Must there be conflict here too? Must one see the world divided in two hostile camps? Are spirit and beauty opposed to each other?

THE PRIOR: They are. I speak the truth, learnt in suffering. (*A pause. It has grown dark.*) Would you know a sign, manifest when two worlds are eternally strange to each other and may not be reconciled? Longing is this sign. Where abysses yawn, she spans her rainbow, and where she is, are abysses. Learn, learn, Lorenzo de' Medici: The spirit can yearn towards beauty. In hours of weakness and self-betrayal, in the sweetness of shame, then it happens. For she, who is blithe and lovely and strong, she who is life, she can never understand spirit, she shrinks from it, perhaps would fear it and put it away from her; even mock it pitilessly and drive it back upon itself. But then, Lorenzo de' Medici, it can renounce, it can grow hard under torture and great in solitude and return in power so that she gives herself.

LORENZO: Why do you stop? I am listening—I am closing my eyes to hear. I am hearing the melody of my life. Will you stop so soon? It is so sweet to listen thus, without an effort, to oneself. I scarcely see you. Perhaps it is darkness, perhaps my sight is failing, but my spirit is awake, I listen. And I hear a song: my own song, the deep low song of longing. Girolamo, yet do you not know me? Whither the longing urges, there one is not, that one is not—you know? And yet man likes to confuse himself with his longing. You have heard that people call me the lord of beauty? But I myself am ugly. Yellow, ugly and weak. I adore the senses—and one lacks me, a precious one. I have no sense of smell. I know not the scent of the rose nor of a woman. I am a cripple, a deformed object. Is that only my body? Nature thrust me forth in a contortion; but I have compelled the frenzy and the staggering to measure and rhythm. My soul was a smouldering torment of desire and a flame of lust; I have fanned it to a clear flame. Without my longing I should be but a satyr; and when my poets put me with the company of the Olympians, not one of them dreams of the long, stern discipline which went to bridle my wild nature. It was well so. Had I been born beautiful, I had never made myself the lord of beauty. Hindrance is the will's best friend. To whom do I say that? To you, who know so painfully well that the hero's garland is not won by him who is merely strong. Are we foes? Well, then, I say that we are warring brothers.

THE PRIOR: I am not your brother. Have you not heard me say it? Let lights be brought, if the darkness weakens you. I hate this contemptible balancing, this lewd intellectuality, this blasphemous toleration of extremes! It shall not move me. Let them be still. I know it, this spirit—too well, too well! I put it behind me. I hear Florence, I hear your time—subtle, daring, easy-going—but it shall not weaken my powers, shall not disarm me, not me, not me—know that once and for all!

LORENZO: You hate the time, it understands you. Which is greater?

THE PRIOR (*savagely*): I am, I am!

LORENZO: Perhaps. You, then. I did not summon you to quarrel with you. And yet—forgive me: I would gladly see you at one with yourself. You rave at the spirit by which you rose to greatness, by which you *let* yourself be borne upwards—am I right? I cannot see your face. But this is how things seem to me: in times like these, such as you have said they are—subtle, sceptical, tolerant, inquisitive, vacillating, manifold, without clear limits—in such a time limitation can seem like genius. Forgive me. I am not fencing, I seek not to offend, I seek but clarity as between you and me. A power that resolutely holds itself aloof from the general scepticism can work wonders. All these subtle little people—they have no faith, do not believe it—they feel a *power* and they bow before it. Once more, forgive me! And again: you revile art, yet use it for your ends. Your name and fame are cried aloud because the city and our time worship the man who proudly dares to be himself. Never, anywhere, has there been such rich reward, so much response, for him who strives in his own way after fame. That you grew great in Florence was only because this Florence is so free, such a spoilt child of art, as to take you as her lord. Were it less so, were it only a very little less lapped in art, it would tear you to pieces instead of paying you homage. You are aware of that?

THE PRIOR: I will not be aware of it.

LORENZO: May one will not to be aware? You rail at the indifference, at the refusal to see, at the shamelessness. But are you not yourself ashamed to win such power, knowing by what means you win it?

THE PRIOR: I am chosen. I may know and still do it. For I must be strong. God performs miracles. You see the miracle of detachment regained. (*Looking at the bust of Cæsar*) Did *he* ask by what means he climbed?

LORENZO: Cæsar? You are a monk. And you have ambition!

THE PRIOR: How could I not have, I that suffered so? Ambition says: My sufferings must not have been in vain. They must bring me fame.

LORENZO: By God, that is it! Have I not known it? You have understood all that to a miracle. We rulers of men are egoist, and they blame us for it, not knowing that it comes of our suffering. They call us hard and understand not it was pain made us so. We may justly say: Look at yourselves, who have had so much easier a time on this earth. To myself I am torment and joy sufficient.

THE PRIOR: But they do not rail. They marvel. They reverence. See them come to the strong ego, the many who are only *we*, see them serve, see them tirelessly do his will—

LORENZO: Although his own advantage is plain to any eye—

THE PRIOR: Although he leave their services quite unrewarded and take them for granted—

LORENZO: Cosimo my forebear—I was old enough to know him; he was a cold and clever tyrant. They gave him the title *pater patriæ*. He took it with a smile and never a word of thanks. I shall never forget it. How he must despise them, I thought. And since then I have despised the folk.

THE PRIOR: Fame is the school of scorn.

LORENZO: Ah, the worthlessness of the masses! They are so poor, so empty, so selflessly self-forgetful.

THE PRIOR: So simple, so easy to dominate.

LORENZO: They know nothing better than to be dominated.

THE PRIOR: They write to me from all the quarters of the earth, they come from far to kiss the hem of my robe, they spread my fame to the four winds. Do I ever ask them for it, have I ever thanked them?

LORENZO: It is amazing.

THE PRIOR : Quite amazing is it. Are you so futile, one thinks, so vacant yourselves, that you know nothing prouder than to serve another?

LORENZO: Just so, just so! One cannot believe one's eyes, to see them bowing low and willingly—so satisfied.

THE PRIOR: One might laugh at the docility of the world...

LORENZO: And laughing, laughing, one takes the world as willing instrument on which to play.

THE PRIOR: To play one's own tune.

LORENZO (*feverishly*): Oh, my dreams! My power and art! Florence was my lyre. Did it not resound? Sweetly? It sang of my longing. It sang of beauty, it sang of great desire, it sang, it sang the great song of life. ... Hush! On your knees. ... There! I see her. She comes, she draws near to me, all the veils fall and all my blood flows out to meet her naked beauty. Oh, joy! Oh, sweet and fearful thrill! Am I chosen to look upon you, Venus Genetrix, you who are life, the sweet world? ... Creative beauty, mighty impulse of art! Venus Fiorenza! Dost thou know what I would? The perpetual feast—that was my sovereign will! ... Oh, stay! Dost thou turn away? Dost pale? I see no more. ... Red waves come ... and a horror ... a yawning abyss. (*Fainting*) Are you still there, by whom I have understood myself? Speak to me! Fear! Anguish! Volterra! Blood! I emptied the treasury of the dowries, I drove the virgins to unchastity. ... Speak quickly. Speak quickly. The conditions of grace....?

THE PRIOR (*beside him, low, eagerly*): *Misericordiam volo.* ... There are three. The first, repentance.

LORENZO (*in the same tone*): I will repent the plundering of Volterra and the theft of moneys....

THE PRIOR: The second: That you return all unjustly owned property to the state.

LORENZO: My son shall do so. Then?

THE PRIOR (*in an awesome whisper, with a gesture of command*): The third: That you make Florence free—at once for ever—free from the lordship of your house.

LORENZO (*as softly; there is a silent, passionate struggle between the two*): Free—for you!

THE PRIOR: Free for the King who died on the Cross.

LORENZO: For you. For you! Why do you lie? We understood each other. Fiorenza, my city! Do you love her, then? Say quickly. You love her?

THE PRIOR: Fool! Child! Lay yourself to bed in the grave with the ideas which are your playthings. A torrential love, a hate all-embracingly sweet—I am this complex, and this complex wills that I be lord in Florence!

LORENZO: Unhappy one—to what end? What can be your purpose?

THE PRIOR: Eternal peace. The triumph of the spirit. I will break them, these great wings—

LORENZO (*anguished, desperate*): You shall not. Wretch! You shall not. I forbid you—I, the Magnifico. Oh, I know you now, you have betrayed yourself to me. It is the wings of life you mean. It is death whom you proclaim as spirit, and all the life of life is art. I will prevent you. I am still master.

THE PRIOR: I laugh at you. You are dying, I am on my feet. My art won the people. Florence is mine.

LORENZO (*in a paroxysm*): Ah, monster! Evil spirit! Then you shall see me strong and ruthless. (*He shrieks, pulling himself up in the chair by both hands on the arms*) To me, to me! Come, come! Seize him! Bind him! He will break the great wings. Dungeon and chains! The lions' den! Kill him, he would slay all! Florence is mine . . . Florence . . . Florence! (*He collapses, his head rolls upon his neck. His eyeballs turn in, his arms describe a last all-embracing motion. Several servants with wax torches come from the right along the gallery into the room. The stage is suddenly full of flickering light. Pico, Ficino, Poliziano, Pulci, Pierleoni, and the artists hasten in horror down the steps.*)

PICO: Lorenzo!

PIERLEONI: He is gone.

POLIZIANO (*in despair*): My Lauro, my Lauro!

(*A new movement in the gallery. Four or five men, dust-covered, make their way hastily in.*)

ONE OF THEM: Hear ye, hear ye! We are sent by the high and noble Signoria. The city is in an uproar. It is reported that the Prophet Girolamo has been betrayed, taken, murdered. The populace are on their way to Careggi. They demand to see the Frate.

THE PRIOR (*looking down at the body of his foe*): Here am I.

FIORE (*appearing like a vision in the torchlight, at the top of the steps*): Monk, do you hear me?

THE PRIOR (*stiffly upright, without turning round*): I hear.

FIORE: Then hear this: Descend! The fire you have fanned will consume you, you yourself, to purify you and the world of you. Shudder before it—and descend. Cease to will, instead of willing nothingness. Void the power! Renounce! Be a monk!

THE PRIOR: I love the fire.

(He turns. They make way. A lane opens for him, timidly. He strides slowly through it in the torchlight, upwards, away, into his destiny.)

THE TABLES OF THE LAW

1

HIS BIRTH was disorderly. Therefore he passionately loved order, the immutable, the bidden, and the forbidden.

Early he killed in frenzy; therefore he knew better than the inexperienced that, though killing is delectable, *having* killed is detestable; he knew you should not kill.

He was sensual, therefore he longed for the spiritual, the pure, and the holy—in a word, the *invisible*—for this alone seemed to him spiritual, holy, and pure.

Among the Midianites, a nimble tribe of shepherds and merchants strewn across the desert, to whom he had to flee from Egypt, the land of his birth, because he had killed, he made the acquaintance of a god whom one could not see but who saw you. This god was a mountain-dweller who at the same time sat invisible on a transportable chest in a tent and there dispensed oracles by the drawing of lots. To the children of Midian this numen, called Jahwe, was one god among many; they did not bother very much about serving him. What service they undertook they did to be on the safe side, just in case. For it had occurred to them that among the gods there could possibly be a bodiless one whom one did not see, and they sacrificed to him so as not to miss anything, not to offend anybody, to forestall any unpleasantness from any quarter.

But Moses, because of his desire for the pure and the holy, was deeply impressed by the invisibility of Jahwe; he believed that no visible god could compete in holiness with an invisible one, and he marvelled that the children of Midian attached so little importance to a characteristic which seemed to him full of immeasurable implications. While he minded the sheep belonging to the brother of his Midianite wife, he plunged himself into long, deep, and violent cogitations. He was moved by inspirations and visions which in one case even left his inner consciousness and returned to his soul as a flaming vision from without, as a precisely-worded pronouncement, and as an unshrinkable command. Thus he reached the conviction that Jahwe was none other than El'eljon, the Only-Highest, El ro'i, the God who sees me, He who had always been known as El Schaddai, "the God of the Mountain," El 'olām, the God of the World and the Eternities—in short, the God of Abraham, Isaac, and Jacob, the God of the Father. And that meant the God of the poor, dumb, in their worship completely confused, uprooted, and enslaved tribes at home in Egypt, whose blood, from his father's side, flowed in the veins of Moses.

Full of this discovery, his soul heavy with command but trembling also with the wish to fulfil the mission, Moses ended his stay of many years with the children of Midian. He placed his wife Zipporah (a sufficiently noble woman because she was a daughter of Reuel, the priest-king of Midian, and the sister of his herd-owning, son, Jethro) on a mule. He took along also his two sons, Gershom and Eliezer, and returned, travelling westward in seven day-journeys through many deserts, to the land of Egypt. That is to the lower land, the fallow country where the Nile branches out into the district called Kos, and variously known as Goschem, Gosem, and Goshen. It was here that the tribes of his fathers lived and drudged.

Here he immediately began to communicate his great experience to his kinsfolk; he talked to them whenever he went and stood, in their huts, their grazing grounds, and their workplaces. When he spoke he had a certain way of letting his arms hang limp at his sides, while his fists shook and trembled. He informed them that the God of their Fathers was found again, that He had made himself known to him, Moscheh ben 'Amram, on the mountain Hor in the desert Sin from a bush which burned but never burned out. This God was called Jahwe, which name is to be understood as "I am that I am, from eternity to eternity," but also as flowing air and as mighty sound. This God was inclined towards their tribe and was ready under certain conditions to enter into a covenant with them, choosing them above all other peoples. The conditions were that they would devote themselves in full exclusiveness to him, and that they would form a sworn brotherhood to serve him alone in worship of the invisible, a worship without images.

Moses stormed at them and the fists on his broad wrists trembled. Yet he was not completely honest with them, and kept under cover much, indeed the essential thought, he had in mind. Fearing he might scare them off, he said nothing of the implications of invisibility, that is, its spirituality, its purity, its holiness. He preferred not to point out that as sworn servants of the invisible they would have to be a separated people, a people of the spirit, of purity and of holiness. Afraid to frighten them he kept silent. They were so miserable, so oppressed, and in their worship so confused, this kin of his father. He mistrusted them though he loved them. Yes, when he announced to them that Jahwe the Invisible was inclined towards them, he really ascribed to the God and interpreted for the God what possibly was true of the God but what certainly was true of him: for he himself was inclined to his father's kin, as the sculptor is inclined towards the shapeless lump from which he hopes to carve a high and fine figure, the work of his hands. Hence his trembling desire, hence too the great heaviness of soul which filled him directly after his departure from Midian.

He also kept back the second half of the secret; for it was a double secret. It included not only the message to his tribe of the rediscovery of their father's God and the God's inclination toward them; it included also his own belief that he was destined to guide them out of Egypt's house of bondage, out into the open, and through many deserts into the land of promise, the land of their fathers. That destiny was part of the mission, inseparably linked with it. God—and liberation for the return home; the Invisible—and release from foreign yoke: to him these were one and the same thought, but to the people he as yet said nothing of this second part of the mission, because he knew that one would inevitably follow from the other; also because he hoped that he himself could negotiate the release with Pharaoh, King of Egypt, with whom he had not-too-remote connection.

Was it, however, that his speech displeased the people—for he spoke badly and haltingly and often could not find the right word—or did they divine, while he shook his trembling fists, the implications of invisibility as well as those of the covenant? Did they perceive that they were being lured towards strenuous and dangerous matters? Whatever the reason they remained mistrustful, stiff-necked, and fearful of his storming. They ogled their Egyptian whip-masters and mumbled between their teeth:

"Why do you spout words? And what kind of words are these you spout? Likely somebody set you up as chief or as judge over us? Well, we want to know who."

That was nothing new to him. He had heard it from them once before he had fled to Midian.

2

His father was not his father, nor was his mother his mother. So disorderly was his birth.

One day the second daughter of the Pharaoh, Ramessu, was amusing herself—under the watchful eye of the armed guard and in company of her serving maidens—in the royal garden on the Nile. There she espied a Hebrew labourer who was carrying water. She became enamoured of him. He had sad eyes, he had a young beard encircling his chin, and he had strong arms, as one could clearly see when he drew the water. He worked by the sweat of his brow and had his troubles, but to Pharaoh's daughter he was the image of beauty and desire. She commanded that he should be admitted to her pavilion. There she plunged her precious little hands through his sweat-drenched hair, she kissed the muscles of his arms and charmed his manhood to wakefulness, so that he took possession of her; he, the foreign slave, took possession of the child of a king. When she had had enough, she let him go. But he did not go far; after thirty paces he was slain and quickly buried, so that nothing remained of the pleasure of the Sun-Daughter.

"The poor man," said she when she heard about it. "You are always such busybodies. He would have kept quiet. He loved me." After that she became pregnant, and after nine months she gave birth in all secrecy to a boy. Her serving woman placed the boy in a box fashioned of tarred reeds, and they hid the box in the bulrushes on the edge of the water. There in due time they found it and exclaimed, "O magic! A foundling, a boy from the bulrushes, an abandoned child! It is like the old tales, exactly as it happened with Sargon, whom Akki the Water Carrier found in the rushes and reared in the goodness of his heart. Such things happen all the time. What shall we do now with our find? It would be wisest if we gave it to a nursing mother, a woman of simple station who has milk to spare, so that the boy may grow up as her son and the son of her lawful husband." And they handed the child to a Hebrew woman who carried it down into the region of Goshen and there gave it to Jochebed, the wife of Amram, who belonged to the tribe of the Tolerated Ones, to the descendants of Levi. She was nursing her son Aaron and had milk to spare. Therefore, and also because once in a while and quite secretly substantial gifts arrived at her hut from sources higher up, did she rear the unclassified child in the goodness of her heart. Before the world Amram and Jochebed became his parents and Aaron became his brother. Amram possessed cattle and fields, Jochebed was the daughter of a stonemason. She did not know how she should name the questionable child. Therefore she gave him a half-Egyptian name, that is to say, the half of an Egyptian name. For the sons of the land were often called Ptach-Moses, Amen-Moses, or Ra-Moses. They were named as sons with the names of the gods. Amram and Jochebed preferred to omit the name of the god, and called the child simply Moses. Thus he was called plain "Son". The only question was, whose son?

3

He grew up as one of the Tolerated Ones, and expressed himself in their dialect. The ancestors of this tribe had come into the land long ago at the time of the Drought. They whom Pharaoh's historians described as the "hungry Bedouins from Edom" had come with the due permission of the frontier officials. They had received pasture privileges in the district of Goshen in the lower land. Anybody who believes that they received these privileges for nothing does not know their hosts, the children of Egypt. Not only did they have to pay taxes out of their cattle, and that so heavily that it hurt, but also all who had strength were forced to do manual services at the several building operations which in a country like Egypt are always under way. Especially since Ramessu, the second of his name, had become Pharaoh in Thebes, excessive building was going on, for building was his pleasure and his royal delight. He built prodigal temples all over the land. And down in the Delta region he not only renewed and greatly improved the long-neglected canal which connected the eastern arm of the Nile with the Bitter Lakes and thus the great ocean with the corner of the Red Sea, but he also constructed two arsenal cities on the banks of the canal, called Pithom and Rameses. It was for this work that the children of the Tolerated Ones were drafted. They baked bricks and carried them and drudged in the sweat of their bodies under Egypt's cudgel.

This cudgel was hardly more than a symbol of the authority vested in Pharaoh's overseers. The workers were not unnecessarily beaten with it. They also had good food with their drudgery: much fish from the Nile, bread, beer, and beef, quite as plentiful as they needed. Nevertheless, they did not take to or care for this work, for they were nomads, full of the tradition of a free, roaming life. Labour by the hour, labour which made them sweat, was foreign and insulting to their nature. The tribes, however, were far too tenuously connected and insufficiently conscious of themselves to be able to signal their dissatisfaction to each other, or to become of one firm mind about it. Because several of their generations had lived in a transitional land, pitching their tents between the home of their fathers and the real Egypt, they were now unanchored souls, wavering in spirit and without a secure doctrine. They had forgotten much; they had half assimilated some new thoughts; and because they lacked real orientation, they did not trust their own feelings. They did not trust even the bitterness that they felt towards their bondage, because fish and beer and beef made them uncertain.

Moses, also, as the supposed son of Amram, was destined to form bricks for Pharaoh as soon as he had outgrown his boyhood. But this did not come to pass; the youth was taken away from his parents and was brought to Upper Egypt into a school, a very elegant academy where the sons of the Syrian town kings and the scions of the native nobility were educated. There was he taken, because his real mother, Pharaoh's child, who had delivered him into the bulrushes, was, though somewhat lascivious, not devoid of sentiment. She had remembered him for the sake of his buried father, the water carrier with the beard and the sad eyes. She didn't want Moses to remain with the savages, but wished him to be educated as an Egyptian and to achieve a court position. His half descent from the gods was thus to be half recognized in silence. Clothed in white linen and with a wig on his head, Moses acquired the knowledge of stars and of countries, the art of writing and of law. Yet he was not happy among the snobs of the elegant academy, but lonely was he among them, filled with aversion towards all of Egypt's refined culture. The blood of the buried one who had been sacrificed to this culture was stronger in him than was his Egyptian portion. In his soul he sided with the poor uncertain ones at home in Goshen, who did not even have the courage of their bitterness. He sided with them against the lecherous arrogance of his mother's kin.

"What was your name again?" his comrades at the school asked him.

"I am called Moses," he answered.

"Ach-Moses or Ptach-Moses?" they asked.

"No, simply Moses," he responded.

"That's inadequate and paltry," said the snobs. And he became enraged, so that he almost wanted to kill and bury them. For he understood that with these questions they simply wished to pry into his uncertain history, which in nebulous outlines was known to everybody. He himself could hardly have known that he was the discreet result of Egyptian pleasure, if it had not been common though somewhat inexact knowledge. Pharaoh himself was as well aware of the trifling escapade of his child as was Moses of the fact that Ramessu, the master builder, was his illegitimate grandfather, and that his paternity was the result of iniquitious, lecherous, and murderous pleasure. Yes, Moses knew this, and he also knew that Pharaoh knew it. And when he thought about it he inclined his head menacingly, inclined it in the direction of Pharoah's throne.

4

When he had lived two years among the whelps of the school in Thebes, he could stand it no longer, fled by night over the wall, and wandered home to Goshen to his father's tribe. With severe countenance he roamed among them, and one day he saw at the canal near the new buildings in Rameses how an Egyptian overseer beat with his cudgel one of the workers, who probably had been lazy or obdurate. Moses paled. With flaming eyes he challenged the Egyptian, who in short response smashed his nose so that Moses all his life had a nose with a broken flattened bridge. Moses seized the cudgel from the overseer, swung it mightily, and demolished the man's skull so that he lay dead on the spot. Not even once did Moses glance about to find out if anybody had observed him. Fortunately it was a lonely place and not a soul was near. Alone he buried the murdered man; for he whom Moses had defended had instantly taken to his heels. After it was over, he felt that killing and burying were what he had always desired in his soul.

His flaming deed remained hidden at least from the Egyptians, who never did find out what had become of their man. A year and a day passed over the deed. Moses continued to roam among his people and to probe into their frays with a peculiar air of authority. So it happened that once he saw two slaves quarrelling with each other. They were at the point of violence. "Wherefore do you quarrel and seek to strike each other?" he said to them. "Are you not miserable enough and neglected? Would it not be better for kin to side with kin, instead of baring your teeth to each other? This one is in the wrong: I saw it. Let him give in and be content; nor let the other triumph."

But as usually happens, suddenly both of them were united against him, and they said, "What business is it of yours?" Especially he who was in the wrong was extremely snappy and shouted quite loudly, "Well, this caps everything! Who are you that you stick your ugly nose into things that don't concern you? Ahah! You are Moscheh, son of Amram, but that means very little. Nobody really knows who you are, not even you yourself. Curious are we to learn who has appointed you master and judge over us. Perhaps you want to choke me too, as you choked the Egyptian and buried him?"

"Be quiet," whispered Moses, alarmed. And he thought, "How did this get out?" But that very day he understood that it would be no longer possible for him to remain in the country, and he fled across the frontier where the frontier had a loophole, near the muddy shallows of the Bitter Lakes. Through many deserts of the land of Sinai he wandered, and came to Midian, to the Midianites, and to their priest-king, Reuel.

5

When he returned to Egypt, fraught with his discovery and his mission, he was a man at the height of his powers, sturdy, with a sunk-in nose and prominent cheek-bones, with a divided beard, eyes set far apart, and wrists that were unusually broad. He had a habit when he meditated of covering his mouth and beard with his right hand, and it was then that those broad wrists were especially noticeable. He went from hut to hut and from workplace to workplace, he shook his fists at the sides of his body and discoursed on the Invisible One, the God of the Fathers, who was ready for the covenant. Actually Moses did not speak well. His nature was halting and pent-up, and when he became excited he was apt to stammer. Nor was he master of any one language, but floundered in three. The Aramaic-Syro-Chaldee, which was the language of his father's kin and which he had learned from his parents, had been glossed over by the Egyptian which he had had to learn at school. And to this was added the Midianitic-Arabic which he had spoken so long in the desert. All of these he jumbled together.

Very helpful to him was his brother Aaron, a tall man with a black beard and with black curls at the nape of his neck. Aaron was gentle and held his large and curved eyelids piously lowered. Moses had initiated Aaron into all his beliefs and had won him over completely to the cause of the Invisible and all its implications. Because he knew how to speak from under his beard fluently and unctuously, he accompanied Moses on his preaching tours and did the talking for him. Admittedly, he spoke in a somewhat oily fashion, and not nearly transportingly enough to suit Moses, so that Moses, accompanying the speech with his shaking fists, sought to put more fire into his brother's words, and sometimes would blurt helter-skelter into the oration with his own Aramaic-Egyptian-Arabic.

Aaron's wife was named Elisheba, daughter of Amminadab. She too partook of the oath and the propaganda, and so did a younger sister of Moses and Aaron called Miriam, an inspired woman who knew how to sing and play the timbrel. Moses was especially fond of yet another disciple, a youth who devoted himself body and soul to his plans, and who never left his side. His real name was Hosea, son of Nun (that means "fish"), of the kin of Ephraim. Moses, however, had given him the Jahwe name, Jehoschua—Joshua for short. Joshua was erect and sinewy and curly-headed, had a prominent Adam's-apple and a clearly defined wrinkle between his brows. He carried his new name with pride, though he had his own view of the whole affair, views which were not so much religious as military. For him Jahwe, God of the Fathers, was first of all God of the fighting forces. The idea connected with the God, that is, the idea of flight from the house of bondage, was to him identical with the idea of the conquest of a new grazing ground which would belong solely to the Hebraic tribes. This was logical enough, for they had to live somewhere and nobody was going to hand them any land, promise or not, as a gift.

Joshua, young as he was, carried all the salient facts in his clear-eyed, curly head, and discussed them unceasingly with Moses, his older friend and master. Without having the means of carrying out an exact census, Joshua was able to calculate that the strength of the tribes tenting in Goshen or living in the slave cities, Pithom and Rameses, and including also the slaves who were farflung over the country, was about twelve or thirteen thousand people. This meant that there were possibly three thousand men capable of bearing arms. Later on these figures were immeasurably exaggerated, but Joshua knew them fairly correctly, and was little satisfied with them. Three thousand men—that was no terror-inspiring fighting force, even if you count on the fact that once on the way several kindred tribes roaming the desert would join them for the sake of winning new land. With such a force one could not dream of any major expeditions; with such a force it was impractical to hew one's way into the promised land. Joshua well understood that. His plan, therefore, was to seek first of all a spot in the open, a marking time and resting place, where the tribes could settle and devote themselves to the business of natural multiplication under more or less favourable circumstances. This natural growth amounted to—as Joshua knew his people—two and a half per cent. per year. The youth was constantly on the lookout for such a hedged-in hatching place where they could grow further fighting forces. In his frequent consultations with Moses it appeared that Joshua saw with surprising clarity where one place in the world lay in relation to another place. He carried in his head a kind of map of all the interesting districts; he knew their dimensions measured in daytime marches, their watering places, and especially the fighting strength of their inhabitants.

Moses knew what a treasure he possessed in Joshua, knew also that he would have need of him, and loved his ardour, though he was little concerned with the immediate objectives of that ardour. Covering mouth and beard with his right hand, he listened to the strategic theories of the youth, thinking all the while of something else. For him also Jahwe meant an exodus, but not an exodus for a war of land seizure; an exodus rather for seclusion. Out in the open Moses would have his father's kin to himself, those swaying souls confused in their beliefs, the procreating men, the nursing women, the awakening youths, the dirty-nosed children. There in the open he would be able to imbue them with the holy, invisible God, the pure and spiritual God; there he could give them this God as the centre which would unite and form them, form them to his image, form them into a people different from all other peoples; a people belonging to God, denoted by the holy and the spiritual, and distinguished from all others through awe, restraint, and fear of God. That is to say that his people would hold in awe a restraining, pure, spiritual code, a code which, since the Invisible One was in truth the God of the entire world, would in the future bind and unite all peoples, but would at first be given to them alone and be their stern privilege among the heathen.

Thus was Moses's inclination towards his father's blood; it was the sculptor's inclination, and he identified it with the God's choice and the God's desire for the covenant. Because Moses believed that the education towards God must precede all other enterprises, such enterprises as the young Joshua carried in his head, and because he knew that such education would take time—free time out in the open—he did not mind that there was so far many a hitch to Joshua's plans, that these plans were thwarted by an insufficient number of fighters. Joshua needed time so that his people could multiply in a natural way; he also needed time so that he himself could become older, old enough to set himself up as commander in chief. Moses needed time for the work of education, which for the God's sake he desired. So they both agreed, if for different reasons.

6

In the meantime he, God's delegate, and his immediate followers, the eloquent Aaron, Elisheba, Miriam, Joshua, and a certain Caleb, who was Joshua's bosom friend, of the same age, and also a strong, simple, courageous youth—in the meantime, they were not idle, not a single day. They were busy spreading Jahwe's message and his flattering offer of alliance among their people. They continued to stoke the people's bitterness against slavery under the Egyptian cudgel, and they planted ever deeper the thought that the yoke must be thrown off through migration. Each of them did it in his own way: Moses himself through halting words and shaking fists; Aaron in unctuously flowing speech, Elisheba with persuasive chatter; Joshua and Caleb in the form of military command, in short and terse slogans; and Miriam, who was soon known as "the Prophetess," in elevated tone to the accompaniment of the timbrel. Their preaching did not fall on barren ground. The thought of allying themselves with Moses's agreeable god to become the chosen people of the Invisible One and under his and his proclaimer's banner to depart for the open—this thought took root among the tribes and began to be their uniting centre. This especially because Moses promised, or at least put it forth as a hopeful possibility, that he would be able to obtain the permission for their departure from Egypt through negotiations in the highest place, so that this departure would not have to take the form of a daring uprising, but of an amicable agreement. The tribes knew, if inexactly, Moses's half-Egyptian birth in the bulrushes. They knew, too, of his elegant education and of his ambiguous connections with the court. What used to be a cause of distrust and aversion, namely the fact that he was half foreign, and stood with one foot in Egypt, now became a source of confidence and lent him authority. Surely, if anybody, he was the man to stand before Pharaoh and plead their cause. And so they commissioned him to attempt to obtain their release from Ramessu, the master builder and master. They commissioned both him and his foster brother, Aaron. Moses planned to take Aaron along first because he himself could not speak fluently while Aaron could; but also because Aaron had at his disposal certain tricks with which he hoped to make an impression at court in Jahwe's honour. He could take a hooded snake and by pressing its neck make it rigid as a rod. Yet as soon as he cast this rod to the ground, it would curl up and "it became a serpent". Neither Moses nor Aaron took into account the fact that these miracles were quite well known to Pharaoh's magicians, and that they therefore could hardly serve as frightening proof of Jahwe's power.

Altogether, they did not have much luck—it may as well be mentioned beforehand—craftily as they had planned their campaign in counsel with the youths Joshua and Caleb. In this council it had been decided to ask the king for permission only that the Hebrew people might assemble and voyage three days across the frontier into the desert so that they could there hold a feast of offering to the god who had called them. Then they would return to work. They did not expect, of course, that Pharaoh would swallow such a subterfuge and really believe that they would return. It was simply a mild and polite form in which to submit their petition for emancipation. Yet the king did not thank them for it.

However, it must be counted to the credit of the brothers that at least they succeeded in getting into the Great House and before Pharaoh's throne. And that not once but again and again for tenaciously prolonged conferences. In this Moses had not promised too much to his people, for he counted on the fact that Ramessu was his secret and illegitimate grandfather, and that they both knew that each knew it. Moses had a trump card in his hand which, if it was not sufficient to achieve from the king permission for the exodus, was at least potent enough to grant him audience again and again with the mighty one. For he feared Moses. To be sure, a king's fear is dangerous, and Moses was playing a dangerous game. He was courageous—how very courageous and what impression he was able to make through this courage on his people, we shall soon see. It would have been easy for Ramessu to have had Moses quietly strangled and buried, so that at last really nothing would remain of his child's escapade. But the princess cherished a sentimental memory of that hour, and very obviously did not want harm to befall her bulrush boy. He stood under her protection, ungrateful as he had been for her solicitude and for all her plans of education and advancement.

Thus Moses and Aaron were able to stand before Pharaoh, even if he refused categorically the festival-vacation out into the open to which their god had supposedly summoned them. It availed nothing that Aaron spoke with unctuous logic, while Moses shook his fists passionately. It availed nothing that Aaron changed his rod into a snake, for Pharaoh's magicians without further ado did the same thing, proving thereby that the Invisible One in whose name both of them were talking could claim no superior powers, and that Pharaoh need not listen to the voice of such a lord.

"But pestilence or the sword shall visit our people if we do not voyage three days and prepare a feast for our God," said the brothers.

The king responded, "That is not my affair. You are numerous enough, more than twelve thousand strong, and you will be able to stand some diminution, whether it be by pestilence or sword or hard work. What you, Moses and Aaron, really want is to permit slothfulness to your people, and to allow them to idle in their lawful labours. But that I cannot suffer nor permit. I have several unprecedented temples in work; furthermore I want to build a third arsenal city in addition to Pithom and Rameses. For that I need the arms of your people. I am obliged to you for your fluent recital, and you, Moses, I dismiss more or less with particular favour. But not a word more of desert festivals."

The audience was terminated, and not only did it result in nothing good but it afterwards had decidedly bad consequences. For Pharaoh, his zeal for building affronted, and annoyed because he could not very well strangle Moses to death—for otherwise his daughter would have made a scene—issued the order that the people of Goshen were to be more pressed with labour than before, and that the cudgel was not to be spared should they be dilatory; on the contrary, they should be made to slave until they fell exhausted, so that all idle thoughts of a desert festival would be driven out of them. Thus it happened. The drudgery became harder from one day to the next for the very reason that Moses and Aaron had talked to Pharaoh. For example, the straw which they needed for the glazing of bricks was no longer furnished to them. They themselves had to go into the fields to gather the stubbles, nor was the number of bricks to be delivered diminished. That number had to be reached or the cudgel danced upon their poor backs. In vain did the Hebrew foremen protest to the authorities because of the exorbitant demands. The answer was, "You are lazy, lazy are you. Therefore you cry and say, 'We want to migrate and make offerings.' The order remains: Gather the straw yourselves—and make the same number of bricks."

7

For Moses and Aaron this was no small embarrassment. The foremen said to them, "There you have it. And this is all the good the pact with your god has done us. Nothing have you accomplished except that you have made our savour worse before Pharaoh and his servants, and that you have given the sword into their hands for them to slaughter us."

It was difficult to answer, and Moses had heavy hours alone with the god of the thorn bush. He confronted the god with the fact that from the very beginning he was against this mission, and from the beginning he had implored that whomsoever the god wanted to send, he should not in any case send him, for he could not speak properly. But the god answered him that Aaron was eloquent. True enough, Aaron had done the speaking, but in much too oily a fashion, and it appeared how absurd it was to undertake such a cause if one had a heavy tongue and was forced to have others plead as deputy. But the god consoled Moses and meted punishment to him from his own soul. He answered Moses from his own soul that he should be ashamed of his half-heartedness. His excuses were pure affectation, for at bottom he himself had longed for the mission, because he himself was as much inclined towards his people and the forming of them as the god. Yes, it was impossible to distinguish his own inclination from the inclination of the god; it was one and the same. This inclination had driven him to the work, and he should be ashamed to be despondent at the first misadventure.

Moses let himself be persuaded, the more so as in counsel with Joshua, Caleb, Aaron, and the inspired women they reached the conclusion that the greater oppression, though it did cause bad blood, was, rightly understood, not such a bad beginning. For the bad blood would form itself not only against Moses but also and especially against the Egyptians. It would make the people all the more receptive to the call of the saving God and to the idea of the exodus. Thus did it happen. Among the workers the discontent caused by straw and bricks was fomented, and the accusation that Moses had made their savour worse before Pharaoh and had only harmed them took second place to the wish that Amram's son should once again exploit his connections and once again go for them to Pharaoh.

This he did, but not with Aaron. Alone he went, not caring how haltingly he spoke. He shook his fists before the throne and demanded in stammering and plunging words permission for the exodus for the sake of the festival in the desert. Not once did he do so but a dozen times, for Pharaoh simply could not deny him admission to his throne, so excellent were his connections. It came to a combat between Moses and the king, a tenacious and protracted combat, the result of which was not that the king agreed to the petition and permitted the departure, but rather that one day he drove and chased the people of Goshen from his land, very glad to get rid of them. There has been much talk about this combat and the various threatening measures which were employed against the stubbornly resisting king. This talk is not entirely without basis, though it has been subjected to much ornamentation. Tradition speaks of ten plagues, one after the other, with which Jahwe smote Egypt, in order to wear down Pharaoh, while at the same time he purposely hardened Pharaoh's heart against Moses's demands, for the sake of proving his might with ever-new plagues. Blood, frogs, vermin, wild beasts, boils, pestilence, hail, locusts, darkness, and death of the first-born, these were the names of the ten plagues. And any or all of them could have happened. The question is only whether any of them, excepting the last, which has an opaque and never fully elucidated explanation, did contribute materially to the final result. Under certain circumstances the Nile takes on a blood-red colouring. Temporarily its waters becomes undrinkable and the fish die. That is as likely to happen as that the frogs of the marshes multiply unnaturally or that the propagation of the constantly present lice grows to the proportion of a general affliction. There were plenty of lions left in Egypt prowling along the edge of the desert and lurking in the dried-up stream beds of the jungle. And if the number of their rapacious attacks on man and beast suddenly increased, one could very well designate that as a plague. How usual are sores and blains in the land of Egypt, and how easily uncleanliness causes cankers which fester among the people like a pestilence! The heavens there are usually blue, and therefore the rare and heavy thunderstorm makes all the deeper an impression, when the descending fire of the clouds mixes with the sharp gravel of the hail, which flails the harvest and rends the trees asunder—all this without any definite purpose. The locust is an all-too-familiar guest; against their mass advance man has invented many a repellent and barricade. Yet again and again these yield to greed, so that whole regions remain gaping in bare baldness. And he who has experienced the dismal darkling mood which a shadowed sun produces on the earth can well understand that a people spoiled by the luxury of light would give to such an eclipse the name of a plague.

With this all the reported evils are accounted for. For the tenth evil, the death of the first-born, does not properly belong among them. It represents a dubious by-product of the exodus itself, one into which it is uncomfortable to probe. Some of the others, or even all of them, if spread over a sufficient period of time could have occurred. One need consider them as merely more or less decorative circumlocutions of the only actual pressure which Moses could use against Ramessu, namely and quite simply the fact that Pharaoh was his illegitimate grandfather and that Moses had the means to bruit this scandal abroad. The king was more than once at the point of yielding to this pressure; at least he made considerable concessions. He consented that the men depart for the feast of offering if their wives, children, and cattle remained behind. Moses did not accept this; with young and old, with sons and daughters, with sheep and cows, would they have to depart, to do justice to the feast of the Lord. So Pharaoh conceded wives and brood and excepted only the cattle, which were to remain as forfeit. But Moses asked where they were expected to find offerings to be burned and slaughtered if they lacked their cattle. Not one single hoof, he demanded, might remain behind, whereby, of course, it became apparent that it was not a question of a holiday but of a departure.

This resulted in a last stormy scene between His Egyptian

Majesty and Jahwe's delegate. During all the negotiations Moses had shown great patience, though there was fist-shaking rage in his soul. It got to the point that Pharaoh staked all and literally showed him the door. "Out," he screamed, "and beware lest you come again into my sight. If you do, so shall you die."

Then Moses, who had just been fiercely agitated, became completely calm, and answered only, "You have spoken. I shall go and never again come into your sight." What he contemplated when he thus took leave in terrible calm was not according to his desire. But Joshua and Caleb, the youths, they liked it well.

8

This is a dark chapter, one to be voiced only in half-whispered and muffled words. A day came, or more precisely a night, a wicked vesper, when Jahwe or his destroying angel went about and smote the children of Egypt with the tenth and last plague. That is, he smote a part of them, the Egyptian element among the inhabitants of Goshen and those of the towns of Pithom and Rameses. Those huts and houses whose posts were painted with the sign of blood he omitted, passed by, and spared.

What did he do? He caused death to come, the death of the Egyptian first-born, and in doing so he may well have met half-way many a secret wish and helped many a second-born to the right which would otherwise have been denied him. One has to note the difference between Jahwe and his destroying angel. It was not Jahwe himself who went about, but his destroying angel, or more properly, a whole band of such, carefully chosen. And if one wishes to search among the many for one single apparition, there is much to point to a certain straight, youthful figure with a curly head, a prominent Adam's-apple, and a determined, wrinkled brow. He becomes the traditional type of the destroying angel, who at all times is glad when unprofitable negotiations are ended and deeds begin.

During Moses's tenacious audiences with Pharaoh, the preparations for decisive deeds had not been neglected. Moses's part in them was limited: he merely sent his wife and sons secretly to Midian to his brother-in-law, Jethro. Expecting serious trouble, he did not wish to be burdened with their care. Joshua, however, whose relationship to Moses was recognizably similar to the relationship of the destroying angel to Jahwe, had acted according to his nature; though he did not possess the means or as yet the prestige to get three thousand arm-bearing comrades ready for war under his command, he at least had selected a group, had armed them, exercised them, and reared them in discipline. For a beginning, a good deal could be accomplished with them.

What then occurred is shrouded in darkness—the very darkness of that certain vesper night which was supposed to be a holiday night for the slave tribes. The Egyptians assumed that these tribes wanted to have some compensation for the festival in the desert which had been denied to them, and thus had planned to hold a celebration enhanced by feasting and illumination. For they had even borrowed gold and silver vessels from their Egyptian neighbours. Instead of this there occurred that appearance of the destroying angel, that death of the first-born, in all those dwellings unmarked with blood by the bundle of hyssop. It was a visitation which caused so great a confusion, and so sudden a revolution of legal claims and property rights, that in the next hour the way out of the land not only stood open to the people of Moses, but they were actually forced on the way. Their departure could not be quick enough for the people of Egypt. Indeed, it seems as if the second-born were less zealous to avenge the death of those to whose place they succeeded than to hasten the disappearance of those who had caused their advancement.

The word of history has it that the tenth plague at last broke Pharaoh's pride so that he dismissed Moses's people from bondage. Soon enough, however, he sent after the departed ones a pursuing armed division which miraculously came to grief.

Be that as it may, it is certain that the exodus took the form of expulsion. The haste with which it happened is indicated by the fact that nobody had time to leaven his bread for the journey. The people were provided only with unleavened emergency cakes. Later Moses formed of this occurrence a memorial feast for all time. But in other respects everybody, great and small, was quite prepared for the departure. While the destroying angel went about, they sat with girded loins near their fully packed carts, their shoes already on their feet, their staffs in their hands. The gold and silver vessels which they had borrowed from the children of the land they took with them.

My friends, at the departure from Egypt there was killing and there was theft. It was Moses's determined will that this should happen for the last time. How can people free themselves from uncleanliness without offering to that uncleanliness a last tribute, without soiling themselves thoroughly for the last time? Now Moses had the unformed mass, his father's kin, out in the open. He, with his sculptor's desire, believed that out in the open, out in freedom, the work of cleansing could begin.

9

The migrants, though their number was much smaller than the legend narrates, were yet numerous enough to be difficult to manage, to guide, and to provision. They were a heavy enough burden for him who had the responsibility for their fate and for their survival out in the open. The tribes chose the route which chose itself, for with good reason they wanted to avoid the Egyptian frontier fortifications, which began north of the Bitter Lakes. The way they took led through the Salt Lake district, a district into which projects the larger, more westerly of the two arms of the Red Sea. These arms frame the Sinai peninsula. Moses knew this district because on his flight to Midian and on his return from there he had passed and repassed it. Its characteristics were better known to him than to young Joshua, who knew it only as a map he had learned by heart. Moses had seen these strange reedy shallows, which sometimes formed an open connection between the Bitter Lakes and the sea, and which at other times and under certain peculiar conditions could be traversed as dry land. If there was a strong east wind and if the sea was at low tide, the shallows permitted free passage. The fugitives found them in this condition, thanks to Jahwe's favourable disposition.

Joshua and Caleb were the ones who spread the news among the multitude that Moses, calling to God, had held his rod over the waters, had caused the waters to divide and make way for the people. Very probably Moses actually did this, and thus assisted the east wind with solemn gesture and in Jahwe's name.

In any case, the faith of the people in their leader could at this moment well do with confirmation, because right here it was subjected to the first heavy trial. For it was here that Pharaoh's mighty battalion, the mounted men in those grim, scythe-studded chariots all too familiar to the people, caught up with the fugitives and were within a hair's breadth of putting a bloody end to the whole pilgrimage to God.

The news of their coming, announced by Joshua's rear guard, caused extreme terror and wild despair among the people. Regret at having followed "that man Moses" immediately flared up, and the mass murmuring arose which was to occur, to his grief and bitterness, at every succeeding difficulty. The women whined, the men cursed and shook their fists at the sides of their bodies as Moses himself was wont to do when he was excited.

"Were there no graves in Egypt," thus was the speech, "which we could have entered peacefully at our appointed hour if we had stayed at home?" Suddenly Egypt was "home", that very Egypt which used to be the foreign land of slavery. "For it had been better for us to serve the Egyptians than that we should die in the wilderness."

This Moses had to hear from a thousand throats. The cries even galled his joy in the deliverance, which when it came was overwhelming. He was "the man Moses who has led us out of Egypt" —which phrase was a paean of praise as long as everything went well. When things went badly the phrase immediately changed colour and became a menacingly murmured reproach, a reproach never far removed from the thought of stoning.

Well, then, after a short fright everything went miraculously and shamefully well. Through God's miracle Moses stood before his people in all his greatness and was "the man who has led us out of Egypt," once again with a different connotation. The people pushed through the dry shallows, after them the might of the Egyptian chariots. Suddenly the wind dies down, the flood returns, and man and horse perish gurgling in the engulfing waters.

The triumph was unprecedented. Miriam the prophetess, Aaron's sister, played the timbrel and led the round dance of the women. She sang: "Praise the Lord—a wondrous deed—steed and man—he has flung them into the ocean." She had written this herself. One has to imagine it to the accompaniment of the timbrel.

The people were deeply moved. The words "mighty, holy, terrifying, praiseworthy, and miracle-dispensing" fell incessantly from their lips, and it was not clear whether these words were meant for the divinity or for Moses, delegate of the god. For they now believed that it was Moses's rod which had drawn the drowning flood over the might of Egypt. This substitution was ever present. At those times when the people were not murmuring against him, he always had his troubles trying to prevent them from looking on him as God instead of as God's proclaimer.

10

At the bottom this was not so ridiculous. For what Moses began to exact of those wretched people went far beyond the humanly customary, and could hardly have sprung from the brain of a mortal. They stood agape at hearing it. He immediately forbade Miriam's dance of triumph and all further jubilation over the destruction of the Egyptians. He proclaimed: Jahwe's heavenly hosts were at the point of joining in the song of victory, but the holy one had rebuked them. "How so! My creatures sink into the sea, and you want to sing?" This short and surprising pronouncement Moses spread among the people. And he added, "Thou shalt not rejoice over the fall of thine enemy, nor shall thy heart be glad over his misfortune." This was the first time he addressed the entire mob, some twelve thousand people with three thousand capable of bearing arms, with "Thou." It was a form of speech which embraced them in their entirety and at the same time designated each individual, man and woman, the aged and the child, pointing a finger against each one's breast.

"Thou shalt not utter a cry of joy over the fall of thine enemy." That was to the highest degree unnatural! But obviously this unnaturalness had some relation to the invisibility of Moses's god, who desired also to be their god. The more thinking ones among the dark-skinned mob began dimly to perceive that it meant to have allied themselves with an invisible god, and what uncomfortable and exigent matters they could expect.

The people were now in the land of Sinai, in the desert of Shur, an unlovely region which once left behind would only lead to yet another lamentable district, the desert of Paran. Why these deserts had different names is inexplicable. Barrenly they joined one another, and were both quite the same, that is, stony, waterless, and fruitless—accursed plains, dotted with dead hills, stretching for three days or four or five. It was lucky for Moses that he had fortified his reputation by impressing them with the supernatural occurrences at the shallows. For soon enough was he again "that Man Moses who has led us out of Egypt," which meant "into misfortune." Loud murmurings rose to his ears. After three days the water which they had taken along gave out. Thousands thirsted, the inexorable sun above their heads, and under their feet bare disconsolateness, whether it was the desert Shur or by this time the desert Paran.

"What shall we drink?" they called loudly, without consideration for the leader, who suffered because he was responsible. Gladly would he have wished that he alone had nothing to drink, that he alone would never drink again, if only he did not have to hear continually, "Why did you carry us forth out of Egypt?" To suffer alone is little torment compared to the trial of having to be responsible for such a multitude. Moses was a much tried man, and remained so all his life, tried more than all the other people on earth.

Very soon there was nothing more to eat, for how long could the flat cakes which they had taken with them last? "What shall we eat?" Now this cry arose, tearful and abusing, and Moses had heavy hours alone with God. He complained how unfair it was that God had placed all the burden of all the people on one servant alone, on Moses.

"Did I conceive all these people and give them birth," he asked, "so that you have the right to say to me, 'Carry them in your arms'? Where can I find the nourishment to give to all? They cry before me and speak, 'Give us meat that we may eat!' Alone I cannot bear the weight of so many people; it is too heavy for me. And if you demand this of me, it would be better that you strangle me to death so that I need not see their misfortune and mine."

Jahwe did not entirely leave him in the lurch. On the fifth day they espied on a high plateau a spring surrounded by trees, which incidentally was marked as the "spring Marah" on the map which Joshua carried in his head. Unfortunately, the water tasted vile, because of certain unsalutary additions. This caused bitter disappointment and far-rumbling murmurs. However, Moses, made inventive by necessity, inserted a kind of filter apparatus which held back the foul additions, if not entirely, at least largely. Thus he performed the miracle of the spring, which changed the plaints into paeans and did much to cement his reputation. The phrase, "He who has led us out of Egypt," immediately took on again a rosy glow.

A miracle occurred also with the nourishment, a miracle which at first caused exultant astonishment. It appeared that great stretches of the desert Paran were covered with a lichen which was edible. This "manna-lichen" was a sugary tomentum, round and small, looked like coriander seed and like bdellium, and was highly perishable. If one did not eat it at once, it began to smell evil. But otherwise it made quite tolerable emergency food, mashed and powdered and prepared like an ash cake. Some thought that it tasted almost like rolls with honey; others it reminded of oil cakes.

This was the first favourable judgment, which did not last. Soon, after a few days, the people became wearied of this manna and tired of staying their hunger with it. Because it was their only nourishment, they sickened of it; it made them nauseated and they complained, "We remember the fish which we got in Egypt for nothing, the squash, the cucumbers, the leeks, the onions, and the garlic. But now our souls are weary, for our eyes see nothing but manna." This, in addition of course to the question, "Why did you carry us forth out of Egypt?" Moses had to hear in pain. What he asked God was, "What shall I do with the people? They no longer want their manna. You will see, soon they shall stone me."

11

However, from such a fate he was tolerably well protected by Jehoschua, his youth, and by the able guards whom he already had called on in Goshen and who surrounded the liberator as soon as the menacing murmurs rose among the crowd. For the time being this armed guard was small and consisted only of young men, with Caleb as lieutenant. Joshua was waiting for the right occasion to set himself up as commander in chief and leader of the battle, and to bind into a regular military force under his command *all* those capable of bearing arms, all the three thousand. He knew that such an occasion was coming.

Moses owed much to the youth whom he had baptized in the name of God. Without him he would have been lost many a time. He himself was a spiritual man and his virility, though it was strong and sturdy, though it had wrists as broad as a stonemason's, was a spiritual virility, a virility turned inward, nourished and fired by God, unconscious of outer happenings, concerned only with the holy. With a kind of foolhardiness, which stood in peculiar contrast to his reflective musings when he covered mouth and beard with his hand, all his thoughts and endeavours dealt only with his desire to have his father's kin alone for himself in seclusion, so that he might educate them, and sculpt into God's image the amorphous mass which he loved. He was little or not at all concerned with the dangers of freedom, the difficulties of the desert, and with the question how one could safely steer such a crowd out of the desert. He did not even know precisely to what spot he must guide the people. In short, he had hardly prepared himself for practical leadership. Therefore he could be doubly glad to have Joshua at his side, who in turn admired the spiritual virility in his master and placed his own direct, realistic, and useful virility unconditionally at his disposal.

It was thanks to him that they made planned progress through the wilderness and did not stray or perish. He determined the direction of the marches according to the stars, calculated the distances of the marches, and arranged it so that they arrived at watering places at bearable if sometimes even just bearable intervals. He it was who had found out that the round lichen was edible. In short, he looked after the reputation of the leader and master. He saw to it that when the phrase, "He who has led us out of Egypt," became a murmur, it would soon again take on a laudatory meaning. He kept the goal clearly in his head, and there he steered with the help of the stars and in accord with Moses, on the shortest route. Both of them were agreed that a first provisional goal was needed. Even if this was a temporary shelter, it would be an abode where one could live and where one could gain time. Much time had to be gained, partly (in Joshua's view) that the people might multiply and furnish him as he grew older a stronger number of warriors;

partly (in Moses's view) that he might lead the mass towards God and hew them into a shape that would be holy, decent, and clean. For this his soul and his wrists longed.

The goal was the oasis Kadesh. Just as the desert Shur touches the desert Paran, so does the desert Sin adjoin Paran in the south. But not on all sides and not closely. Somewhere in between lay the oasis of Kadesh. This oasis was like a precious meadow, a green refreshment amid waterless waste, with three strong springs and quite a number of smaller springs, a day's march long and half a day's march broad, covered with fresh pasture and arable ground, and enticing landscape rich in animals and in fruits and large enough to quarter and nourish a multitude like theirs.

Joshua knew of this attractive spot: it was scrupulously marked out on the map which he carried in his head. Moses too had heard something about it. But it was really Joshua who had contrived to select Kadesh as their destination. His opportunity—it lay there. It goes without saying that such a pearl as Kadesh was not without its owner. The oasis was in firm possession. Well, perhaps not too firm, Joshua hoped. To acquire it, one had to fight those who possessed it, and that was Amalek.

A part of the tribe of Amalek held Kadesh occupied and would most certainly defend it. Joshua made it clear to Moses that this meant war, that a battle between Jahwe and Amalek was inevitable, even if it resulted in eternal enmity from generation to generation. The oasis they would have to have; it was their predestined place for growth and consecration.

Moses had his reservations. In his view one of the implications of the invisible god was that one should not covet the house of one's neighbour. He said as much to the youth, but Joshua responded: Kadesh is not, strictly speaking, Amalek's house. He knew his way about not only in space but in historic pasts, and he knew that long ago—though he could not precisely say just when—Kadesh had been inhabited by Hebrew people, and that they had been dispossessed by the people of Amalek. Kadesh was property through robbery—and one may rob a robber.

Moses doubted that, but he had his own reasons for believing that Kadesh truly was the property of Jahwe and should belong to those who were allied to him. The place bore the name of Kadesh, which means "sanctuary", not only because of its natural charm but also because it was in a certain sense a sanctuary of the Midianitic Jahwe, whom Moses had recognized as the God of the Fathers. Not far from it, towards the east and towards Edom, lay the mountain Horeb, which Moses had visited from Midian and on whose slope the god had appeared to him in the burning bush. Horeb the mountain was the dwelling-place of Jahwe—at least it was one of them. His original dwelling was Mount Sinai in that range which lay towards midday. Thus between Sinai and Horeb there was a close connection—that is, that they both were Jahwe's dwelling places. You could perhaps name one after the other, you could call Horeb Sinai. And you could call Kadesh what it was actually called because, speaking somewhat loosely, it lay at the foot of the sanctified mountain.

Therefore Moses consented to Joshua's scheme and permitted him to make his preparations for the combat with Amalek.

12

The battle took place—that is an historic fact. It was a bloody, fluctuating battle. But Israel emerged the victor. Moses had given this name Israel, which means "God makes war", to his people before the battle, to strengthen them. He had explained that it was a very old name which had slipped into oblivion. Jacob, the original father, had first won it, and had thus called his kin. Now indeed it benefited Moses's people. The tribe which previously had only loosely held to each other, now that they were all called Israel, fought united under this armoured name. They fought grouped in battle ranks and led by Joshua, the war-worthy youth, and Caleb, his lieutenant.

The people of Amalek had no illusions as to the meaning of the approach of the wanderers. At all times such approaches have only one meaning. Without waiting for the attack on the oasis, they burst in bulging bands into the desert, greater in number than Israel, and better armed. Amid swirling dust, amid tumult and martial cries, the battle began. It was an uneven battle, uneven also because Joshua's people were troubled by thirst and had eaten nothing but manna for many days. On the other hand, they had Joshua, the clear-seeing youth, who led their movements, and they had Moses, the man of God.

At the beginning of the engagement Moses, together with Aaron, his half-brother, and Miriam, the prophetess, retired to a hill from which he could view the field of combat. Virile though he was, his duty was not to do battle. His was a priest's duty, and everyone agreed without hesitancy that that could be his only duty. With raised arms he called to the god, and voiced enflaming words, as "Arise, Jahwe, appear to the myriads, to the thousands of Israelites, so that your enemies shall scatter and those who hate you flee before your sight."

They did not flee nor did they scatter. Or if they did, they did so only in a few places and temporarily. For though Israel was made fierce by thirst and by satiety with manna, Amalek disposed of more "myriads". And, after a brief discouragement, they again and again pressed forward, at times dangerously close to the commanding hill. It clearly appeared that Israel conquered as long as Moses held up his arms in prayer to heaven. But if he let his arms sink, then Amalek was victorious. Because he could not continuously hold up his arms with his own strength, Aaron and Miriam supported him under the armpits, and even held his arms so that they might remain raised. What that means one can measure by the fact that the battle lasted from morn to evening, and in all this time Moses had to retain his painful position. Judge from that how difficult is the duty assigned to spiritual virility, up there on the hill of prayer—in truth more difficult than the duty of those who hack away below in the turmoil.

Nor was he able to perform this duty all day long. Intermittently, and for a moment only, his helpers had to let down the arms of the master. And immediately this caused much blood and affliction among Jahwe's warriors. Then the arms were again hoisted, and those below took fresh courage. What also helped to veer the battle in their favour was the strategic gift of Joshua. He was a most ingenious apprentice of war, a youth with ideas and vision. He invented manœuvres which were utterly novel and quite unprecedented, at least in the desert. He was also a commander stoical enough to be able to view with calmness the temporary loss of territory. He assembled his prize warriors, the carefully chosen destroying angels, on the right flank of the enemy, pushed against this flank determinedly, deflected it, and harried it sufficiently to be victorious in that one spot. It mattered not that the main force of Amalek had the advantage against the ranks of the Hebrews, and storming ahead gained considerable territory from them. Because of the break-through at the flank, Joshua penetrated to the rear of Amalek's force so that now they had to turn around towards him, without being able to cease fighting against the main might of Israel. And they who a moment ago had almost been vanquished now took new courage. With this the Amalekites lost their head and despaired. "Treason," they cried, "all is lost. Do not hope any longer to be victorious! Jahwe is above us, a god of unbounded malice." And with this password of despair, the warriors of Amalek let their swords sink and were overcome.

Only a few succeeded in fleeing north towards their people, where they found refuge with the main tribe. Israel occupied the oasis Kadesh, which proved to be traversed by a broad, rushing stream, rich with nut bushes and fruit trees and filled with bees, song birds, quails, and rabbits. The children of Amalek who had been left behind in the village tents augmented the number of their own progeny; the wives of Amalek became Israel's wives and servants.

13

Moses, though his arms hurt him long afterwards, was a happy man. That he remained a much tried man, tried more than all the people on earth, we shall soon see. For the time being he could well be pleased with the state of affairs. The exodus had been successful, Pharaoh's avenging might had drowned in the sea of reeds, the desert voyage was mercifully completed, and the battle for Kadesh had been won with Jahwe's help. Now he stood in all his greatness before his father's kin, in the esteem which springs from success, as "the man Moses who has led us out of Egypt." He needed this esteem to be able to begin his work, the work of cleansing and shaping in the sign of the Invisible One, the work of hewing, chiselling, and forming of the flesh and blood, the work for which he longed. He was happy to have this flesh and blood at last all to himself out in the open, in the oasis which bore the name "sanctuary". Here was his workplace.

He showed his people a certain mountain which lay towards the east of Kadesh behind the desert. This was Horeb, which one could also call Sinai. Two-thirds of it was overgrown with bushes, but at the summit it was bare, and there was the seat of Jahwe. This was plausible, for it was a peculiar mountain, distinguished among its neighbours by a cloud which never vanished and which lay like a roof on its peak. During the day this cloud looked grey, but at night it glowed. There, he told the people, on the bushy slope beneath the rocky top, Jahwe had talked to him from the burning thorn bush, and had charged him to lead them out of Egypt. They listened to the tale with fear and trembling. They could not as yet feel reverence or devotion. All of them, even the bearded men, shook at their knees like cowards when he pointed to the mountain with the lasting cloud, and when he taught them that this was the dwelling of the god who was inclined towards them and was to be their sole god. Moses, shaking his fists, scolded them because of their uncouth behaviour, and endeavoured to make them feel more courageous towards Jahwe, and more intimate with him, by erecting right in their midst, in Kadesh itself, a shrine in his honour.

For Jahwe had a mobile presence. This was another attribute of his invisibility. He dwelt on Sinai, he dwelt on Horeb. And hardly had the people begun to make themselves at home in the camp of the Amalekites when Moses gave him a dwelling even there. It was a tent right next to one's own tent. He called it the meeting or assembly tent, and also the tabernacle. There he housed holy objects which would serve as aids in the service of the Invisible. Most of these objects traced back to the cult of the Midianitic Jahwe as he remembered it. First, a kind of chest carried on poles, on which, according to Moses's explanation (and he was the man to know such things), the invisible divinity was enthroned. This chest they could take along into the field and carry before them in battle, should Amalek approach and endeavour to seek revenge. Next to this chest he kept a brass rod with a serpent's head, also called the "Brass Serpent". This rod commemorated Aaron's well-meant trick before Pharaoh, but with the additional import that it be also the rod which Moses had held over the sea of reeds to part the waters. He also kept in the tent a satchel called an ephod, from which the oracle lots were drawn. These were the yes and no, the right and wrong, the good and bad, the "Urim and Thummim" judgments which were Jahwe's direct decisions in those difficult disputes which man alone could not solve.

For the most part Moses himself did the judging in Jahwe's stead, in all kinds of controversies and contentions which arose among the people. As a matter of fact, the first thing he did in Kadesh was to erect a tribunal where, on designated days, he passed judgment and settled differences. There, where the strongest spring bubbled, the spring which was already called Me-Meribah, meaning "water of the law", there he pronounced his verdicts and let the holy judgment flow even as the water flowed from the earth. If one considers that there were twelve thousand five hundred souls who looked up to him alone for justice, then one can well imagine how sorely tried was he.

For more and more of them sought their rights and pressed towards his seat near the spring, as the idea of right was something utterly new to these forsaken and lost souls. Up to now they had hardly known that there was such a thing. Now they learned first that right was directly connected with the invisibility and holiness of God and stood under his protection, and second that the conception of right also included the conception of wrong. The mob could not understand this for a long time. They thought that there, where right was dispensed, everybody had to be in the right. At first they could not and did not want to believe that a person might obtain his right through the very fact that he was judged in the wrong and had to slink away with a long face. Such a man regretted that he had not decided the matter with his adversary as he used to decide in former times, that is, with stone in fist, even if the affair might then have had a different outcome. With difficulty did this man learn from Moses that such an action was offensive to the invisibility of God, and that no one should slink away with a long face if right had declared him wrong. For right was equally beautiful and equally dignified in its holy invisibility whether it said yea or nay to a man.

Thus Moses not only had to pass judgment but to teach judgment. And greatly was he tried. He had studied law in the academy in Thebes, and knew the Egyptian law scrolls and the Code of Hammurabi, king of the Euphrates. This knowledge helped him to a decision in many a case. For example: if an ox had gored a man or a woman to death, then the ox had to be stoned and his meat could not be eaten. But the owner of the ox was innocent unless he knew that that ox previously was wont to push with his horns and had not kept him in. Then his life was forfeit, except that he could ransom it with thirty shekels of silver. Or if somebody dug a pit and did not cover it properly, so that an ox or an ass fell into it, then the owner of that pit should make restitution in money to the other man for his loss, but the carcass should belong to the first man. Or whatever else occurred in matters of violence, mistreatment of slaves, theft and burglary, destruction of crops, arson, or abuse of confidence—in all these and a hundred other cases Moses passed judgment, leaning on the Code of Hammurabi, and decided what was right and what wrong. But there were too many cases for one judge, and his seat near the spring was overrun. If the master probed the various cases only half-way-conscientiously, he was never finished and had to postpone much. Ever-new problems arose, and he was tried above all people.

14

Therefore, it was a stroke of great good fortune that his brother-in-law, Jethro, came from Midian to visit him in Kadesh and give him good counsel, counsel in such as the overconscientious Moses could never have found for himself. Soon after the arrival in the oasis, Moses had sent to Midian to his brother-in-law for the return of his wife Zipporah and his two sons, who had been entrusted to the safety of Jethro's tent during the Egyptian tribulations. Accommodatingly, Jethro came in person to deliver wife and sons, to embrace Moses, to look around, and to hear from him how everything had gone off.

Jethro was a corpulent sheik with a pleasant mien, with even and deft gestures, a man of the world, a paladin of a civilized, mundane, and experienced people. Received with much splendour, he put up at Moses's hut. There, not without astonishment, he learned how one of his own gods—peculiarly enough, the imageless one—had done so extraordinarily well for Moses and his people, and had, as he already knew, delivered them from Egypt's power.

"Well, who would have thought it?" he said. "Obviously this god is greater than we suspected, and what you tell me now makes me fear that we have cultivated him too negligently. I shall see to it that we shall accord him more honour in future."

The next day public sacrifices were ordered. Moses arranged these seldom, as he had little use for a custom common to all the people in the world. Sacrifice was not essential, said he, to the Invisible One. "Not offerings do I want," spoke Jahwe, "but that ye shall listen to my voice, and that is the voice of my servant, Moses. Then shall I be your God and ye my people." Nevertheless, this once they did arrange slaughter and burnt offerings in Jahwe's honour as well as to celebrate Jethro's arrival. And again the next day, early in the morning, Moses took his brother-in-law along to the Spring of the Law so that he could attend a court session and observe how Moses sat and judged the people. And the people stood round him from morn to evening, and there was no end to it, no question of being finished.

"Now, let me ask you one thing, my honoured brother-in-law," said the guest when, after the session, he walked home with Moses. "Why do you plague yourself like that? There you sit all alone and all the people stand around you from morn until evening. Why do you do it?"

"I have to," answered Moses. "The people come to me that I may judge one and all and show them the right of God and his laws."

"But, my good friend, how can you be so inefficient?" said Jethro. "Is that the way to govern, and is it right that the ruler should have to work himself to the bone because he does everything himself? It is a shame that you drive yourself so that you can hardly hold your head up. What is more, you lose your voice with all that judging. Nor are the people any less tired. That is no way to begin. As time passes you will not be able to transact all business yourself. Nor is this necessary—listen to my voice. If you act as the delegate of your people before God, and personally bring before him only the most important cases, those cases which concern everybody, that is all you can possibly be expected to do. As for the other cases—well, look around you," said he with easy gestures, "look around among the mob and search for respectable men, men of some standing, and place them as judges above the people. Let one of these men rule a group of a thousand, another a hundred, still another fifty and even ten, and let them all rule according to the law and tenets which you have set up. Only if it is a great matter should you be called. The lesser questions they can settle themselves; you do not even need to know about it. That is how we do it, and so shall it be easier for you. I would not to-day have been able to get away to visit you, if I took it into my head that I had to know about everything that is going on and if I burdened myself as you do."

"But the judges will accept gifts," answered Moses with a heavy heart, "and will declare the godless ones in the right. For gifts blind those who see and turn awry the cause of the just."

"I know that," answered Jethro, "I know it quite well. But one has to close one's eyes to that, just a little. Wherever order reigns, wherever law is spoken, wherever judgments are made, they become a little involved through gifts. Does that matter so much? Look, those who accept presents, they are ordinary folk. But the people themselves are ordinary folk; therefore they understand the ordinary and the ordinary is comfortable to the community. Moreover, if a man has been wronged because the judge of the ten has accepted gifts from his godless adversary, then let that man pursue an ordinary process of law. Let him appeal to the judge who rules over the fifty, then to the one who rules over the hundred; and finally, to the one who rules over the thousand: that one gets the most gifts and has therefore the clearest vision. Our man will find his rights with this last judge, that is, if in the meantime the fellow has not wearied of the whole affair."

Thus did Jethro discourse with even gestures, gestures which made life easier if one but saw them. Thus did he show that he was indeed the priest-king of a civilized desert people. With a heavy heart did Moses listen and nod. His was the pliable soul of the lonely spiritual man, the man who nods his head thoughtfully at the cleverness of the world and understands that the world may well be in the right. He followed the counsel of his deft brother-in-law—it was absolutely necessary. He appointed lay judges who, according to his tenets, let judgment flow next to the great spring and next to the smaller one. They judged the everyday cases (such as if an ass fell into the pit); only the capital cases came to Moses, the priest of God. And the greatest matters were decided by the holy oracles.

Moses no longer had his hands tied with everyday affairs; his hands were free for the larger work, the work of sculpting for which Joshua, the strategic youth, had won the work-place, Kadesh the oasis. Undoubtedly, the doctrine of right and wrong was one important example of the implications inherent in the invisible God. Yet it was only one example. Much work remained to be done. Mighty and long labour lay ahead, labour which would have to be achieved through anger and patience before the uncouth hordes could be formed into a people who would be more than the usual community to whom the ordinary was comfortable, but would be an extraordinary, a separated people and a unique monument erected to the Invisible One and dedicated to him.

15

The people soon learned what it meant to have fallen into the hands of an angrily patient workman who held himself accountable to an invisible god. They began to realize that that unnatural suggestion to omit the shout of triumph over the drowning of the enemy was but a beginning, though a portentous beginning, which already lay well within the domain of holiness and purity. It was a beginning which presupposed a certain understanding; the people would have to acquire that understanding before they could view Moses's command as anything less than unnatural.

What the mob was really like, to what degree it was the rawest of raw material and flesh and blood, lacking the most elementary conception of purity and holiness, how Moses had to begin at the beginning and teach them beginnings, that is to be deduced from the simple precepts with which he started to work and chisel and blast. Not to their comfort, certainly, for the stone does not take sides with the master but against him; to the stone the first stroke struck to form it appears as a most unnatural action.

Moses, with his wide-set eyes and his flattened nose, was always in their midst, here, there, in this and that encampment. Shaking his broad-wristed fists, he jogged, censured, chided, and churned their existence; he reproved, chastised, and cleansed, using as his touchstone the invisibility of the God Jahwe who had led them out of Egypt in order to choose them as his people and make them into a holy people, even as holy as himself. For the time being they were nothing more than rabble, a fact which they proved by emptying their bodies simply wherever they lay. That was a disgrace and a pestilence. Ye must have a place outside the camp where ye shall go when ye need to. Do ye understand me? And take along a little scoop and dig a pit before ye sit down, and after ye have sat then shall ye cover it. For the Lord your God walks in your camp, therefore your camp must be holy. And that means clean, so that the Lord need not hold his nose and turn away from you. For holiness begins with cleanliness, which is purity in the rough, the rough beginning of all purity. Dost thou comprehend this, Ahiman, and thou, wife Naemi? The next time I want to see everybody with that scoop, or ye shall have to reckon with the destroying angel.

Thou must be clean and wash thyself often with live water for the sake of thy health. For without water there is no cleanliness or holiness, and disease is unclean. But if thou thinkest that vulgarity is healthier than clean custom, then thou art an imbecile and thou shalt be visited by jaundice, fig warts, and the boils of Egypt. If ye do not practice cleanliness, then evil black blains shall grow up in you and the seeds of pestilence shall travel from blood to blood. Learn to distinguish cleanliness from uncleanliness, or else ye shall fail before the Invisible One and ye are nothing but rabble. Therefore if a man or a woman have a cankerous sore or an evil fistule, if he suffer with rash or ulcers, then he or she shall be declared unclean and not permitted in the encampment, but shall be put outside, separated in uncleanliness even as the Lord has separated you that ye may become clean. And whatever such a one has touched, on whatever he has lain, the saddle on which he has sat, that shall be burned. But if he has become clean again in separation, then he shall count seven days to make sure that he be truly clean, then he shall bathe thoroughly in water and then may he return.

Distinguish, I say unto you, and be holy before God. For how else can ye be holy as I want you to be? Ye eat everything together without choice or daintiness, and to me who have to watch you that is an abomination. There are certain things that ye may eat and others that ye may not, for ye shall have your pride and your disgust. Those animals which have cloven hoofs and chew their cud, those ye may eat. But those which chew their cud and divide not the hoof, like the camel, those shall be unclean to you and ye shall not eat them. Notice well: the good camel is not unclean as a living creature of God; it is merely unfit for food, as little fit as the pig, which, though it has cloven hoofs, does not chew its cud. Therefore distinguish! What creatures in the water have fins and scales, those ye may eat, but those which slither in the element without fins or scales, the entire breed of salamanders, they, though they also are from God, ye shall shun as nourishment. Among the birds disdain ye the eagle, the hawk, the osprey, the vulture, and their ilk. Furthermore, all ravens, the ostrich, the night owl, the cuckoo, the screech owl, the swan, the horned owl, the bat, the bittern, the stork, the heron, and the jay, as well as the swallow. Who would eat the weasel, the mouse, the toad, or the hedgehog? Who shall be so gross as to eat the lizard, the mole, and the blindworm—in fact, anything which creeps on the earth and crawls on its belly? But ye do it, and turn your souls into loathsomeness. The one whom I shall next see eating a blindworm I shall deal with so that he will never do it again. For though one does not die from eating it, though it is not harmful, yet it is reprehensible, and much shall be reprehensible to you. Therefore ye also shall eat no carcass, for that is even harmful.

Thus did he give them precepts of nourishment and circumscribe them in matters of food, though not alone in those. He did likewise in matters of lust and love, for there too were they disorderly in rabble fashion. Ye shall not commit adultery, he told them, for marriage is a holy barrier. But do ye really know what that means: ye shall not commit adultery? It means a hundred curbs out of regard for the holiness of God. It does not mean only that thou shalt not covet the wife of your neighbour: that is the least. For though ye are living in the flesh, ye are allied in oath to Invisibility. And marriage is the essence of all purity of flesh before God's visage. Therefore thou shalt not take unto thyself a wife and her mother, to name only one example; that is not seemly. And thou shalt never and under no conditions lie with thy sister so that thou shalt see her shame and she yours. For that is incest. Not even with thine aunt shalt thou lie. That is not worthy of her nor of thyself: thou shalt keep clear from it. If a woman have a sickness, then thou shalt shun her and not approach the fountain of her blood. And if something shameful should happen to a man in his sleep, then shall he be unclean until the next evening, and he shall bathe carefully in water.

I hear that thou causest thy daughter to be a whore and that thou takest whore money from her? Do this no longer, for if thou perseverest, then shall I let thee be stoned. What art thou thinking of, to sleep with a boy as well as with a woman? That is iniquity and rabble depravity. Both of you shall be put to death. But if somebody consort with an animal, be it man or woman, they shall be completely exterminated, and they and the animal choked to death.

Imagine their bewilderment over all these curbs! At first they felt life would hardly be worth living if they should observe them all. Moses struck at them with the sculptor's chisel so that the chips flew. Deadly serious was he about meting out the chastisements which he had placed on the worse transgressions. And behind his ordinances stood the young Joshua and his destroying angels.

"I am the Lord thy God," said he, risking the danger that they might in truth take him for God, "who have led thee out of Egypt and separated thee from all the peoples. Therefore shall ye separate, the clean from the unclean, and not follow in whoredom the other tribes but be holy to me. For I, thy Lord, am holy, and have separated you so that ye shall become mine. Of all the unclean actions the one most unclean is to care for any other god. For I am a jealous god. The most unclean action is to make yourself an image, be it the likeness of a man or a woman, of an ox or a hawk, a fish or a worm. In doing that ye shall become faithless to me, even if the image shall be in my likeness, and thou mightest as well sleep with thy sister or with an animal. Such an action is not far removed and soon follows quite by itself. Take care! I am among you and I see everything. Whosoever shall whore after the animal-and-death gods of Egypt, him shall I drown. I shall drive him into the desert and banish him like an outcast. And the same shall I do with him who sacrifices to the Moloch, whom I know ye still carry in your memory. If ye consume your force in its honour, I shall deem it evil, and heavily shall I deal with you. Nor shalt thou let thy son nor thy daughter walk through fire according to the stupid old custom, nor shall thou pay attention to the flight of the birds and their cry, nor whisper with fortune-tellers, destiny predictors, or augurs, nor shall ye question the dead nor practise magic in my name. If one among you is a scoundrel and takes my name in false testimony, he shall not profit by such tale-bearing, for I shall devour him. It is even magic and abomination to print marks on one's body, to shave one's eyebrows and make cuttings on one's face as a sign of sorrow for the dead—I shall not suffer it."

How great was their bewilderment! They were not even allowed to cut their faces in mourning, not even allowed to tattoo themselves a little bit. They realized now what it meant by the invisibility of God. It meant great privation, this business of being in league with Jahwe. But because behind Moses's prohibition stood the destroying angels, and because nobody wanted to be driven into the desert, that which he prohibited soon appeared to them to be worthy of fear. At first it was fearworthy only in relation to the punishment, but by and by the action itself took on the stamp of evil, and if they committed it they became ill at ease without even thinking of the punishment.

Bridle your hearts, he said to them, and do not cast your eyes on somebody else's possessions. If ye desire them, it soon follows that ye take them, be it through stealthy purloining, which is cowardice, or by killing the other, which is brutality. Jahwe and I do not want you either cowardly or brutal, but ye shall be in the middle between these two; that means decent. Have ye understood that much? To steal is slinking wretchedness, but to murder, be it from rage or from greed, or from greedy rage or from raging greed, that is flaming wrong, and against him who shall commit such a wrong shall I set my countenance so that he will not know where to hide himself. For he has shed blood and blood is holy awe and a deep secret, offering for my altar and atonement. Ye shall not eat blood nor any meat in the blood, for blood is mine. And he who is smeared with the blood of human beings, his heart shall sicken in cold terror and I shall drive him that he run away from himself unto the ends of the world. Say ye Amen to that.

And they said Amen, still hoping that with the ban on murder killing alone was meant. For few of them had the desire to kill, and those who did had it only occasionally. But it turned out that Jahwe gave that word as wide a meaning as he had given the word adultery and that he meant by it all sorts of things, so that "murder" and "killing" began with almost any transgression of the code. Almost every wound which one man inflicted upon another, whether through deceit or through fraud (and almost all of the people hankered a little after deceit and fraud), Jahwe considered bloodshed. They should not deal falsely with one another nor bear false witness against their neighbours, and they should use just weights, and just measures. It was to the highest degree unnatural, and for the time being it was only the natural fear of punishment which gave an aspect of naturalness to all this bidding and forbidding.

That one should honour one's father and mother as Moses demanded, that also had a wider meaning, wider than one suspected at first blush. Whosoever raised his hand against his progenitor and cursed him, well, yes, he should be done away with. But that respect should also be extended to those who merely could be your progenitors. Ye shall arise before a grey head. Ye shall cross your arms and incline your stupid head. Do ye understand me? Thus demands the decency of God. The only consolation was that since your neighbour was not permitted to kill you, you had a reasonable prospect of becoming yourself old and grey, so that the others would have to arise before you.

Finally, it appeared that old age was a symbol of what was old in general, everything which did not happen from to-day to to-morrow but which came from long ago: the piously traditional, the custom of the fathers. To that one had to pay the tribute of honour and awe in God. Ye shall keep my sabbaths, the day on which I led you out of Egypt, the day of the unleavened bread, and the day when I rested from the labours of my creation. Ye shall not defile my day with the sweat of your brow: I forbid it. For I have led thee out of the Egyptian house of bondage with mighty hand and with outstretched arm, where thou wert a slave and a work animal. And my day shall be the day of thy freedom, which thou shalt keep holy. Six days shalt thou be a tiller or a plough-maker or a potter or a coppersmith or a joiner. But on my day shalt thou put on clean garments and thou shalt be nothing, nothing but a human being who raises his eyes to the Invisible.

Thou wert an oppressed servant in the land of Egypt. Think of that in your behaviour towards those who are strangers amongst you: for example, the children of Amalek, whom God gave into your hands. Do not oppress them. Look on them as ye look on yourself and give them equal rights, or I shall crash down upon you. For they too stand under the protection of Jahwe. In short, do not make such a stupid, arrogant distinction between thyself and the others, so that thou thinkest that thou alone art real and thou alone countest while the others are only a semblance. Ye both have life in common, and it is only an accident that thou art not he. Therefore do not love thyself alone but love him in the same way, and do unto him as thou desirest that he do unto you. Be gracious with one another and kiss the tips of your fingers when ye pass each other and bow with civility and speak the greeting, "Be hale and healthy." For it is quite as important that he be healthy as that thou be healthy. And even if it is only formal civility that ye do thus and kiss your finger-tips, the gesture does leave something in your heart of that which should be there of your neighbour. To that say ye Amen!

And they all said Amen.

16

Actually, that Amen did not mean very much. They only said it because Moses was the man who had led them successfully out of Egypt, who had drowned Pharaoh's chariots, and had won the battle of Kadesh. It took a long time before what he had taught them, what he enjoined upon them—all those barriers, laws, and prohibitions—sank into their flesh and blood. It was a mighty piece of work which he had undertaken, the work of changing the rabble into a people dedicated to the Lord, and to a clean image which could pass muster before the Invisible. In the sweat of his brow he worked in his workplace, Kadesh. He kept his wide-set eyes on all. He chiselled, blasted, formed, and smoothed the unwilling stone with tenacious patience, with repeated forbearance and frequent forgiving, and also with flaming anger and chastising sternness. Yet often did he almost despair when once again the flesh relapsed into stubbornness and forgetfulness, when once again the people failed to use the scoop, when they ate blindworms, slept with their sisters or their animals, painted marks upon themselves, crouched with fortune-tellers, slunk towards theft, and killed each other. "O rabble," said he to them, "ye shall see. The Lord shall appear above you and devour you." But to the Lord himself he said, "What shall I do with this flesh and why have you withdrawn your graces from me, that you burden me with a thing I cannot bear? I would rather clean a stable untouched for years by water or spade, I would rather clear a thicket with my bare hands, and turn it into a garden, than try to form for you a clean image out of them. Wherefore must I carry these people in my arms as if I had given them birth? I am but half related to them from my father's side; therefore I pray you let me enjoy my life and free me from this task. Or else strangle me rather!"

But God answered Moses out of his inner consciousness with so clear a voice that he could hear it with his ears and he fell upon his face:

"Just because you are only half related to them from the side of the buried one are you the man to form them for me and to raise them to a holy people. For if you were wholly and only one of them, then you could not see them as they are nor work upon them. Anyway, that you complain to me and wish to excuse yourself from your work is pure affectation. For you know quite well that your work is beginning to take effect. You know that you have already given them a conscience so that they are ill at ease when they do ill. Therefore do not pretend to me that you do not desire your travail. It is my desire, God's desire, which you have, and lacking it you would sicken of life as our people sickened of manna after a few days. Of course, if I decided to strangle you, then yes, then would you be rid of that desire."

The much-troubled Moses understood this, nodded his head at Jahwe's words as he lay there, and stood up once again to his travail. But now he had problems, not only in his capacity as a sculptor of the people; trouble and grief began to creep into his family life. Anger, envy, and bickering arose around him and there was no peace in his hut. Perhaps it was his own fault, the fault of his senses. For his senses, stirred up by overwork, hung on a Negro girl, the well-known Negro girl.

One knows that at this time he lived with an Ethiopian girl as well as with his wife Zipporah, the mother of his sons. She was a wench from the land of Kush who as a child had arrived in Egypt, had lived among the Hebrew tribes in Goshen, and had joined the exodus. Undoubtedly she had known many a man, yet Moses now chose her as the companion of his bed. She was a magnificent specimen of her type, with erect breasts, with rolling eyes, thick deep lips, to sink into which may well have been an adventure, and a skin redolent of spice. Moses doted on her mightily; she was his recreation, and he would not let go of her, though he drew upon himself the enmity of his whole house. Not only his Midianite wife and her sons looked askance at the affair, but also and especially his half-sister Miriam and his half-brother Aaron. Zipporah, who possessed much of the even worldliness of her brother Jethro, got along tolerably well with her rival, particularly since the Ethiopian girl knew how to hide her feminine triumph and conducted herself most subserviently towards her. Zipporah treated the Ethiopian girl more with mockery than hate, and adopted towards Moses a light tone of irony which hid the jealousy she felt. His sons, Gershom and Eliezer, members of Joshua's dashing troop, possessed too much sense of discipline to revolt openly against their father; yet they let it be known unmistakably that they were angry and that they were ashamed of him.

Matters stood yet differently with Miriam the prophetess and Aaron the unctuous. Their hatred towards the Ethiopian mistress was more venomous than that of the others, because that hatred was the expression of a deeper and more general grudge which united them against Moses. For a long time now had they envied Moses his intimate relation with God and his spiritual master. That he felt himself to be God's elect worker they thought was largely conceit; they deemed themselves just as good as he, perhaps better. To each other they said, "Does the Lord talk only through Moses? Does he not also talk through us? Who is this man Moses? that he has exalted himself above us?" That then was the real cause of the indignation which they manifested towards this affair with the Ethiopian. And every time they noisily reproached their unfortunate brother with the passion of his nights, they soon departed into more general complaints. Soon they would be harping on the injustice which was their fate because of Moses's elevation.

Once as the day was drawing towards an end, they were in his hut, and harassed him in a way I said they were wont to harass him: the Ethiopian here and the Ethiopian there, and that he was thinking of nothing but her black breasts, and what a scandal it was, what a disgrace to his wife Zipporah, and what exposure for himself who claimed to be a prince of God and Jahwe's sole mouthpiece on earth....

"Claimed?" said he. "What God has commanded me to be I am. How ugly of you, how very ugly, that you envy my pleasure and my relaxation on the breasts of the Ethiopian. For it is no sin before God, and there is no prohibition among all the prohibitions which he gave to me which says that one may not lie with an Ethiopian. Not that I know of."

But they answered that he chose his own prohibitions according to his own tastes, and quite possibly he would soon preach that it was compulsory to lie with Ethiopians. For did he not consider himself Jahwe's sole mouthpiece? The truth was that they, Miriam and Aaron, were the proper children of Amram and the grandchildren of Levi, while he, when all was said and done, was only a foundling from the bulrushes; he might learn a little humility and not insist quite so much on his Ethiopian nor ignore their displeasure quite so offhandedly. Such behaviour was proof of his pride and his conceit.

"Who can help it that he is called?" answered he. "Can any man help it if he comes upon the burning thorn bush? Miriam, I have always thought highly of your prophetic gifts and never denied your accomplishments on the timbrel...."

"Then why did you disallow my hymn 'Steed and Man' and why did you prohibit me from leading the round dance of the women? You pretended that God forbade his flock to triumph over the downfall of the Egyptians. That was abominable of you."

"And you, Aaron," continued the hard-pressed Moses, "you I have employed as the high priest in the tabernacle, and I have entrusted the Chest, the Ephod, and the Brass Serpent unto your care. Thus do I value you."

"That was the least that you could have done," answered Aaron. "For without my eloquence could you never have persuaded the people to the cause of Jahwe, nor won them for the exodus. Consider how awkward is your mouth! But now you call yourself the man who has led us out of Egypt! If you really valued us, if you really did not exalt yourself so arrogantly over your blood relatives, then why do you not pay heed to our words? Why do you remain deaf to our admonition that you imperil our whole tribe with your black paramour? To Zipporah, your Midianite wife, she is a draught as bitter as gall, and you offend all of Midian with your action, so that Jethro your brother-in-law might soon declare war on us—all for the sake of your coloured caprice."

"Jethro," said Moses with restraint, "is an even man of the world who well understands that Zipporah—praised be her name!—no longer can offer the necessary recreation to a highly overworked and heavily burdened man. But the skin of my Ethiopian is like cinnamon and perfumed of carnation in my nostrils; all my senses long for her, and therefore I beg of you, my good friends, grant her to me."

But that they did not want to do. They screeched and demanded not only that he should part from the Ethiopian and forbid her his bed, but also that he drive her into the desert without water.

Thereupon veins of anger rose on his forehead and terribly did his fists begin to tremble. But before he could open his mouth to respond, a very different trembling began—Jahwe interposed and set his visage against the hard-hearted brother and sister, and came to his servant's aid in a way they never forgot. Something frightful, something never before seen, now happened.

17

The foundations trembled. The earth shook, shivered, and swayed under their feet so that they could not stand upright but tottered to and fro in the hut, whose posts seemed to be shaken by giant fists. What had been firm began to waver, not only in one direction but in crooked and dizzying gyrations. It was horrible. At the same time there occurred a subterranean growling and rumbling and a sound from above and from outside like the blare of a great trumpet, followed by a droning, a thundering, and a rustling. It is very strange and peculiarly embarrassing if you are on the point of breaking out into a rage and the Lord takes the words out of your mouth and himself breaks out much more mightily than you yourself could have done it, and shakes the world where you could only have shaken your fists.

Moses was the least pale with fright, for at all times he was prepared for God. With Aaron and Miriam, who were deathly pale, he rushed out of the house. Then they saw that the earth had opened its jaws and that a great gap yawned right next to their hut. Obviously this rent had been destined for Miriam and Aaron, and had missed them only by a few yards. And they looked towards the mountain in the east behind the desert, Horeb and

Sinai—but what was happening on Horeb, what was taking place on Sinai? It stood there enveloped from foot to summit in smoke and flames, and threw glowing crumbs towards heaven, with a far-off sound of fearful crackling. Streams of fire ran down its sides. Its vapour, crossed by lightning, obscured the stars above the desert, and slowly a rain of ashes began to descend upon the oasis Kadesh.

Aaron and Miriam fell upon their foreheads; the cleft destined for them had filled them with terror. This revelation of Jahwe showed them that they had gone too far and had spoken foolishly. Aaron exclaimed:

"O my master, this woman my sister has jabbered ugly words. Accept my prayer and let not the sin remain upon her, the sin with which she sinned against the man anointed by the Lord."

Miriam also screamed to Moses and spoke: "Master, it is impossible to speak more foolishly than spoke my brother Aaron. Forgive him and let not the sin remain upon him, so that God may not devour him just because he has twitted you a little about the Ethiopian."

Moses was not quite certain if Jahwe's revelation was really meant for his brother and sister and their lack of love, or if it was the call meant for him, the call for which he had waited hourly, the call that summoned him to commune with God about his people and the work of their education. But he let them suppose what they supposed and answered:

"There, you see. But take courage, children of Amram. I shall put forth a good word for you up there with God on the mountain, whither he calls me. For now you shall see, and all the people shall see, whether your brother has become unmanned by his black infatuation or if the courage of God still dwells in his heart stronger than in other hearts. To the fiery mountain shall I go, quite alone, upward to God, to hear his thoughts and to deal without fear with the fearful one, on familiar terms, far from the people, but in their cause. For a long time have I known that he wishes to write down all that I have taught you for your salvation into binding words, into an eternal condensation, that I might carry it back to you from his mountain, and that the people may possess it in the tabernacle together with the Chest, the Ephod, and the Brass Serpent. Farewell. I may perish in God's tumult, in the fire of the mountain; I have to reckon with that. But should I return, then shall I bring out of his thunder the eternal word, God's law."

Such was his firm resolve; whether for life or death, that had he decided. For in order to root the obdurate, always backsliding rabble in God's morality, in order to make them fear his laws, nothing was more effective than that he, bare and alone, should dare to climb up to Jahwe's terror, up the spewing mountain, and thence carry down the dictates. Then, thought he, would they observe the laws.

When the people came running from all sides to his hut, trembling at the knees, frightened by the signs and by the terrible undulations of the earth, which occurred once and twice again, though weaker, Moses forbade them their commonplace quaking and admonished them to decent composure. God called him, said he, for their sake, and he was to climb up to Jahwe, up to the summit of the mountain, and bring something back for them, with God's will. They, however, should return to their homes and should prepare for a pilgrimage. They should hold themselves clean and wash their garments and abstain from their wives, and to-morrow they should wander out from Kadesh into the desert near the mountain. There should they encamp and wait for him until he returned from the fearful interview, perhaps bringing something back for them.

And thus it happened, or at least almost thus. Moses in his fashion had only remembered to tell them to wash their garments and to abstain from their wives. Joshua, the strategic youth, had remembered what else was necessary for such an excursion; with his troop he provided the proper quantities of water and nourishment needful to the thousands in the desert. And he also established a line of communication between Kadesh and the encampment near the mountain. He left Caleb his lieutenant in Kadesh with a police detail to supervise those who could not or would not come along. When the third day had dawned and all preparations had been made, all the others set out with their carts and their slaughter animals. They journeyed towards the mountain, a journey of a day and still a half. There, at a respectable distance from Jahwe's fuming dwelling, Joshua erected an enclosure. He enjoined the people most strictly, and in Moses's name, not to think of climbing that mountain nor even to set foot upon it. The master alone was privileged to approach so near to God. Moreover, it was highly dangerous, and whoever touched the mountain should be stoned or pierced with the arrow. They took this command in their stride, for rabble has no desire whatever to come all too near to God. To the common man the mountain did not in the least look inviting, neither by day, when Jahwe stood upon it in a thick cloud crossed by lightning, nor certainly by night, when the cloud and the entire summit glowed.

Joshua was extremely proud of the courage of his master, who the very first day and before all the people set out on his way to the mountain, alone and on foot with his pilgrim's staff, provided only with an earthen flask, a few crusts, and some tools, an axe, a chisel, a spade and a stylus. Very proud was the youth, and pleased at the impression which such holy intrepidity would surely make on the multitude. But anxious was he too about the man he worshipped, and he implored him not to approach too near to Jahwe and to be careful of the hot molten streams which ran down the sides of the mountain. Also, said he, he would visit Moses once or twice and look after him, so that the master would not in God's wilderness lack the simplest necessities.

18

Moses, leaning on his staff, traversed the desert, his wide-set eyes fixed on God's mountain, which was smoking like an oven and spewed forth many times. The mountain was of peculiar shape: it had fissures and veins which seemed to divide it into terraces and which looked like upward-leading paths, though they were not paths, but simply gradations of yellow walls. On the third day, after climbing several foothills, God's delegate arrived at the bare foot of the mountain. Then he began to ascend, his fist grasping the pilgrim's staff which he set before him. He climbed without path or track many an hour, step by step, higher, always higher, towards God's nearness. He climbed as far as a human being could, for by and by the sulphurous fumes which smelled of hot metals and which filled the air choked him, and he began to cough. He arrived at the topmost fissure and terrace right underneath the summit, where he could have a wide view of the bald and wild mountain ranges on both sides, and out over the desert as far as Kadesh.

Closer by he could see the people in their enclosure, far below and small.

Here the coughing Moses found a cave in the mountain wall, a cave with a projecting roof of rock which could protect him from the falling stones and the flowing broth. There he took up his abode and arranged himself to start, after a short breathing spell, the work which God had ordered from him. Under the difficult circumstances—for the metal vapours lay heavily on his breast and made even the water taste of sulphur—this work held him fast up there not less than forty days and forty nights.

But why so long? Idle question! The eternal had to be recorded, the binding word had to be briefed, God's terse moral law had to be captured and graved into the stone of the mountain, so that Moses might bring it down to the vacillating mob, to the blood of his buried father, down into the encampment where they were waiting. There it was to stand from generation to generation, unbreakable, graved also into their minds and into their flesh and blood, the quintessence of human decency.

From his inner consciousness God directed him to hew two tablets from the rock and to write upon them his dictate, five words on the one and five words on the other, together ten words. It was no easy task to build the two tablets, to smooth them and to shape them into fit receptacles of eternal brevity. For a lone man, even if he had drunk the milk of a mason's daughter, even if he had broad wrists, it was a piece of work subject to many a mishap. Of the forty days it took a quarter. But the actual writing down was a problem the solution of which could well have prolonged the number of Moses's mountain days far over forty.

For in what manner should he write? In the academy of Thebes he had learned the decorative picture writing of Egypt with all its current amendments. He had also learned the stiffly formal arrow script of Euphrates, in which the kings of the world were wont to exchange their thoughts on fragments of clay. In Midian he had become acquainted with still a third magic method of capturing meaning. This one consisted of eyes, crosses, insets, circles, and variously formed serpentine lines. It was a method used in Sinai which had been copied with desert awkwardness from the Egyptians. Its marks, however, did not represent whole words or word pictures, but only their parts. They denoted syllables which were to be read together.

None of these three methods of fastening thought satisfied him, for the simple reason that each of them was linked to a particular language and was indigenous to that language. Moses realized perfectly well that it would never under any conditions be possible for him to set upon the stone the dictate of ten words either in Babylonian or in Egyptian language, nor yet in the jargon of the Sinai Bedouins. The words on the stone could be only in the language of his father's blood, the very dialect which they spoke and which he himself employed in his teachings. It did not matter whether they would be able to read it or not. In fact, how could they be expected to read a language which no one could as yet write? There was no magic symbol at hand to represent and hold fast their speech.

With all his soul Moses wished that there existed such a symbol, one which they could learn to read quickly, very quickly; one which children, such as they were, could learn in a few days. It followed, then, that somebody could think up and invent such a symbol in a few days, with the help of God's nearness. Yes, because it did not exist, somebody had to think up and invent this new method of writing.

What a pressing and precious task! He had not considered it in advance, had simply thought of "writing" and had not taken into account that one could not write just like that! Fired by his fervent search for symbols his people could understand, his head glowed and smoked like an oven and like the summit of the mountain. It seemed to him as if rays emerged from his head, as if horns sprang from his forehead, so great was his wishing exertion. And then a simple, illuminating idea came to him. True, he could not invent signs for all the words used by his kin, nor for the syllables from which they formed their words. Even if the vocabulary of those down in the enclosure was paltry, yet would it have required too many marks for him to build in the span of his mountain days and also for the others to learn to read quickly. Therefore he thought of something else, and horns stood upon his forehead out of pride over the flash of God's inspiration. He gathered the sounds of the language, those formed by the lips, by the tongue, by the palate, and by the throat; he put to one side the few open sounds which occurred every so often within the words, which in fact were framed by the others into words. He found that there were not too many of these framing sonant sounds—hardly twenty. If one ascribed definite signs to them, signs which everybody could alike aspirate and respirate, mumble and rumble, gabble and babble, then one could combine these signs into words and word pictures, leaving out the open sounds which followed by themselves. Thus one could form any word one liked, any word which existed, not only in the language of his father's kin, but in all languages—yes, with these signs one could even write Egyptian or Babylonian.

A flash from God. An idea with horns. An idea such as could be expected from the Invisible and the spiritual one, him to whom the world belonged, him who, though he had chosen those down below as his people, was yet the Lord of all the earth. It was an idea also which was eminently fitting to the next and most pressing purpose for which and out of which it was created: the text of the tablets, the binding briefed text. This text was to be coined first and specifically for the tribe which Moses had led out of Egypt because God and he were inclined towards them. But just as with a handful of these signs all the words of all the languages of all the people could, if need be, be written, just as Jahwe was the God of all the world, so was what Moses meant to brief and write of such a nature that it could serve as fundamental precept, as the rock of human decency, to all the peoples of the earth.

Moses with his fiery head now experimented with signs loosely related to the marks of the Sinai people as he remembered them. On the wall of the mountain he graved with his stylus the lisping, popping, and smacking, the hissing, and swishing, the humming and murmuring sounds. And when he had all the signs together and could distinguish them with a certain amount of assurance, lo! with them one could write the whole world, all that which occupied space and all that which occupied no space, all that was fashioned and all that was thought. In short, all.

He wrote. That is to say, he jabbed, chiselled, and hacked at the brittle stone of the tablets, those tablets which he had hewn laboriously and whose creation went hand in hand with the creation of the letters. No wonder that it took him forty days!

Joshua, his youth, came to see him several times. He brought him water and crusts, without precisely telling the people of his visits.

The people thought that Moses lived up there in God's proximity and communed with him quite alone. And Joshua deemed it best to let them believe this. Therefore his visits were short and made by night.

From the dawn of the light of day above Edom to its extinction, Moses sat behind the desert and worked. One has to imagine him as he sat up there with bare shoulders, his breast covered with hair, with his powerful arms which he may have inherited from his ill-used father, with his eyes set far apart, with his flattened nose, with the divided now greying beard—chewing his crust, now and then coughing from the metal vapours of the mountain, hammering, scraping, and polishing his tablets in the sweat of his brow. He crouched before the tablets propped against the rocky wall, and painstakingly carved the crow's-feet, then traced them with his stylus, and finally graved the omnipotent runes deep into the flatness of the stone.

On one tablet he wrote:

> I, Jahwe, am thy God; thou shalt have
> no other gods before me.
> Thou shalt not make unto thee any
> image.
> Thou shalt not take my name in vain.
> Remember my day, to keep it holy.
> Honour thy father and thy mother.

And on the other tablet he wrote:

> Thou shalt not murder.
> Thou shalt not commit adultery.
> Thou shalt not steal.
> Thou shalt not harm thy neighbour by
> false witness.
> Thou shalt not cast a covetous eye on
> the possessions of thy neighbour.

That is what he wrote, omitting the open sounds which formed themselves. And always it seemed to him as if rays like two horns stood out from the locks of his forehead.

When Joshua came for the last time to the mountain, he remained a little longer, two whole days. For Moses was not finished with his work and they wanted to descend together. The youth admired whole-heartedly what his master had accomplished. He comforted him because a few letters were cracked and unrecognizable in spite of all the love and care which Moses had expended. Joshua assured him that this did no harm to the total impression.

The last thing that Moses did while Joshua looked on was to paint the sunken letters with his blood so that they would stand out better. No other pigment was at hand. Therefore he cut his strong arm with his stylus and smeared the trickling blood into the letters so that they glowed rosily in the stone. When the writing had dried, Moses took one tablet under each arm, gave his pilgrim's staff, with which he had ascended, to the youth, and thus they wandered down from the seat of God towards the encampment of the people near the mountain in the desert.

19

When they had arrived at a certain distance from the encampment, just within hearing distance, a noise penetrated to them, a hollow screeching. They could not account for it. It was Moses who heard it first and Joshua who mentioned it first.

"Do you hear this peculiar clatter," he asked, "this tumult, this uproar? There is something doing, I think, a brawl, a bout, or I am much mistaken. And it must be violent and general, that we hear it as far as this. If it is what I think it is, then it is good that we come."

"That we come," answered Moses, "is good in any case. But as far as I can make out, this is no scuffle and no tussle, but something like a feasting or a dance of triumph. Do you not hear the high-pitched jubilation and clash of timbrels? Joshua, how is it that they celebrate without my permission? Joshua, what has got into them? Let us hurry."

He grasped his two tablets higher under his arms and strode faster with the puzzled Joshua.

"A dance of triumph ... a dance of triumph," he repeated uneasily and finally in open terror. For it appeared all too clearly that this was not an ordinary brawl in which one person lay on top and the other below; this was a general united carousal. And now it was only a question of what kind of unity it was in which they thus revelled.

Even that question answered itself too soon, if indeed it need ever have been asked. The mess was horrible. As Moses and Joshua passed the high posts of the encampment they saw it in shameless unequivocalness. The people had broken loose. They had thrown off everything that Moses had laid upon them in holiness, all the morality of God. They wallowed in relapse.

Directly behind the portals was a free space which was the assembly place. There things were happening, there they were carrying on, there they wallowed, there they celebrated their miserable liberty. Before the dance they had all stuffed themselves full. One could see that at first glance. Everywhere the place showed the traces of slaughtering and gluttony. And in whose honour had they sacrificed, slaughtered, and stuffed themselves? There it stood. In the midst of barrenness, set on a stone, set on an altar pedestal, an image, a thing made by their hands, an idolatrous mischief, a golden calf.

It was no calf, it was a bull, the real, ordinary stud bull of all the peoples of the world. A calf it is called only because it was no more than medium size, in fact rather less, and also misshapen and ludicrously fashioned; an awkward abomination, yet all too recognizable as a bull.

Around this thing a multitudinous round dance was in progress, a dozen circles of men and women, hand in hand, accompanied by timbrels and by cymbals. Heads were thrown far back, rolling eyes were upturned, knees jerked towards chins; they screeched and they roared and made crass obeisance. In different directions did the dance turn, one shameful circle turning towards the right, another towards the left. In the very centre of the whirlpool, near the calf, Aaron could be seen hopping around in his long-sleeved garment which he used to wear as the guardian of the tabernacle, and which he had gathered high so that he could jig with his long, hairy legs. And Miriam led the women with her timbrel.

But this was only the round dance near the calf. Farther on what was to be expected was taking place. It is difficult to confess how far the people debased themselves. Some ate blindworms, others lay with their sisters and that publicly, in the calf's honour. Others simply squatted and emptied themselves, forgetting the scoop. Men offered their force to the calf. Somewhere someone was cuffing his own mother.

At these gruesome sights, the veins of anger swelled to bursting on Moses's forehead. His face flaming red, he cut his way through the circles of the dancers—straight to the calf, the seed, the fountain, the womb of the crime. Recognizing the master, they gaped with embarrassed grins. High up he lifted one of the tablets of the law with mighty arms, and smashed it down on the ridiculous beast, so that its legs crumbled. Once again did he strike, and with such rage that though the tablet broke into pieces, nothing but a formless mass remained of the thing. Then he swung the second tablet and gave the abomination a final blow, grinding it completely to dust. And because the second tablet remained still intact, he shattered it with a blow on the pedestal. Then he stood still with trembling fists, and deeply from his breasts he groaned: "Ye rabble, ye Godforsaken! There lies what I have carried down from God, what he has written for you with his finger as your talisman against the misery of ignorance. There it lies in ruins near the fragments of your idol. And what shall I now tell my Lord so that he will not devour you?"

He saw Aaron the jumper standing near with downcast eyes, and with oily locks at the nape of his neck; he stood silent and stupid. Moses seized him by his garment, shook him, and spoke: "Where did the golden Belial come from, this excrescence, and what did the people do to you that you push them to their destruction while I am up on the mountain? Why do you yourself bray before them in their dance of debauchery?"

And Aaron answered, "O my master, let not your anger be heaped on me and on my sister. We had to give in. You know that the people are evil. They forced us. You were away so long, you remained an eternity on the mountain, so that we all thought that you would never return. Then the people gathered against me and screamed, 'Nobody knows what has become of that man Moses, who has led us out of Egypt. He shall not return. Probably the spewing mouth of the mountain has swallowed him. Arise, make us gods which shall go before us when Amalek comes. We are a people like other peoples, and want to carouse before gods which are like the gods of other peoples!' Thus they spoke, master, for if you pardon me, they thought they were rid of you. But now tell me what I could have done when they banded together against me. I asked them to break off the golden earrings from their ears. These I melted in the fire and made a form, and cast the calf as their god."

"It is not even a good likeness of a calf," interposed Moses contemptuously.

"They were in such a hurry," answered Aaron. "The very next day, that is, to-day, they wanted to hold their revels in honour of the sympathetic gods. Therefore I handed over to them the image as it was, a piece of work to which you ought not deny a certain amount of verisimilitude. And they rejoiced and spoke, 'These are your gods' Israel, which have led you out of Egypt.' And we built an altar and they offered burnt sacrifices and thank offerings and ate, and after that they played and danced a little."

Moses let him stand there and made his way back to the portal through the scattered circles of dancers. There with Joshua he placed himself beneath the birchen crossbeam and called with all his might:

"Who is on the Lord's side, let him come unto me."

Many came, those who were of sound heart and had not willingly joined the revels. Joshua's armed troop assembled around him.

"Ye unfortunate people," said Moses, "what have ye done, and how shall I now atone for you before Jahwe, that he shall not blot you out as an incorrigibly stiff-necked people and shall not devour you? As soon as I turn my back, ye make yourselves a golden Belial. Shame on you and on me! Do ye see these ruins—I do not mean those of the calf, let the pest take them!—I mean the others? That is the gift which I had promised you and which I have brought down to you, the eternal condensation, the rock of decency, the ten words which I, in God's nearness, wrote down in your language and wrote with my blood, with the blood of my father; with your blood did I write them. Now lies the gift in fragments."

Then many who heard this wept and there was a great crying in the encampment.

"Perhaps it will be possible to replace them," said Moses. "For the Lord is patient and of infinite mercy, and forgives missteps and trespasses. But"—he thundered of a sudden, while his blood rose to his head and his veins swelled to bursting— "he lets no one go unpunished. For, says the Lord, I visit the iniquity of the fathers upon the children unto the third and fourth generation as the jealous God that I am. We shall hold court here," exclaimed Moses, "and shall order a bloody cleansing. It shall be determined who were the ringleaders who first screamed for golden gods and insolently asserted that the calf has led you out of Egypt, where I alone have done it, says the Lord. They shall all have to deal with the destroying angels, regardless of their rank or person. To death shall they be stoned and shot by the arrow, even if there are three hundred of them. And the others shall strip off their ornaments and mourn until I return—for I shall again ascend the mountain of God, and shall see what in any case I can do for you, ye stiff-necked people."

20

Moses did not attend the executions which the golden calf had made necessary. That was the business of the dashing Joshua. Moses himself was once again up on the mountain in his cave underneath the rumbling summit. While the people mourned he again remained forty days and forty nights alone among the vapours. But why so long? The answer is thus: not only because Jahwe directed him to form the tablets anew and to write down the dictate afresh—that task went more quickly because he had acquired practice and knew how to write—but also because he had to fight a long fight with the Lord before he would permit the renewal. It was a wrestling in which anger and mercy, fatigue over the work and love for the undertaking, were in turn victorious. Moses had to use much power of persuasion and many clever appeals to prevent God from declaring the covenant broken. For almost did God cast himself loose from the stiff-necked rabble, almost did he smash them as Moses in flaming anger had smashed the first tablets of the law.

"I shall not go before them," said God, "to lead them into the land of their fathers. Do not ask this of me—I cannot depend upon my patience. I am a jealous God and I flame up, and you shall see one day I shall forget myself and I shall devour them altogether."

And he proposed to Moses that he would annihilate these people, who were as miscast as the golden calf and as incorrigible. It would be impossible, said he, to raise them into a holy people, and there was nothing left but to consume Israel and rot it out. But of him, Moses, he would make a great nation and live with him in covenant. But this Moses did not want, and he said to him, "No, Lord," said he, "forgive them their sins; if not, then blot me out of the book also, for I do not wish to survive them. For my part, I wish for no other holy people but them."

And he appealed to the Lord's sense of honour and spoke: "Imagine, holy one, what is going to happen. If you kill these people as one man, then the heathen who shall hear their screams will say, 'Bah! The Lord was not able to bring the people into the land which he had promised them. He was not powerful enough. Therefore did he slaughter them in the wilderness.' Do you want that said of you by all the peoples of the world? Therefore let the power of the Lord appear great, and be lenient with the missteps of your children according to your mercy."

It was this last argument which won God and decided him towards forgiveness. With the restriction, however, that of this generation none except Joshua and Caleb should ever see the promised land. "Your children," decided the Lord, "I shall lead there. But all those who are above twenty in their age, they shall never see the land. Their bodies shall fall in the desert."

"It is well, Lord, all shall be well," answered Moses. "We shall leave it at that." For because this decision agreed with his and Joshua's purposes, he argued against it no longer. "Now let me renew the tablets," said he, "that I may take your brevity down to the human beings. After all, perhaps it was just as well that I smashed the first in my anger. There were a few misshaped letters in them. I shall now confess to you that I fleetingly thought of this when I dashed the tablets to pieces."

And again he sat, secretly nourished and succoured by Joshua, and he jabbed and he chiselled, he scraped and he smoothed. Wiping his brow from time to time with the back of his hand, he wrote, hacking and graving the letters into the tablets. They came out a good deal better than the first time. Then again he painted the letters with his blood and descended, the law under his arms.

It was announced to Israel that the mourning had come to an end, and that they again might put on their ornaments, except of course the earrings: these had been used up to bad purpose. And all the people came before Moses that he might hand them what he had brought down, the message of Jahwe from the mountain, the tablets with the ten words.

"Take them, blood of our fathers," said he, "and hold them sacred in the tent of God. But what they tell ye, that hold sacred in your actions. For here is briefed what shall bind you; here is the divine condensation; here is the alpha and omega of human behaviour; here is the rock of decency, which God has inscribed in lapidary writing, using my stylus. In your language did he write, but in symbols in which if need be all the languages of all peoples could be written. For he is the Lord of all, and therefore is the Lord of ABC, and his speech, addressed to you, Israel, is at the same time a speech for all.

"Into the stone of the mountain did I grave the ABC of human behaviour, but it must be graved also into your flesh and blood, Israel. So that he who breaks but one word of the ten commandments shall tremble before his own self and before God and an icy finger shall be laid on his heart, because he has stepped out of God's confines. I know well and God knows in advance that his commandments will not be obeyed, and they will be transgressed at all times and everywhere. But at least the heart of everyone who breaks them shall turn icy, for the words are written in every man's flesh and blood and deep within himself he knows that the words are all-valid.

"But woe to the man who shall arise and speak: 'They are no longer valid.' Woe to him who teaches you: 'Arise and get rid of them! Lie, murder, rob, whore, rape, and deliver your father and mother to the knife. For this is the natural behaviour of human beings and you shall praise my name because I proclaim natural licence.' Woe to him who erects a calf and speaks: 'This is your god. In his honour do all of this, and whirl around the image I have fashioned in a round dance of debauchery.' He shall be mighty and powerful, he shall sit upon a golden throne, and he shall be looked up to as the wisest of all. For he knows that the inclination of the human heart is evil, even in youth. But that is about all that he will know, and he who knows only that is as stupid as the night and it would be better for him never to have been born. For he knows nothing of the covenant between God and man, a covenant that none may break, neither man nor God, for it is unbreakable. Blood shall flow in torrents because of his black stupidity, so much blood that the redness shall vanish from the cheeks of mankind. But then the people shall hew down the monster—inevitably; for they can do naught else. And the Lord says, I shall raise my foot and shall trample him into the mire, to the bottom of the earth shall I cast the blasphemer, one hundred and twelve fathoms deep. And man and beast shall describe an arc around the spot into which I have cast him; and the birds of the heavens, high in their flight, shall shun the place so that they need not fly over it. And he who shall speak his name, he shall spit towards the four corners of the earth and shall wipe his mouth and say, 'Forfend!' That the earth may again be the earth, a vale of want, yes, but not a sty of depravity. To that say ye Amen!"

And all the people said Amen.

Also available in the Landmark series:

THE GRAPES OF WRATH
by John Steinbeck

A TOWN LIKE ALICE
by Nevil Shute

BRIGHTON ROCK
by Graham Greene

TO KILL A MOCKINGBIRD
by Harper Lee

SONS AND LOVERS
by D. H. Lawrence

THE TRIAL AND METAMORPHOSIS
by Franz Kafka

THE DAY OF THE LOCUST AND HIS OTHER NOVELS
by Nathanael West